HER DEADLY ANGELS

HER DEADLY ANGELS

THE SEVEN SINNERS OF HELL'S KINGDOM, BOOK TWO

by

GINNA MORAN

ISBN 978-1-951314-45-3 (soft cover)
ISBN 978-1-951314-46-0 (hardcover)

Cover design by Silver Starlight Designs
Cover images copyright Depositphotos

For Inquiries Contact:

Sunny Palms Press
9663 Santa Monica Blvd Suite 1158
Beverly Hills, CA 90210, USA
www.sunnypalmspress.com
www.GinnaMoran.com

Dedication

This book is dedicated to all you pretty, dark souls who have come back for another round of punishment. Good girls (and boys). You deserve all of the delicious, painful pleasure eternity has to offer. I'm not even sorry that some of your standards have been raised to devilish proportions or that some of your significant others now how to compete with the devils themselves. You will thank me. Now.

I'd also like to thank all the freaky-ass sex toys out there. You have helped many beautiful people (myself included!) get through times when normal isn't enough.

1

Past Life

RAVEN

"**G**OD, PLEASE FORGIVE me for my sins. I know I deserve the path I walk and the fate of Hell that burns at my back, but please, I'm asking you to show your mercy. I've changed." Elias quietly prays the words on the other side of the closet door, his soft voice sounding like a broken man.

I've been listening to him talk to God since the fog from my mind cleared. He's been going on and on, and the sheer annoyance of having to listen to him sobers me up from the intoxicating effect Dante had on me in our moment of passion. Anger grips my chest just thinking about Elias's brutal interruption. How could we have been bested by someone like him? I know Dante is freaking the fuck out. Kase might even do something crazy. His wrath might ruin the world for me.

"God, please." Elias's desperate pleas get under my skin the longer he rambles, sharing with the universe all the reasons why he should get salvation. How he's been righting his wrongs and doing the almighty's work.

But fuck. I want to holler at him. He's not the good man he claims to be. Good men don't kidnap people, no matter who the woman is. They don't hurt them like he hurt me, injuring me with a blessed arrow of some sort to steal me away from Dante. They also don't slap a measly bandage over the wound nor do they slap the remaining medical tape over people's mouths to shut them up. At least I managed to lick the adhesive enough to get it off my lips. But I won't scream. Not yet.

"I don't know what else to do to prove my loyalty, love, and unwavering faith toward you, your Almighty Grace," he continues. A haggard cough bellows through the air, and he wheezes, catching his breath. He sounds awful, and it gets worse, but it doesn't stop him. "I need guidance. Help me see what I need to do. I've been fighting the darkness in your name for as long as I remember, and yet, my repentance doesn't feel like enough. I don't feel any closer to your forgiveness and light for my recent mistakes. How can my moment of weakness undo a life of hard work? Please. It can't end like this."

It takes everything in me not to break it to him that no one is listening. If they were, one of the saviors would've revealed themselves already. Maybe. Why would they? I can imagine Cassius would claim this to be a miracle since he never got the chance to smite me. The bastard angel.

Ethereal light hazes the room through the small crack of space between the sliding closet doors, drawing my attention. I twist and rub the ropes together on my wrists, trying to loosen the knots. My assumption about Elias being a devil was completely wrong. No devil would kneel before a religious shrine, light candles, and pray for forgiveness. Nor would a devil have an aura of angelic light surrounding him—light that fades with each passing minute as my head clears. I can almost see him as the man he is.

"Lord, I'm begging you to give me a sign. A chance. Something, anything, that will bring me into your favor. I'm running out of time. I don't know how much longer I will last. Please, God. Let her be the answer to my prayers to you. Please," Elias says, clutching his hands together. He's talking about me as if I will bring him a miracle of some sort, and it confuses the fuck out of me. Why would he think that? I wish I understood what is going on in his head. Maybe if I did, I could reason with him. Or maybe I can offer him a different deal, one on Dante and Kase's behalf. Because I can't have a savior answer his prayers. I can't.

I hope I'm right about them staying away.

Tipping his head toward the ceiling, Elias stares upward like he'll find the answers to his questions on the water-stained ceiling. The brown ring declares that the roof might not last through another rainstorm in this hellhole worse than where the saviors lived. I wish I knew how this supposed former angel got to this point. What has happened to him since he fell? How is it possible that he's mortal now? And sick. Not knowing how sick he is leaves me with a dozen more questions. It's obviously bad enough to act in desperation. The only way I'll find out the answers to my questions is if I break free and call upon my devils to extract it out of him.

"Damn it! What do I need to do?" Elias shouts. Something crashes. "Do you want me to end her?"

I groan and yank the ropes harder. I really fucking hope he doesn't start trying everything he can think of to get his heavenly response. It's one thing holding me hostage and praying. It's another trying to assume what the Higher Power wants.

Elias falls silent, and I still. The eerie quiet of the room ignites rising panic inside me. I wonder if he can hear things I can't. Maybe one of the saviors responds to him through a telepathic link like Micah would speak to me.

Micah.

With the thought of his name, I can't help thinking about

him and what he's doing in Hell. Kase and Dante never told me what claiming a throne in Hell's Kingdom involved, but I can't imagine it being anything good. Lucian is a dick. Hell will get to Micah, especially being away from the Mortal Realm. I hate to even think about what kind of torture Micah might inflict on the souls that land in his newly formed level, created from his descent.

I shudder.

Pushing all my thoughts of Micah away, I concentrate on trying to break my hands free from the rope bindings. Unlike when Dante restrained me to his bed, these makeshift restraints feel as if they will loosen if I continue to pull and twist. Elias is clearly not an expert in any sort of bondage—or kidnapping, for that matter—because he did nothing about my legs and when I break free, only he will lie between me and my freedom. And right now, he looks like he's drunk or something by how much he wobbles.

Sighing, Elias finally stops meditating or whatever he's doing and pushes to his feet. He turns away from his shrine, ignoring the fact that he's strung me up in a closet among his smoky clothes, reeking of cigarettes. I think it's been hours since he's last checked on me, and I'm lucky I don't have to go to the bathroom yet. I plan to be out of here before that kind of urge overtakes me. I'd rather dislocate my thumbs than face standing in my own filth.

Elias strolls to a cluttered dresser and swipes a beer bottle from the mess and takes a swig. Coughing, he clutches onto the furniture, sounding like he hacks up a lung. He wheezes and huffs, clearly in pain now that I have a better look at him. His skin lacks any warmth or color, pale like he might have the flu. He's on the thin side, his muscles sinewy instead of buff. I also catch sight of his hands trembling.

"Fuck," he grumbles under his breath. "Fuck this bullshit!" Swinging his arm, he clears off the dresser, knocking the trash to the floor.

I grimace, a million questions running through my mind as he swears and trashes the place, knocking over the lamp and throwing shit off the nightstands in heaps of garbage on the carpet. Could it be possible that I was wrong, and this man isn't the supposed angel who loved me enough that he gave me part of his essence in another life and had fallen? Maybe. But seeing his soul shining brightly, hearing him pray, and now getting a better look at him with a clearer head, I know that this man is *the* Elias—the one Cassius blames me for destroying.

It's strange. It feels like a part of me recognizes him, but he's a complete stranger. A man from another life I have no recollection of or even want to know about. If he had loved my soul enough to fall, he obviously didn't fight for me or whatever. I don't know. None of that matters anyway. My eternity is sealed and my soul now rests in the hands of the devils. The only important thing now is getting out of here, so Elias doesn't figure out how to call upon the saviors to send me to Hell before I can complete my end of Lucian's contract.

Like Elias senses I watch him, he turns his attention toward the closet and eyes me through the crack. I stop struggling against the ropes, afraid he'll notice I've loosened the knot on my left wrist some, and I'm almost free. The last thing I need is for him to re-tie and tighten them even more.

But he doesn't move from his spot. He continues to stare at me in a silence so heavy that it weighs on my soul, making me uncomfortable. I don't even feel this exposed and vulnerable under Kase and Dante's scrutiny. With them, I feel sexy. Desired. Hotter than the levels of Hell they rule. With this guy? Goosebumps crawl across my skin in a bad way. He reminds me of how I felt with Cassius aiming a flaming sword at my heart.

I inhale a few long breaths, calming my racing heartbeats the best I can. Elias's light gray eyes search over my face until they finally meet mine. The beautiful color reminds me of stormy skies lit by the white glow of lightning bolts. He remains unmoving, just gawking at me like he enjoys making me feel uncomfortable and awkward.

Hanging my head, I break his stare. I consider my options as to what I should do. It might be best to wait things out. Kase and Dante will find me. I know it. I just have to survive whatever Elias has planned until they do. And right now, he's not doing anything that scares me. If he's Hell-bound like he thinks he is, then I doubt any savior would arrive at his call.

"You're a creep," I finally say, squirming under his attention. It feels better than I imagined it would to speak again. "Whatever you expect to get out of this won't work."

"Don't say another word," he mutters, glowering. "You don't get to speak, you demon's little slut."

"That's offensive to my devils. They're far more powerful than those bottom feeders." The hem of my dress dances along my thighs, and I try not to move too much to keep it from hiking up. I want to kick myself for thinking something so short was a good idea all because I wanted to tease Dante. At least I wore a thong. I almost went commando. "Why are you even doing this? My devils will get here before anyone can even consider answering your bullshit prayers."

Elias remains expressionless, his scruffy face handsome without the scowl he wore when he kidnapped me. I don't know what happened or how he—or I, for that matter—looked like in our former lives, but he still carries an otherworldly attractiveness. "What did I say about talking? I don't want to hurt you. If the neighbors hear you, we're going to have a problem, darlin'. You don't want to be responsible for a couple deaths by demon."

Demon? He's praying to God. This whole situation is

fucked. If I knew what was going on, I might be able to save myself.

I narrow my eyes, ignoring his comment. "You know, praying is useless. No one is going to come to your call because you've asked for forgiveness. My soul keepers said that once someone is Hell-bound, that's it for them. You're better off just letting me go and bartering whatever it is that you want with my devils."

"Your devils? Mortals can't own demonic entities." Elias's brows lower on his forehead with his anger. "They own you. I should know."

Clenching his jaw, Elias strides the short distance to me but doesn't widen the space between the closet doors. I try to stay calm under his new level of scrutiny. His eyes travel down my face and to my body, lingering on the short hem of my dress. Elias swallows and drags his gaze back up, shifting his mouth. A dimple peeks on his cheek. While he doesn't look buff or brawny like Kase and Dante, he also looks nowhere near what the saviors look like in comparison. Elias is mortal, obviously sick, and the last person I want to deal with.

"I'm not just any mortal, fuckhead, and neither are you. So obviously you don't know. I'll give you one last chance. It'll be in your best interest if you let me go unharmed." My innate need to prove myself consumes me. I shouldn't be the only one curious about this situation. "You don't want to make Lucian mad."

"Lucian?" Elias tilts his head slightly, sending his rich brown hair onto his forehead. His gray eyes rapidly blink like he's running the name through his mind. "Who the fuck is he?"

"Most people know him as Lucifer." I wiggle my fingers, trying to keep the feeling in my hands. "If you hurt me or give me to the saviors, all it does is guarantee your eternal punishment."

"God will pardon my sins. He has to. I know your importance to Hell. The demons have spoken of you. You have a bounty on your soul." Elias grips one of the sliding doors, easing it open wider, turning his fingers pale with his grip. "If the demons want you so much, surely so does Heaven."

My expression falters, and I flare my nostrils. This is all Lucian's fault for putting me in this situation. Had he trusted Kase and Dante with the task of helping me make the angelic brethren fall, word would've never gotten out. And whoever Elias is now...fuck, I need to know. He doesn't remember our past life, his mind a blank slate the same as mine toward him. If he knew, maybe things would be different. But telling him now? I doubt he'll believe anything I say.

"Elias, please. It's not what you think. I can help you. We can help each other," I beg, shaking my body against the restraints. "There is so much I have to tell you. You just need to release me and let me call my devils. They will help you with whatever it is you need."

"Only God can save me!" Elias yells, his handsome face twisting in rage.

He grinds his teeth and punches the slider door, knocking it off its tracks. I startle and fall backwards, putting all of my weight on the clothes rod. It cracks in half, and I fall to the closet floor. Elias hollers at me, trying to open the door, but it doesn't budge. Twisting the broken rod, I hold it between my knees and wiggle the ropes up the length. If I can just get it off, I can fight.

"God, please. I'm begging you. Save me. That's all I ask of you. Forgive me for my sins. I never intended to go against your grace." Elias continues to pray instead of trying to force open the closet. "I will do anything."

The floor rumbles under my ass, and I squeak in fear, rushing as fast as I can to free myself from the binds. Elias chants his words over and over again. Bright light flashes through the crack in the door. I ignore it, bracing my back to the closet wall and using my feet to push the clothes rod away until the rope falls free. Panic tightens my chest. Shit. Shit. Shit. No good for me comes with bright light such as the glow stinging my eyes through the crack.

"Elias." The sultry voice of a woman hums through the air. Why am I surprised? Maybe because this is the first woman I've encountered in the last couple weeks. "You are looking unwell.

I bet your keeper just loves it. Slow and agonizing without having to put in the work."

Elias groans without responding with words.

"Aww, baby. Come on. I don't even have your tongue." A purr sounds through the air, rattling the closet door. What I thought was an angel clearly isn't. Fuck. The light must've been hellfire.

"Speaking to you is a waste of breath," Elias says, his voice raspy. He coughs and wheezes like the effort to speak is too much for him.

"Not if you give me the word. Your keeper can be handled. All you have to do is ask, handsome. I heard a rumor that you got your hands on a soul wanted by all of Hell. You do know that to get the freedom you desire, all you must do is show me the woman who became angel-kissed for you. Allow me to help you, Elias. We can help each other. You don't have to spend the rest of your pitiful life ill and in pain. I'll take your contract as my own. Wouldn't you prefer my brand of eternal punishment? It'll be fun," the woman says, the soft taps of her heels clicking over the threadbare carpet. "What do you say?"

I shift on my feet and peek through the crack between the closet doors. My breath catches at the sight of the woman—the demon—as she dangles Elias a foot above the floor. Her long blond hair twists into a braid that hangs down her back. If it weren't for her demonic façade peeking through, revealing her true body, she'd be model-gorgeous. But the patch of rotting flesh on her cheek and her sunken blue eye leave her a freaky hot mess.

"Where is she?" she purrs.

"Fuck off! The only thing you can do for me is prolong my miserable life. My contract is binding. Now go!" Elias manages to unsheathe a blade from his jacket and jabs it into the demonic woman's chest. "Return to Hell!"

Screeching, the demon throws Elias at the wall, sending him crumpling to the floor. She laces her hand, sharp with claw-like nails, around the metal hilt and tugs the knife free. Smoke wafts from her burning fingers, and she drops the blessed dagger to the floor.

She touches the bloody spot between her breasts and glowers at Elias. Sharp, jagged teeth extend from her mouth as she reveals her hellacious glory. "Do you really think such things are so easy, baby? I own a hundred powerful souls. Without your precious light, you can't—"

The closet rod smacks against the sliding door with a thud, cutting off her words. I curse the damn universe, not bothering to whisper. Swiveling her neck, she turns her head at an impossible angle. I meet the demon's yellow eyes. My muscles tighten in anticipation, and I grip the rod as if it can protect me from the suddenly raging beast charging in my direction. I move out of her line of sight, pressing myself to the other side of the empty closet. I need just a few feet of space to add force to my jab. If I get that, I might be able to survive another couple of minutes.

The floor trembles, and the gross scent of rotten eggs permeates through the air, her demonic façade grotesque-smelling instead of hypnotic like Kase and Dante's. I don't even have to glance at the woman through the crack to know she reveals her true body, and I bet it is as gross as all the other demons I've seen. Unlike my devils, who embody dark and delicious power, still enthralling in their Hell forms, the demons I've seen freak me out and make my skin crawl. They just look wrong and smell awful. Instead of being attracted to the alluring darkness, I'm repelled by it. I never asked, but it might have to do with the fact that my devils were once angels, and my soul knows it. Demons are creatures born and bred, created from the fiery pits of Hell. But honestly, I don't know much more than that. It could be the fact that despite their psycho tendencies, my devils are sweet and protective.

A scratching noise claws at the closet door, and I shiver. The demon doesn't rush to yank it off, preferring to torment me for a bit like she knows I can't go anywhere. And while the anticipation of her attack digs painfully deep into my soul, it also gives me time to think about ways to save myself.

"Thank the devils you've found me," I say, keeping my voice low. Sweat prickles along my hairline. I try to summon my bravery, but the demonic woman sets off my human instincts that scream she's a predator, and I'm in danger. "This asshole thinks he could use me to get into the Higher Power's good grace by offering me to the saviors. My soul keepers will heavily reward you for returning me to them."

I clutch the rod, preparing for the worst. Demons are tricky. They don't necessarily work together or think about anything other than what they can gain. I'm just hoping she's smart enough to consider the consequences of hurting me compared to the possible rewards for her help.

"Return you to them? No, honey. That isn't happening," she responds, tapping her nail to the flimsy door.

I shuffle away as quietly as I can, realizing she knows I had moved and plans to sneak attack me. A crack sounds through the air, and I startle, deadpanning at the sight of her four-inch claws penetrating the door. Dragging her hand lower, she scratches five jagged lines down the door, letting in beams of light from the torch lamp illuminating the room.

"The reward is far greater if I keep you for myself," the demonic woman says, hacking her nails horizontally, ripping a hole in the door. "Haven't you heard? Lucian is offering a throne to the one who can properly control you."

Purring, the woman jabs her arm into the closet, swiping her furry paw through the empty air. Bone-like spines jut from the inside of her forearm, curling upward. The sharp spines look as if they can gut someone if slashed just right, and the sight of them trembling and twitching twists my stomach into knots.

I do the only thing I can think of. Swinging the rod, I slam it against her arm, my strength powerful enough to break her bone. I've never been so thankful for one of the small perks of being soul-bound to a devil, but I'll take what I can get. Shrieking, the demonic woman jerks her oddly bent arm out, only to replace it with her head. Long, wiry whiskers flutter from the rotting flesh of her face, her hellish glory ripping through the human shell she inhabits. Because demons must use humans to anchor themselves to this plane unlike my devils. Their angelic façades came first. It's their devilish forms they summon instead of the other way around.

The sight of the demonic woman shocks me into swinging the clothes rod again, trying to get her away. This time, she jerks out of the way and instead of entering the closet, she locks her claws to the broken slider and rips it off the track completely.

"Stay back!" I shout, trying to jab her with the splintered end of the rod. "Lucian won't give you a throne unless I make some damn angels fall, and there is no fucking way I'll do it to help you."

Snatching the rod from me, she drags it toward her. I stumble, unable to steady myself, and the demon swipes her clawed fingers at me, snagging the front of my dress. I can't scramble away fast enough, and she yanks me toward her and out of the closet.

I buck and thrash my body, trying to break out of her hold. She bares her fangs at me, yowling like a hungry cat instead of roaring like Kase would in his gigantic feline form. Where he's almost lion-like, this demon is like a feral stray, thinking she's powerful for her ability to catch me like a mouse. But catching mice won't ever prove her power. She'll have to try harder than this to take a devil's throne.

"Is that so?" she mutters, twitching her nose. "Maybe you'll reconsider when I'm through with you."

Slamming my back to the wall, the woman leans into me, capturing me in her yellow gaze. I cringe at the sensation of her rough, sand-paper tongue scratching across my cheek. My skin burns, making my eyes water. She might be a lowly predator, but she can obviously still hurt me.

"Please, you don't have to do this," I say, blinking the tears from my eyes. "There must be another way. We can make a deal."

A smile widens across the woman's face. "Or I can peel every inch of skin off you with my tongue. Maybe then you'll realize you'll do whatever I say. Lucian might have a contract on your soul, but I have your body. You can survive a lot, you know." She draws her tongue across her lips, showing off the blood-red appendage with what look like hair-thin spikes. Shit.

No wonder it hurt. Can I die from a thousand tiny cuts? I'm afraid I'll find out.

"Please," I whisper. "Please."

The demonic woman leans closer, dragging her tongue along my jaw. I scream in pain, thrashing and trying to kick her, but she only tightens her grip.

"Help me!" I yell, tensing as she draws her tongue closer, aiming for my neck next. "God, please! Please!"

Too bad the Higher Power will never hear my prayers.

Why do I even bother?

Reincarnation

RAVEN

YELLOW LIQUID SPLASHES across my face, stinging my skin. I stare in shock as a long blade protrudes from the woman's neck, spilling her weird-colored blood down the front of her torn shirt. Stretching open her mouth, she tries to scream, but no sound escapes her thin lips. I can't pull away from her before a bucket of water cascades over us. My skin cools as I watch the demon burn. A cloud of putrid smoke wafts through the air, and the demonic woman falls to her knees. Elias stands behind her, a bucket by his feet and his long blade clutched in his hand.

I recoil, trying to back up, but the wall traps me in place.

I can't do anything except for watch as Elias swings the long dagger with enough force to cut the demon's head clean off. I heave a breath, retching at the disgusting sight. My empty stomach does nothing to help me. Elias flicks his gaze at me for a split second and shakes his head like he can't believe my reaction. Locking his fingers to the demon's severed head, he lifts it up and drops it into the bucket.

My mind is total mush as I try to process what's happening. He doesn't even look fazed by decapitation, which reminds me of Dante. This man has clearly done this before, because he lifts the bucket from the floor and strolls from the room like he has a plan. I watch in silence and without moving as Elias struts away.

From my spot, I get a good view of the empty living room and open kitchen. Elias flings open a cupboard, revealing dozens of jugs of water. While I can guess that they're not intended for drinking, I still can't process what's going on. He snags a jug from the lowest shelf and begins pouring the water into the bucket. My only thought is that the stuff is holy water. I can't think of anything else that might hurt a demon like this. I'm also nearly certain it's what he used to get me away from Dante.

Smoke billows from the bucket, and I cover my nose and mouth, trying to filter the awful air the best I can. Elias abandons the demon's head on the counter, returning to me—or

I guess the demon's body—and he drags it toward the small bathroom.

"Grab the candle from the dresser, will you?" he asks, twisting to glance at me still frozen in my spot. "There is a lighter next to my smokes on my nightstand." No wonder he's constantly hacking.

My feet automatically start taking me across the room to follow his instructions despite my mind yelling at me to get my shit together. I shouldn't be helping this asshole. I should be running as fast as I can and getting away from him.

But then I catch sight of the demon's body in the tub. What if I leave only to run into one? Right now, I know Elias doesn't want me dead. He wants to use me to somehow get into the Higher Power's good grace, but I highly doubt one of the angelic brethren will be coming around soon. I should just wait until Kase and Dante find me or until I can catch Elias off guard and steal his phone. Whether the ideas are good is another story. But I'm in survival mode, and this guy killed a demon. My chances are better with him. And who knows? Maybe I'll get some answers I can use to help me.

"There's a box of salt under the sink. Grab that too, will you?" Elias asks, arranging what looks like dried sage over the corpse. "Hustle. I have to move fast."

I do as he commands and pull out the heavy box of salt from beside more jugs of water. I knew this guy was crazy, but fuck.

It's obvious he isn't just some man on a mission to summon a miracle. Elias has experience taking care of demons in what I can tell is a very human way. With Kase and Dante, they open a portal to Hell and basically shove them back in.

And damn it. I have so many questions.

"Pour the salt around the edge of the tub. Be careful not to leave any breaks. I don't want the fucker escaping because you don't know how to draw a salt circle." Elias motions to me with a wave of his hand, getting me to stand by his side. "You know how it goes. They'll take whatever opportunity they can to avoid returning to the pits, and I don't want to risk the lives of my neighbors. It's not their fault you're damn demon bait."

Anger rushes through me, and I drop the salt, letting it clatter to the floor. "You're right. But it's *your* damn fault because you shouldn't have kidnapped me in the first place. So don't try to blame me."

He grunts in annoyance and snatches the box of salt, pouring it along the ledge of the tub until it creates a salt ring around the demon's body. "I didn't kidnap you. I relocated you to a place more accessible to the divine. You can't honestly tell me you enjoyed being a sex slave to a demon. I saw how rough he was, trying to tear your throat out with his cock."

Blush burns over my chest and cheeks at his comment.

"I bet his demon juice tastes as bad as demon's smell," he adds, turning his head to grimace at me. "It fucked you up. I wasn't sure you'd ever come down from that fucking high."

How do I even respond to that? For one, the bastard watched me give Dante a blowjob. What a fucking creep. But why am I surprised? Elias was an angel in another life, and those halo-heads love to watch in silence, being their creeper selves. I learned that from Micah.

"Of course this would be easier if you hadn't," Elias adds, lifting the candle I brought from the dresser.

I notice strange, unfamiliar symbols carved into the black wax, shining golden with the light from the flame. He whispers something under his breath and tilts the candle until it touches the corpse and sets it ablaze. The room rumbles and shakes, and I nearly fall over as the flames in the tub shoot toward the ceiling. Unholy fuck. It's all I can think as the demon's body melts and disappears in what I can only describe as a human-made portal to Hell.

The fire disappears with the body, leaving the empty tub with the ring of salt still in place. My mouth opens, my jaw slack, and a dozen thoughts swirl through my mind.

"How in the hell?" I ask, my mouth rebelling to speak what's on my mind.

Elias's stern expression breaks, and a grin cuts across his brooding face. "You've never seen a banishing circle before?"

I press my lips together. I hate admitting he's right, but my reaction is obvious. "I didn't even know humans could do that."

"Most can't, but I'm a hunter, darlin'. It's in my blood to send these Hellraisers back to the pits. It's the least I can do for..." Elias's voice trails off with his thought. He scrubs his hand into his beard and shakes his head.

"A hunter? As in a demon hunter?" Why can't I get my curiosity in check? Elias kidnapped me and hurt Dante. I shouldn't be socializing with him. If anything, I should kick him in the balls and create my own banishing circle to send his ass to Hell.

Elias arches a brow at me like I've asked the dumbest question in the universe. "What else would I hunt? These evil bastards are everywhere. They will do anything to gain power over humans to use us against Heaven. I want nothing more than to send all of them back to Hell, but especially the one who has a contract on my soul. It's why I borrowed you from that asshole. I need a miracle, and you're the key. I know it. I feel it in my gut."

"Your gut is off." I sigh and shake my head, breaking away from his gaze. "You need more than that. You seem to have experience with demons, but you obviously can't remember shit about angels. This is all a waste of time. You can try to give them me in exchange for your soul to be saved, but you'll be disappointed. Trust me. I asked for help like you and you know what they did?"

Elias scratches the back of his neck, looking just as curious as I am. "Didn't answer?"

I laugh in exasperation. "I wish. The bastard angels wanted to send me to Hell and tried stabbing me with their flaming swords. I barely escaped their vengeance and attempt to force self-sacrifice on me."

Elias's gray eyes darken like thunderous clouds roll over his gaze. He doesn't say anything but stares at me as if he can read my mind for confirmation of the truth. I consider telling him what I know about our past lives and how the same avenging angels blame me for his fall from Heaven, but what's the point? He might turn around and blame me too.

I'll have to try another way to relate to him. He doesn't seem like the same Hell-bound people I've come into contact with before. If I can figure out what is going on, maybe I can get him to release me.

"I know you won't believe me, but they might do the same thing to you," I add, wringing my hands together.

His intensity burns through me like any devil's would, and I shift on the balls of my feet, struggling between loving how his eyes seem to penetrate me on a soul-deep level yet hating it all the same. I have a serious problem that I'm starting to feel bad for the man who kidnapped me. My poor taste in mortal men just won't release me. If anything, it grows stronger.

"I doubt it. I've been working my ass off to prove my

soul's worth. Over the last year, I've sent thirty-six—thirty-seven—demons back to Hell." He curls and uncurls his fingers. "What have you done to repent?"

"I have nothing to repent for," I snap, glowering. "I haven't done anything to deserve this."

"You let a monster fuck your damn face. I'd say that deserves a mark for Hell on your soul." Elias stomps past me, shoving me out of the doorway with his shoulder. "Despicable."

I stand in shock, trying to process what the fuck he just said to me. My annoyance explodes into fury, and I chase after him and grab his arm. Spinning around, Elias scowls at me. I swing my hand and slap him across his handsome face, jerking his head to the side. He cups his cheek, his muscles flexing. I brace for him to hit me back. To do something to hurt me. But he just continues to glare.

So I try to hit him again.

Snatching my wrist, Elias yanks me into him, pinning my hand between us. His heart thumps on the back of my hand, the chaotic beats incredibly strange. I try to tug away from him, but he doesn't let me go. He tightens his fingers and leans in close until we share the same breath.

"Darlin', hitting me won't change the truth of the matter. I know you believe we're somehow on the same level, but you have no fucking idea. Now knock it off and quit talking. Don't make me gag you. We gotta get moving. If the next demon turns out to want a piece of your ass, you're going to find yourself bent over if you want me to send it to Hell. You make a killer distraction."

"You're sick!" I yell, ramming my hand into his chest, getting him to let me go. "I'm not going anywhere with you."

He heaves and coughs, his face turning red. As soon as he catches his breath, he smirks at me in amusement.

"Oh, come on. If these angels don't show up, then I can at least let all my trouble in kidnapping you be worthwhile. Maybe being some demon bait will help put in a good word for your soul too. Couldn't hurt." A smirk plays on Elias's lips as he stares at me, waiting for my reaction. "I already know you can handle it, demon whore."

His words kick me in the ass, and I launch at him, my mind reeling. What right does he have to judge me and belittle me? For being a man looking to repent, he is clearly off base with how to accomplish this.

Elias blocks his face with his arm, so I reach behind me and punch him in his cock. Hollering, he tries to throw me off, but I curl my fingers around his junk and squeeze. If he thinks his life has been shitty up until now, he has no idea. I'm not some weak little demon plaything that can be pushed around. I'm the fucking woman who can make angels fall.

"Call me a name again, and I will rip your damn balls off, you wannabe righteous asshole," I say, heaving a breath as I peer down at him. "You have no idea what you're talking about or who I really am and who I belong to. I didn't make a shitty deal for some mundane thing. I turned Lucian down to begin with, but the bastard devil didn't leave me a choice. It was either make a damn deal or get trapped with my abusive-ex who would've gotten the deal instead. I'd have ended up in Hell regardless. So don't you fucking judge me. There is nothing wrong with having a good time to make up for the bullshit that people like you put me through. I bet you're jealous because this is probably the closest a woman's ever been to your cock."

"Screw you, devil slut," he growls.

Patting his cheek with my free hand, I say, "I'll save that for the angels. Because guess what? They're going to be mine too. That's my thing and why Hell wants me so badly. I break angels, just like I broke y—"

Elias flips me off him and onto my back. I gasp as the air escapes my lungs. Yanking a dagger from his belt, he aims it at my throat. I hold utterly still, not putting it past him to try to send me to Hell on Heaven's behalf. He seems psycho enough to do it.

"No more talking, darlin'. You're getting to be a real fucking pain in my ass." He pushes to his feet and clutches his chest, coughing like crazy. He clears his throat several times, glaring at me. "Say one more word, and I'll gag you. Go sit at the table and wait for me to finish packing."

I huff a breath and roll to my knees, taking my time to get off the floor. As much as I want to swear at him, I resist for the sole reason that I don't want him shoving another dirty rag in my mouth. I shuffle my way to the tiny table and plop down in one of the chairs. Pill bottles litter the glass top, and I try not to let them get to me. Pills remind me of Joel and what he did. What if Elias tries to do something the same to make me comply?

"Don't even consider touching my shit," Elias mutters, swiping his arm across the table and gathering the medication into a bag before I can read the labels.

"I wouldn't. I don't have a pill problem, thanks." I regret saying anything with the death glare he gives me and snap my mouth shut. I just can't get my mind to comply and keep quiet like he demands.

"Neither do I. So stop fucking judging." This. Guy. Elias telling me not to judge him is laughable.

"I'm not." I push away from the table, preparing to fight him if he even considers trying to gag me again. "I was just curious. My ex was a pharmacist. Shoot me for trying to figure you out."

"Guns are too noisy, and I don't kill humans. The pills are part of my pain management, among other things. Cancer is a fucking asshole." His jaw tightens as he presses his lips together. I don't think he intended to tell me any of this by how quickly he abandons me to rush to the bedroom.

I watch Elias head to his dresser and pull the top drawer

open. Easing out of the chair, I only hesitate for a second. I thought I'd wait around for Kase and Dante to find me, but with this guy choosing to leave...fuck this. It might be harder for my devils to track my soul, if they even can. With the way the demonic woman spoke, it sounded like Lucian still keeps a bounty on my soul.

Racing across the living room, I charge to the door and flip open the deadbolt before unhooking the chain. I twist the knob and pull, but it doesn't budge. A doorstopper is shoved under the crack, preventing me from escaping fast enough. I swear under my breath and twist at the sound of Elias's thudding footsteps.

"If you stop now, I'll only tie your hands up," he calls, coughing as he runs toward me.

"Fuck you!" I kick the stopper out of the way and swing the door open.

Cool air engulfs me. Rushing down the driveway, I race toward the sidewalk. I thought Elias lived in a crappy apartment, but I find myself in the middle of a quiet neighborhood in the suburbs. I don't recognize anything. All I can hope for is that I can manage to run and find someone willing to let me use their phone.

"Get back here!" Elias yells from behind me.

A car door slams and the engine starts.

Shit. Fuck. Damn.

How will I escape him if he chases me in a car? I can't run that fast, and I'm out of shape.

But I need to try.

Peeking over my shoulder, I glance at Elias barreling out of the driveway. The only thing I can count on is that he was being truthful about not killing humans. I ignore the blare of his horn and keep running despite knowing he follows behind me. Tires squeal, and he zooms past, jerking left into the next driveway.

"Help!" I scream, hoping to cause a commotion.

I spin to run, but hands lock into my hair.

"Damn it. Why can't you just do as you're told?" he asks, hoisting me onto his shoulder.

Kicking and screaming, I try my best to fight him off, but it's no use. It's like his determination makes him the most powerful asshole in existence in this moment. Elias pops open his trunk and prepares to throw me into it. If he locks me in, my life could be over. My soul will be done for.

In one last attempt to fight, I jab my fingers into his eyes. Pain explodes in my back as I hit the sidewalk. Elias can't get to me fast enough.

Once again, I run.

3

Lust and Sin

RAVEN

SWEAT DRIPS FROM my hairline and down the back of my neck. I swear to the devils, if I survive this bullshit, I'm going to work on my strength and stamina. And not just in the bedroom like Kase and Dante want. I'm talking about treadmills, cardio, and weights. The works.

Pushing my thoughts away, I try my best to keep a steady pace. Elias shouts from behind me. He's pissed, but I'm determined. There is no way I'm letting him catch me again, even if he has a car. I can go places by foot that he can't. And with how hard he's coughing and wheezing? Maybe I'll get lucky and he'll just die and go to Hell, solving my demon hunter problem.

Headlights flash as a red sedan turns onto the street at the stop sign. I hop from the sidewalk, my feet slapping on the asphalt. Waving my arms above my head, I get in the middle of the road. The light stings my eyes, and I pray the driver doesn't decide to run me over. I need someone to pity my ass right about now. A Good Samaritan, soccer mom, whatever. I'll even take a creepy uncle as long as he has a phone.

"Stop! Please, stop! I need help!" I hop up and down, waving my hands. "There is a man after me!"

The sedan slows to a stop, and the driver's side door flings open. I don't hesitate, jogging closer. Blinking my eyes, I clear the hazy light from my vision. A man stands halfway out of his red vehicle, clutching the doorframe.

"Please, help me. My husband has lost his mind. I need help." I swivel and look behind me, spotting Elias finally getting his shit together to pull from the driveway. "Please. You don't have to take me far. Just long enough to make a phone call."

"Let me call the police," the man responds, pursing his mouth.

Shaking my head, I rush toward the passenger's side door. I fling it open and slide into the front seat, thankful for the unlocked doors. The man only stares at me for a second before climbing back in. A car horn blares, and I screech and smack my hands on the dashboard.

"Hurry, please! He'll hurt you if you try to call the cops here. Please. Go! Go! Go!" I bounce on the seat, anxiety clinging to me. If the man doesn't drive soon, I don't know what Elias will do. He could really hurt the older man or do something insane like crash his car into this one. "Go!"

The man groans and slams his door closed, stomping the throttle of the sedan. He peels forward with a holler, clearly not used to driving under this sort of pressure. I can't stop the laugh from escaping my mouth, and I smack my hands on the dashboard again, cheering as we barrel past Elias.

My relief and excitement rubs off on the man, because he starts laughing too...okay, it's not exactly the same. He sounds scared out of his mind and maniacal, but it's far better than hearing him scream in terror. Hysterics, I can handle. Acting like a chicken? I need someone that can get me at least a mile away.

I shift in the seat and peer through the back window. Elias pulls into another driveway to turn around. "Faster! Run the stop sign."

"Ah shit," the man says, barreling through the stop sign like I ask. "He is crazy, isn't he?"

"You have no idea. He's tripping. Tied me up in the closet and claimed that—never mind. Where's your phone?" I glance at the side of the man's face. "Please. I need to call my...brot hers. They can calm my husband down. He listens to them. I don't want the cops involved."

The man grips the steering wheel tighter. "But—"

"Now!" I don't mean to screech, but I'm running out of time. If Elias catches up, or another demon, I'm screwed. "Give me your damn phone!"

Hollering in surprise, the man scrambles to grab his phone from the cup holder and drops it on my lap. If a horn didn't honk from behind us, I'd throw my arms around the man and hug him. Hell, I'd kiss the damn phone. Instead, I shout for him to unlock it and tap my finger across the digital keypad. Who knew the number of my devils would be one of the handful that I've memorized.

It doesn't even ring before Kase growls into the line and says, "This better fucking be Raven or I'll rip your spine out through your asshole for calling this number."

I blow out a breath. "Kase..." His name comes out a whisper from my lips. Just hearing his voice sends tears watering my eyes. It's like my body knows that I'll soon be in the safest place in the world, sandwiched between my sexy devils.

"Where the fuck have you been? We've been trying to locate you. You okay?" Kase's deep voice wraps around me, his concern palpable enough to twist my soul strings. "It wasn't the bird-brains. I had them in my sight."

"I've been better, but I've also been worse," I manage to spit out as I flick my attention behind the car again. I don't see Elias's headlights but that doesn't mean anything. "I'll explain everything. Just come and get me. I'm…" I lean forward and peer at the man's navigation system within the dash. "I'm near Seraphim Drive and Main in Angel Canyon." Now that I see the street names, I realize I'm not that far from my old apartment that I had to give up when I lost my office manager job. "I'm going to head to Tony's and wait for you—"

The man slams the brakes, sending me crashing against the dash. I lose the phone, the small device flying from my grip to land somewhere on the floor. Kase's muffled voice calls my name, but I don't attempt to look for the phone. It'll do nothing to help me, not if Elias cut us off.

Bright light illuminates the dark world, snagging my attention.

Fuck. The man didn't stop because of Elias.

I tense and stare out the window as Andre unfurls his brilliant wings, expanding them from one side of the road to the other. The headlights set his white wings aglow, the tips sparkling with iridescent rainbow color as if holographic glitter coats each of his feathers. Heavenly light engulfs him in a golden halo. Crossing his arms over his chest, he looks steeled and ready against anything I could possibly pull with him. I guess my angelic hand job didn't make the impression I had hoped for. I'm going to have to work on that.

The man beside me inhales a sharp breath. "My God. Is that...?"

"A righteous bastard on a hellish mission?" I quip, popping open the glove compartment. "Yeah. Now put the car in reverse. He's just as bad as the guy chasing me."

"No. My savior requests a moment of your time." The man snatches my wrist, stopping me from digging for a makeshift weapon. "Come on. He's asked me to bring you to him."

My chest tightens at the strange monotonous tone of the Good Samaritan's voice. I had no idea that angels could influence mortals in such a way. If I had, I would've scrambled out of the car immediately, not letting this man get a hold on me.

I yank my arm away from him. "No. I'm not going. Now get out if you're going to turn all high and mighty."

Unbuckling his seatbelt, the man flings his door open. The tropical scent of coconut wafts on a breeze, and I swing my attention to Andre. He flaps his enormous wings, sending the fragrance of his body to me. And damn it. He smells so fucking delicious, reminding me of my short time with him when the brethren kidnapped me.

"Raven, listen to the mortal. He is one of the Higher Power's faithful and will stop at nothing to obey what he feels is his purpose." Andre's voice bellows through the night, sounding like a supervillain or some shit. "Right now, his mission is bringing you to me."

I twist in the seat and kick my foot at the man. "Then make him stop!"

"I can't. A servant of God will only stop when their mission is complete. Don't make this any harder on him than it has to be, little hellion. Haven't you been enough trouble? I just want to speak with you. Your soul keepers have been blocking you from us." Andre takes another step closer.

The man grumbles under his breath and laces his hand around my ankle. Hoisting me over the center console, he attempts to drag me out of his vehicle. I yell and thrash, locking my fingers to the steering wheel.

There is no way I'm leaving this car. Andre could swoop at me and fly me away to a remote island that he and the other brethren spoke about. I refuse to spend the rest of my mortal life alone and waiting for it all to end. Andre has a whole lot of Hell coming to him if he even thinks for a second I'll accept that it's his mission in the universe to send me to Hell before I can hold up my end of the contract. I will not be a damn demon slave. I won't. The only plans I have for Hell are taking my own throne and rising as the ruler of Purgatory.

"Last chance to call him back," I say, hanging on with all my devilish strength. "If Kase and Dante show up and see his hands on me, they'll surely cut them off. I don't want that as much as you don't."

"Then stop resisting," Andre argues.

I swear talking to angels is like shouting at a brick wall. They're dense as fuck. Naïve. So full of faith that it's infuriating.

"Fuck off, Andre! I thought I could like you, but you're just another one of Cassius's bitch boys. Where is the righteous psycho, anyway? I highly doubt he'd send you to retrieve me alone, knowing how you nearly stuck your dick in my mouth." I kick my leg again, managing to finally knock the mortal man away.

He lands on his ass and yells in exasperation. "Don't speak to the divine with your vile, Hell-tongue."

Leaning out of the car, I grab the door and slam it shut. Revving the engine, I lock my fingers around the steering wheel and glower at Andre. His eyes shine metallic gold in the headlights, and he still doesn't move, choosing not to back down.

And neither do I.

The man slaps his hands on the window and tugs the door open. I screech and stomp the throttle, sending me barreling forward. To my utter shock, the man doesn't let go of the door and lets me drag him as I zoom forward at Andre. Flapping his wings, Andre stands tall in place, squaring his shoulders. Even though I will plow into him in seconds, he refuses to move. Yelling, the man steals my attention from Andre's hard features, and I ease my foot on the brake pedal and roll to a stop. I can't crash into the angel, nor can I risk hurting the man.

Andre's chest rises and falls, and he locks his gaze to mine. "I knew you would do the right thing, Raven. You might have darkness claiming you, but your soul still shines so brightly. It's the most mesmerizing, enchanting thing I've ever seen."

"Why is he even out here?" I mutter to myself, popping the car into reverse.

"You know why." Andre's voice remains even. I can't believe he heard me. I know that Micah could speak to me telepathically, but this isn't the same. Andre's voice came clearly through the air.

I flick my gaze in the rearview mirror. "I'm going to need confirmation. As far as I know, all I can think is that you have a hard-on for my soul and want to spirit fuck me once more before Cas—"

"You devil's whore!" The man startles me, throwing open the door.

I stomp my foot on the pedal, sending the sedan in reverse. He hollers and chases after me, waving his hands and shouting for me to stop in the name of God. I ignore him and swivel in my seat to peer out the back window.

My heart slides into my stomach.

Elias eases his car forward, blocking the street, not giving me a way to drive in that direction. I hit the brakes again and shove the gear into drive. Annoyance rushes through me, and I swing my attention back to the road in front of me. But it's too late.

I don't have time to slam the brakes before a heavy body hits the windshield, cracking it. Rolling forward, the man tumbles down and off the hood, landing on the street. I thrust the car door open and hop out. I knew this shit would happen. All I wanted was to get away from Elias and return to my devils. Now, Andre forced my hand by hypnotizing this guy into thinking he is some sort of angelic soldier. This is all so messed up.

I don't bother paying attention to whether or not Elias approaches us and rush around the front of the car to where the man lies on his back. His features twist in pain, and a tear seeps from the corner of his muddy brown eyes, disappearing into the graying hair on his temple. I kneel beside him and trail my gaze over his body, looking for signs of blood and trauma.

"I'm so sorry," I say, trying to keep my shit together. Maybe he'll be okay. People survive worse. It was just a tap. "You should've stayed out of the way."

The man blinks his eyes, staring up at the sky instead of at me. Golden light grows brighter with the all-consuming coconut fragrance of Andre. I don't look up, but I know he meanders closer, cautiously, treating me like the wild abomination his brethren think I am.

Andre sighs. "Raven, I tried to warn you. Once a man is—"

"Lucifer's slut!" Ramming his hands into my chest, the man

shoves me hard, knocking me off balance.

I scream in surprise, the strange haze in the man's eyes freaking me out. He acts possessed, but it's obviously nothing demonic. Either way, he's terrifying all the same.

"I cast you away from the presence of grace and into Hell," the man says, tackling me. Light glows from his eyes and crawls over his face as if something illuminates him from within. His fingers warm around my throat as he squeezes, cutting off my airway.

And then I hear it.

Elias's raspy voice chants something from behind me in a language I've never heard. Goosebumps prickle over my skin, and I open and close my mouth, trying to gasp for air that won't come. I writhe and move, fighting against the man's hold as Elias continues to chant the strange words from somewhere nearby.

Shadows crowd my vision. My already tired body grows weak. Giving up fighting, I let my arms thump to the ground and close my eyes. This is pointless. Heaven's army will send me to Hell before my devils can save me.

Fuck. This can't be it.

Like the Higher Power finally answers one of my silent prayers, the man's grip on my throat eases away. I remain frozen and confused, wondering why he didn't end my life. My eyelids turn red with the brilliant glow of Andre strolling closer. It's now that I realize he might've stopped the man, or at least distracted him. But then…I also don't hear Elias chanting either.

Snapping my eyes open, I inhale a sharp breath. My throat burns, and I cough and roll onto my side. From his spot hidden beneath the shadow of a tree, I spot Elias's gray eyes sheening with tears. He clutches his chest, his brows low on his forehead. I realize what has happened with one look at him. It wasn't the Higher Power or Andre intervening. It was Elias succumbing to his sickness which stopped his chant.

Scowling, I watch Elias gasp a deep breath, making him wince in pain. It doesn't stop him from moving his mouth again, and once more, his eerie chant drifts through the night. I brace myself at the low groan of the man and roll, moving out of the way fast enough that he misses grabbing onto me again. I scramble to my feet and peer around. Andre blocks the street going one way, and Elias's car and the man stand in the way of my other escape route.

"Stop! Please, I don't want to fight!" I yell, clenching my hands into fists. "You have to stop!"

"Go to Hell, Satan's slut!" the man hollers, rushing me.

Swinging my fist, I use all my strength to punch the guy in the face. My hand explodes in pain as my fist connects with the man's jaw. No one ever mentioned how much punching someone like this would hurt, and I wish I'd have slapped him instead.

At least my punch was enough to knock the crazed, overzealous man on his army of God mission away. He flails his arms like pinwheels, trying to steady himself, but he can't. He trips over his feet and falls face-first toward the sidewalk. My stomach twists at the sound of his head smashing against the curb. Covering my mouth with my hand, I gawk in shock as blood pools in the gutter, dripping from the man.

He doesn't yell or try to get up.

He doesn't move.

Elias stops chanting and the glow of Andre's wings fades away. Silence fills the world around me as if time stops. My whole body trembles as I try to process what happened. I was only trying to protect myself. I never wanted to hurt the man. He was only here because he was nice enough to stop and help me.

Tears burn my eyes, and I shuffle closer, peering at the man like he'll wake up and try to attack me. I nearly hope he does. But still, he doesn't move. His back doesn't rise and fall with his breathing. Blood stains the ground.

"Fuck," I murmur, nudging his rigid body with my toe.

"I'm sorry, Raven. It was his time. There was nothing you could've done. He was meant to go to everlasting paradise." Andre's soft voice trickles to me, and his glorious light illuminates the world again, bathing me in a stinging glow.

I inhale and exhale a few deep breaths, trying to get my anger under control. Is he for real? He speaks as if it wasn't his fault for getting in the way of the car. He doesn't even mention the fact that Elias was chanting something that I'm nearly fucking sure put Heaven right into the man to turn him into one of God's warrior followers. And it pisses me off. I can't believe he just pulled the "it was his time" bullshit. Because it wasn't. It shouldn't have been.

Whipping my head back, I peer up at Andre and clench my jaw, forcing my mouth to stop trembling. "You're crazy! How was this supposed to be his time? This was your fault. Had you not gotten into his head, he'd be alive. You should've just left me alone."

I swipe a stray tear from my face, hating how much my eyes water despite me not wanting to cry over this man and in front of this angel. Unfurling his wings, Andre flaps them once, sending a gust of coconut scented air over me. And then he reaches out and touches my shoulder, his own eyes watering like mine.

"Perhaps it was my fault," Andre admits, sighing and drooping his wings. "I shouldn't have come here, but I heard your yells. I heard your call for help. I've seemed to grow in tune to your voice and it brought me here. It was like you responded to my own prayers for answers of what to do."

I grimace, confusion getting the best of me. "What does any

of that mean, Andre? I don't understand."

He stiffens and digs his fingers into my shoulder, his eyes locking onto mine. Without a word, he shows me exactly what he means by drawing his heavenly sword. It bursts into flames, lighting the world around us even more.

Raising his arm, he aims his weapon at me.

I close my eyes and brace for Hell. "Please, just make it quick."

4

Fall from Grace

ELIAS

ANGEL FIRE DANCES over the long sword of one of the most glorious bastards I've ever seen. I don't know what I was expecting an angelic warrior to look like, but it was nothing like the giant man in front of me, standing at least half a foot taller than my five-eleven frame. I tense in anticipation as the looming man lifts his sword over Raven, her Hell-bound soul quivering as hard as her body. Her aura swirls in ribbons of light and dark, the seductive dance of the devil entrancing even the angel.

I clear my throat, the pain tight in my chest, screaming that I need to sit my ass down and rest before I keel over. "My grace.

I've waited so long for this moment. Please accept this offering on my behalf. I've done everything I could for the chance to earn my place back in Heaven's light. I—"

Scowling, the angel flaps his wings, knocking Raven over as he launches at me. I duck and cower, hitting my knees to the asphalt. I'm not against groveling and praying. I have nothing else to lose as my soul is tethered to a demon who can't wait to drag me to Hell.

Bright light illuminates the world so intensely that I have to shield my eyes from the godly being, far more terrifying than I'd expect of an angel. "Please, forgive me. Show me mercy. I'm a dying man who has made mistakes in my life. I—"

"Elias? No. It can't be," the angel whispers, his towering body lighting the world around me with his heavenly glow. He knows my name. This must be a good sign.

"Yes, your grace. My name is Elias. You must know I've been fighting on your behalf, sending dozens of demons to Hell in Heaven's honor." My chest clenches, and I rasp a cough, my ribs and back aching. The pain has gotten worse over just the last month. I can barely sleep as the cancer consuming my lungs tortures me with a slow and painful death. But I wouldn't wish for a swift end. Not now. I need every second I can get. "I've taken Hell's most wanted soul from its keepers to bring to you. All I ask is for redemption and your mercy."

The angel folds his wings, cocking his head to stare down at me. His thick brows pinch together, and he remains silent as he processes my words. Shifting on his boots, he swivels and glances at Raven, shaking and crying at his feet, and then back to me. Heavenly light radiates from his very essence. If I crawl close enough, maybe some of it will spill onto me and help me through my final days.

I press my palms together. "Please—"

"Elias," the angel says, repeating my name. "You've been here all along? We thought Lucifer bound you to Hell." Uh...what the fuck is he talking about?

"Who's *we*? And Lucifer? I think you have the wrong Elias." It's my turn to frown. I should continue to plead and beg for forgiveness, but the way this angel looks at me has my mind spinning. I thought he knew me from my constant prayers and acts on God's behalf. Unfortunately, he looks angry. Confused. Like he might backhand me across the country. "I haven't made a deal with the devil. It was—"

"It's pointless, Andre. He doesn't remember shit." Raven's soft voice cuts me off, drawing my attention to her. She wipes her hands over her glistening cheeks, settling down faster than I expect her to. "Not me or anything that happened. Humanity took everything from his memory like it had with me. I doubt he'd have done this to me if he did remember...right? Instead, looks like we both screwed up our clean slates."

"Raven," the angel, Andre, says. "I can't speak with you

about things I don't know."

"But it is Elias. *The* Elias, right?" she prods.

What the fuck is she talking about? Me remembering her? I've never met Raven before I saw that monster fucking her mouth. I'd remember a woman like her. Despite the whole demonic sex slave thing, she's hot. Definitely fuckable. I can see why she's been chosen to play with. But as for everything else? She's mistaken. Even if I did know her—hell yeah, I would've still done this regardless of who she is. I need someone I can use to barter with to help regain possession of my soul. Unlike Raven, I really don't want to be a demon's bitch for eternity. She looks bendy and tough as nails. My ass puckers at even the thought. Fuck my life.

"Come on, Andre. Just tell me. I heard what Cassius said, you know. He blames me for Elias. You probably do too." Raven's black hair curtains her face, blocking her tear-stained cheeks. Andre breaks his ethereal gaze from me and turns to her. Tipping her head back, she stares up at the tall, muscular angel, her mouth puckering in a pathetic pout. And then her bottom lip trembles. Damn. I wonder if that could work for me.

"I could never. Cass was speaking out of hurt, little hellion. He knows even angels can rise and defy, making their own choices if they want them badly enough." Andre strokes her damp cheek with his knuckles. If I didn't know any better, I'd think he was doing it out of his need to be close to her and not his empathy.

"Then why are you here? You said you wanted to talk." Raven covers his hand with her own. "You went through a lot. The man..."

"I never wanted that to happen. I'm sorry," Andre says.

It's like I'm no longer here, and I don't know how to feel about it. This was supposed to be my chance to receive salvation, yet he won't look at me for more than a second. He's enthralled with her. Keeps stroking her cheeks and getting all up in her space. This is far beyond being close to her for comfort.

I can't exactly blame him if he wanted her attention. She's beautiful, even crying. It's always the hot mortals who get seduced by demons. I don't get it. Those fuckers are horrendous. But then again, it could be something else with the way they speak as if they know each other.

Does he have a boner? I think he fucking does. No, not think. He's pitching a damn tent. And I was starting to lose faith that miracles happen. Maybe I have been going about all this wrong. Maybe Hell is after Raven because of this, and I can use her to get through to the angel.

I shake off my curiosity about angelic boners, because fucking A. It doesn't matter. None of this does.

"I didn't even know it was you who accepted his grace, but

it's obvious neither of you are truly to blame. You've even managed to find each other despite death and time itself," Andre murmurs, stretching out his free hand to comb her hair behind her ear. He glances at me, and I dart my gaze to the ground. I need him to keep talking so I can plan my redemption accordingly. "And you're both bound to Hell. I thought perhaps it was more than what you said about your deal with Lucian and that maybe you were drawn to Hell because of your soulmate, but it seems I was wrong since he wasn't there. I don't have a good answer for any of this."

"Why do you need a good answer?" Raven asks, flicking her gaze to mine, trapping me in place. I've never felt captured by anyone as much as I do in this moment. "Can't you just accept that maybe it's more than about my Hell-bound soul?"

"How the fuck so?" I mutter under my breath. "Who are you anyway? How do you know me?"

She either doesn't hear me, chooses to ignore me, or maybe I never even said the words out loud because she doesn't respond to my question. Her blue-green depths sheen with unshed tears, yet she keeps her face expressionless, no longer affected by the angel or the man she killed. I think Andre's presence calmed her as much as it has me. It's strange, feeling evil my sick lungs chill out for a moment, letting me breathe.

"I'd have to get a better reading of your soulmate to be certain." Andre flaps his wings again. "The Higher Power never does things without reason."

Releasing me from her enchantment, Raven shifts her attention back to Andre. "You can't possibly think this asshole bastard is my soulmate. He wants to sacrifice me to save his own soul. You have no idea what I've been through."

I'm going to have to agree with her. Sure, she's attractive. I'd fuck her harder than any of her soul keepers. But my soulmate? Impossible.

"Too much, little hellion. Far more than you should've ever had to bear," Andre says softly, ruffling his brilliant feathers, sparkling like a damn rainbow prism even in the dark, "and I'm sorry. Things should've never shifted this way. Your beautiful soul is too light and pure to experience such torment. I wish there was something I could do, but you are bound. You must understand why I can't intervene...with either of you."

I tense and curl my fingers into fists at his words. Anger gets the best of me, and I stomp forward and surprise both of them by grabbing Raven by the back of her dress. Hoisting her off the ground, I restrain her to me and unsheathe my blessed dagger from beneath my jacket. It won't do jack-shit to the angel—at least not like how it'll burn a demon—but I don't like the way things are going or what he's saying. I'm running out of time.

"This is bullshit! I've done nothing but serve in God's name, and you're going to deny me the one thing I need." I aim the dagger at Andre. "If you can't help me, then I'm going to find someone who will."

Raising his hands, Andre admits defeat and steps back. A strange look crosses his face, and he flicks his eyes toward the starry sky. I remain firm in my place, refusing to let the quick look toward the heavens distract me. Angels are supposed to be trustworthy, but there is something about this guy that makes me want to keep my guard in place. I don't know if it's the way he looks at Raven or if it's the way he doesn't just give up and abandon us. Whatever it is about him leaves me on edge. I need to get out of here while I can still force Raven to go with me.

Raven locks her slender fingers over my arms, trying to break my hold on her. "There is no angel on this plane who will help you, Elias. But if you let me introduce you to my devils—"

I holler my frustration in her ear, giving her a shake. "I've already made a shitty fucking deal with a demon. I need divine intervention. I deserve it. I'm only in this mess because I was trying to do the right thing." My chest aches, my lungs tight and clenching. I can't suppress the cough as much as I want to, and Raven uses it against me to jab me with her elbow.

I heave and bow forward. My eyes uncontrollably water, and I swing my blade, ensuring the damn angel doesn't try anything stupid. Blinding light illuminates the world. Shielding my eyes, I shuffle away, putting space between us. Raven surprises me by sauntering closer with her outstretched arm.

"It's serious, isn't it?" she asks, risking my fury to touch my shoulder.

A shockwave courses through me, stealing my breath even worse than the cough. I stumble out of her reach, my fear forcing me to put distance between us once again. I don't know what kind of bullshit this is, but I want no part of it.

"It's none of your damn business," I snap, my words coming out gruff.

Andre expands his wings, startling me. I jerk my attention to the angel and rush him. He doesn't dodge me and launch into the sky like I expect. The fucker surprises me by enveloping me within his wings. Standing in shock and awe, I steady myself by gripping the front of his shirt. Maybe he changed his mind. Maybe he's decided he can show me mercy and free my soul of its demonic bind.

Wrapping his arms around me, the angel pulls me close in what I can only describe as the most awkward hug I've ever felt in my god-damned life. I remain rigid under his flexing muscles as he releases a breath near my ear. I shudder at the sensation, hating how he smells like a tropical drink without the alcohol.

And then the angel sniffles and pulls away.

I grimace and peer into his glossy eyes as he leans in close enough to see the ring of metallic gold around his dark irises. "Why are you fucking crying? Is this part of the whole save my soul and prepare me for Heaven thing? Because if it is, I don't feel any closer to God. Only your…" Fucking damn it. I ram my hands into the angel's chest, shoving him back. "Don't rub that thing against me. Not cool, man. Save it for her. She looks like she'd enjoy it as much as she enjoys the damn demons."

"We both do," he says simply, so seriously, that it throws me off. I had no fucking idea that angels could get a boner, and this guy nearly stabbed me with his. "The body is a magnificent thing, but also so frail. I'm sorry yours has failed you."

"The fuck?" I obviously found the wrong angel. "It only failed me because—"

"You only have weeks left on this plane." He cuts my comment off and tries to close the space to me once more. "But you know that, don't you."

Stumbling away from him, I raise my palms. "This is why I'm asking for your help. I've been working my ass off in God's name. I'm not asking you to save my life or give me more time. I'm asking you to cancel my demonic contract. You can do that. I know you can. You're an angel and demons don't have anything on you."

"I'm sorry, Elias. Your assumptions are untrue," Andre whispers, flapping his wings hard enough to stir up fallen leaves from the ground. He doesn't try to hug me again despite looking like he wants to. Fuck, he doesn't even adjust his meat rod to get it in line. All he does is blink his eyes, shedding a damn tear. "I wish the Higher Power had led me to you sooner before you succumbed to a demon's clutches. You will face far worse eternal torment than any mortal ever would."

I stiffen at his words, wondering why he thinks that. It's pointless to ask him. He already steps away and stares at the sky. "You should be fucking sorry. It's like you want me to burn." I wave my blessed dagger at him. "You can offer me a miracle and choose not to. You're a fucking bastard."

Another tear sparkles on Andre's cheek. "I can't."

"Then fuck off!" I rush forward, planning to test my theory on whether or not my blessed dagger will harm an angel. I want this son-of-a-bitch to feel the pain I feel. The agony he guarantees on my soul.

"Elias, stop!" Raven shouts, stepping between me and Andre. If the angel didn't flap his wings, sending me falling on my ass, I might've gutted her by accident.

Pain swells through me, and I punch my fists into the hard ground. My vision hazes, my eyes uncontrollably watering. I shout in anger again, so pissed off by the way my plans to save myself unravel before me, and nothing I do can stitch up my mess of fate's strings unless someone offers to cut me free of them.

Raven stomps closer and snatches my discarded dagger from the ground. "Are you fucking insane? What do you think would happen if you stab him? He's an angel for fuck's sake. He can flick his damn hand and smite you straight to the pits of Hell."

I flare my nostrils and glower. "Then why doesn't he do that instead of cry on my behalf like it'll somehow make a damn difference?"

"Because it hurts him that he can't do anything," Raven says, surprising me. "He's not lying—he can't lie—Elias. Andre would save both of our souls if it were possible."

Swiveling, she peers over her shoulder at Andre, and he offers her a whisper of a smile. One just obvious enough to get under my skin. How can she stand up for him? How can she be okay and have accepted the fact that she's just as damned as I am? She can't love demon cock so much that she'd be okay getting fucked, punished, and who knows what else for the rest of time...can she?

I shudder. I don't even want to know.

"I would," Andre says, affirming Raven's words. "You don't deserve this fate—"

An earthquake rocks the world around me, and Raven stumbles at the suddenly shaking ground. With a quick shriek, she catches herself on the road and remains there, not bothering trying to get up. I scoot away from her as Andre unsheathes his flaming sword. White light glows from his eyes, radiating across his skin. Fear tightens my chest, and I cough, my ribs aching with the force.

Red fire cascades through the air and into Andre, knocking

him back with the hellish force. I scramble to get up, my body hollering to give it a break. It nearly forces me back to my knees, but the deep-seated urge to run keeps me moving. This isn't an earthquake. Demons are coming, and they're powerful enough to scare the angel.

Shit.

Waving her arms, Raven gets Andre's attention from the ground. "Go! Get out of here. They'll try to take your wings."

Andre tightens his jaw, standing tall and stiff. His muscles ripple and flex. I search the area in the direction he studies, wondering what the fuck I'm dealing with. I don't see any-thing yet, but I know whatever demon it is closes in on us because Andre relents to Raven's words and bends his knees, launching into the air.

"Wait!" I shout, tipping my head back. "Take us with you!"

Andre disappears.

A guttural roar echoes through the night with another ex-plosion of red fire crashing into the ground where the angel had stood. Pushing myself off the ground, I manage to grab my knife and steady myself. The loud thuds of the demonic beast fade until I only hear the soft sound of bare feet.

I rush toward Raven and lock my arm around her waist, pulling her into my chest. I'm torn between wanting to protect her, so I can see if I can find an angel powerful enough to help me, or using her to get my ass out of the demon's way. A gust of wind blows from behind me, and I twist, expecting to see that Andre returned, but a tall, scaly, freaky-as-fuck demon folds black wings on his back.

And then I recognize him. It's the demon I kidnapped Raven from.

Fuck my life.

Shoving her away, I break into a sprint to make a run for it. Something snags my ankle, sending me sprawling to the asphalt. I feel around for my knife, but it's out of my reach, and whatever restrains my legs doesn't break no matter how hard I fight against it.

Red light explodes above my head and rains sparks over me. I blink and cringe, trying not to react as it burns my skin. A looming shadow cuts over me, blocking out the glittering stars above. I feel across my jacket, looking for my last chance to save myself.

"I should rip you open to see if your intestines taste like Heaven or the bowels of Hell," a sharp voice says. "Or better yet, I will feed them to you, and you can tell me."

I heave a few breaths and tilt my head up to face the demon head-on. "Fuck off."

"You were always a brave bastard, Elias," the demon says, narrowing his red-glowing eyes. "It makes things more fun."

Bending down, the demon grabs the front of my shirt and yanks me upright. My stomach twists at the sight of his skin rippling and moving as his demon body starts to break free. Shoving my hand in my pocket, I finally manage to find what I've been looking for.

The demon is too concerned with flexing his evil in an attempt to scare me that he doesn't see me pop open the cap of my flask. Summoning my own damn miracle, I throw the blessed water into the demon's face.

I hit my back on the ground and laugh. There is nothing else to do as the demon hollers and prepares to kill me.

He unleashes Hell.

5

Demon Bound

KASE

"**W**HAT THE ACTUAL fuck!" I yell, shooting red hellfire from my palms to light a circle around Elias. I can't remember the last time someone doused me with holy water, and the stuff this shithead used is legitimate, demon-burning, blessed with heavenly light by some asshole angel. But I know he isn't one. He would've flown away with the coward Andre.

"Oh, shit! Kase!" Raven's frantic voice screams through the night, dragging my attention away from Elias and to her.

I don't have a chance to brace myself before she throws herself at me, jumping into my arms like the sexy maniac she is. The world could be exploding, and she'd still make me want to fuck her brains out, especially because it feels like years have passed by since Dante screwed up.

She cups my face, her eyes searching over the blisters from the holy water. I want to spank her for her hesitation, her need to coddle me outweighing her desire.

"You better fucking kiss me instead of trying to baby something that doesn't bother me," I murmur, leaning in.

She snaps out of her concern and attacks my face, teasing me with a dozen light kisses. I slide my hand through her hair and guide her to my mouth, getting sloppy on purpose, sensing Elias glaring. I want him to see my unholy fucking tongue slip in her mouth and show him how much she enjoys me being a devil. If he doesn't stop, I'll fuck Raven with my tail right here until I get her to squirt all over him and then I'll light him on fire. He should fucking burn for this.

"Are you okay? I'm going to kill him." She squirms like she wants me to set her down, but there is no fucking way I'm letting her wild ass loose. Twisting in my arms, Raven glowers at Elias. "I'm going to kill you! You should've just made a deal with me."

The fuckhead looks like he would enjoy her wrath too much. She is capable of hurting him, sure, but her kind of pain can go either way, and I'm not risking giving him an ounce of pleasure. She can't help it that she's hot as fuck. And right now,

I want him to suffer.

Raven shakes her fist at Elias, wiggling more. I laugh and bury my face into her shoulder for a moment. She's far from intimidating, but she tries her best, and I fucking love the hell out of her threatening to murder someone on my behalf.

I tangle my hand through her midnight hair and force her to pay attention to me. She tries to resist for only a second until I tease her thong with my tail, snapping the fabric. Gasping, she clutches my face and kisses me again, crashing her soft lips to mine. I growl deep in my throat, so turned on by the taste of her tongue slipping against mine that I nearly do shift her panties to fuck her right here and now. I fucking want to. Desperately.

"Forget about that asshole, angel-girl. I have things to do, and by things, I mean you. We can leave him in the damn circle until it burns out." I give her a little hump. "Please."

I glide my tail along the outside of her panties. She creams already, the fabric soaked with her excitement. My cock presses against my pants, throbbing with need. I lick my lips and bend her neck enough to glower at Elias. I disguise the gesture by sucking her throat. Moaning, she tightens her arms around me. It doesn't take long to wear her down, her body rubbing against my raging wood. I can't wait to see the damn wet spot she'll leave behind.

"But what if—" She snaps her mouth shut as I tease her again. "We can deal with him tomorrow."

A smile curls my lips, and I nod. "First thing."

Maybe.

I don't tell her as much though, because the shock of seeing Elias digs under my skin. He obviously doesn't have wings, and he hasn't claimed his rightful throne in Hell, which means...I don't even fucking know. I need to talk to Dante, but first, Raven needs me.

Releasing a whistle, I call for Dante to return to us and to stop chasing the blasted angel. Andre will be back. He's been circling around us since Micah abandoned his grace just as I expected him to. He's far better about hiding his intentions. From the second Raven told us that Andre got a hard-on from touching her soul, I knew he would be the easiest of them all to make fall. I just have to get Dante on board. The longer we're with Raven, the more jealous and possessive he becomes and letting Andre have a piece of Raven is important for his descent. I just have to remind him.

A gust of wind bats at my back, blowing Raven's hair from her face. She wiggles in my arms, but still, I don't let her go. There is no way in Hell Dante's going to distract her with his pouty face and apology for letting Elias best him instead of getting her off. She's probably suffered for hours, unable to get the relief she deserves. If anything, he's going to suck my cock while I get her off. Damn. My nuts clench just thinking about it.

"Fly us the fuck home. I can't wait much longer," I snap, clutching onto Raven's ass with one hand and raising my other one into the air.

"Let me carry her, Kase," Dante says from behind me. I don't bother to look at him. I'm still pissed.

"Fuck no. I got her. Maybe I'll be nice and let you kiss her if you hurry your ass up, though." I start jogging and kiss Raven's throat, working my way up to her jaw until she finally accepts that she's mine for the ride.

The swooshing flap of Dante's wings pushes me forward, and he snags my raised hand and pulls me off my feet. Hugging me from behind, he tries to cop a feel of…one of us. I groan at his damn hand running over my boner in his attempt to get in on the action. His cock presses against my ass, and I swear to unholy Hell if he accidentally makes me a bottom, I'll cock-block him from Raven for the rest of time. Ass play is all him and our girl. I wouldn't have risen from Hell with my mighty dick and even mightier tail if I wasn't meant to be the one fucking.

The world blurs with Dante's sudden descent, and I don't get the chance to threaten his good time because Raven screeches. Kissing her again, I shut her up, stealing her breath until she turns malleable in my arms, all fucking cuddly and submissive. My perfect angel-girl, all ready to let me take care of her.

We land with a thud outside of the apartment, and Dante silently guides me while I continue to kiss Raven, massaging my tongue over hers. It's not until the door slams shut that I break away from her mouth and spin her around to face Dante.

"No talking. I don't want either of you to ruin this moment with apologies. I can feel that your soul's been through a lot, angel-girl, and I want to ensure you don't lose focus because of it. Is that okay?" I already know she will agree, but I know she likes when I ask her.

She slaps her hand over my mouth and smiles. "Shut up and take me to the shower. I'm filthy, my body hurts, and I want both of your attention right now."

Damn. I lift an eyebrow and shift my gaze toward Dante. Snatching Raven's wrist, I yank it from my mouth and lace my fingers with hers. "You heard our soul. Go start the shower. Have her favorite soap ready. You're helping me clean every inch of her before I fuck her every which way."

I expect Dante to argue because I don't include him in the fuck Raven fest, but he doesn't. I'm sure I'll hear about it later after he gets his balls back to stand up to me. I've been cock-blocking him more times than I can count, but it's because I can sense Raven's hesitation. She has fun with Dante, and they fool around, but she has yet to take his ten-inch cock anywhere but down her throat.

"And be naked," Raven adds, wiggling her fingers at him.

"I'm not going to let you just stand watch. That fucker hunter was obsessed with catching me with your dick in my mouth and I want to experience it again and again."

Dante's eyes flash green, and a smile curls his lips. "Whatever you want, pretty soul. I owe you."

Gliding her tongue over her bottom lip, she responds, "Just to be with you two."

She knows exactly what to say and do to him to suppress his innate envy over her giving me whatever I want before him. It's not even about the fucking for Dante. It's about wanting something another bastard has and keeping it from him to get him truly riled up. He knows he has Raven, and as long as he doesn't feel like he's left out, he's good. It has always been our thing. I'm the one who blows the fuses, not him. He's chill with small gestures of affirmation. We both know when it's him who loses his shit that we're in trouble, which is why I'm always hard on him. Thankfully, we know each other better than anyone. If we didn't, Raven might've found her soul ripped in half.

"You gotta tell me now, angel-girl. Are you ready for Dante to bang you yet?" I ask her, lowering my voice. "I need to know."

"If I say yes, does that mean you two will each take a hole? Because my ass isn't ready for that adventure. You're both too big." She eases away and smirks at me. "I'm serious. No D.P.

unless it's..." Reaching behind me, she sneaks her hand under my shirt and digs her fingers into my lower back until I reveal my tail.

I never should've fucking showed her where to tease to get me to do it, because she loves using it against me. Lacing her fingers around the base, Raven slides her hand up my tail as she pulls it to her. My nuts tighten, and I uncontrollably moan at how brazen she's become with my hellish nature. She loves it. Loves what she can do to me. It's one of the few things in her life she can control, so I let her get away with it, even if she fucking gives me a hard case of blue balls.

"If you take Dante's dick, you're taking mine. I'm sure he will be happy to help you stretch," I tease, pulling her close so I can draw my finger between her ass cheeks. She puckers that naughty back hole of hers and locks me out. "I will not wait in fucking line when there is enough of you for the both of us."

Her blue-green eyes widen, and she purses her lips. "Then I won't fuck either of you."

That's what she thinks.

Lifting her into my arms, I use my free hand to unzip my pants and whip my cock out. I grind her damp panties up and down the length of my shaft, making her moan and bow forward, tightening her grip on my tail.

I press my tip against the thin fabric of her thong. "I'm fucking someone, and if you don't want it to be you, then

Dante wi—"

Raven silences my threat with her mouth, kissing me hard and deep with enough passion to heat up the room hotter than Hell. Releasing my tail, she reaches between us and shifts her panties out of the way, inviting me in before we make it to the bathroom. I slowly slide into her, wanting to enjoy how tight her pussy feels as it stretches around my girth. Fuck she's so wet. I can feel her dripping on my balls, and I fucking love it.

Her warmth sets off every nerve-ending in my cock, and I moan through her kiss, rocking her body to me. Steam from the shower fogs the air, and I break away from Raven's mouth to meet Dante's gaze. His muscles ripple as he stands hard and naked like Raven commanded him to, and I motion for him to come help me undress her.

Raven arches her back and stretches her arms over her head. "Kiss me, Dante. I've missed you too."

Dante tugs off her dress and kisses her bare shoulder, sliding his hand around her neck to guide her face to his mouth. Bowing down, I suck her tit, rolling my tongue over her nipple. She moans hot and loud, locking her ankles together behind my back like she only wants me to push deeper inside her.

"Wanna ride me, angel-girl? Let me see how much you can take of me?" I ask, turning around.

Dante helps me slide my pants off without me having to ask, and I spin Raven around and sit on the edge of the tub.

I brace myself in place as Raven bounces on my cock, moaning in quick bursts. Dante hums under his breath and steps into the shower, massaging his fingers into my shoulders in anticipation. He's so damn lucky Raven fucks me like she's riding me in my beast form. If I didn't have to concentrate on not dropping her through the intense pleasure, I'd flick his fucking balls for him resting them on my shoulder.

But damn that sexy body of our soul.

Raven parts her pouty mouth and sucks Dante's tip between her lips. I have one helluva view and watch as she slobbers all over his cock until he locks his fingers into her hair and gets her to deep throat him. Her moans gurgle, but she doesn't stop bouncing on me. I've never seen, heard, or felt anything as incredibly sexy as she is in this moment, treating us as her kings instead of her soul keepers the world claims us to be.

"My fucking beautiful angel-girl," I murmur, weaving my tail around her waist until I slide it between us to rub her clit. "I hope you know I will worship every inch of you as you deserve."

She responds with a moan of agreement, and I hook my hands to her hips and take over, guiding her up and down my cock, giving her a chance to enjoy the ecstasy of our passion.

Dante keeps her hair out of the way, gathering it to use it to guide her mouth over his dick. His balls slap against my shoulder with his rocking, but I no longer care. We're all having a fucking amazing time with each other, and that's all that matters.

Our moans of passion fill the air, and the three of us merge together almost as if Raven shares the light of her soul, tangling it with our darkness and ensuring nothing can ever tear us apart. Raven's body tenses, and she clenches me, the tightness of her pussy pulsating around my cock, making me cum with her. She gasps and leans away from Dante, feeling the power of my orgasm zinging through her.

Dante moans and rubs himself, blowing his load across her chest instead of in her mouth like I know he wants. But after last time, he won't for a while. Raven's high enough on our passion, and he knows as well as I do that she needs to be clear-headed. Because now that we all got off, we have some catching up to do. Dante knows it. I know it. If only Raven did.

Fucking Elias. He's going to continue to be a buzzkill even if he's not here. Unfortunately, none of this can wait.

Raven stretches her arms over her head, silently asking Dante to lift her off of me. I quickly rinse off, unable to ruin Raven's mood this second, and kiss her cheek. She frowns, realizing that I'm leaving.

"I'm going to make you something to eat. Check to ensure no one is stupid enough to try anything else tonight. Why don't you let Dante wash your hair like he wants, okay?" I sling a towel around my hips and twirl my finger at Dante. "Don't get carried away. I know you. Once you start, you won't want to stop, and she needs food."

Dante waves me away. "We're waiting until we know there won't be any damn interruptions, so don't worry. All of the fun stuff is in my room anyway."

He doesn't have to say it, but when Raven finally lets him fuck her, it's going to be when I'm gone and can't join in. The bastard can't help it. Once he knows the pleasure her pussy brings, he won't want to share with me. Neither of us has time to deal with that bullshit.

Raven giggles, her voice light and breathy. "I don't know, Dante. Your tongue is…"

I shut the door, leaving Raven and Dante to finish showering together. If I listen to her tease him, I'm going to want to fuck her all over again. If I do, I'll lose my nerve to tell her about Elias.

Fuck. I really don't want to. I had no idea that he had fallen from grace and had refused his throne in Hell for mortality. Not even Lucian would've known he chose to die on this plane to return as a mortal. The asshole. Elias's decision might've ruined everything.

Scrubbing my hands over my face, I head to my room and grab a pair of underwear, choosing to only wear the boxer-briefs because Raven loves seeing me in them. I listen to

Dante chuckle and groan, and then Raven crack up, laughing maniacally, and I force myself to stroll to the kitchen. I pop a frozen dinner in the microwave and grab the pitcher of water from the fridge, knowing she likes cold water over room temperature from the tap.

The microwave dings at the same time Raven and Dante emerge, both wearing towels and not stopping to get dressed.

Raven beats me to the microwave and pulls out the hot food. "I'm so fucking hungry. The douche didn't even offer me a sip of water. For being a former angel and the one who fell for me, Elias is a real fucking asshole."

I drop the glass of water, nearly shattering it on the floor. I catch it with my tail and toss it in the sink. "What did you say?"

Dante hisses, squaring his shoulders as the realization hits him at the same time as it does me. Raven just said that Elias was the reason for her angel-kissed soul. And fuck. That means this is worse than I thought.

"Elias is an asshole?" Her brows pucker together as she thinks about her comment, trying to decipher what exactly I want her to repeat. "Or that he's why my soul is angel-kissed? I thought you knew. Cassius...shit. What am I missing?"

I slam my palms on the counter and look at Dante. "We need to find him. Now. If the saviors go back for him, they'll—"

"Probably get their wings hacked off." Raven shuffles closer, tugging her hot TV dinner with her until she stands next to me. "He's pissed off that Andre wouldn't help break his contract with a demon."

My boiling blood chills at her comment. Unholy Hell.

"Fuck," Dante says, speaking the only word that swirls in my mind. "Fuck!"

I rub my hand on the back of my neck and turn to him. "The hellfire would've gone out by now. He could be anywhere."

"And we won't even be able to fucking sense him." Dante unfurls his black wings and ruffles his feathers. Turning to Raven, he flicks his tongue, unable to control his devil façade. "Do you think you can show us where he kept you?"

She shrugs. "I think so, but you guys said he would be okay until tomorrow. What changed? Don't lie to me. I know something is up."

I look at Dante again, seeing if he's on the same page as me. We like to keep things on a need to know basis, but she's proven herself capable of keeping her shit mostly together. And this? Fuck. She needs to know, even if I'm nearly certain the bomb I'm going to drop might be her breaking point.

"Kase, Dante, knock it off and tell me. We're supposed to be a team. If we can fuck and get each other off, then we can face whatever you're hiding." Strolling the distance to me, she cups my junk and surprises me. "Now don't make me squeeze it out of you."

I flick my gaze from Dante to Raven and then down to my

cock and nuts as she gives me a little bounce on her palm. "You naughty little angel-girl. What gives you the idea that you can control me by my balls? Threaten my manhood for unimportant information that we can handle, so you don't have to worry about it?"

She tightens her fingers. "You're lying, Kase. You did that twitch thing with your cock. You're testing whether you can free yourself without being castrated by my hand."

I narrow my eyes at her. "The only thing I've heard come from your mouth is that you want me to spank your ass until you're the same shade as my devilish form, which might take a while, and we don't have much time."

"Why not?" Raven asks, meeting my glare with her own.

"Because we need to figure out who claims Elias's soul," Dante says, acting like the good little blabbermouth he is to her. He can't help it, but now it makes me want to bend him over and whip his ass with my tail. "It'll be easier to bring him here until we possess it."

Sticking her tongue out at me like the sexy brat Dante's been teaching her to be, Raven turns to him and slides her arms over his shoulders. "Why would you even want it?"

I swing my tail at him, getting it right in his mouth, shutting him up. I expect him to sink his fangs into it as punishment for pulling the move, but the fuckhead sucks it, making me shiver. Locking his hands around it, he pulls me to him and Raven, sandwiching her between us.

We each use a free hand and cover one of her ears to try to block out our conversation. "Dante, you're going to unnecessarily stress her out," I whisper, ignoring her attempt to break free. "Let's see exactly what we're dealing with first."

He groans. "She's going to hold it against me. It's easy for you to pull this shit when you're not trying to fuck her."

"If you take my side, I'll give you my night with her, so you can have an extra day to convince her to spread her legs for more than just your tongue." I smirk with my words. "Maybe I'll even leave."

"You'd do that?" Dante cocks an eyebrow suspiciously. He doesn't believe me. I wouldn't either. We both know how pissed off she was last time I disappeared and left him in charge.

"Yes." I remain expressionless.

"I want a blowjob from you too," he adds.

This fucker.

I flick my tongue at him. "Fine, but Raven will watch, and you have to finish yourself."

"You know I won't do shit without her." He's right about that. Neither of us will. She's ours and we won't leave her out. Before was just getting off. Now, it means something.

"Also, I'm not swallowing," I add, almost forgetting. He'd enjoy cumming in my damn mouth way too much.

"Aw, come on. You love it when you're high off my bite.

You'll love my jizz," he teases.

"You guys, I mean it! Knock this shit off!" Raven shoves her ass into my cock and wiggles it, trying to use my favorite asset on her against me.

Dante and I look at each other once more, and he nods his head. If giving him a damn blowjob will get him to do things my way, then I'll slobber his knob. Maybe it'll drive Raven crazy and she'll let us have her together. Double penetrating her is only a few sweet words and a couple more orgasms away. I can feel it in my dick.

"Tell me why you want Elias's soul or you're never getting to stick anything in me for the rest of eternity. I don't have a problem fucking myself." This naughty soul.

Pulling my hand away from her ear, I take a step back and cross my arms, bracing for her bitch-fest. "You're full of shit, angel-girl—"

"We need to find who owns Elias's soul and get it back because he is supposed to take a throne in Hell. If he dies and is under a demonic contract, he can't take a throne and you will fail. It takes the power of one of the angelic brethren to create a level of Hell." Dante spits out the words faster than I can stop him.

"What?" Raven asks, her eyes widening. "Why can't the demon do it? Lucian's already threatened to give up your thrones."

Dante sighs. "Our kingdoms are already made."

I slap my hand over Dante's mouth and turn, peering down at Raven. "I'm going to gag you both if you don't chill and let me assess the situation. I don't need either of you freaking out on me."

"Of course I'm freaking out! Elias is supposed to be an angel. I'm supposed to make him fall. And now, he's dying or some shit and bound to a demon. This—"

Grabbing her by the neck, I pull her to my mouth and kiss her, silencing her panic until she stops trying to talk. "This is something we can handle. Now trust me. I'll summon Lucian and find out what asshole is trying to fuck up our eternity."

Raven groans and rests her head on my shoulder.

I hug her. "Don't worry. You're ours, Raven. There is no fucking way I'm letting an asshole demon ruin our plans. We'll get Elias's soul, and when we do, you can do what must be done."

"Which is?" she asks, pouting her kissable lips.

Looking into her blue-green eyes, I peek at her bright soul. "Nothing difficult. You will be the one to kill him and send him to Hell."

His Soul to Keep

RAVEN

"TRY AGAIN. OPEN the gates and drag him here if you have to." I point at the empty ring of hellfire in the middle of the living room floor. The scent of rotten eggs trickles in through a measly crack with no sign of Lucian trying to break free.

Kase growls and strolls along the perimeter. He'd never admit it, but he doesn't want to cross the barrier. I wouldn't put it past Lucian to purposely fuck with us and wait until we do something that exposes us to his dangerous fury. He was pissed off that Kase and Dante managed to keep my contract intact, giving me a lifetime to complete my task of baiting angels to join Hell.

And now that I think about my deal with the worst devil, I recall the moment with the female demon and how she mentioned there was a price on my soul.

"Or if you prefer I enter it and call for him, I will. The bastard has some explaining to do anyway. I forgot to mention it, but Elias came after me because he heard that Hell had a bounty on my soul, which is why he thought he could use me to get the Higher Power's attention. A demon even tried to collect, but he killed her."

Red fire shoots from Kase's palms, and his true devil form explodes free. I close my eyes and tense, half-expecting guts and remnants of his human façade to rain over me, but nothing happens. Well, except for more red fire and an earthquake violent enough to send me crashing to my ass.

A looming shadow towers over me. Kase bares his fangs and roars, blowing my hair from my face. The gourmand scent of his vanilla breath bathes me in a way that I can't help inhaling, trying to drink it in. He smells so fucking delicious. I wonder if he tastes the same. He hasn't cum in my mouth ever like he prefers to see if we can conceive the antichrist—though we can't...I think. No one's mentioned it, and I assume because I know they've been fucking mortals before me and I think something like spawning a satanic heir would be something a bit hard to hide.

"How the fuck could you forget to tell us that?" Kase says, thumping his big paws on each side of my head. His guttural voice used to freak me out in this form, but I've grown used to his wrath lashing out at least once a day.

I stretch up, not letting him intimidate me, and lock my fingers to the outside horns of his three-pronged crown of blunt bones jutting from his forehead. "Do I have to remind you that Dante kind of had my mouth full?"

Dante howls a laugh from the spot he quietly stands, watching the two of us. He didn't want to be within the vicinity of the summoning circle either. Whipping his head toward Dante, Kase unleashes his wrath and roars at him next. Dante unfurls his breathtaking black wings and flaps them, using the force to push him forward. He knocks Kase off me and flashes his snake fangs, matching Kase's Hell façade with his own. The floor shakes under their wrestling match, and I scramble to get out of the way.

"No wonder the three of you fail to get anything done." The soft, musical voice swirls through my mind. I almost had forgotten how melodic Micah's thoughts were sneaking into my head. "You are either having intercourse or fighting. I thought by now things would have progressed and you would have brought one of my brethren to me. Lucian wouldn't be so attentive if you had. And to be honest, I'm growing tired of his need to flex his power."

I jerk my attention to the summoning circle and spot Micah towering so tall that he has to hunch to stand on two legs. My heart kicks into overdrive, the frantic beats trying to freak me out at the sight of Micah in all his hellish glory. Seeing him like this—with two long tusks curving from his wide mouth, hooves instead of hands and feet, bristly hair, orange glowing eyes instead of gold, and a tail that looks ready to flog me if I get any closer—reminds me of the angel I broke to turn him into this beast. I blink the tears away before they can sheen my eyes and suck up my mortal instincts that scream at me to run and hide. Instead, I want to prove to him that no matter the form he takes, he is still the stalker angel I've gotten to know and that seeing him now...I've missed him.

"Do you have anything to say for yourself, heathen?" Micah asks, his voice swirling through my mind.

Kase and Dante continue to fight, rolling around the floor in an attempt to see who calls mercy first. With one look at them, I gather my nerve and step closer to the summoning circle. Hellfire dances around Micah, heating the air. I stop short of him and tip my head back, staring into his orange-glowing eyes.

"It's really fucking weird to hear you say intercourse," I say, responding to his prodding a little late. "Does Hell not automatically give you a filthy mouth?"

"I could've said fornicate." A smile widens his mouth, giving me a view of his sharp teeth.

I crinkle my nose. "Can you please just call it sex and then we can move on? This wasn't exactly the conversation I expected to have with you when—"

Reaching through the ring of hellfire, Micah hooks his thick arm around me and drags me across. I gasp in surprise, a yelp escaping my lips. Lucian couldn't cross the barrier, and I had assumed Micah couldn't do it either.

"I'm not tethered to Hell, Raven," Micah says, his voice dancing through my head as he reads my mind.

And fuck. I knew he could speak telepathically but this? I grab one of his massive tusks like it's going to somehow make a difference. It's not like I can control him. Maybe I do it to try to stay calm. I don't know. But feeling the heat radiating from him ignites a strange sensation in my core.

"Get out of my head, Micah. I did not give you permission to listen to my thoughts," I snap, saying the words out loud. "And put me down."

He huffs a hot breath in my face. "No and no. I need to know what you think of me now that I control the power you demanded I take."

"And what have you found out, sneaking into my mind?" I try not to let it get to me, but having him able to peek into my head to discover things I'm not even sure I know unnerves me. What if he sees something he doesn't like? What if—

"You want to see me as I was," he responds, interrupting my thoughts without commenting on my nerves.

"I've missed you, Micah. I've been thinking about you every chance I get." I suck my bottom lip into my mouth. I don't know why I admit it, but it's like a part of me opens up to him, even in his devil form.

"You've been worried about how I've been handling Hell," he thinks to me as if he doesn't want me to hear the sound of his voice coming from his monstrous form. "You shouldn't be. It's not an eternity of punishment like you think. I'm stronger than ever. Let me show you."

A part of me wants to resist him, because I'm afraid of what I might see. Too bad I'm curious as fuck. It suppresses my urge to protect myself and encourages me to feel him on a soul-deep level and feel exactly what his jump from grace did to him. His alluring darkness weaves around me, prodding my essence until I meet his orange glowing eyes.

His beastly façade melts away, leaving me staring into the metallic gold depths of his penetrating gaze. Glowing against his dark skin, Micah's eyes capture me and refuse to let me go, not that I want them to.

"You really did miss me, Raven," he says, greeting me with a smile that lights his face. "I thought that perhaps I might've been a means to an end for you."

His words steal the lightness from my heart at seeing him in his former angelic glory. It hurts me deeper than I expect it to, and I wonder if his harsh honesty is because of Hell or because I'm the one who sent him there. Maybe both.

"Of course, I missed you, Micah," I say, keeping my voice low. I don't want it to break. "I never wanted you to actually go to Hell and stay. I just thought—I don't know what I was thinking, to be honest. I'm just happy you're here and are okay."

He twists his lips into a cocky smile. "Does this mean you will get your act together and do your job in a timely manner?" The fact that he doesn't say anything about me doesn't go unnoticed. "I'd prefer you not to wait decades."

Maybe the part of him that cared enough about me and my soul is gone now, and I'm just the woman who is supposed to break angels. Whatever I am now...I don't like it. It might be selfish of me, but I miss the angel who turned me into his purpose. The man—the devil standing before me—is far from being that same person.

"I have been doing my job. Why do you think we've been trying to summon Lucian?" I press my hands to his bare chest, the smoothness of his pecs pointing out the fact that he stands naked before me. Markings decorate his velvety-smooth skin, and I notice a red and black tattoo on his arm—one forged from Hell, I guess, representing the gluttonous boar-like beast he encompasses. I was so caught up in his gaze that nothing else mattered.

But now that I realize it, I look down to see him in all his delicious glory. He's as buff, if not more so, than ever. The sharp definition of the V of hips point directly at his cock, the thick rod of flesh at least eight inches semi-hard. I narrow my gaze, willing it to grow to its full length, so I can see how big he truly is.

Micah pinches my chin, guiding my face back up to look into his eyes. "I don't know why. You haven't brought one of my brethren." It takes me a minute to realize he's answering my remark about why we're trying to summon Lucian. I need to get my shit together. These devils need to keep their cocks covered or I'm just going to be brain fucked forever.

"Any other reason doesn't matter, and Lucian will not be coming to your call," he adds, tightening his jaw, his eyes flashing with fire.

A dozen questions flit through my mind, and I frown. Lucian is confusing as hell. He was nearly overbearing before, demanding things happen instantly, but now he's absent. What is wrong with him?

"I will, though. Mostly. If you make the journey from my kingdom worth my while." Micah rubs his thumb across my lip and graces me with a grin that leaves me weak in the knees. I love the way he looks at me way too much, and his comment? His desire for me gets to me in a good way. "For now, all I ask from you is a kiss. I mean, if you want me to come at your summons."

I don't even have to think about it before I lean in and caress my lips to his. His fingers tighten on my hip, and he slides his other hand from my face and into my hair. My soul zings at his closeness. I slide my hands from his taut pecs and to his shoulders, letting his presence consume me. It's not our bodies that truly tangle and touch in this moment, but my soul with his essence as he experiences me on another level.

"I can't wait to have your body," he thinks, his voice coming from everywhere and nowhere as his lips tease and taste mine, sweetly but with a devastating passion I know he'll unleash at any moment. "I need you in your corporeal form. It's all I have thought about, Raven. I never did get enough from you, especially with your soul keepers standing in my way."

A blip of fear blooms from my middle as his heat ignites a blaze around my soul.

He hums, deepening our kiss. "They think they somehow have a right to you—"

Fire shoots around me, engulfing Micah and cutting him off from me. Screams of pain rip through the air. I stand frozen in shock at the strange world around me. Heat licks my skin, but it doesn't burn. It warms my being and sinks into my bones, caressing my soul.

"Micah?" I ask, squinting through the bright glowing

flames. I should be freaked the fuck out standing alone in what I'm pretty sure might be Hell. I should scream for Kase and Dante to get me out of here, yet I can't. Curiosity makes me its bitch once again, and I shuffle a few steps forward along the burning coal-like path leading into a tunnel. My gut says this isn't the main gateway to Hell. It's the entrance of Micah's portion of the fiery kingdom.

"Micah?" I call again, raising my voice over the heart-wrenching cries of the damned. "Micah, please. Where are you?"

Strolling deeper into the tunnel, I focus on the firelight at the end. I wonder how many Hell-bound souls mistake the flames for the expected light at the end of the tunnel crap. They're probably surprised at first, thinking about how the fuck they made it into Heaven and then when they realize it's fire and not heavenly light, they probably bitch and bemoan all their life choices. I know I would.

"All right, Micah. You need to stop this. I know I'm not actually here." Like a new level of awareness, I sense a disconnection within myself. Micah plays with my soul, tangling my light with his darkness, but I know I'm anchored to the Mortal Realm. No one has said as much, but I'm nearly fucking certain I have to die to enter Hell completely. This is all just a mind fuck—and not a good one.

Micah doesn't respond, and annoyance courses through me.

I summon my bravery and remind myself that none of this is real, so I can get my legs to take me through the veil of fire. I rush through and spin, patting my arms instinctually. Nothing burns and my...damn it. I'm still wearing my towel. At least Micah didn't undress me in my mind. If it were Kase or Dante, I'd be butt-ass naked. Probably bent over. They wouldn't hide from me either.

Screams echo through the air around me, pulling me from my freaky thoughts. Spinning on the balls of my bare feet, I drink in the...far from hellish palace. I expected lava and skeletons, beasts and tortured souls strung up every which way, and not the sleek throne room of what must be a palace within Micah's level of Hell. Towering obsidian walls stretch what seems like miles above me, climbing toward a ruby vaulted ceiling with what might be flames dancing on the other side, setting the room aglow in blood-red light. Huge arched doorways, with hellish beasts carved into the frames, lead into pitch-black chambers. My curiosity doesn't get me to step closer to any of them because it checks out and calls to my fear to return my better sense to me.

I catch sight of an eerie throne on a raised platform with stairs leading to it. It seems like such a ridiculous sight. I have to sit in it and see what it's like. I'm not one to pass up the opportunity to sit in a fancy chair. I used to do it all the time at furniture stores growing up, tours of places my parents took me to, and once at a museum of an old mansion—chains blocking the entrance be damned. But Micah's throne is far superior than the head seat at a table for fifty people. All I'm missing is a scepter...or pitchfork, I guess.

I climb the massive, shiny black stairs wide enough to accommodate Micah's huge devil body. Reaching the platform, I gawk at how huge the throne is up close and personal. The seat itself reaches my boobs. It doesn't stop me from swinging my leg up and shimmying my out-of-shape ass onto it.

I plop my butt down and place my hands on the armrests, having to spread my arms wide to do so. A jolt of energy shocks me to the core, kicking the world on around me like the throne transports me to another plane. I scream as agony seizes me, shadowing my vision. Voices hum through the air, the cacophonous wails of the damned pleading and begging for forgiveness, for help, for an end to their very existence.

It steals my breath, the pain and torment cascading over me as if it is mine, and mine alone. My head spins with the noise, and I try to throw myself from the throne, but dozens of hands break through the stone and lock onto me, restraining me in place.

Firelight and black smoke fill the air. Hundreds of figures roam the room, lost and defeated. Unlike those screaming, these souls have succumbed to their fate in Hell, taking their eternal punishment in silence while flaming monsters weave through the masses, inflicting unimaginable torture. I heave, my stomach clenching in disgust. I can't believe Micah allows this to go on. Is this how it is for Kase and Dante? I know they are psychos, but to see the demons beneath them declaring punishment on the devils' behalves leaves me reeling. There is no way in literal Hell I want to experience what it's like to watch a demon shove what might be some sort of demonic animal carcass down someone's throat until they explode. The endless loop of torture shatters my soul.

I can't do this.

I can't be here.

But what choice do I have? The angels were right about me. I'm far too selfish to sacrifice myself to Hell to stop it from growing.

"Micah! Micah, please!" I scream, trying to pull free of the hands restraining me. I try to close my eyes only to have bony fingers pry at my lids. "Micah! Let me go!"

My ears pop and a wave of icy darkness swallows me whole only to spit me out in the living room of the apartment. I stumble through the hellfire and into Dante's arms. Gasping, I rub my eyes, trying to rid the vision of Hell from my mind. The scent of rotten eggs clings to me and smoke wafts from my sweaty skin.

"Hey, look at me," Dante says, pinching my chin, forcing my face away from the blazing summoning circle. "It's okay. It wasn't real."

Tears burn my eyes. "You're lying! It was real. Those souls—"

A roar lashes through the air, reverberating through my bones. Kase clomps toward the circle, where I spy Micah's silhouette in his mortal façade. His gold eyes meet mine, a strange look crossing his face.

"What the fuck, Micah!" Kase hollers. "What did you do?"

Micah doesn't respond to Kase. He doesn't even look at him.

And then he whispers, "I'm sorry, Raven. I'm so sorry," into my mind.

The summoning circle vanishes, leaving a ring of ashes in Micah's wake as he abandons me without an explanation as to why he put me through that. My body and mind reel, trying to grasp reality, but my soul feels as if it resists and remains in Micah's kingdom. Every time I blink, I see the demons. I hear the screams of the damned.

"Raven, look at me. I need you to focus on me. Come on," Dante pleads, carrying me down the hallway and toward his room, not allowing me to stare at the empty space where Micah had stood.

I finally gather my nerve and meet Dante's vibrant green gaze. "I did this to him."

"He chose his fate. He made his kingdom to reign. Do not blame yourself." Dante's diamond-shaped pupils expand and retract. "I mean it, Raven. What he chooses to do is not your fault."

Then why does it feel like it?

Another roar sounds from the living room, and I catch the scent of Hell as Kase opens the gates again. "Micah! Lucian! Come and face me!" he yells, his guttural, growly voice shaking the whole apartment.

Neither responds, and a part of me is thankful.

Closing his door, Dante cuts me off from Kase as he unleashes his wrath, his anger palpable, heating the room.

Something inside me shuts down.

In a moment like this, I want to pray. I want to ask for guidance and help. But my faith is gone, and only vengeance waits for my calls in the form of righteous avenging angels.

So instead, I sit in silence.

I push the world away completely.

7

What Dreams May Come

RAVEN

"LITTLE HELLION," ANDRE whispers, his voice lacing around me, tugging me from darkness.

Bright light turns my dark eyelids red, and I flutter my lashes and open my eyes. Engulfed in a halo of light, Andre kneels over me with the brilliant blue sky behind him. I sit up and shove him away, confusion washing over me. Where am I? The last thing I remember is falling asleep in Dante's arms what feels like minutes ago. There is no way it can be light out—or possible that Andre kidnapped me to bring me to this colorful meadow of yellow flowers overlooking the vast sapphire ocean.

"Settle your soul. There's no need to fight me. This is only a dream. I heard your prayer as you drifted off to sleep. You invited me here." Andre raises his hands in surrender, scooting back a foot out of my reach.

"Like hell I did," I snap, pressing my palms against the soft grass. It feels more like a downy pillow than the itchy blades I'm used to. "I would not pray to you."

"You might not have, but your soul did, and little hellion, I must ask why you allow the devils to sully and break what should be your most precious possession? Hell might have a contract for your soul, but no devil owns it yet. I would think you'd save this kind of torture for when you descend." Andre puckers his bottom lip, his pout turning his handsome face cuter, gentler. He's not the badass angel warrior in this moment, and I'm not sure what to make of him.

"I don't think it was on purpose," I say, building my guard up as Andre tries to tear it down. The comment comes from my mouth before I have time to think about it, and now that it's out there, I realize the truth to it. Micah might've showed me his kingdom, but I don't think he purposefully intended to hurt my soul. If he had, he wouldn't have apologized...right? Fuck. I don't know. It doesn't exactly make me feel better either. Actually, I feel like shit.

"Even so, you've experienced agony at the hands of the merciless tormentors of Hell, and your soul fissures with its darkness. I bet it feels awful." Andre risks getting shoved again to scoot closer.

"What the fuck? Are you listening to my thoughts? Get out of my head," I say, squeezing my eyes shut. I wouldn't put it past him to read my mind like Micah had.

Andre's thick brows lower on his forehead. "I don't understand. I can't hear what you think and only what you choose to tell me here. I'm dream-walking, little hellion. Telepathy isn't my forte."

"So I really am dreaming? And you're here?" I can barely wrap my mind around it. "Why? How?" I have so many questions.

"Like I said. Your soul called to me. I wanted to help heal you while I still can. I might not be able to grant you a miracle or save your soul from eternal damnation, but I can offer you this small mercy. Please let me." Andre's voice lowers, and he extends his hand to me, everything about him so sincere.

As much as I want to tell him to screw off, another part of me begs to stop being stubborn for the sake of it and to let this sexy angel do what he pleases. He wants to fix my pain, so I might as well accept it. It's not the first time he's healed me.

Rubbing my lips together, I slowly meet his unintentionally seductive coffee gaze. His eyes search mine as he waits for my response, and I nod my head in agreement. A smirk lights up his features, his relief over my acceptance like a warm bath soaking me in comfort and peace. Andre opens his arms and unfurls his glorious, rainbow-prism wings, inviting me closer. Anticipation builds inside me, my soul practically throwing itself at the angel. I force myself to chill out and let him pull me to him instead of tackling him. His smile widens at my closeness. Leaning in, he cups my face, and I brace for his lips to press to mine. He disappoints me by resting his forehead to mine instead, leaving a torturous inch of space between our mouths.

"This will only take a moment," Andre murmurs, locking me in his gaze.

I don't get a chance to respond as angelic light glows from the depths of his eyes and sets my world aglow, chasing the lingering Hell residue from my essence. I gasp and clutch onto him, my lips accidentally caressing his as he leaves me breathless. Static shocks me, humming through my whole body. Andre tenses but doesn't recoil. He doesn't pull away either like he savors the sensation of my closeness, of my lips against his, and how we share the same breath—perhaps more in this dream world.

"Raven," he whispers, his coconut scent strong enough to taste as he talks against my mouth. "You have the most beautiful soul I've ever been blessed enough to experience. You do unexpected things to me, even in this state."

"Like what?" Because damn it. I want nothing more in this moment in the entire universe than to hear him say what I can already feel in the world around us.

Gently combing his fingers through my black tresses, he pushes my hair from my face to get a better look at me without the veil I like to hide behind. "I don't know how to put it into words. Can I show you?" His cool breath tickles my mouth, and I swear I feel his lips quiver in anticipation, being so close to mine.

Like my soul knows what he means before he can explain what he wants to do, I find myself leaning into him completely, kissing him harder, more fervently. Andre moans against my mouth, devouring my affection like it's the only thing that matters in the universe. Desire courses over me in a hot wave, emanating from Andre as he shows me what he feels inside him—the lust new and unexpected, uncontrollable and wild, and completely all-consuming.

I push him back, my body buzzing and humming as he lets me take control. His hands tangle in my hair, and he slips his tongue in my mouth, his kiss sweet yet passionate and unlike anything I've ever experienced. It's almost addicting how sugary his mouth tastes, how I can't think about anything else but kissing him until he pleads for more.

Andre's body awakens under mine, and I squeeze him between my thighs, loving what I do to him. Hooking his fingers to my hips, he grinds my body against his, letting me feel the length of his shaft.

I moan and kiss him desperately, rocking my body, my clit tingling and wanting more. Sliding lower, I reach down and hook my fingers to his pants. He arches up and cups my breast through my shirt, his wild need prodding at me at a soul-deep level.

"I want to undress you," Andre says, playing with the hem of my shirt. "May I?"

I open my mouth to respond, but an electric bolt of lightning blasts the ground beside us. The world explodes in darkness. Andre disappears from beneath me, taking his light with him. My soul aches in his absence. I can't dwell on it long, because a rumble shakes me, tugging me from sleep.

I bolt upright and gasp, my clit aching like I was close to an orgasm only to be denied. I huff a breath and can't stop myself from rubbing between my legs to try to cure myself from my need of relief.

"Damn, pretty soul. Let me help you." Dante shifts on the bed next to me and greets me with a lust-filled gaze that only worsens my desire.

I automatically nod my head, because this is one of those moments where I desperately want someone else to take care of me. Humming deep in his throat, Dante flicks his tongue like a snake and rolls on top of me. His hot body warms the cool absence Andre left behind. Dante leans down and brushes his lips to mine before jerking away and touching his hand to his smoking lips.

I cover my mouth in surprise. "What the fuck?"

"You taste like Heaven. Who was it, Raven?" Dante remains on top of me, his voice more curious than accusing, but I can tell a dozen thoughts cross his mind. "Who do I need to hunt down and tie up for you to pay back for not finishing your fantasy?"

I laugh in exasperation. "Wait, you don't want to pluck someone's wings for dream walking, but punish them for abandoning me before giving me a wet dream?"

"Yes, exactly. Because the bastard's soul bonding went far longer than it should've and now unless you want me to burn you, we can't fuck like I want. I can feel his essence radiating from my favorite parts of you. What were you doing? It wasn't a hand job." Dante touches his fingers to mine without recoiling.

I blink a few times. "I have so many questions. We just kissed."

"You sure? We can test it, but it could hur—"

"Get up. Both of you." Kase knocks his knuckles to the open door. "You were supposed to call me the second she woke up, Dante."

Snatching a pillow, Dante chucks it at Kase, hitting him right in the face. "You try to remember that when the first thing she does is start masturbating."

I whack Dante with my pillow next and roll out of bed. He lunges toward me, trying to bring me back to him, but Kase retaliates and chucks the pillow hard enough to knock Dante off his feet. I screech and take cover, knowing well enough that devils make even pillow fights deadly, and there is no way I'm risking getting sent to Hell early because I got between Kase and Dante fucking around.

"She wouldn't have to masturbate with me, fucker," Kase teases, whipping his tail toward me. He snags me by the waist and tugs me to him. "Isn't that right, angel-girl?"

Dante watches in anticipation as Kase captures my mouth with his, only to realize something is wrong. Kase groans and pulls away, his mouth pink. I touch my swollen lips and sigh. Fucking Andre should've come with a warning label. Dream foreplay cock blocks demons.

Tipping his head back, Dante howls a laugh. "You want to discover where else the bastard angel touched on our pretty soul?"

Kase runs his fingers through his hair. "Don't tempt me. I can make the exploration painfully fun, but I need Raven to be able to keep up with us. If I start, she won't want me to stop and we need to go. Elias has been out there long enough. We need him here."

I tense at his mention of Elias, and the desire Andre awakened in me fades like I jump into a cool lake. Shivering, I face the possibility of failing to complete Lucian's contract all because my dumbass already made Elias fall in a past life in which he didn't claim Hell and chose to get reincarnated or whatever. I obviously have too, but I don't know much more. I will ask later. It's nice having life's answers at my fingertips. I just have to rub my devils the right way and they'll give me what I want.

"Dante will take us back to where we found you, but you will need to guide us from there," Kase continues, touching my cheek like he knows I lose myself in my thoughts instead of paying attention. "I hope Micah and...Andre didn't melt your brain too much with their messing with what is ours." He means my soul.

I almost ask how he knows for certain it was Andre to dream-drop, but I don't get the chance. Kase scoops me up and slings me onto his shoulder. I hang upside down and listen as Dante grabs a few weapons for us until he takes me into his arms.

He grins with a wicked glow in his eyes. "This is going to be fun, pretty soul. Elias will piss his fucking pants when he sees me again."

I crinkle my nose. "We want to get him to come with us, not make him put up a fight."

Narrowing his eyes, he unfurls his wings. "That's no fun."

Tightening my arms around his neck, I purposefully lean in,

testing to see if he'll kiss me despite knowing my lips will sear him. He doesn't hesitate, and I stop short. "Dante, I mean it. He's mortal now. You can break him."

"That was the plan," he responds, wagging his eyebrows.

I purse my lips. "Not anymore. You're leaving Elias up to me."

I stand between Dante and Kase, staring at what I'm about seventy-percent sure is Elias's house. No light filters through the curtains, and I'm uncertain whether he's home. His car isn't in the driveway, nor was what was left of the car crash and the Good Samaritan who...I can't think about it. If I do, then I'll feel bad. I don't have time for that. Andre can carry the guilt of the man dying. I don't need that kind of bullshit piled on with everything else.

Kase unsheathes a dagger and motions for me to take it. "The fucker is clever. I can feel the protective shields from here, so I need you to break them. When we have him, I'm going to force him to tell us where he learned this shit from. We don't have time for wannabe saviors screwing with us, trying to do the Higher Power's work."

"No torturing him," I say, straightening my shoulders. "I

mean it."

Kase scowls and clenches his fingers into fists. "Why the hell not? He deserves it."

"Because there are better ways to get information. He's sick, Kase. Desperate. He doesn't want his soul in the claws of a demon as much as we don't. If we go running in, whipping tails and threatening to impale him with your horns, he'll never be on our side." I lace my fingers through Kase and Dante's fingers, bringing their hands to my chest. "Please, you guys. I know you have bad history with him, but apparently I don't. Andre says Elias is my soul—"

Dante covers my mouth, cutting off my words. "Don't you say it, Raven. He lost his chance when he abandoned your soul. We would never do that. You are ours."

I smirk against his hand. "Dante, there's no need to envy Elias for falling from grace for me. Had he not, I wouldn't even be in this position. You don't have to thank him or anything. You don't have to like the guy. All I'm asking is that you don't torture him and let me do my job."

"You're lucky I'm trying to be good for the chance to get in your pants," he mutters, flaring his nostrils.

I kiss his palm before tugging his fingers from my lips. "Keep telling yourself that. I think you might be keeping your psycho in check because you like me."

"Not only like you. I'm obsessed." His diamond-shaped

pupils expand and retract. "Enamored. You have no idea of all the things I want to do on your behalf and in your name like the goddess you are to me. You can always count on me to kneel before you to worship that pretty soul and sinfully seductive body of yours."

I laugh and shake my head. "You're too much."

"I have to be with the bastard traitors creeping in and cock blocking me. If I didn't love having your mark, I would show Andre exactly what this pain is like. I have just the contraption in my collection." Opening his hand, he reveals the reddish, puckering burn from my kiss. The effects must last longer on devils, because the only thing I felt was the tingling of my soul from his closeness.

"Enough, you two. He's coming. Let's wait for him inside." Kase doesn't give me the chance to peer around to see what he sees. Tightening his hand around mine, he tugs me, and Dante by default, along with him.

Transforming his fingers, he extends his dagger-sharp claws out and uses one to pop the lock. Headlights flash behind us, and Kase and Dante usher me inside. Kase pushes me behind him protectively, and the three of us stand just out of the way of the door, ensuring that Elias won't see us when he comes in.

A strange clicking noise sounds through the room, and Dante and Kase tense. Hissing, Dante expands his wings and pulls me to him, wrapping me in the protection of his muscular body. Kase explodes into his monstrous feline form but doesn't get far. Water rains from the ceiling, soaking everything.

"I cast you back to Hell, demons," Elias says, flicking his thumb over a lighter.

Whipping his tail, Kase locks it around Elias's neck and drags him closer. The lighter falls from Elias's hand. Bright flames ignite across the floor, eating away at something in the carpet that creates a circle with symbols out of the flames until it dissipates and causes Kase to release Elias.

"Nice try, Elias. You should know better than to try a holy banishment on us. Instead of sending us to Hell, you really just pissed me off." Kase bares his sharp fangs with another growl. "Now fucking break the circle and make things easier on yourself or I'm going to ram my fucking horns up your—"

"Kase." I smack Kase's muscular hindquarters from the safety of Dante's arms. "I told you to let me handle it."

Red light sparks his devilish gaze, and he shifts back into his handsome human façade. "You have thirty seconds, angel-girl. I've run out of patience."

I wiggle from Dante's arms, silently begging him to help me keep Kase in control. "I need at least two minutes."

"You can have three," Dante says, digging his fingers into Kase's shoulder. With his other hand, he nudges me forward and pulls Kase against his chest, making him swap places with me.

And damn. I kind of don't want to face Elias when Dante is pinning Kase to him. I would have more fun seeing what I could get away with while Kase is restrained.

My wandering thoughts distract me too much. I miss Elias raising a silver dagger at me. Rushing forward, he tries to jab the knife into my stomach. I scream and stumble out of the way, holding my hands up in surrender instead of trying to fight.

"You're dead, you bitch. This is your fault. Heaven won't help me because of you," Elias accuses. He swings his arm, slashing at the air.

"Are you kidding me? Heaven won't help you because you abandoned the Higher Power." I glower and reach into my jacket for the dagger Dante gave me for protection. I meet his threat with my own. "I should be the one blaming you, dickhead. You doomed me to Hell with you."

"You're out of your damn mind!" Elias charges me, his face sharp in anger.

I brace for him to stab me. I expect to see the fiery gate to Micah's level of Hell.

But then the floor shakes, knocking Elias off his feet. Kase and Dante stomp together. I'm so thankful for their help, even if I did say I wanted to handle this on my own.

Launching from the floor, I tackle him. I aim the blade at his throat. "You have five seconds to chill out or I'll give your soul to your demon master earlier than you want." I have the urge to nick him with the point, but I force myself to hold steady. I will not let Kase and Dante hang that psycho urge over my head.

Elias's eyes widen in fear, his jaw tensing and hiding his lips in his beard. "Please, no."

Tightening my fingers around the hilt, I shift the dagger. Blood drips from the small cut, and I try not to react. But damn it. The accidental hit works. I can see it in his eyes that he believes I'm as crazy as my devils. And maybe I am. "Fuck off, Elias. I'll see you in Hell."

"Wait!" he hollers, reaching to grab my wrist.

My faking him out works, leaving him open. Swinging my fist, I punch him in the face hard enough to jerk his head to the side.

Elias's eyes roll to the back of his head. He passes out.

8

Soulmates

RAVEN

"**Y**OU SAID NO torture, pretty soul. I thought that included us." Dante comes up behind me and rests his chin to my shoulder. "If I have to sleep on the couch another night instead of in my bed, I'm going to—"

"Be heavily rewarded," I say, twisting on my feet to face him. "Especially if you take him to the bathroom again. He's been bitching for ten minutes."

Elias hollers from Dante's bed, learning exactly what it feels like to have been kidnapped and restrained. He's lucky he's not hanging in the closet like he had done to me and also that Kase and Dante take him to the bathroom when he needs to go, and we're not starving him. He just can't leave. Ever. I haven't told him as much yet. I'm waiting until the urge to pummel him unconscious again subsides before facing him. Knowing that we had a thing for each other in another life blows my mind. What the hell is it about me that draws me to bastards. Who knew that my sweet yet psychotic devils would be an upgrade?

"You're going to finally let me have my way with you?" Dante asks incredulously, narrowing his eyes. "Don't get my hopes up. It is hard enough for me. Here. Feel."

Grabbing my hand, Dante gets me to rub my palm against the length of his shaft through his jeans. I bust up laughing, practically cackling, loving exactly what I do to him.

I stroke him harder. "If you do this favor for me, I'll—"

"Fucking please!" Elias shouts, cutting off my words. "I've had enough. Just tell me what it is you want from me or kill me already. I'll suffer enough in Hell."

"Not if I show you how to train your asshole, you won't," Dante quips, leaning into the doorway of his bedroom. "You might even have fun if you stop thinking butt play is torturous. I have a strap-on for Raven to use. If you're a good boy, she'll—"

I whack him on the shoulder. "Dante! Do not offer my services to him without asking me first. Don't think I won't turn that supposed strap-on on you."

"Be my guest. I'm only offering to help. Remember that

with your reward." He chuckles, pinching my ass. "I have a couple double-ended dildos. We could fuck each other."

"Yeah, no. Not happening as part of your reward for your attempt at being helpful. It was a nice try. But honestly, no one really wants to think about their ass belonging to a demon." I try to remain expressionless, knowing that I just set myself up for one of his dirty responses. "Except for me when it comes to you."

Flicking his tongue, he grazes my bottom lip, his barbells sparkling with the green light in his eyes. "I can't wait. That sexy asshole of yours is going to feel so good. So tight. I promise you'll welcome me in just fine."

I clench my ass, the hum of his voice sending tingles through my body. I shouldn't even get off on the idea, but he makes it seem like fun.

"Please," Elias calls again, cooling the rising heat inside me. "Please."

Sighing, I gather my nerve to confront him. Dante stays on my heels, following me into his room. Elias tips his head up to look at me. My mouth dries, my body turning rigid. In this moment, he looks utterly and completely defeated. Defenseless. And I feel bad.

I stop in my tracks as a storm of emotions crashes through me. How can I feel so hot and cold toward a man who has done nothing to deserve my sympathy? I should let Kase and Dante have at him and just let them handle it. But a part of me knows better. Whatever place in Hell he is supposed to take means that he will be a part of my eternity if I succeed. I don't want to hate him. I truly don't. I just want to secure my soul in a place that doesn't mean eternal torment.

Shifting on my feet, I turn to Dante. "Can you give me a moment with him? You don't have to go far, but maybe just a few feet of space?"

Dante looks ready to deny me. Like Kase can somehow sense my needs, he shouts Dante's name from the living room. Raising his hand, he points at Elias. "Say anything disrespectful to my soul, hurt her feelings, try to lie or manipulate her, and you'll learn the art of contortion to suck your own cock. Understand?"

Elias presses his lips together in a thin line and nods his head.

Damn. I love protective psycho on my jealous devil. I'm also a bit curious about this art form he speaks of. Blinking a few times, I push thoughts of Dante sucking his own dick from my mind and nudge him to go to Kase, who calls his name again.

"I'll yell if I need you, okay?" I murmur, stretching on my tiptoes until he meets me for a kiss.

Reacting with passion, he slips his tongue in my mouth and makes a show out of it by squeezing my ass. I bat his chest, getting him to stroll out of the room. Dante glances at me from the doorway and winks. I swivel on the balls of my feet. Elias stares at me in silence, a frown plastered on his face.

I straighten my shoulders. The bastard won't get to me. I won't let him. I've already been called an abomination. A demon slut. Nothing he can say will break me, because in the end, I'm breaking him. He will die and go to Hell by my hands.

"Before you go judging me like every other righteous, entitled bastard, you should know that Dante and Kase have been here for me when everyone else thought I was a lost cause. They've faced Lucian on my behalf and have lifted me up and taught me how to summon strength I didn't know I had. So whatever the fuck you have to say about my affection toward them, you can shove it down your throat."

"Were you always so hostile," Elias quips, sarcasm dripping from his voice.

I just glare at him.

"While your assumptions about what I think of your...un holy relationship with these evil creatures aren't wrong, you should know that I can't blame you. We are in similar positions, except my deal with a demon derives from selflessness and not self-preservation. I've been also trying to do God's work while you've been serving your soul keepers in body and mind." Elias smirks at me, waiting for my reaction.

And fuck it. If he wants one, he's going to get one. He shouldn't play with the soul he ultimately damned if he doesn't want me to drag him into the fire to burn right alongside me.

Climbing onto the bed, I surprise Elias by jumping on top of him. He struggles against Dante's restraints but isn't strong enough to break out of them. I lock my fingers onto his shirt and pin him in place. Raising my hand, I pretend as if I'm going to slap him. He flinches and closes his eyes. I stop short of his face and pat his cheek, enjoying fucking with his head. My devils were right. He deserves a little torture, but not in the way they see fit.

"Hit me already," Elias mutters, peeking through his eyelashes. "Just kill me and be done with it if you want so badly to send me to Hell. I'm dying anyway."

I press my hands into his chest, pushing myself off of him. A racking cough heaves from him, stealing his breath. His face reddens with the coughing fit, startling me a bit. I can't help myself from trying to re-position him to sit up.

He groans and shakes his head, wheezing and clearing his throat. "I knew you didn't have it in you. I saw how you handled killing that man. Be thankful I took care of the wreckage you left behind."

His comment leaves me speechless, and I sit beside him, staring into his stormy gray eyes. He doesn't look away. If anything, he uses it as an excuse to stare at me more intently. My whole body tingles under the weight of his gaze, and I shiver.

"I do what I have to do," I finally say, rubbing my lips together.

The fucker rolls his eyes. "You didn't have to kidnap me."

"Actually, I did. My soul depends on yours not going to Hell, and with the way you're acting like a lunatic on a mission of self-sacrifice trying to do the impossible, well, you're staying here. At least, until we find the demon controlling your soul." I poke him in the stomach, startling him. It's like he can feel the same shockwave of my touch like I can with his. "So why don't you make things easy and just tell us? I can help you."

"Help me? Help me how? I think I'd rather take my chances with my soul keeper over yours. They're pissed that I bested and outsmarted them." He lifts his chin and motions toward Dante's shelves of sex toys. "And by the looks of this room, my farts would sound like a fucking wind tunnel after what they'd have in store."

Did he just really say that? I tip my head back and laugh in exasperation. I fucking hate that I find so much amusement in his comment. He cracks a smile like he can't help it, knowing damn well what an absurd turn this conversation has taken.

"At this point, I doubt they will touch you with a ten-foot pole. They only show that kind of affection to people they like, so relax. Your ass—"

"Is only going to get kicked if you don't listen and do what we say." Kase crosses his arms in the doorway, resting his back on the frame.

"Kase, you said I could handle it." I huff a sigh through my nose.

"You're getting distracted, angel-girl. He doesn't need ass-urance. He needs to know what the fuck is at stake and why he's been targeted by a bottom feeder. His little trip and fall into humanity ruined him, and I don't have the patience to ease him into knowing the truth." Kase strides forward, and Dante takes his place, leaning against the doorframe. While Kase takes the lead, Dante backs him up, and they look ready to toss me out of the room to do things their way.

I get off the bed and block Kase. "This is my job."

"And it's my job to help you. I'm not putting your fate in the hands of the fucker who abandoned your soul once. I won't put it past him not to do it again." Red light flickers across Kase's burgundy irises.

Elias rattles the restraints. "What the fuck are you going on about? I don't even know her. I heard about her—"

Growling, Kase lifts me up and spins me around, setting me on my feet out of his way. Elias cowers under Kase's towering threat, proving that he might act like a hard ass, but he's just as human as I am.

Locking his fingers to Elias's chin, he turns his head for him and points at me. "Do you see that soul—I mean, really see her?"

"It doesn't matter what I see," Elias says, scrunching his nose.

Kase blows a hot breath, sending a tendril of smoke wafting through the air. Pointing to Dante, he says, "Come on. Give him a little bite, Dante. Show him the Hell that we see when looking at the two of them."

What is he talking about? Dante strides past, not giving me a chance to stop him. Elias hollers at the sight of Dante's fangs, and I stand frozen and watch Dante sink his teeth into Elias's arm. I gasp at the same time Elias does. Jealousy cascades over me at the sight of Dante's mouth on Elias. It kicks my ass out of my state of shock. Locking my hand to the back of Dante's shirt, I yank him back, summoning the strength of Hell.

"Hey, now. Those fangs are mine." I wrap my arms around his broad shoulders, trying to lock him to me.

Pulling me up higher, he kisses my wrist, teasing my skin with his sharp fangs. I shiver, remembering how he left a mark on my thigh, which still makes me clench my vagina in anticipation if anyone gets near it.

"If you want me to bite you, all you have to do is ask." Dante flips me over and into his arms, cradling me like a bride.

Elias groans, his lolling head stealing my attention. "What did you do to me? I feel weird."

Kase plops down beside him on the bed and drapes his arm over Elias's shoulders. Leaning into him, Kase fucks with Elias by ruffling his fingers through his hair. "You'll feel great in a minute. High and mighty as the angel you used to be until you fell for that soul right over there." Twirling his finger, Kase motions at me. "Don't you see it?"

Elias slowly blinks, squinting his eyes at me. "What do you mean I fell for her?"

"Not Raven—at least, not in this lifetime. The soul." Kase pinches Elias's chin and keeps him in place. "Look at that sexy bright thing."

"All I see are the bands of darkness choking the light of that soul. The same darkness radiating from you. Her light has only grown darker since I first laid eyes on her. Nothing you say, and I mean, nothing, will ever attract me to an abomination."

Dante releases a vibrating hiss. "I suppose you'd have to be a narcissist, considering it belongs to you."

"What?" Elias's head bobs before he touches his chin to his chest. "I'm too fucked up to follow." His words slur and he attempts to raise his head again.

Kase pulls him by the hair, getting him to flop back and stare at the mirror on the ceiling. I can't help following his line of sight. Catching my gaze, Elias smiles lazily, his hard features softening to expose how cute he looks, even under the influence of Dante's venom.

"My God, my love. You haven't changed, my breathtaking soulmate." Elias stretches his arms in an attempt at coaxing my reflection to him, but the restraints lock him in place. A flash of anger steals the gentleness of his features, and he thrashes. "Let me go! I have to get to her. The darkness claims her because of me. Please, don't hurt her."

I shift in Dante's arms. "I think he's tripping."

"Grace! My Grace, listen to me. They will come for you to use you against me. You must never give in to their temptation. They will only lure you to your doom. Run and don't look back. I will come for you." Elias's eyes rim with tears, and he struggles again. "Promise me, Grace. You won't let the saviors tempt you. You will do as we planned. I can't live without you, and if they get what they want, they will use life and time to try to keep us apart."

"He's hallucinating, Dante. There has to be something you can do. I'm afraid he'll hurt himself." I try to shrug out of Dante's arms, but he doesn't let me go.

Kase scoots between the two of us and Elias, ensuring I don't try anything crazy. Tilting his head toward the mirror on the ceiling, Kase watches Elias watch me. Dante watches too. It's so strange to hear him call me by another name and treat me like I'm the most precious person to him, even if it's not real.

"It's a memory, Raven," Kase finally says. He twists and waves his hand in front of Elias's face, grabbing his attention. "You hear me, Elias? Whatever you see isn't real."

Whipping his head down, Elias breaks my stare in the mirror, widening his eyes at the sight of Kase like he just now realizes he sits in front of him. "Kase, my brethren. What are you doing here? Have you come for me?"

Kase clears his throat. "It took you long enough. You should've followed us and leaped."

I gawk at the back of Kase's head. I can't believe he's playing along, pretending to know what the hell Elias rambles on about in his venom-induced memory hallucination. It takes everything in me not to whack him on the back, because I want to find out how Elias's memory of me in another life played out without devil intervention. Dante laces his fingers through mine and stops me.

"It wasn't my time. Please, you have to understand," Elias says, fighting against the chains. "I couldn't. But I'm ready now. I need your help. Cassius—"

"You want a deal with the devil?" Kase says, cutting him off.

"No, Kase. I want your help, not a deal. You must keep Lucifer out of it. I know your alliance is strong, but he is Hell's anchor, and I don't want him touching my beautiful Grace." Elias grinds his teeth, still fighting the restraints. "Please, will you help me?"

"Under one condition," Kase says, swiveling his torso. "You must tell Dante who holds your mortal soul."

I don't get a chance to react before Dante drops me on the bed beside him and hisses, letting his devil façade break through his skin. I know one of his specialties is entrancing humans into a state of hypnosis to bend them to his will, but I'm not sure it will work on Elias. It didn't work on me.

"I don't have a mortal soul. I barely have my light. I gave it to Grace." Elias heaves a breath and coughs, hacking so hard that blood spatters across his shirt. Fuck. It's worse than I thought. He wasn't joking about being sick and dying.

Dante towers over Elias and grabs him by the throat, getting him to stop fighting. Leaning in, he captures him with his gaze. "Snap out of it. You're human and you sold your soul to a bottom feeder demon. Tell us who owns it, so we can handle the situation."

Like Dante knocks sense back into him, Elias's wide eyes narrow, and his features twist from fear and into hatred hot enough that I expect the world to ignite in flames around us. Flaring his nostrils, Elias jerks his attention back toward my reflection on the ceiling. I nearly dive into Kase's arms, half expecting the fallen angel, now reborn as a mortal, to still have the capability to smite me.

"What the actual fuck! What have you done to my head?" Elias asks, his voice rising with his fury. "Just kill me and get it over with. I can't give you the information you seek. It's in my contract."

Kase grows and snakes his tail toward Elias, wrapping it around his neck, constricting his airway. "Just because you can't speak of it, doesn't mean there aren't other ways to extract the information. Now, about a deal."

"No. I've sold enough to Hell." Elias bucks his body, trying to break free.

"Damn it, you son-of-a-bastard," Dante snaps, flashing his fangs. "We are trying to help you—and your *soulmate*." He hisses the word soulmate like it pains him to say it. "You've already failed her once. Don't try to dismiss what you saw."

"You messed with my head," Elias accuses. "You want me to fucking pity the abomination."

Annoyance grows inside me, and I climb across the bed, dodging out of Kase's way. I slip under Dante's arm and get into Elias's face, meeting his eyes dead on. He stills under my closeness, sending my body buzzing. I nearly throw myself back. The intensity is too much. But like I'm trapped in some sort of magnetic hold, I can't break away. All I can do is stare into Elias's stormy gray eyes and how they look almost silver in the light.

"Elias, please. I don't know what happened to us, but I do know what will happen to me if you don't accept that what you remember is true. My soul depends on you. I depend on you. Please, if you won't make a deal with my devils, then make one with me. As much as you piss me off and get under my skin, I wouldn't wish your soul burning with mine when we can help each other." I search his gaze for something, anything, to let me know that my words get to him, but he remains expressionless.

"You can't honestly want to deny the chance to free your soul from a demon," Kase says, his growly voice rumbling across my shoulder as he leans in to peer at Elias from behind me.

"Going from one demon to another isn't freeing my soul. I know how contracts work. I want fucking redemption." Elias tightens his scruffy jaw.

"We don't want your soul. Just your mortality," Dante says. He moves even closer, looming over Elias. "In exchange, we will free you from your demonic contract."

"That sounds shitty. I want more." Elias turns his attention to me, his eyes narrowing. The greedy bastard. "I want you to treat me like an equal. Give me one helluva good time until the end of my life, my own room, anything I can think to ask for...and time with my soulmate."

"Fuck no," Kase and Dante say in unison. "She's ours."

Be still, my black heart. I love how automatic their denial was in regards to me. "They're right. I'm not something to possess. I want the same thing as you—my soul free from Hell's binds."

"Do we have a deal or not?" Elias asks, narrowing his eyes at the three of us. "Those are my terms."

Red fire ignites in Kase's palms, and I throw myself at him, knocking him on his back. I shove my palms into his thighs and push upright, giving Dante one look. He flashes his fangs at me, but doesn't say anything. I hate to use the possibility of sex against him, but it's a real motivator and gets him to keep himself in check as he desires to prove he doesn't let his envy control him.

"Time does not mean sex, being your slave to do your bidding, or anything like that, understand?" I say, my heartbeat picking up speed. "I don't even have to talk to you if I don't want to."

Elias dips his chin. "Don't worry. I'm not some twisted as fuck demon. The only thing I want from your time is to get you away from them. You deserve a moment of not being under their constant control and demands. Maybe you'll see things clearly."

Is he for real? "Are you k—"

"Is it a deal or not?" he asks, locking his gaze on mine.

I sigh and look at my devils. It could be worse, right? "Fine, whatever. You have yourself a deal."

9

Demon Bait

DANTE

"COME ON, ANGEL-GIRL. Don't be a tease." Kase's voice trickles from his cracked open bedroom door.

Raven squeals and laughs. "Watch your fucking tail, or I'll tie it in a knot."

I stop short, seeing one of my cock rings hanging on the handle. That fucker. I leave the room for ten minutes to shower, and he takes advantage by declaring he's taking some alone time with our girl. Sure, it might be his day, but I endured torture during my time with Raven all because she didn't want Elias seeing us getting it on in the living room, and Kase would want to join in his room. It might be petty that I want her to myself, but I can't see things going as perfect as I want them to otherwise. Kase is more dominant out of the two of us, and he will control both Raven and me. It's not worth the power struggle.

"Twist it, tie it, suck it, fuck it. I love all the ways you think you can punish me." Kase purrs deep in his throat. "We have to pass the time somehow until our sources get back to us."

Clenching my hands into fists, I swivel on my feet and stare at the living room. If that's what we've been waiting on, then it's time for a better plan. Kase doesn't mind waiting around, but I'm fucking tired of having to resort to hanging out in my least favorite area of the apartment now that Raven abandoned sleeping alone on the couch. I'm sure Kase will devour the rest of his time with our girl, considering she's supposed to hang with Elias next.

"How about we go angel watching instead?" Raven asks, her comment helping to ease the jealousy rising inside me. It's like she can sense it and chooses not to test me, for which I'm thankful. "As much as I have fun riding you like the beast you are, if we start, I won't want to stop. It'll cause problems in approximately four hours and twenty-seven minutes."

Kase groans and something thuds against his bedroom wall. "Elias is a lucky bastard that we can't kill him. You deserve a powerful devil and not some half-alive mortal who has as much sex appeal as your father in a speedo."

"Kase, ew!" Raven laughs again.

"If you think that thought is gross, let me get started on your uncle L—" Something cuts off Kase's teasing, and I hear Raven's whispery voice offer him a deal.

I rub the back of my neck and wait until I can hear a soft moan from Raven. They're not getting it on, but she's giving Kase the affection I crave.

Forcing my attention away from their bedroom, I redirect my focus on the bigger problem in my existence. It's already been three fucking days since Elias made Raven the deal without consulting me and Kase. And because the dickwad was already in my room, I had no choice but to suck it up and let him remain there—not like Elias could stay anywhere else. It's the only room without an easy exit. Sure, he could try to climb through the window, but he'd step right into a trap I set to keep bastard Hell-bound souls out. No matter what, I'm over it. I want my space back, and the only way to get it is to find the demon who owns his soul.

Curling my fingers into fists, I barge into my room and drop my towel to the floor. Elias gawks at me from my bed, reading one of my old Kama Sutra manuals like he could even successfully perform any sex position beyond missionary—or if he could survive the act at all. I have a sense for death, especially with Hell-bound souls, and his will come soon.

"Have you ever heard of knocking?" Elias asks, getting the nerve to speak to me.

"What for? This is my room and I don't need a fucking invitation in." I stroll to my dresser and pull out a T-shirt, shrugging it on first, knowing my swinging cock makes him uncomfortable. I purposefully give him a show, swaying my hips as I close the space. I stand at the end of the bed. "Now I want you to get ready. You're coming out with me."

"No way. This was part of the deal. You take care of my contract, and I hang out." Elias closes the book and tosses it on the nightstand.

Snatching his ankle, I drag him toward me and dangle him upside down high enough that he can't take his eyes off my cock. It's like he's afraid it'll strike him, and it might if he doesn't do what I need.

"Nothing about the deal says you get to sit on your ass all day in my room." I set him on his shoulders and ease him onto floor, despite my raging desire to drop his ass. "Our contracted contacts are taking too long to find answers, so it's up to you."

I leave him in shock on the floor and head back to my dresser to grab a pair of jeans. I slide them on commando and adjust my junk. Watching me in silence from the floor, Elias remains frozen. I hiss and startle him, loving how he's lost his tough-ass attitude. He realizes he's the prey, and I won't hesitate to devour him if he gets under my skin. I know how to keep him alive and complacent during the process.

"I'm incapable of telling you anything about my master. I've told you this." Elias scoots back until he hits my bed.

"I can use other information. Like where you signed your deal," I mutter, stomping closer. Crossing my arms, I tower over him. "If you tell me what you got in exchange for your soul, that could help me as well. Demons have specialties. Now get up. We're going hunting."

"I'm not feeling good enough. You didn't let me take my pain meds," he says, scratching his arms. "I can barely function without feeling like I'm suffocating, you asshole."

Elias grips the bed frame, trying to pull himself to his feet. His pathetic attempt fails, and I crack my neck, bend down, and help him up. I don't want to do it, but I also don't want him giving up and lying on my bedroom floor until he keels over. I don't want him in my room at all. I'll carry him if I have to.

"We will stop by and grab them. Until then, let me bite you. A bit of my venom will help. I won't release as much as last time, because I don't need you soaring like you grew your wings back." I adjust him like a big-ass angel baby. This is far less fun with him than it is with Raven. It doesn't help that he smells like cigarettes, the fucker really not caring about dying. "Give me your wrist."

"Fuck no. Put me down." Elias shoves his palm against my

cheek. "Keep that filthy mouth away from me."

"Don't be a weak-ass ball sack and accept my help. It just makes me want to toughen you up when you resist. It's just a nip." I lean away as he tries to swing at me.

"It's more than that. I bet you get off on sinking your teeth into anything you can. It's not going to be me." Elias raises his voice and manages to clock me in the jaw.

Clenching my teeth, I stride toward the hallway and toss him out of my room. "You ungrateful piece of shit. I'm trying to help you with no fucking strings attached for the sake of Raven and you're being a dickhole. Why suffer through pain when I can help you? I don't get it."

"You're only trying to help yourself," he says, groaning from the floor.

I swing and punch the wall in anger.

"Dante, Elias. What the hell is going on out here?" Raven hovers in the doorway to Kase's room wearing only one of his shirts. "Why are you fighting?"

It takes everything in me to control my anger, especially when Raven helps Elias off the floor. I want to cut off his hand for even having the chance to touch hers. My jealousy gets the best of me, and I spin and storm away. I know I'm fucked up when I start hating something as little as a gesture. Hell, I might even hate Kase's shirt, because it's where I want to be, wrapping myself around her.

Raven chases after me. "Dante, come back here."

I slow to let her catch up but don't turn to face her. Hopping onto my back, she ensures I can't escape by clinging to my shoulders and hooking her legs around my torso. She stretches and presses her lips to my ear. I shiver under the sensation of her breath as she kisses my lobe.

"What did the asshole do?" she asks, keeping her voice low. "Did he fuck with your stuff?"

I groan and flip her around to face me. The fact that she assumes it was Elias's fault lights a fire inside me. I fucking love her. She understands me on a level no one else does, and even if she knows I might be caught up in my own emotions, she will never make me feel bad about it.

"He's in pain and wouldn't let me help him. I figured the two of us could go demon hunting since our contracts haven't responded yet, but I need him in better shape. A little bit of my venom will take the edge off until we can get his pain meds." I look past Raven and glower at Elias. "He only wants to lie around, waiting to die."

Something indecipherable crosses Raven's face. Her bottom lip puffs out with her pout, and she knits her eyebrows together. I wish I could hear her thoughts in this moment to know what she's thinking. If I could, I might be able to figure out how to return her breathtaking smile to her beautiful face.

Raven shifts slightly in my arms, trying to look behind her.

"Why didn't you tell us you were suffering, Elias?"

"Because I didn't think it mattered to you." Elias wobbles on his feet and leans against the wall for support.

"Of course it does. We're not monsters, despite what you think. Now stop being stubborn and let Dante help you. He's right about the contracts. If he has a plan to hunt your demon down, we should go for it." Raven smirks at me, her eyes lighting with her words. "I'll come too."

I scowl, unable to control my reaction. "Like hell—"

She slaps a hand over my mouth, cutting me off. "Kase mentioned he had some business to take care of, so you don't have a choice. I'm coming."

"Not in the way you think," I mutter under my breath, peering toward Kase's shadow looming in the hallway. I don't know what kind of business he claims he has to do, but it better be important.

"If you're good, maybe I'll say the same about you." Licking her lips, she bows closer. "Kase promised he'd look into a bigger place for us. He feels bad about you giving up your room...though I like being in the middle of you two. It's hot."

"Don't let him fool you. It's about his need to have you to himself," I murmur.

"Maybe it's also about me having you to myself as well. I know you and Kase have fun together, but I love having your undivided attention." Her voice lowers with her words, and she slides her hand across my shoulder and to the back of my neck. "He won't let me have it if we have to share a room."

I hum in my throat, her whispery voice awakening my cock. And damn it. I want to prop her on the wall, tug my pants down, and fuck her until she screams my name like I'm the one she worships.

Sliding my hand down her back, I pull up her shirt and dig my fingers into her ass cheek. "If you're teasing me or trying to distract me—"

Her lips mold over mine as she silences me. Kissing me deeper, she explores my mouth with her tongue, not giving me the control I crave. Raven knows exactly what she's doing to me and she relishes every second of turning me on. She even reaches down to feel my cock through my pants, not caring that we're being watched by Elias.

She breaks away from my mouth. "Kase, grab Elias. I need you to pin him down, so Dante can help him."

Elias raises his hands up. "That's not necessary. I'll fucking let him bite me as long as you swear I don't have to go alone with him."

Raven nods. "I promise. I'm not letting you out of my sight."

I flash my fangs at Elias. "At least for now."

"Are you sure it was here? It's a playground." Raven tightens her jacket around herself, peering at the dozens of children playing while their parents, nannies, and other relatives watch them. "It's fucking creepy."

"Parks, stores, bars, restaurants—demons will go where the humans go, pretty soul. This park happens to be the breeding ground for a lot of despicable behavior. I mean, look at that asshole over there. He's been stalking the babysitter for weeks, waiting until he catches her alone." I blink my eyes, letting loose my Hell power to get a better reading on the souls in the area. The stalker is bound to Hell without even a contract.

Raven covers her mouth with her hand. "Oh, my God. We have to do—"

"The woman's soul isn't exactly shining. She's done some shitty things too," Elias says, speaking up. Reaching into his back pocket, he pulls out a pack of smokes and waves the box.

Before he can light up, Raven surprises the both of us and steals the pack and hands it to me. I wonder if she knows and has been ignoring the fact that he's been sneaking cigs in my room.

"You can see her soul?" Intrigue laces Raven's voice. Look at her, not giving him a hard time. I'm torn between wishing she would and knowing if she did that it might mean she cares more about his health than she lets on. The guy is dying already. There is no stopping it.

Elias rubs the back of his neck and shifts on his boots. "I read auras. Always have. It's how I got into hunting demons."

"You mean it's what got the demons hunting you." I crack my knuckles and peer around the park. "Your soul matches Raven's. You're a beacon, and it's getting on my nerves."

Raven smacks my arm. "Knock it off."

I return the gesture, but instead of her arm, I spank her ass hard enough to make her jump. "Make me."

Her eyebrows peak on her forehead. "Don't test me."

Elias twitches his fingers, bouncing with anxiousness. "Yeah, don't. Anytime she gives you a little attention, you try to devour her completely. We don't have time. I don't want to be out here longer than I have to. My demon—"

Unfurling my wings, I flap them and throw him off his feet with a gust of wind. Raven tries to dodge out of my reach, but I'm faster. I hook my arm around her waist and scoop her into my arms. She doesn't get a chance to fight me to stay before I launch us into the air. Wind whips Raven's hair into my face, and I inhale a breath of her floral fragrance like the cherry blossom shampoo she picked out.

"Hey! Wait! Don't leave me here!" Elias swings his arms over his head and runs a dozen feet like he'll sprout wings to chase after us.

I adjust Raven's legs around me and wave. "You'll be fine, demon bait. Get your master to come out, and I'll get you."

Raven screeches as I fly us higher and land on a nearby roof. No one notices our dramatic exit, the power of Hell compelling them to mind their damn businesses. Raven gasps a few deep breaths, her heart thudding against mine. She clings on tighter, burying her face into my shoulder. Fuck, I love it. I love it so much that I plop her sexy ass on the ledge, so her instincts kick in and refuse to let me go.

"Dante, what are you doing? We need to go back." Raven eases away and realizes there is a four-story drop behind her.

Huffing, she tightens her ankles across my ass and pulls me so close that if I tugged down my zipper and shifted her emerald green thong an inch, I could fuck her right here. And damn, do I want to. It's been days since I've been alone with her with no chance of interruption. I hadn't realized how starved for her attention I was.

"Relax, pretty soul. We're demon repellant. If someone senses us, they'll think we've stuck a claim on their domain. Elias needs to be alone for this to work. If his demon offers deals here, then he'll come around. We just have to wait."

She grips the front of my shirt. "Dante."

"Keep saying my name. I love it." I slide my hand up her back until I tangle my fingers through her hair.

She moans a breath as I pull it, forcing her to tip her head back to look at me. Her big blue-green eyes sparkle in the light of the sun, and she yanks me closer by my shirt until I crash my mouth to hers, our lips and tongues battling for dominance. She loves being controlled. Her pleasure. Her needs. As long as it's in ways she enjoys from the clothes I pick out to the shade of red lipstick she wears. But she also loves feeling power, my power, especially when I give it to her. Right now, I'm willing to compromise and give her what she wants. If she wants to taste my mouth and bruise my lips, I'll take it to make her happy.

These last few days have made me realize the kind of power she holds over me and how I'm willing to gut anyone who tries to get between us. I need my piece of her soul. I'm not willing to give it up. If other fuckers like Elias want even a molecule of Raven, they're going to have to earn it. Fight for it, even. She only deserves the best from the bastard who will go to Hell for her. Elias isn't there yet. Maybe after today when I find his demon and disembowel him in a way that keeps him on this plane but also makes him wish he were in Hell—and then get the fucker to give me Elias's contract—will I consider it okay for him to share her breathing space. For everything else? He better horn up.

Raven moans dragging her fingers down my abs until she cups my hard-on through my pants. "I should punish you for getting me worked up."

Grinning, I flex my cock to tease her palm. "Punish me? You've been testing my strength for weeks. Giving me only a taste before pulling back. You're driving me batshit crazy with need for you. If anyone is getting punished, it's going to be you. And don't think I won't. I bought a spanking bench to restrain you too. As soon as we get the chance—"

I feel the shockwave of Hell pulsing through the air as a demon taps into Lucian's kingdom to secure a human façade. Raven senses my distraction and stops rubbing my aching cock, my balls screaming at me to ignore the demon's approach down below for a couple more minutes. If I knew Raven would be up to the challenge, I'd fuck her while flying and fighting to show her how talented I really am.

"Dante! It's not him!" Elias's yell catches on the wind.

I jerk my attention to the park below and spot Elias breaking into a jog, running in the opposite direction of what I can only describe as one of Hell's shit piles of a demon. If the fucker is here, it can only mean that it's trying to scrounge up a couple of deals Elias's demon didn't care to negotiate before moving on. And if he moved on...fuck.

Raven tries to twist in my arms to see what's going on. I don't let her and push her back, startling her. She screams as she freefalls a dozen feet until I swoop down and catch her. I need her a bit scared to kick her adrenaline on. She's feistier this way. More likely to fight. It'll also piss her off, and when she's angry, she can summon a bit of Hell's strength.

Skidding my boots on the grass, I slow to a stop behind the demon. I flap my wings, sending a gust of wind in his direction, but the bastard only uses it to push himself forward instead of eating shit on the ground like I had hoped.

"Dante!" Elias shouts, feeling his jacket for the knife I took from him.

The demon explodes from his human façade, shaking the ground. Like a demented rhinoceros with blood-red skin and two heads, the beast charges at Elias on four legs. It doesn't bother trying to do anything except attack, knowing Elias's soul is already bound to another.

Lowering his head, the demon rams into Elias with his massive horn, throwing Elias a dozen feet.

Raven screams, her voice ripping through the air.

Elias hits the ground.

He doesn't move.

The demon shrieks and tramples over Elias, realizing I'm chasing him. The damn demon will have more than a little Hell to pay.

10

Lust

ANDRE

"HOW COULD YOU be so careless? Fuck, Dante. He's hurt." Raven races the dozen feet it takes to get to Elias and drops to her knees.

"It was a risk we needed to take. I don't think you understand the severity of his fucking condition. I was trying to help." Dark green and gold scales sprout from his arms as he unleashes his Hell body, turning into the serpent he truly is.

"He almost died and we didn't even get any answers." Raven caresses her knuckles across Elias's cheek.

"Stay here with him. Don't go anywhere. Do you understand?" Dante flashes his fangs while he speaks. "You'll be safe enough."

"Where are you going?" Raven asks, her voice rising in panic.

"To get answers." Without waiting for Raven to respond, Dante launches into the air, sending a gust of his burning pinewood scent in my direction.

Raven slaps her hands into the grass and growls, taking out her frustration on the ground. Hanging her head, she lets her midnight hair veil her face, shielding the world from seeing her tears sparkling on her cheeks. A couple splash on Elias's face, stirring him back to consciousness, and he just stares up at her.

"Darlin', you look like an angel," Elias murmurs, reaching up to comb Raven's hair from her face. "For a second, I thought my prayers were finally answered."

Raven groans and sniffles, tipping her head toward the sky. If I didn't know she was looking for her soul keeper, I'd think she was about to pray to the Higher Power. Blinking the tears from her eyes, she clears her vision only to catch sight of me. I don't hide from her like I should, but her fear is palpable, shuddering through my essence. She needs to know that she isn't alone. With me, no demon will risk coming closer.

I rub my hands together and thin the veil between planes, pushing out the rest of the world from Raven's view. She gawks at me in shock. And then what feels like a miracle happens. Raven raises her arm and motions to me.

"Andre, you have no idea how happy I am to see you." She invites me over with her trembling voice. I can feel her need for my closeness deep in my bones. It awakens a part of me that has lain dormant for as long as I've existed. "Please, can you help him? If he dies…" A sob escapes her ruby lips and tears at my essence. How can I deny such a plea?

Folding my wings, I stroll closer and tower over her and Elias, staring down at his frozen form. Blood seeps from his ear, threatening to drip into his hair the second I close the veil and put the world together. Raven's desperation sinks inside me, and I find myself kneeling beside her. Seeing Elias like this, an angel once so powerful that demons ran in his presence, guts me on a level I didn't know possible. The same sorrow I felt over Micah's discarded grace crashes over me, and I can't stop the tears from burning my eyes.

"My friend, what have you done? What was worth trading your existence for?" I ask, hovering my hand over Elias's forehead.

"Please, Andre. There has to be something you can do." Raven rests her hand on my knee, sending electricity coursing through my body, awakening every inch of me under her touch.

I tilt my head and meet her gaze. "I can heal his wounds, but the sickness devouring his lungs is bound by a demonic contract."

"What?" Raven's surprise softens her features. "He's sick because of a demon?"

"I will let you know more if you give me your permission to read his soul. It does partially belong to you in a way." I summon my heavenly light in my palm, setting Elias's face aglow. The halo reminds me of another one of his lifetimes, when he would've never resorted to a demonic deal.

"Yes, of course. Do what you have to." Raven scoots closer to me, sliding her fingers through Elias's. The gesture tugs at me, capturing my attention. I know she doesn't remember the history of her soul—and neither does Elias for that matter—and I can't help basking in the bright light they create together. Their souls know they are fated even if they don't, and I want nothing more than to live in their light.

"It'll only take a minute, but he will remain out of sorts. Will you be able to manage with your soul keeper acting so carelessly?" I search Raven's eyes. I can't tell her that I'll stay with her regardless, but I also need to know she can handle it. I don't want her to think I've abandoned her.

She hides her lips, tightening her mouth. "I don't know. I'm scared. Can you stay until Dante returns? We flew here, and I'm not even sure I can find my way back to our apartment."

"You want me to stay?" My heart flutters, the sensation stealing my breath. A wave of pure joy envelops me as if Raven hugs me. But it's just her essence. Her need of protection. It's in this moment I realize how dangerous her effect is on me. If I didn't feel so strongly about my path and what my mission is, I might lose myself to her completely.

"If that's okay," she says, squeezing my knee.

Her touch shoots pleasure to my groin, and I tense, losing focus with my erection. It happens more and more lately, but especially with her closeness. I don't mind as long as my brethren don't notice. Such a simple thing is an unnecessarily big deal to Cassius. He acts as if it's a bad omen. I consider it a connection to humanity. I can serve mortals better knowing what simple things like a body's reaction to another is like.

"It would be my honor, little hellion. How else am I supposed to influence some good into the dark spots the devils carve into your soul?" I remain expressionless with my words, trying not to let the truth of them get to me.

My lack of expression does nothing to help Raven, and she reacts with a scowl. "Don't act all high and mighty, Andre. You're the one with a damn erection. If anything, you're a bad influence, reminding me of how enormous your angelic cock is. Now just get on with it. This isn't about my soul. It's about Elias."

Releasing my leg, she cups Elias's hand between her palms. I wonder what her warmth would feel like to have her hands on me, if I'd feel better or worse. Shaking my head, I push the thoughts of her touching me from my mind only to have the memory of her exploring my erection snap back front and center.

I roll my shoulders, ruffling my wings. "My apologies. I can't seem to control this common reoccurrence with you. I don't know how to get it to stop."

She groans and shifts, hiding her face from me. "Next time you're alone, rub one out or something."

"Rub one out?" I ask, continuing on my mission to heal Elias even through this fascinating conversation. I'd love to possess her knowledge on the matter. "Perhaps you can show me what that is."

Her shoulders shake, and I frown, wondering why she's crying. I reach out with my free hand and graze my fingers over her forearm. Whipping her attention to me, she bursts out in laughter. I misjudged her body language. She finds great amusement in this moment, and her melodious, contagious giggling eases the worry clinging to me.

"Can you please just finish healing Elias?" she asks, twirling her finger. "We can get into the relief and fun of masturbation some other time."

"Oh." Warmth heats my cheeks at her words.

I should've understood her comment far quicker than I had. Why does it bother me in such a way? Perhaps because I lack the mortal experiences she's grown accustomed to, especially with the devils. They enjoy suffering and pain, but I also know how much they savor pleasure and bliss, which might be the closest thing they could ever experience now that the joy of grace is out of their reach.

Raven bumps me with her hip, sending a shockwave of something indescribable through me. My groin tenses at the sensation and my desire turns uncomfortable almost. Persistent. Nagging. The absurd need to touch myself consumes me.

"You have no idea how much I want to corrupt you, Andre," she comments, watching my heavenly light set Elias aglow. Squinting, she peeks at me through the strands of her dark hair veiling her face.

"Enlightening and educating me on certain physical aspects of humanity wouldn't corrupt me." I suck in my bottom lip as Raven touches my leg again. Swallowing, I focus on reading Elias's soul, the darkness clinging to him so foul that I jerk my hand away and unfurl my wings. "But digging deeper into Elias's Hell-bound soul might."

Raven's eyes widen and she gently sets his limp hand on the ground at his side. "What did you see? Are you okay?"

I shiver. "I will be. His soul was just...so tormented. He traded his soul for the health of someone close to him. Someone like a brother. I couldn't remain focused long enough to read further. I'm sorry. He is healed as best as I could manage though. Hopefully it'll buy you time. The demon with his contract hid a stipulation which transferred the lung cancer to him."

She blinks her eyes, working through the swelling emotions inside her. "That bastard demon. He must've learned from Lucian personally on crappy deals."

I sigh and scrub my hand over my face. Shedding the darkness of Elias's soul is harder than I expected. "Perhaps. I—" A strange wave of dizziness washes over me. "I'm sorry. His soul—"

Warm fingers sink into my cheeks, and I narrow my attention on Raven's glorious soul shining before me. She cradles my face between her palms, saying my name, and I manage to use her light to destroy the lingering darkness. Electricity zings through us, and she gasps, falling into me. I automatically engulf her in my arms and pull her up, not letting her slide to the ground.

"Healing Elias had a worse impact on me than I expected. It's one of the reasons we tend to leave Hell-bound souls be," I murmur, adjusting my legs until I sit on the ground with her on my lap.

Raven surprises me by hugging me tighter, burying her face into the crook of my neck. "Thank you for helping us despite it. I owe you."

The pressure of her body sinking onto my erection sets me off with a deep-seated ache that forces me to tighten my hands on her hips to adjust her. I can't stop the breath of a moan escaping my lips, my body reacting so intensely to Raven. I consider abandoning her to do what she recommended, despite my promise.

"You owe me nothing, little hellion," I manage to murmur, my thoughts whirling with a dozen scenarios of what I desire to happen next. "But if you'd like to help me in return, I'd gladly appreciate it. The brilliance of your soul brings me great relief."

She tilts her head. "Even though Lucian taints me with his evilness?"

I smile and touch her cheek. "Your soul happens to be the one exception, it seems."

"Then do what you need. I don't mind." Her stunning blue-green eyes capture mine, the deep navy rings around her irises a dark contrast to the mixture of emerald and turquoise.

Drawing my eyes lower, I memorize her slender nose and full ruby lips, painted with makeup. I suddenly crave to taste her mouth, wondering if her lips are as sweet as their cherry color. And then her pink tongue glides along the seam of her mouth like she anticipates me leaning in and recreating our moment alone in her dream world.

"Raven, I desire to kiss you," I say, running my thumb across her pout.

"Are you sure that's what you want? I wasn't joking about wanting to corrupt you. It's my mission," she says, her honesty the purest thing in the moment. I appreciate it more than she could know. As long as we're both aware of our desires and the grim possibilities that can occur, I can navigate my mission without losing sight.

I offer her an assuring smile. "You can try your best, but that's an impossible task, Raven. The only bad thing about you is Lucian's chain, and even then, it does nothing to me. So to answer your question, yes, I'm most certain. I yearn to know what it's like to kiss you on this physical plane."

With a small nod, Raven tilts her head and caresses her lips to mine, the feather-softness of her caress prodding at something warm inside me. Goosebumps prickle over my body, and I deepen our kiss, tasting the sweet sugar flavor of her tongue. Just the simple gliding of her tongue across mine ignites an undeniable desperation inside me, and I slide my hand down the length of her back and pull her into me, needing the pressure and weight of her body against mine to stop me from floating away on this ride of excitement.

She combs her fingers through my hair, rocking her hips like she wants to feel my desire for her. I moan and dig my fingers into the soft skin of her waist. The pleasure she brings with such a simple gesture sets my body off, each touch, each shift, even just the sensation of her breath on my mouth as she pulls away makes me feel as if I'm ascending to the point where I'll have nowhere to go except back down.

She gasps and eases away, clutching onto my shoulders like I'm the only thing keeping her grounded as our essences try to soar away together. "I have to stop," she mumbles, her heaving chest grazing her breasts against me—breasts I imagine are as perfect as the parts of her I see now. "If I don't..." She shivers. "You're not ready for that."

I try to keep her in place. "I'm ready for anything, my little hellion."

"Then maybe I'm not." Raven shifts out of my arms and gets to her feet, kicking our private world back into motion. "Thank you, Andre. For everything."

I frown and use my wings to launch me up. Towering over her, I look into her eyes, trying to get a read on her soul, but she steps away. "Have I done something wrong? I apologize if—"

I shudder, my words cutting off as I sense the quivering darkness of Hell rising from my right. Without finishing my thought, I launch into the air, leaving Raven standing over Elias in the grass. Dante stalks in their direction, his body soaked in the filth of demon guts. I only watch for a second as Raven throws her hands up at Dante, her shouts lost on the whistling wind.

I can't bear to witness the most breathtaking soul I've ever seen lose itself to a devil's darkness, especially after reminding me of Heaven. My body still buzzes and aches, and I fly to a rooftop and bow against an access door, clinging onto Raven's light and the memory of her closeness. Unzipping my pants, I pull out my erection and stroke my fingers along the length of my shaft, taking care to massage myself in the fast, exciting strokes I get from my thoughts of Raven.

My body tenses, and I moan, staring at my release splattering on the door. My vision turns white, the pleasure and relief from a simple act helping to clear my mind. I inhale a few long breaths and slow my racing heart. It feels as if it wants to escape my chest to chase the soul that calls to me, wanting nothing more than to feel my light and love and grace but a soul so afraid of unleashing darkness that Raven will deny what could be something glorious and pure between us. She doesn't see it, but I'm good for her and her soul. She can't corrupt me.

It makes me more determined to prove it.

I will show her that there is hope beyond her binds to Lucifer. She can experience good grace and Heaven with me.

"Andre, I've been calling to you. What has kept you from responding?" Cassius's deep voice cuts through the air behind me.

I stiffen and adjust my pants, not allowing him to see he caught me in an act intended for humanity. "Raven." I cannot lie to Cassius despite knowing he'll be displeased. "Her soul keepers are up to something."

"You are not to be around her." Cassius scowls and gives me a once over, trying to figure out what I hide from him. "She—"

"She could be useful." I cross my arms over my chest. "I know you worry, Cass, but I know my purpose, and I will not allow a single soul to ruin that. Yet, I also can't seem to get the thought of gaining her trust out of my mind. My instincts believe she can do what we have been incapable of accomplishing. She can keep us informed about Hell's plans. Kindness goes a long way. So does mercy. Have you thought about that? Instead of disregarding her, we should see what she is willing to do to help the Higher Power."

I press my lips together, the suggestion hiding my alternate desire to get to know Raven on a physical level. That is none of Cassius's concern as the knowledge will do nothing apart from worry him for no reason.

Cassius studies my face for a moment before nodding. "I suppose you're right. But I want you to be careful. Don't get too close. You know why her soul shines so brightly."

I nod without response.

Like he must confirm it out loud, he adds, "She is an abomination. Her essence born from our own brethren's fall from grace. It isn't good, Andre."

"Yes, Cassius." Except he's wrong.

Cassius unfurls his wings. "It's deceptive. If you're not careful—"

Anger lashes through me, and I scowl. "Enough! Do not speak to me as if I don't know and understand my purpose.

I will not fail."

"I pray so," he whispers, glancing at the sky. "I can't lose anyone else."

Without another word, Cassius launches into the air, taking flight. He might not want to lose anyone else, but I don't want to lose Raven. He will see her importance. And when he does, he will realize what I know on a soul-deep level.

Raven isn't a lost soul.

She's a force that'll take on Hell.

She's angel-kissed for a reason.

With her, I know the Higher Power will continue to rise.

11

Punishment

RAVEN

"**D**ON'T TOUCH ANYTHING. If you smear your polish, I will punish you." Dante twists the cap back on the glittery purple nail polish. Usually I'd deny him the chance to doll me up the way he wants, but I know he needs a little extra agreement and submission from me to help ease his wild emotions. "Your hand will look so fucking sexy around my cock. I can't wait."

I smirk and carefully grab his wrist, lacing my fingers around his arm. "I never knew how much I wanted a manicure from a devil. You're so talented."

He chuckles and guides my hand to stroke his arm. His cock

hardens under me as I sit on his lap with him gazing at my slow movements from over my shoulder. "Not so much talented as I have quirofilia. Your hands are especially sexy and so fuckable."

"You're such a kinky ass," I tease, wiggling my ass. "I can't wait to see what you have in store for me in your new room."

"Our new room," he corrects, shifting my hair to kiss my shoulder. "I've demanded our own bathroom, balcony, and a kitchenette. I want to ensure we never have to leave if we don't want to, my pretty soul."

"You sound like you plan to keep me all to yourself." I continue to grind on him, turning myself on so much that my nipples ache, their tightness grazing against the thin fabric of my lace bra.

He hums. "After seeing you with Andre and Elias a few days ago, I need to make the most of my time alone with you."

I tip my head back, exposing my throat to him. "You're worried."

"Not worried. I just want to keep my envy in check. It's why I don't push you more. I know you think I might let it get the best of me, which is why you don't let me have my way." Dante snuggles close, sliding his hand over my thighs and up the bare skin of my stomach, leaving a blazing trail of warmth in his wake. "But trust me, Raven. I won't do anything to jeopardize our growing relationship, even if I have to suck it up and share you beyond how I do with Kase. Don't forget where I come from. I was created to love a single power who loved many. You are far more worthy of my worship."

I shift in Dante's arms, yearning to face him. "Please don't place me on a pedestal. I don't want to be a god. I just want to be an equal. We can worship each other."

Turning me around completely, Dante meets me for a kiss, filling me up with warmth and affection. I devour his attention, combing my fingers through his hair as I straddle him, rocking my body on the length of his shaft over the towel. It would be so easy to sink on top of him. I almost do.

If a knock didn't thud on the bathroom door, I'd give into my sinfully hot desire to test his resolve as the embodiment of envy and build new boundaries to test.

"You said to give you an hour," Kase says, cracking the bathroom door open. "I've given you two, and Elias is getting on my nerves."

I expect Dante to hiss and complain, but all he does is lean in and whisper, "The wait will be worth it. The power of my desperation to claim you as mine will leave you creaming for years."

I shiver and rest my head on his shoulder, letting him stand with me in his arms. Kase grabs my dress from the hanger on the door and motions for me to spin around. Digging his fingers into my hip, he slowly uses his other hand to zip up the body-forming number, short enough that my vagina will show if I bend over. Hell, my devils better be careful. If they mess with me too much while I sit on one of their laps, they'll end up with a puddle on their pants because lace does nothing to prevent such occurrences.

"She's so fucking enchanting. I can't get over how we can have her whenever we want for the rest of time," Kase murmurs to Dante. "Why don't we have Elias drive and we can have some fun in the backseat?"

I release a breath of desire and push my way out from between them. "He doesn't deserve that kind of show yet."

Kase smirks. "You're right, angel-girl. The bastard has far from earned anything. He's lucky he didn't fuck up his deal with us or he'd be staying in a closet."

Swatting my ass with his tail, Kase herds me from the bathroom and into the living room. Several quiet men work at packing up the place, and I can't help but think good riddance to this whole apartment complex. My devils promise that the summoning circle will no longer bring Hell into the house we move in to tonight. I can't wait. Like, I really fucking wish we could just go there now.

But alas, we have a demon to hunt and angels to tease.

Elias stares at me in silence as he stands by the door, dressed in a button-down shirt and dark jeans Kase probably forced him to borrow. I give him a long once-over, drinking in how much better he looks now than what he looked like this morning. Dante's venom definitely helps him some. If I didn't know any better, I'd never guess he was terminally ill.

Elias opens the door for me and murmurs that I look good under his breath. I can't blame him for being nervous about complimenting me in front of Kase and Dante. I almost wish he hadn't. A part of me wants to keep my distance. I can't trust him, not like I can trust Dante and Kase.

Kase grabs Elias and drapes his arm over his shoulders, making him stiffen. "Raven looks far better than good. If you can't think of a compliment worthy of her, then keep your mouth shut."

I can't stop the laughter bubbling from my throat as I climb into a car I've never seen before. The black Maserati looks fitting for Dante, and I wonder if he'd ever let me drive. Surprisingly, Kase and Dante take the front, leaving Elias in the back with me. I wonder if it has to do with keeping their desire in check...maybe mine. I wasn't kidding about not allowing Elias to watch and judge my intimacy with my soul keepers, but shit happens. Sometimes I can get on board with dropping my inhibitions and letting loose my filthy, naughty side.

Elias watches me the entire ride to the Demon's Den, one of the many establishments owned by the demonic legion under Kase and Dante. A man in an all-black suit opens my door for me, but Dante hisses and towers behind him faster than my mind can even grasp that he abandoned the passenger's seat. I realize how I must be cautious, even with my devils protecting me, and I inwardly kick myself for almost letting the man take my hand.

"These two mortals are off limits," Dante snaps, flashing his fangs. "Make it be known. I will gut anyone who dares even glance at them. Understand?"

Dante helps me from the car and touches his hand to my lower back. I can't tell if he's being protective or possessive, but either way, I love having my psycho devil on my arm. Knowing that he saves his soft side for me makes me weak in the knees.

"There will always be one to disobey," Kase says, coming up on my other side. He keeps his hand locked on Elias's shoulder, forcing him to walk in front of him instead of behind. "I call dibs on gutting them."

I widen my eyes. "Seriously? You're going to gut someone for looking at me?"

"Or him. But mostly for you." Kase gives Elias a shake.

"Always you." Dante pulls me closer until I practically melt into his side. Bowing down, he presses a kiss to the top of my head and waits for me to tip my face up so he can meet my mouth.

Scooping me up, he hums, teasing me with his tongue the entire way inside. Music blares through the bar, but Dante doesn't let me look around. His mouth doesn't leave mine until my heart raps against my ribcage, and I'm breathless.

A deep, familiar roar echoes over the pulsing music, and a woman laughs, her melodious voice like a sultry singer. Dante slides into a booth and finally lets me pull away. I gawk at Kase tossing the head of a man into the air with his tail. Spinning, a gorgeous woman in a sparkly silver dress catches the demon's head and plants her burgundy lips to the man's.

I cover my mouth, trying not to gag. Elias stands rigid at the edge of the booth, his face losing color by the second.

"Three o'clock, my king," the woman calls, throwing the head toward another male demon.

The demon unleashes his Hell façade in an attempt to fight, but Kase towers over the demon and sends a breath of red fire over his beastly form. With a slash of his claws, Kase rips the demon's middle open, spilling its innards across the shiny black floor.

"Yeah, babes! You see that? Look what happens when you disobedient pricks try to test our kings!" The woman picks up the decapitated head from the gut pile and swings it as she saunters behind Kase in our direction. She drops the head on the table in front of me. "A gift, my liege. For your queen and her...jester. It's a displeasure to see you again, Elias. You look like shit."

I continue to gape at the severed head on the middle of the table. Who the fuck is this demon and how is it possible she might be more psychotic than my devils?

"Uh-oh. You haven't spoiled her with presents yet, have you?" the demonic woman asks, leaning closer. She doesn't look at me, keeping her gaze down as Kase had instructed the man outside to tell everyone. "The poor doll is in awe. She doesn't even know how to react."

"Uh, thanks?" My voice rises in question. The demon is right. I have no fucking clue how to react.

Dante shifts me onto the booth seat beside him and bumps his shoulder to mine. "Now what do you expect, Gia? Raven has no use for a severed head."

Gia laughs and shakes her head. "Of course she does. She can use it for entertainment. Come on, my gorgeous queen. Pick it up by the hair and give it a good throw. Hit any bastard here you please, and they will bow before you." Gia taps her coffin-shaped nail to the tabletop. "You can pierce the eyes, if you prefer. Give it a good toss."

I glance from Dante and then to Kase, sliding into the booth across from me. The two of them shrug at the same time, leaving the decision up to me. A part of me wants to throw up at the idea of touching such a repulsive thing, but damn it. I don't want to seem weak. Mortal. I love the fuck out of being called the queen to my devils, and if this is how I should accept a gift, I guess the heads will roll—or fly. I'm not messing up the manicure Dante spent time giving me.

Sucking in a breath, I reach for the severed head and lock my fingers through the demon's oily hair. It's heavier than I expect it to be, and I ignore the black liquid dripping onto the table. Kase and Dante grin with so much pride I expect them to pat their own backs or at least each other's that I don't back down. Elias, on the other hand, grimaces at me like I'm about to catch the plague.

"That's it, my queen. Look at the bastards and pick which one you want to bow at your feet," Gia encourages, standing beside me. Heat radiates from her body, her brunette hair shining in the dim light. Her light brown complexion complements her dark eyes, sparkling with a red glow similar to Kase's. Even though I study her face, she still takes care not to look at me. It's a bit uncomfortable, because I'm used to eye contact, but I'm not pressing anyone's buttons. She seems loyal enough to gut herself if she fails to comply with my devils' demands.

I dangle the head in front of me, trailing my eyes across the crowded bar. None of the demons look in our direction, and I kind of feel like I used to as a teen in school, silently praying that if I don't look that the teacher won't call my name. The demons act exactly like that, which makes me only want to pick the one sweating the most.

"Any suggestions? Who pissed you off today?" I ask, deciding to use this chance to discover a bit more about the demonic lifestyle. "I'd like to see them bow before us."

Gia claps her hands and bolts forward, running so effortlessly in her tall stilettos I consider asking her for pointers.

"Now you've done it, angel-girl," Kase mutters from behind me. "Gia takes her commands very seriously."

I swivel my torso to look at him. His smile never fades. In fact, it widens at the grunts and growls rumbling behind me. Scrunching my nose, I slowly spin back around to face Gia. She shoves two demons on the floor and grabs a third one from a table by the bar and drags him closer, her strength freaky as fuck with her petite frame.

"Meet the fuckers who think they can swoop in on my territory and steal souls out from under me." Gia kicks the middle demon and steps on his back, impaling him with her high heel between the shoulder blades. "Fuckers, this is your queen."

The two demons kneeling growl and threaten me. My body screams to run but my head reminds me that these predators love a game of chase. So I do the only thing I can think of. Swinging the severed head, I clock the two demons across their faces.

Gia pumps her fist and shakes her ass in a happy dance. "It looks like the queen has chosen. Bow to your superior."

Dante hisses from the table, his threat getting the two demons to join the third one bowing on the floor. I drop the severed head in front of them and step back, my adrenaline pumping like crazy. This feels like a freaky-ass nightmare, or a twisted fantasy, but I can't wake up. If I could, I wouldn't even want to. Gia's excitement is contagious, and I laugh and kick the head at the guy on the right.

"Look at her and swear your loyalty," Gia adds, straightening her back.

The three demons all tilt their heads up.

Unsheathing a long sword from nowhere, Gia brings it up only to swing it with enough force to cut off the three demons' heads at once before they can utter a word. I gasp and hop back, covering my mouth in surprise.

"Disobedient fuckers. I'm not their ruler. They shouldn't have obeyed me."

I blink a few times.

This. Bitch. She's awesome.

"You're evil," I say, laughter lightening my voice. "I love it."

Gia's features light up with a wicked grin. "I've been at it for over a century. Being female means you gotta really cement your place. Be ruthless. Don't let any asshole push you around. And if he tries, take their heads." Peering over her shoulder, she glances at Dante and Kase. "May I have permission to look at the queen?"

Before either of them responds, I say, "Of course you can. You don't have to ask them. You've proved yourself fucking badass, and I think I want you to teach me more."

Gia still looks in their direction, waiting for them to respond. It annoys me more than it should, and I strut between her and the booth and meet her face straight on. Fire lights her eyes, and we stare at each other in silence for a moment.

"I want you to tell me more about what it's like for you," I add, nudging her back. "All I've been currently taught is things about breaking angels."

"That sounds more entertaining than dealing with desperate mortals." Gia click-clacks a few feet away from me and stops next to a man hunched over a glass of whiskey at the bar. "I mean, look at Mr. Douchebag. He just wears away at this bar because when he made a deal to have a demon kill his boss so he could get a promotion, he didn't think to include the part about being able to succeed at the new position. Isn't that right, little dick? No soul and now no job."

The man doesn't look up or respond, continuing to stare at his glass of whiskey.

"And he's not even the most pathetic." Gia slaps the man on his shoulder and turns back to me. Her dark eyes flicker with red light, and she draws her gaze over my face, taking advantage of the ability to look at me. "If you speak with the kings, I'll gladly arrange for some one-on-one training with you, my queen. We would have a blast putting all of these bottom feeders in place. Under one of his majesties supervision, of course."

"That won't be necessary." Dante's voice drifts from behind me before the heat of his body blazes at my back. "Raven's time is better served—"

I spin around to face him. "I'm sure it won't be that time consuming. It could be helpful—"

Dante's second lids blink with the release of his devil form. It's been a while since I noticed them. "There is no need for you to get involved in demonic affairs more than you already are."

I place my hands on my hips. "But—"

Flicking out his forked tongue, Dante hisses. "The answer is no. We already split your time enough as it is. Gia serves us well, and I'd like it to stay that way. She—"

"You don't need to be jealous." I grab the front of his shirt, cutting him off.

Dante locks his fingers around my wrist. "It's not that."

"It is and you know it." Yanking my hand away from him, I spin on my heels and storm toward the booth Kase and Elias sit at, silently watching us.

"Raven," Dante calls, striding behind me. "Get back here. We're not done talking."

"Oh, yes we are—" The breath knocks from my lungs as something smashes into my back, knocking me forward.

Kase roars, jumping from the booth. Red fire explodes from him, devouring his human form, leaving his feline beast in its wake. The building shakes as he launches in my direction, and I expect him to crash into Dante to shove him off me. Kase flies over us, and Dante drags me from the floor and into his arms.

"Don't let him escape!" Dante shouts, closing the space to Elias. Ushering me into the booth, Dante stands protectively in front of us, unfurling his wings.

I climb up on the seat and peer over his make-shift barrier. "What's going on?"

Kase blasts fire at a man near the door. Without having to ask who he is, I know the man is the demon with a contract on Elias's soul.

In a tornado of fire, the man splits the floor open and dives into a pit of Hell

Kase dives in after him.

The two of them disappear.

12

Jealousy Bites

RAVEN

"**S**HIT, WHERE DID they go?" I ask, trying to get up.

Dante folds his wings and plops into the booth next to me, eyeing the room. He doesn't respond to my question and leans his elbows on the table. I scoot over to give him space, his body radiating with the heat of Hell. Elias sits rigidly, clutching onto the edge of the table. His eyes dart from the spot Kase chased the demon into some sort of Hell portal and to me.

"Hell," Elias murmurs, swallowing his hoarse word.

A dozen thoughts cross my mind. If Kase entered Hell, could Lucian take advantage of it and force him to stay? Fuck.

The room rumbles and the putrid scent of rotten eggs trickles through the air as fiery cracks fissure across the shiny black floor. Dante closes the foot of space I put between us and drapes his arm across my shoulders like we hadn't just gotten into an argument about his reaction toward me showing Gia my attention. I could try to shove him away out of spite, but the more sensible part of me knows he has his reasons and will explain them to me. Right now, I want to be as close to him as possible before Hell breaks loose.

"Relax, pretty soul. It's only Kase. You know the realms break easily under his wrath," Dante says, stroking his hot fingers up and down my arm.

"Apparently, the same goes for Elias's master." I sink into Dante, relief flooding through me at the sight of Kase materializing from a burst of flames.

"Not without a price. He'll be weakened." Turning his gaze toward Kase, Dante shares a silent look with him. It's obvious from his quick return that the demon managed to get away. And now he knows Elias is with us.

Kase remains expressionless as he strides to the booth. I try to lock my gaze to his, but he trains his glowing glare on Elias. Shifting on the seat, I prepare to intervene if Kase decides to unleash his wrath. It's no one's fault the damn demon got away...sort of. I push the thought of my weird-ass fun with Gia to the back of my mind. I know it could've distracted Kase and

Dante, and I don't want to think that something so small will be the cause of my downfall.

"Elias, get up. You're going hunting with me," Kase says, crossing his arms over his chest. "I can use his hold on you to track him now that I know who he is. Fucking bottom feeder. I'll give him credit for his determination but he's sloppy."

Elias remains in his spot, his complexion pale, his body trembling. He looks worse than he had only an hour ago. My chest tightens with worry. The unknown stability of his terminal cancer scares me. What if something happens and we can't get his contract in time? Fuck.

"Can you do it without him? He doesn't look so good," I say, tapping my fingers to the table to get Kase's attention.

Flaring his nostrils, Kase finally meets my gaze. "Why work harder when he can help me pinpoint his new territory? I hate to sound like an asshole to you, angel-girl, but the dickhead isn't getting any better. He'll never look good."

Dante stands up and towers over the table. "I'll give you another dose of my venom. It'll keep you going."

"Until his body just gives out," I exclaim, tugging on Dante's jacket. "You guys are going to kill him faster than—"

"Raven, it's fine. They're right. I'm not getting any better. I'd rather fight my hardest and fail than waste away, praying to God for mercy when it's now more obvious than ever that my prayers will never be answered." Elias slowly gets up, using the table to support himself with one hand. Lifting his other, he gives his arm to Dante to bite.

I clench my jaw, forcing my face to stay in check instead of frowning. I can sense the dozens of gazes penetrating me as both demons and Hell-bound souls alike try to eavesdrop on our business. No one must look at me fully, watching the devils instead, because I spot Gia keeping watch over the crowded bar like she's antsy to make more heads roll.

Stroking my cheek with his tail, Kase grabs my attention away from the room. "Try not to test Dante too much. I like this bar and would prefer not to see it crumble into the fiery pits of Hell because he couldn't control his envy in regards to you asking for someone to teach you something we're plenty capable of handling."

I stand in silence, letting his words hang in the air. I can't believe the bastard called me out. They both damn well know that they don't want to share their demonic affairs with me. This is the first real outing I've been on that wasn't chasing angels. I had no idea that demons like Gia worked for them. They have entire legions that work for them, Hell-bound souls, and who knows what else.

Kase leans over and kisses me, cutting off my argument. Dante grabs his tail and makes him jump and back away like he thinks if Kase starts something, neither of us will stop. It wouldn't be the first time Kase did as much with Dante in the middle.

"If Elias gets hurt, I'm restraining you to Dante's bed and screwing him in front of you, Kase," I say, sucking in my bottom lip to stop from reacting. "I mean it. I know he's your least favorite, but take it easy on him."

"Good luck following through, angel-girl," he quips, giving Elias a nudge forward. He peers at Dante from over his shoulder. "Take our soul to the new place. I'll meet you two there later."

Dante doesn't give me a chance to say anything and blocks my view of Kase and Elias leaving. Like the demons around us finally give up on their nosiness, voices pick up again, blending with the pulsing music. It grows louder in volume, proving I was right. Fucking demons.

Dante sits down and pulls me onto his lap, hooking his arms around my stomach. "You have no idea how frustrated I am with you. I want so badly to bend you over my knee and spank you until you lose feeling in your ass."

I shiver at his words. "The humiliation of getting spanked in front of your minions might be worth it if it helps you get under control enough to have a conversation that won't make you spit acid on anyone who looks at me."

Dante groans deep in his chest at the thought, his body awakening beneath mine. "Don't tease me like that."

A figure moves in the edge of my vision as Gia struts up to

the booth. "My king, can I—"

"Get the fuck back to work," Dante snaps, slapping his hands on the table. "I know what you're doing, and it won't work. I think you've forgotten your place. This soul is mine."

I scrunch my nose. "Dante."

Dante covers my mouth with his hand. "Do not argue, Raven. Gia is a demon of deception and manipulation. She is excellent at her job for a reason. Just because she doesn't try to get to you the way others have tried doesn't mean she doesn't plan to. I swore to protect you, and that's what I'm doing."

"Are you sure it's not about controlling me, Dante? Because that's what this feels like." I swivel to look at him. "You got pissed off because I was giving her my time."

His eyes flash green, and he drops his gaze away from mine. "It's more than that. It's not about controlling you. It's about controlling them. Yes, I'm jealous that you chose to give her time doing things you didn't seem interested in before, but if Gia thinks she can take something, she will. Whether it's your time or attention, she is a demon of my domain and will always want what others have."

"But she can't have me," I say, touching his chin to get him to look up. "I belong to you."

His hard features light with the fire of lust. Dante might be a tough-ass. He might push boundaries and do psychotic things. But even through the fire and envy, there is a part of him that needs the reassurance only I can give. I don't know if it's our bonding of souls or what, but with him being my soul keeper, it's like my humanity prods at him. Instead of pointing it out or making him resent it, I tend to it. I work with it and use it to grow our relationship beyond me being a possession. I want more, and it's obvious so does he.

"Damn straight," he confirms, combing his hand into my hair.

I bend my neck slightly, exposing my throat to him. "Why don't you show them? Give me a mark that they can always see."

"My perfect soul," he murmurs, kissing my neck. "You're the one with the power over me, you know? It's you who controls me."

I exhale a small breath, my body tingling with anticipation as he teases me with his fangs, preparing to bite me. I shift on his lap and squirm, wishing we weren't in this booth in the middle of a crowded club. I can't stop my curiosity from getting the best of me, and I glance toward the bartender serving drinks. I catch sight of Gia glaring at me, her once friendly demeanor now gone with the blazing fire dancing in her dark eyes.

"Relax," Dante murmurs, tugging me by the hair more, positioning me how he wants to bite. "It'll be a little pinch. I'm not going to bite you with venom either."

"You're not?" I ask, almost whiny. The reminder of how he

can get me high blooming front and center in my mind. It's strangely exciting.

"I want you clear headed for me." He kisses my neck again. "All I'll do is drink. Taste you as I crave. Feel you as I've always wanted."

I moan at the pressure of his bite as his fangs sink into my throat. I expect him to pull away, but he doesn't. He loosens his mouth enough to retract his fangs and molds his lips over his bite mark, sucking hard enough to drink my blood. The act sends pleasure shooting right between my legs.

"And I thought you were worthy of the kings of Hell, but here you are acting as prey in the snake's grip." Gia appears at the booth with her hands on her hips. "I knew I should've grabbed you when I had the chance, but I'm willing to fight."

Gia unsheathes a dagger before Dante has a chance to react. She slashes it at me, but Dante's arm gets in the way and she cuts him. My body kicks into action, and I kick my leg, knocking her blade away. Lifting me up with him, Dante gets to his feet, towering over Gia. She freezes and raises her hands in surrender, and the awe I had for her vanishes.

Something dark and deadly comes over me. The world hazes red and it's as if my soul separates from my body. I watch myself launch from Dante's arms at Gia, landing on top of her. Instead of dragging me away, Dante strolls to Gia's head and grabs a long sword from somewhere hidden on his devil form breaking free.

"Do not underestimate me, demon," I say, my voice seemingly snapping my soul back to my body. "Dante is my king. Mine. I should cut you to pieces."

Gia remains placid beneath me.

"Do it," Dante encourages, pointing his sword.

I narrow my eyes, training my gaze to the unpredictable demon. "I have a better idea. I will spare your life but you will now serve me as your queen. If you betray me, you will know the true Hell given to me by my kings."

"Yes, your majesty," Gia says, tightening her jaw.

"And let this be a lesson on how to control my legion," Dante says, pulling the sword away. "If you kill all our servants, we will have no one left to serve us."

I push my palms into Gia's chest and get to my feet, dusting myself off. I expect her to blast me with fire or some shit, but all she does is bow her head in respect. My emotions run wild. I was foolish to think that maybe I could befriend a demon. She was obviously testing me. For the first time in weeks, I feel a bit bad. I mean, my ex basically made me ruin all my friendships and relationships outside of him that it made keeping it that way easier. But now? Will it ever be possible again?

"All right, pretty soul. Time to leave this hellhole and go somewhere worthy of your presence." Dante scoops me into his arms and strides from the bar without another glance around.

Outside, he sets me on my feet and kneels in front of me, surprising me. He takes my hands between his and brings them to his chest, sandwiching them to his pecs. His heart beats furiously against my palms, and his eyes shine with his devilish light.

"What are you doing?" I ask, his weird gesture stealing the sadness from me.

"Groveling. Pleading. Begging for you to forgive me and also allow me to show you my appreciation. Drinking your blood opened you up in a way I'm unused to, and it's getting to me." Dante squeezes my fingers. "Your protectiveness of me has me so hot right now. It's taking all of my power not to ravish you right here, but I'm also afraid that if I take you home, I will lose control, and I know I fucked up in there. I know you might not want to fuck me if you think I'll pull that shit again."

"You mean the shit where I was naïve? We both made mistakes. I'm not going to hold that against you, Dante. I should bend you over and spank you myself for thinking that. You have been so good to me, even if it's sometimes in weirdly psychotic ways." I grin with my words.

He pulls me closer, stretching to bury his face in my cleavage. I laugh and link my fingers through his hair, tipping his head back. The smile he graces me with could melt the panties right off me. He's so sexy on his knees, looking ready to lift my dress and make me scream with his tongue.

"If that's what you want, pretty soul. You can teach me a lesson," he murmurs, sliding his hands to my ass. "I'm yours."

I love the sound of that. "I do...just not here. I don't want to risk interruptions, especially when you're on your knees before me."

"Worshipping you inch by inch," he teases, testing my resolve by sliding a finger between my legs to feel what he does to me. "Mind, body, and soul."

I pull him to his feet and kiss him, savoring his devotion. Feeling him on a level I never imagined possible. "And then it'll be my turn."

A bright flash of light steals my attention, and I stiffen. Dante hisses and spins, not hesitating to throw acid in the direction of the saviors coming into view. Red flames explode across the ground in front of us, creating a barrier, and I stare in surprise as Gia stands by the entrance of the club.

It's enough to steal Cassius and Zade's attention from us, and they turn their heavenly fury toward the demon.

Gia growls and unsheathes two small daggers hidden on her hellish form. Without hesitating, she throws them at Cassius, hitting him in his wing. The demon is quickly making up for her bullshit inside, and I nearly cheer for her.

"Time to go, pretty soul," Dante says, lifting me into his arms.

I don't argue and bury my face into Dante's chest. Launching into the air, Dante avoids the blasts of fire and light, flying me away.

I glance down at the fight below.

Andre steps from the shadows and glances up at me. I tense in anger. Has he been messing with me this whole time, waiting for the opportunity to lead Cassius and Zade to me? Fuck. How could he?

As quickly as my angry thoughts rise, they fade. Andre isn't fighting with his brethren against the demons rushing from the bar. He's hiding. Sneaking around the building and away from his brethren, Andre disappears in a flash of light.

"Looks like he can't get enough of you," Dante says, following my line of sight.

"But you will get everything you want. Everything he can't have." I hug Dante tighter.

He hums under his breath. "I can't wait to see him fall. You're truly Hell's queen."

13

Divine Warning

RAVEN

"KEEP YOUR EYES shut, pretty soul. I mean it." Dante covers my eyes with his hand like he thinks I might try to peek, which he's right about.

I flutter my eyelashes against his palm. "I'm too excited. This place looked huge from the outside. Why did you guys choose to stay in the apartment when this was an option?"

"We didn't need much. The complex was great for being around mortals, and I don't know. We hadn't been there long. Maybe we chose it instinctively because you were there." Dante's breath tickles my neck as he murmurs in my ear. "We also like to save help from our more prominent contracts for the right time. Now watch your step. We're entering the elevator."

"Elevator? What the fuck kind of place is this?" I ask, linking my fingers around his wrist. I try to pull his hand from my eyes, but he doesn't budge.

"A palace for our queen." Dante eases me around and lifts his hand from my face. He doesn't let me get more than a glimpse at the mirrored wall of the elevator as it hums to life and the world shifts with its ascension. "Somewhere more worthy. Plus, there are enough rooms that we won't ever have to share, even if all of Hell decides to come to the Mortal Realm." Scooping me into his arms, Dante caresses his lips to mine, using the soft sweetness of his tongue to hold my attention hostage.

I kiss him deeper, stroking my tongue over the barbells in his mouth until he forks his tongue and kisses me in a way he never has before. The new sensation feels almost like I'm kissing two people at the same time, but it's not a fight for affection but more like teamwork to explore every inch of my mouth.

The elevator stops and Dante blindly carries me down a warm hallway that seems to go on for miles. My curiosity prods at me, and I slow our kiss and try to ease away. Dante tightens his fingers through my hair and holds me in place. His diamond-shaped pupils expand and retract, and he smiles at me in amusement.

"You're driving me crazy. I'm dying to see everything," I say, fake-glaring.

"If you feel like I'm driving you crazy now, just wait. I'll give you a tour after I'm done having my way with you. I will not waste another second." Dante glides his tongue across his bottom lip, drawing my attention back to his pouty, kissable mouth. "I'm already jealous enough by how excited you are about the place that you haven't even considered what I'm about to do to you now. I should punish you for spending more time trying to disobey me than attempting to rip off my clothes."

My mouth forms an O as I let his words sink in. The whole angel invasion thing stole the thoughts from my mind. "Are you sure it's safe?" I regret my comment immediately. Of course it's safe.

Dante groans deep in his throat and picks up his pace until we reach the end of a corridor. "Do you doubt my capability to protect you?"

I bare my bottom teeth. "I don't."

Kicking the door closed, he still doesn't let me glance around. "Yet you say such preposterous comments, pretty soul."

I search his eyes, knowing that there is one way to fix this. I can tell my comment bothered him even if it was unintention-al. "Because I don't know how else to ask for punishment. You might not give it to me right now even though I deserve it."

His features sharpen with his desire as I get to him in the best way I know how. "Tell me why. I want to hear all the reasons why you're my naughty girl."

I raise my eyebrows, finding myself speechless for any reason that doesn't sound lame. So instead, I say, "Make me."

"What did you say?" Dante asks, his voice deepening.

I grin. "Make. Me."

Growling, Dante hooks his arm around my waist and carries me to a bed finally fit for a beast of his size. I expect him to bend me over his knee, but he surprises me by setting me on the bed. I watch him open a couple of unpacked boxes until he pulls out some sort of sex positioner, covered in black velvet with four restraints.

"I've been dying to punish that bubble butt of yours on our new spanking bench," Dante says, his smile widening as he watches my reaction.

Heat warms my cheeks, my whole body going haywire just thinking about how he restrained me in a sex swing. And now this? I'm nervous yet excited. The thrill of learning how to embrace this darkly delicious wild side of myself gets to me in a good way. I never even thought about liking this kind of thing, but Dante's anticipation is enough for me to want to do anything to see him happy. Satisfied. He's always so good to me even with his self-proclaimed flaws that I want to be the naughty girl he desires.

"I deserve it, don't I?" I ask, lowering my voice to a breathless whisper.

"You do. Now come here, pretty soul. I'm going to spank the Hell into you until you scream halo." Dante grabs me by my ankles and drags me to him.

I wiggle my ass, teasing him by moving and not making it easy to lock the cuff restraint around my wrist. "You can try."

"But first, after you're nice and secure, I'm going to plug you with something to encourage me." Dante pops open a box with a small silicone butt plug.

I gasp a laugh in exasperation. I thought he was joking about having a butt plug for me with the words spank me etched into the pink heart-shaped jewel adhered to the bottom of the base. "You're seriously going to bling-out my ass?"

He traces his fingers over the back of my thong. "You know I love you dolled up from lips to asshole."

Fuck me. This is nuts. And so fucking hot.

Sliding his big hand under me, Dante lifts me onto the firm spanking bench he positions on the middle of his king bed. He gathers my hair in his hands and ties it up out of my face, giving me nothing to hide behind. Goosebumps prickle over my skin, and he teasingly hikes my dress up until he exposes my ass.

He hums and licks my butt cheek, working his mouth up until he hooks his fangs to the thin band of my panties. "I hope you're ready for all the things I plan to do to you, pretty soul."

"I don't know about your brand of punishment...sir. You speak as if I should shake in fear, but I'm only shaking in anticipation." I crane my neck to peer at him kneeling behind me. Excitement slickens the apex of my thighs at the dark desire turning his eyelids heavy with lust. He loves when I act at his mercy, but he loves that I also push back.

"You're naughty because you crave submitting to my power. Is that why you constantly test my resolve? Why you tease the beast inside me, waiting for it to explode from me to burn the world down?" Using his fangs, he hikes up my dress, exposing my ass cheeks peeking from my thong to him.

The restraints on my wrists and ankles make it impossible to move, and I shiver at air caressing my damp skin.

"Yes, my king. I love when you unleash Hell on the world, especially because of me," I say, keeping my gaze on him.

Cool liquid drips down my butt before Dante caresses my body with his finger, rubbing his lube over my skin. I moan as he slides his finger into my ass, fingering me softly, testing my reaction.

"Such a naughty girl," he murmurs, kissing my shoulder. Leaning closer, he whispers for me to relax as he inserts the plug, the sensation strange yet exhilarating as it stretches me only a teensy bit more than Kase's tail. "How does that feel?"

I stretch to peer at him, gliding my tongue over my bottom

lip. "So good. You'd be jealous if you could read my mind. You might destroy all of your favorite possessions."

He hums. "What did I say about prodding at my envy, pretty soul? You have to be careful. I'll annihilate everything in the universe for you. Maybe I should help you remember with a bit more punishment." Slapping my ass, Dante sends tingles blossoming over my skin. He loves this so much that it's easy to play along with his fantasy and make it my own.

"It's why I bait your envy. I love seeing you riled up. So hot. Possessive. Your jealousy makes me wet." I suck my bottom lip between my teeth. "It turns me on so much so that poking your devil side is now my purpose, you know. It's why I wore this dress. This lipstick. My thong. I knew you would envy how they touch the parts of my body I withhold from you."

"They must go." Dante tightens his fingers to the back of my dress and rips the seams at the zipper. "You will never wear these clothes again." He's not kidding. Proving his point, he leaves my dress in shreds in front of me. Using his teeth, he tears my thong off and stretches the band, snapping it against my ass cheek.

I gasp at the stinging sensation and watch as he ties the flimsy fabric around his wrist like a trophy. "Please, my king. Forgive me."

Grabbing my ponytail, Dante stretches my head back and caresses his lips to mine. "After I have my way with you, starting with another toy from my pleasure box. Only after I test everything on you and make you cum until you scream for mercy will I forgive you for your naughty behavior. Understand?"

I try not to smile and fake a pout. "Yes, sir."

Dante hums his approval and rubs his hot palm across my ass cheek before he spanks me hard enough to feel the fire of his devil side sink into my skin. The bed shifts with his movements, and Dante disappears from my line of sight. He rummages through a couple of boxes. It's like he purposefully takes his time gathering everything, wanting me to suffer with anticipation. He wasn't wrong about this being punishment, and I want more.

I pull against the restraints, testing the durability of his spanking bench, seeing if I can free myself. A shadow falls over me, and Dante twists my ponytail in his fingers, holding me in place with one hand. He presses against me, letting me feel his cock test the strength of his pants. The sound of his zipper sliding down sends tingles bursting between my legs in anticipation. I pant and wiggle, my body so turned on that all I want is for him to hurry up and sink his cock inside me. I want to feel the sensation of him fucking me with the plug in. I wonder how long it'll be until I give in to my devils' desire to take me at once.

He thumps his hard-on on my ass cheek. "You want me, don't you? You regret waiting so long to give in to me. Isn't that right? I bet you thought I'd rush and give you what you want."

"Why don't you? I can't stand waiting." My voice comes out with a bit of a whine. "You're taking forever."

"It's part of your punishment. I want you to ache for me. Savor the anticipation before I fuck you until you see stars. But first, you're going to watch me enjoy myself, pretty soul. That is what you get for your impatience." Damn. Dante's comment digs into me, prodding at a side I didn't think was there. Am I jealous of his hand? Of whatever toys he's going to play with by himself? Fuck yeah, I am.

I groan and rub my legs together, wiggling in an attempt to tease him into being unable to resist me. "So wicked. I don't think I can handle the ache."

"If you ask nicely, I'll let you have your own fun," he responds, drawing the tip of his cock along the seam of my ass, making me clench as he stops too soon. "I'll love watching you squirm as I control your pleasure. Because you're mine. Would you like that?"

"Please, my king. I want it so badly. Let me cum for you," I say, all breathy and excited.

Easing away the tip of his cock and without taking away my backdoor adventure, Dante uses his fingers to spread open the folds of my body as he adjusts something small over my clit and inside my vagina lips, my body holding the toy in place. He moves around to kneel in front of me, now completely naked and glistening with lube as he strokes himself with one hand. I spot a remote in his other hand a second too late. Tensing with a loud moan, I stiffen at the intense vibration against my clit, turning my mind to mush.

Dante leans in and kisses me, stealing my moans. I've never felt a vibrator like this in my life and how it stays in place with only help from my body. Stroking his cock, Dante masturbates while watching me bent over helplessly at the mind-blowing pleasure of the toy. It doesn't take more than a couple of minutes until my muscles spasm and I orgasm.

Dante smiles and strokes his fingers over my chin, reaching around to remove both toys before the intensity of the vibrator turns uncomfortable. He knows exactly how to work my body, and he takes the time to kiss along my spine, just savoring me.

"You're so fucking sexy, Raven," Dante says, spanking my ass again while giving me a moment to breathe. "Are you ready for more?" He seamlessly goes from controlling my pleasure to ensuring it's not too much. I've never been with someone so attentive to my needs that it gets to me in a good way.

"I'm ready for you," I say, stretching to stare at him. "For anything you want."

His eyes soften at my words, and he leans closer and kisses me. "My pretty soul. You're all I ever want. Your attention. Your desire...your love."

"My love?" My heart races at comment. "Dante." I don't know what to say.

"I've never wanted something so much in my existence," he says, his voice nonchalant and matter-of-fact. "Even more than completing the levels of Hell. I hope it's possible. I know mortals love and worship the Higher Power. Perhaps you'll feel that way toward me. The way I feel toward you."

"You love me?" My brows knit together.

"Is that so hard to believe?" he asks, releasing me from the restraints of the spanking bench. "Why do you think the world itself gets to me in regards to you?"

I wobble as I push up. "Because you're obsessed and possessive."

He grins, hooking his arms around my waist to pull me to him. "And psychotically in love with you, Raven. I will disembowel a million men in your honor if that's what it takes for you to accept it as the truth."

I raise my eyebrows, my eyes widening. "Or you could, you know, kiss me and fuck me until I feel your love piercing my soul."

Fire lights his eyes with my words, and he reacts with intense passion, kissing me hard and deep like he wants my lips to ache with the memory of this moment. Sliding his tongue into my mouth, he explores the taste of my need and desire as my tongue dances with his in perfect sync to the melody of our desperation.

Dante flips me onto my back and yanks my hands over my head, pinning me and taking the control he desires. His fangs nip my bottom lip, and he tastes my blood, stirring something wild inside me. He's never said as much, but I know the taste of my blood, my life-force, sets him off in a good way.

I moan and dig my nails into his taut shoulders, mapping my fingers over where I know his wings hide until he unfurls them above me, unleashing his devil side. I stroke the downy black feathers as he works his mouth along my jaw and to my throat. Lacing his warm fingers around my knee, he spreads my body wider, making room for his hips between my legs. With his hand, he exposes my clit and strokes his thumb over it, sending pleasure through me. I stretch my legs wider and he lifts my ass with his palms and curls my torso a bit.

I moan as he pulls me closer, controlling my body instead of thrusting into me. The pressure of his thick girth stretching me ignites ecstasy in every single cell on my body, and I breathe heavily through my parted lips as we watch each other.

"How do I feel?" Dante asks, rocking my body to his.

"Incredible," I gasp, closing my eyes to savor this moment. "Better than I imagined."

He smiles with his lust, picking up speed until he thrusts into me, turning my thoughts to only my pleasure.

"Your pussy is so tight and wet. It makes me want to fuck you so hard that you can't even stand for days," he says, releasing a sexy sound, like a moan, growl, and hiss wrapped into one.

"Do whatever you want. I'm yours," I say, clutching the blankets.

"Forever." Dante tightens his hold on me and picks up his speed, thrusting into me hard and fast, fucking me how I expect a ruler of Hell to screw me—hot, without reserve, and in a way that all I can do is scream in satisfaction.

His devil façade cracks through, and I admire the fiery light shining through his scales. We lock our gazes, and the world around me hazes and shudders until the room disappears, leaving me alone in a world where our essences merge the same way as our bodies. My whole being hums, and warmth builds through me with my release. Dante stretches my legs over my head completely, his muscles bulging and flexing. He grunts, his face scrunching, and I feel his orgasm on a soul-deep level. Shadows and light swirl around us, and I kiss Dante as he slows, every amazing sensation and emotion pooling around us in this strange world where it's only the two of us and our pleasure.

Rolling off me, Dante hugs me to him, continuing to kiss and savor every ounce of my affection like he can't get enough.

"You're the most beautiful, smart, feisty, naughty mortal I've ever known, and I can't wait to give you the power and kingdom you deserve," he murmurs, cuddling me. "But until then, I will give you whatever your body and soul need."

I smile and trace my finger over his hard pec. "How about you draw us a bath?"

He hums and nods. "That sounds like the perfect way to relax until you're ready again. I'm keeping you to myself all night, and I guarantee you won't be leaving my bed tomorrow either. Kase can join us as his reward for catching the demon."

Heat blossoms over my body, and I roll on top of him and kiss him with everything in me. His hard body throbs against me. If he didn't flip me off him, I'd align our bodies again and have my way with him this time.

I try to grab his hand. "I don't need a break yet."

Bowing forward, he laces his hand around my ponytail and manhandles me, dragging me a bit closer. His roughness gets to me in a good way, and excitement builds between my legs, craving more of his devil nature. "Don't worry, pretty soul. I wasn't truly planning to give you one. You'll see." He scoops up a box from the floor and shakes it, rattling the contents.

Arching my back, I stretch, giving Dante a view of my body as he strolls backwards toward the archway to the huge bathroom just for our suite. He flicks his tongue, teasing me, and my body explodes with tingles. I drink in the sight of his perfect ass, watching him fill the spa-like tub and suction cup a few different things to the tiles.

"That thing better be for you," I call, twirling my finger at the dildo he suction cups to the wall.

He chuckles and closes the door partially on me, not letting me see him prepare for our next ride on the Kinkland Express. Dante turns on soft music, and a sweet citrusy scent permeates the air from the bathroom. I crawl out of bed and snatch his shirt to put on, dying to use it against him, knowing how he likes to see me in his things. It'll allow me to peek at what he has in store.

"Don't even think about it, Raven. No ruining the surprise," he says, waving his hand through the crack in the door. "Five more minutes."

"You make me only want to disobey you more," I tease, sauntering toward the door leading to a balcony.

"Good. More reason to punish that sexy ass of yours. I saw how you were fully prepared to let me fuck you like that." He groans, his deep voice vibrating with lust at the thought. "Maybe after I train you to take more than a thumb."

My body trembles in a good way, and I scrub my heated cheeks.

Opening the balcony door, I allow crisp night air into the room, needing to cool off before I melt into a puddle on the floor. If this is what my eternity will be like, I will never miss the idea of Heaven. I don't think the pearly gates have access to spanking benches and restraints. My current idea of eternal paradise is strolling through an archway of sex toys that start vibrating in anticipation upon my arrival. And not to mention having my devils waiting to bend me over.

Wind whips around me, playing with the loose strands of my hair pulled free from my ponytail. I don't get a chance to react or scream as a cold hand clamps over my mouth. A sweet yet tart fragrance envelops me—like apples dipped in caramel—and I stiffen. The halo of light emanating across the balcony with the shadow of wings stretching out proves it's not demonic.

"Don't speak or call for your devil and I won't sink my blade into your back," Cassius mutters, keeping his rumbly voice just about a whisper. "I need to know what you are up to with Andre."

"I don't know what you're talking about." I try to stay calm, speaking into his hand. If I didn't feel the sharp tip of his blade on my lower back, I'd scream for help.

"Did you ask him to save your soul?" he asks, ignoring my comment. "What is your plan? You know you are far from redemption."

"Cass, let her go." Andre lands with a thump on the balcony, his wings flapping with glorious light. "If you have questions, you need to ask me."

"But you withhold information!" Cassius shouts.

A low hiss sounds through the air, and I jerk my head back, clocking Cassius in the chin. Hooking his arm around my waist, he launches into the air, not giving Dante the chance to make it to the door. Thrashing in Cassius's arms, I fight as hard as I can. I know if he kidnaps me, I might never see my devils in this life. He will ensure I fail my mission and turn into a demonic slave.

"Let me go, asshole!" I scream, feeling behind me until I manage to grab his junk. It's squishy and soft, totally vulnerable, and I will inflict a world of agony on his cock.

Cassius grunts, loosening his hold on me. My mission to inflict pain doesn't work, so I go for Plan B. I stroke my hand over his groin and fake a moan, trying to get his body to react to mine. His shaft hardens, surprising the fuck out of him, and he drops me. I scream as I freefall. A loud crack sounds through the air. Hot air blows from beneath me, warming the wind stinging my skin. I flail, stretching my arms for Dante as he spits venom at Cassius trying to catch me.

"Grab her!" Cassius commands, but I can't see anything but bright light.

And then fire.

The gates of Hell open under me, and I wonder if I died without knowing it.

I can't get myself to scream or fight. All I do is brace for eternal punishment. But it doesn't come. Warm, muscular arms catch me, stopping my fall. Jerking his hand out, Micah throws orange fire at Cassius, engulfing him in hellfire. Andre intercepts Dante's attack, locking his arms around his smiting brethren, launching the two of them higher in the sky.

I expect Dante to chase them, but he lands beside us. He tries to take me from Micah, but Micah growls.

"Give her to me. Now," Dante commands, his eyes glowing green.

"After you were nearly the cause for Hell's downfall? No. You can wait until I'm ready to give her up." Micah proves his point by stepping forward and out of a summoning circle drawn in blood on a concrete platform. "Now show me to my living quarters."

"Micah," I whisper, my mind, body, and soul whirling in confusion. "You can't just steal me from Dante. This is our time together."

He glowers but doesn't let me down. "Try me, heathen. I saved your soul. I deserve your immediate time."

I glance at Dante. "But—"

Micah touches my chin, pulling my attention to him. "Stop acting like my presence is unwanted, Raven. You and I both know how much you've missed me."

I don't know how to respond. I don't even recognize him in this moment.

But I guess it doesn't matter, because I've only truly known him as an angel.

Now, it's time I face him as this devil. I need to find out just what kind of monster I created. Maybe then, I can figure out what happens next. Or how to save my soul from him.

Micah smiles at me. "I'm ready to make you mine."

14

Hell's Newest Ruler

MICAH

I CAN'T TAKE my eyes off Raven's shining soul as she sits beside what should be her biggest regret. Elias sinks into the couch and tips his head toward the ceiling. Apparently, I overestimated Raven's bond toward me, because she hasn't looked at me or said a word since I stole her from Dante and interrupted his night of ravishing her body in ways I've thought about every second since abandoning her after she asked for help and instead I gave her access to my kingdom in Hell.

"You might be her mortal soul keepers, but my mark is on her body and the contract with Lucian. I will take what belongs to me if you want to see her succeed," I say, crossing my arms over my chest. I went through Hell to prove to Lucian that Raven should belong to me, including offering my allegiance and souls I procure while in the Mortal Realm. Will Raven hate me for it? Maybe. But I can't lose her and I can't trust Kase and Dante to ensure she completes the task. "You two can take the opportunity to fix the mistakes Elias has made. I will guard them. My connection to Hell still remains strong."

"Which is why you should go with Kase," Dante mutters, his fangs peeking from beneath his lip. "Prove to us that you're capable of handling the Mortal Realm as a devil. You might think you're some powerful son-of-a-bastard, Micah, but your grace still lingers."

"It has not. Fire courses through my veins." I summon orange hellfire between my palms.

Kase growls and whips his tail around my wrists, tugging them over my head. I roar and thrash, annoyance courses through me. It only makes him smile wider and lift me an inch from the ground. It takes everything in me not to reveal my devil body, open a portal to Hell, and shove him in it for testing me in front of Raven. He might be wrath, but I hold on to my angelic vengeance against him.

"Stop it with the pissing match. Angel-girl isn't into watersports," Kase says, spinning me around to look at Raven. She gawks at me from beside Elias, her expression a mixture of indecipherable emotions. "Isn't that right, Raven?"

She opens and closes her mouth and ends up shaking her head.

Kase waves his hand. "See? So get your Hell together. Your demands and attempts at forcing your superiors into obedience will only leave you with a bruised ego and virgin cock for all of eternity. There is no way you can wet your dick in someone else if you claim to want Raven. We don't play games like that."

Kase swings me toward the wall, and I kick off and launch at him. He needs to learn my place as well. Just because he jumped from grace first doesn't mean anything. I have determination and a pure bond to Raven's soul—something he will never have.

"That's enough, you guys," Raven says, pushing to her feet. "I don't want you destroying the place. If you must fight, at least rip each other's clothes off or take this bullshit outside. We're on the same side."

Kase whips his attention to her and then back to me like he considers following her orders. With a glare, he strides away, getting out of my face to stand in front of Raven. "I wasn't aware you were ready for that kind of team building, angel-girl. If our clothes come off, so do yours. There is enough of you to go around. I hope Dante got you nice and stretched."

I expect her to smack him or grimace, but she flushes and

darts her gaze to Dante and then to me like she's thinking about it. My cock pulses, awakening at the lust parting her pouty lips with her wandering thoughts. I shift and adjust myself, not used to the restriction pants now seem to cause me. Raven's gaze trails down my body, and she watches me with such intense fascination that silence fills the room.

"You know what, fine. You can babysit the fuckup while we clean up his mess," Dante says, unfurling his black wings.

Pain lashes over my shoulder blades at the sight, and I stretch my back, suppressing the phantom agony still clinging to me over my lost wings. I rub my prickly jaw and narrow my eyes. His sudden change in attitude was far too easy.

"Raven, I'll bend over and give you power over me if you resist giving into Micah for the next couple hours." Dante smirks with his words. "What do you say? It'll be a lesson on getting his gluttonous ass in control. You thought I'd be bad, but you have no idea. I can already see his lack of restraint consuming him."

"I'm fine," I snap, the vision of Raven mounting Dante to penetrate him with some sort of contraption is something I never imagined would cross my mind. Or that the idea does nothing for my erection. It's not the thought of the act but how that beautiful woman could put him in his place and show him he's not the only ruler around. "Sexual intercourse is not something I'm obsessed about like you. My bond to Raven is soul-deep."

"Fucking lying devil," Elias mutters. "Your hard-on says otherwise."

Raven throws her hands up. "This is enough. No more talking about sex, power, deals, or anything else. I'm about to place an out-of-service sign around my neck." Swiveling to Kase and Dante, she places her hands on their chests. "You two go already and hurry back. When you come back, we're all going to sit down. We need some new rules around here. I don't think I can survive if you guys decide to cock fight around me for access to my body. I love a good pounding and all, but if you haven't noticed, you guys aren't exactly average. You might actually accidentally fuck my brains out."

Dante and Kase laugh in unison, their voices bouncing off the walls. Kase spins Raven into his arms and kisses her. "I think you underestimate how tough you are, angel-girl. I bet you can force all of us to our knees."

"Even if it's just for a taste of your pussy," Dante adds, smacking her glutes. "You'd love that, wouldn't you? If we all lined up."

She laughs in exasperation and drags the two of them to the door by their shirts. I tilt my head in curiosity. They enjoy letting her think she has control over them. I don't understand why. What does it accomplish? I'll have to figure it out, because I don't plan to pretend to fall in line. Raven needs to know I am her king. I jumped from grace to rule, and she will be mine.

"Micah? Hello?" Raven's soft voice snaps my attention away from the front door. She strolls across the space to me and offers me a nervous smile. "You can quit it with the tough asshole attitude now. They're gone. You don't have to pretend with me."

I lock my hand around her wrist and pull her flush against me. "Who says I'm pretending? I don't think you comprehend what it means for me to have claimed my rightful throne in Hell. Or should I remind you?"

Her bottom lip trembles at my intensity, and I can smell the sweetness of her rising fear as potent as her lingering desire. Something indecipherable crosses her fathomless eyes, glassing with her thoughts. I don't know if it's the thought of my kingdom in Hell or how I'm no longer the blessed angel she wrapped around her soul and refused to let go. Either way, she builds an impenetrable shield of light with the depths of her spirit, banishing my essence from merging with hers. Fury whips through me. How can she steal the one thing I've sworn to protect away from me?

I tighten my arm around her, digging my fingers into the soft curve of her hip. "Answer me. What makes you think—"

Swinging her hand, Raven slaps me across the face, the sting of her palm reminding me of the determination and fight she carries with the strength of her soul. "You will not speak to me like this or threaten me with a bond we formed before you gave up your grace."

Elias sucks in a sharp breath from his place on the couch, and it takes everything in me not to unleash Hell on the room. Clenching her jaw, Raven glowers at me, staring at me with her own wrath, surely siphoned from Kase. It awakens my body, and a mixture of emotions and sensations course through me. Where I was calm, composed, and in control of feelings as an angel, I no longer carry that kind of restraint. Hell unleashed something dark and wild, and I'm not sure it can ever be tamed.

"Micah, do you understand? I'm not some possession no matter what you think. You can't do as you please." She yanks herself free of my hold and places her hands on her hips. "And if you for one second think that this whole Hell raising persona is you, then you're extremely wrong."

Damn.

It's the first profane word that has crossed my mind, and Raven is responsible for dragging it out of me.

I swallow and steel myself from her sudden enchantment and the urge to bow at her feet for slapping my devil side into a strange enthralled submission. "While I think you're the one who is wrong, I won't test my theory. There is no point in flexing my power with you, especially because it would be far too risky to lose time with the woman who will give me her soul to keep."

If looks could send me back to Hell, my world would explode into flames.

"You know what? I've been through enough shit. When you're ready to treat me the way I deserve, you can apologize and we'll move past this. Until then, I'm going to binge watch a show about demon hunting with Elias. At least he realized his bullshit wasn't necessary." Raven spins on her feet and stomps away.

Elias looks ready to defecate himself as he watches me with wide eyes. And then the brave sickly bastard grabs a dagger he must've hidden between the couch cushions. Raven whips around, sending her midnight hair sweeping out with her gesture. She doesn't get a chance to even react to my quick movements. Slinging her onto my shoulder, I carry her toward the door, not caring that she screams for me to put her down.

"Wait! What are you doing? You can't leave me!" Elias shouts, struggling to get up off the couch.

I spin and slam my foot into the ground, shaking the world enough to send Elias to his knees. Why Raven wants to spend another moment with a dying traitor, too concerned with himself that he doesn't even ask where I'm taking Raven, is beyond me.

"You can't keep up with us where we're headed," I say, adjusting Raven in my arms as she pummels my back with her fists, screaming every obscene word she can think of. "Now be a good little mortal and stay inside. Don't answer the doors for strangers, and if Kase and Dante return before we do, you better come up with something believable to tell them or your end will be just a glimpse of the agony I can inflict on you."

Slamming the door, Elias swears to the Higher Power. I grin, loving how I've gotten under his skin. It'll serve him right for stealing unwarranted sympathy from Raven.

"Damn it, Micah. I swear to damnation if you don't stop and talk to me, I will make your time here worse than Hell." Raven thuds her fists harder to my shoulder until I bring her down to face me.

Like the action leaves her speechless, she clings onto me, locking her ankles together on my lower back. The closeness of her body sets me off even more, and I wonder what it would take to cure the ache in my testicles aroused from her beauty and fight.

So I drop her down a few inches until our bodies align with only our clothes between us.

"Troubles, Micah?" she asks, her face lighting with amusement. The way she keeps saying my name digs under my skin to bury inside me. I crave to hear her say it over and over again.

I shift her back up and growl under my breath. Just her closeness failed to work, and my body throbs, the hard tightness annoying. "Yes, I'm having trouble. I don't know what kind of devil's curse this is, but I have a persistent erection around you. It's uncomfortable."

Tipping her head back, Raven releases a bout of laughter that echoes through the air. "You sound so proper. It kills me. You're one of the rulers of Hell. You should be shouting boner and blue balls. It's more fun."

I purse my lips, narrowing my eyes. "My word choice causes no harm. Not like you, you wicked heathen. Now stop it with your control over my penis or give me the cure."

She laughs harder, her amusement setting off fiery heat in my face. "For being a stalker, peeping angel who used to watch the devils get me off, you're shockingly naïve."

"I never watched such things with mortal vision. Angels use focus and light as blinders. We grant privacy," I say, rubbing my hard shaft through my pants. It only helps ease the ache a little.

She covers her face with her hands, trying to suppress her laughter. "Okay, okay. How about we make a deal? You stop being so proper, and I'll tell you how to take care of that." Reaching between us, she cups my manhood in such a way that I tense and grunt, the sensation so incredible I crave for her to do more.

But she pulls her hand away.

"Is it a deal?" she asks, prodding at my devilish side with her words.

I swallow and nod. "You're unhelpful and disobedient, you know."

A smile stretches across her full lips and she bobs her head. "Which you obviously like." Again, she touches my erection through my pants. "It's kind of exciting to see what turns you on."

"I don't need it on. I need it off. I can't concentrate on anything but my erec—boner, and I would prefer to not have it in the way for our plans. It's inconvenient." I remain expressionless, hoping she will finally see the seriousness of this moment. "Now, please. Give me the cure."

She smirks and covers her mouth, trying to hide her continuous amusement. "Sex. Masturbation. A blowjob. Those are usually quick fixes, but things I will not be helping you with, so don't even ask."

I sigh. "Surely there is something else."

She shrugs. "Time? Something you dislike?"

I rack my mind for things I find unpleasant.

Patting my cheek, she leans in and whispers, "Why don't you pray about it? Maybe the Higher Power will show you mercy this time around and smite your boner away."

Fire sizzles through my veins at her words, and I flare my nostrils. My hellish façade breaks through my skin. Raven doesn't try to shove away from me. Instead, she clings on as I grow several feet in height to tower over the world around us. Like my monstrous side enchants her, she laces her slender fingers around my tusks and strokes them like they're the most attractive, fascinating things in the world to her.

"Did it help?" she asks, tilting her head as she studies my beastly features.

I close my eyes and regain control over my façade. Licking my lips, I nod. "It'll do until you realize you're only punishing yourself for not letting me have you like Kase and Dante. They might've seen and claimed you first, but we've bonded on another level."

"You keep saying that, but it means nothing if you don't remind yourself that this isn't a competition, nor is it about having me because you think you deserve me. It's about that bond we had—have—Micah. You didn't return to this plane just because you were bored."

Her words slice through my hellish armor, power, and fire, opening me up in a way that leaves me antsy. Because she's right. The sudden change in my existence destroyed everything I thought I knew about humanity and souls. But having my life explode in a raging ocean of hellfire never meant it was over. All it meant was that it was time for me to rebuild and create my existence to better fit my new purpose—Raven.

"I returned because I can't keep away from you," I say, locking away my beast completely. I comb her hair behind her ear with my fingers. "You're my purpose in this existence. Not

Hell. Not this seemingly impossible mission. You."

Her face lights up as if the sun shines from her very being. Clutching my cheeks between her palms, Raven leans in and caresses her lips to mine, the feather-light sensation like a whisper of appreciation before she eases back, not getting carried away. It makes me crave more. Need more. I realize how tightly Raven holds onto me without letting go. I want to prove myself as worthy as Kase and Dante. I know I must if I'm to ever compete with their fire constantly lighting her beautiful eyes.

"I can't get enough of you," I murmur, returning her smile with my own. "Can I take you somewhere? I want to show you something."

"I'd like that," she says, hugging me again. "I've missed you, you know."

I set her on her feet and lace my fingers through hers. "Don't worry about that ever again, my beautiful heathen. I plan to never leave your side."

I shouldn't test Raven. I know I shouldn't. But a dark part of me wants to know her breaking point when it comes to my rule over Hell. I want nothing more than to help mold her into a powerful being that the universe bows down to. I worry about her shutting me out and denying the eternity I've built around her soul, one that calls to me more than my existence.

"What am I looking at?" Raven asks, squeezing my hand like she's afraid she might otherwise fly away if she doesn't.

"The foundation of my power." I study her expression as her brows lower in confusion. "Rising from Hell isn't as simple as you might think. I need an energy source to ground me to this plane while allowing me to tap into the power of my kingdom."

Averting her eyes from a man with a towel around his hips with a woman watching TV in bed, she finally turns to me. "You're talking about their souls?"

"Just his. Before I came to you, I had been busy with negotiations generously given to me by Lucian. This unfaithful man traded his soul for his wife's death, so he didn't have the mess of a divorce and the burden of alimony. We have come to collect." I remain expressionless as Raven pieces things together.

"You're fucking kidding me. Why would you want to show me this?" Raven's voice rises with her words. "I don't want to watch you murder a man and steal his soul."

"I'm not killing anyone, you heathen hypocrite. How is this any different than the things you've witnessed Kase and Dante do to humanity?" I twirl my finger at the man in the window. "We are only here to mark him for his descent. No murder. No soul taking, which I might add is not stealing."

Raven releases my hand and grimaces. She's conflicted because she knows I'm right. If I were Kase or Dante, she wouldn't even bat her eyelashes. "Micah—"

"You need to realize that I'm no longer an angel. The standards you had for me before must not apply to me now. That is why I really brought you here. I need for you to accept me for the devil I've turned into. This job, collecting and marking souls, is necessary for balance in the universe and in Hell." Not to mention keeping my name on her contract with Lucian. I don't say as much. She's already uncertain enough of me as it is.

I turn to face her and test to see if she'll let me take her hand again. Her pouty lip quivers, but she doesn't deny me her touch. Sliding her fingers through mine, she squeezes my hand. I bring it to my mouth to kiss her knuckles.

"I'm sorry. You're right," she says, her uneasy smile remaining instead of turning real.

I yearn to see her face light up as brightly as her shiny soul. "I hope you will still give me the chance to claim your soul regardless." I tug her closer and snake my hand around her waist and to her lower back. "You are the one thing who reminds me of my purpose—not only as a ruler of Hell, but also as one of the protectors of a soul cursed with the light we need to build Hell as it was intended."

"I'm not a possession," she comments, thinning her lips to turn expressionless, "and if you realize that, and understand that I can't be yours alone, then I will give you the chance to continue to grow a bond with me."

My heart races for the first time since my descent. "I accept your compromise."

The brightness of her soul radiates more intensely, and she throws her arms around me. I inhale a breath at the sensation of her body awakening mine. The citrusy fragrance of her hair engulfs me. Burying my face in the crook of her shoulder, I savor how Raven's soul pushes away the darkness inside me, reminding me of the light I once carried.

"I never wanted for you to abandon grace, but I'm happy you did to save me. It means everything to me. I hope you know that," she murmurs, easing away. "I look forward to building something amazing with you."

I smile and capture her gaze. "Does that mean you won't hold this against me?" Waving my hand, I motion to the window.

"Never. Let's mark that bastard." Her lips spread into a beautiful smile. She makes it so easy to drop my guard with her and show her who I truly am, despite the things she might see as flaws on my being.

I hum under my breath and tug her forward. "Careful, my beautiful heathen. You sound so incredibly sexy that I might need an alternative cure for my erect—hard-on for you."

She tips her head back and laughs, her musical voice filling the air. "I think that might be possible. You've earned—"

Glass shatters a second before pain bursts in my side. Whipping my attention toward the house, I catch sight of the man aiming a gun in our direction. He pulls the trigger, the loud gunshot startling Raven, making her scream. Another bullet hits me, exploding across my chest. Rage turns my vision red, and I narrow my focus on the bastard trying to withhold his end of the deal. I should've thought better of the situation. Of course he would fight, and now Raven stands amid danger that can end her life.

My muscles flex and quiver. Releasing a guttural roar, I expel my human façade and embrace my beastly form. I knock Raven to the ground and out of the way of another round of gunfire ravaging my body.

But it doesn't slow me down. It pushes me forward.

Crashing through the wall of the house, I charge forward and launch at the man. He hollers and thrashes, pulling the trigger of his gun in one last-ditch effort to send me to Hell. Raven screams from behind me. I stomp my hooved hand onto the man's hand, crushing it under my weight. Another screech rips through the air, one not belonging to Raven, and I whip around and summon hellfire between my palms. The mistress of my contracted soul tangles her hand through Raven's hair, waving a kitchen knife. She must've come out through the front.

"Leave us be and break Corbin's contract or I'll kill her," the woman shouts, swiping the knife again.

Something dark crosses Raven's face, and instead of pleading with me to do as the woman says, she subtly shakes her head.

I snarl and turn my back on the woman. Bowing, I shove my tusks into the man's gut and toss him out of the house. The woman screams his name, her attention stolen from Raven. Swinging her fist, Raven punches the woman in her breast, winding the wail from her mouth. I stare in utter astonishment as my beautiful heathen snatches the kitchen knife and jabs it into the woman's stomach. Blood splashes over her hand, and Raven does it again and again, screaming at the woman as she takes her life.

Raven kneels beside the woman, shaking and glowering, chains of darkness lacing around the light of her soul. "I didn't want to do this!" she yells, slamming the knife into the woman once more. "You shouldn't have threatened me. You shouldn't have put my eternity at risk. I'm done putting others before me." Tipping her head back, she peers up at the night sky. "Do you hear me? I'm done!"

Her words crack at my burning armor, allowing me to escape the grip Hell has on me. She's not only talking to the dead woman but also the Higher Power. Her threat blooms a need inside me that makes me want to run to her, to lift her in my arms and hold her, to kiss her trembling mouth and let the blood soaking her clothes bleed onto mine, shredded and tattered from unleashing my beast without protecting my human façade from annihilation.

I give in to my innate need and stride closer, peering down at her. Even though I tower over her, she doesn't cower. She's not a frail broken soul.

She is the most enchanting, sexiest woman I've ever had grace me with her presence.

"She shouldn't have tried to hurt me," she says, meeting my gaze.

"No, she shouldn't have." I kneel beside her in a pool of the woman's blood and lift the woman's hand. Twisting the large diamond ring free, I pinch it between my fingers. The woman's soul remains fractured, in shock from her sudden death, and I run my fingers over the hell-bound essence and guide it into the diamond, setting it aglow.

Raven reaches out her hand and caresses her bloody fingers to the ring in silence.

"Which means this is for you. With her soul comes power. Power you deserve." I slide the ring on Raven's finger. It's a perfect fit as if this moment was always intended to be a part of our destiny.

Throwing her arms around my neck, Raven collides into me,

kissing me in a way I never imagined could be so perfect. The sweet taste of her lips, the weight of her body pressing against mine, and the desperation and desire she arouses inside me sends me over an edge I will never return from.

I don't want to.

"Take me home," she murmurs against my mouth. "I want to savor our power for a while. And you."

Our power.

My body buzzes at her words.

"This won't be it. We will get more," I say, lifting her up.

She meets my gaze. "I don't think we can ever get enough."

She's right. I embody gluttony after all.

15

Death at the Door

ELIAS

THE DIGITAL CLOCK on the oven changes to three, and I hunch over my empty plate, wishing that someone would come home soon. Home. It's fucking weird to think that I'm now sharing a huge-ass mansion with evil bastards who have made it their sole purpose to free me of my demonic contract. I should be happy. It's what I've wanted. But then again, I can't help wondering at what cost. No one has told me in any extensive detail why it's important apart from that I was a fuckup to bargain away my soul to begin with.

Don't get me started on the fallen angel and soulmate bullshit. Because damn. I must've really loved Raven to have given her part of my former angelic essence. I only wish I could remember more. I never even believed in reincarnation. It's a lot to think about, but being alone for hours to watch the night drag on to early morning has been plenty enough. I can't sleep comfortably without pain meds, because my chest rattles and aches, and every time I cough, I feel as if my lungs will fall out. I hate how much better I feel from Dante's bite, because now all I can do is think about him sinking his teeth into me. It's strange as fuck. I don't even like the asshole. But the relief? It's better than the painkillers. I feel alive instead of drugged.

Finally getting my ass to move, I pop my dirty plate into the dishwasher and swig water straight from the tap because I couldn't find any glasses. It's obvious these demonic hell raisers don't eat mortal food by the lack of basically anything useful. Poor Raven has probably been surviving on cheese sandwiches, which has to change. I prefer some damn meat depending on how I feel. All I know is that I don't want to keel over with my last meal being something substandard in my mind.

Strolling to the grand staircase, I slowly climb up instead of taking the outrageous elevator. Call me paranoid, but I don't know what kind of evil bullshit Kase and Dante—and now the new guy Micah, who looked ready to toss me into a wall—attract to their bastardly lair. I will not get trapped in an elevator if some man-eating ghost or some shit invades the place with the beasts away. No damn thank you.

I rest for a moment on the landing overlooking the badass living room. I've never watched TV on a screen that takes up the width of an entire wall with surround sound positioned in a way that startled me when I flicked it on the show Raven sucked me into. The woman sure loves her TV, and it speaks to the part of me that just wants to spend the rest of my days curled up with a beautiful woman until the gates of Hell drag me in. At least it's something. It's strange how Raven's presence calls me to her, especially knowing what I do now. I wish my mind would open up and let me know more. I want to feel the things that should come with the knowledge, but it's just not there, and I'm not so sure it ever will be again. I see the way she looks at Kase and Dante and the way they look at her. I'd be stupid to ever consider I could somehow change things.

What am I even thinking? I'm dying. My wishful thinking will only leave me sorely disappointed.

I stroll the long hallway in the direction of my modest room. Kase and Dante have giant suites that are almost like apartments within this mansion. My room, on the other hand, is just a basic room. I have a bathroom that connects to another room, a wall closet with a sliding door, a window with a view of a pool I'll never get to enjoy, and a fucking twin bed barely big enough to fit me. It's like the demons wanted to ensure I will always be alone.

Except I'm not.

I see the monstrous form lying on my bed before my brain registers what the fuck is going on. Reaching for my belt, I come up empty-handed. Weaponless. Fuck. I left my dagger on the kitchen counter.

"My wicked little hunter. Were you ever planning to tell me you had moved?" Vincent Valeka, my very own personal demon, rests on the burgundy flannel comforter with his hands behind his head.

I try to command my feet to turn me around, but I can't move. Vincent twists his fingers, tightening the invisible chain he locks around me until I gasp and heave. I fall to my knees on the tan carpet and hang my head.

"I didn't move," I manage to spit out, my lungs tight and stinging with each shallow breath. "I was kidnapped."

"Then I suppose it's a good thing I found you. We don't want to risk you dying without me. I'm sure you would prefer not to risk a monster devouring your soul before I have the chance to properly reap it." Sitting up, Vincent swings his legs over the edge of the bed and gets to his feet. His skeletal-like frame freaks me out even more with him towering over me, his sunken eyes looking ready to fall into his skull. It sets off the sensation that has turned me into an excellent hunter, because it's like I have a sense for evil, and when I can see it coming, I can strategize how to fight.

Too bad for me, I can't send this dickhead, lying, despicable bastard back to Hell without risking him dragging me down with him. Instead, I do the only thing I can think of. I turn on the balls of my feet and sprint away as fast as I can. If I can keep distance between us, maybe someone will come back and intervene. I hadn't wanted to make a deal with Raven's soul keepers, but now that I have and now that I see they aren't chaining me up, I will fight to stay.

"Wicked hunter, there is no point in running. This is the house of the devils. I'm stronger than ever graced with the darkness that clings to everything. How very lucky I am to have your soul to grant me access. It makes this far easier." Vincent grabs me by the neck and lifts me off my feet.

The sudden theft of my breath slackens my body, my chest and lungs wanting nothing more than to just give up. I know if I put up a fight now, Vincent might collect my soul early. I never added that in my contract the same way I fucked up and didn't include anything about where the lung cancer would go once my best friend and most trusted confidant was healed of this terminal disease.

My eyes bug out with the agony. An image of Preston comes to the forefront of my mind only to have it obliterated with Raven and her bright soul, the perfect reflection of mine. I close my eyes, my body going slack. This is it. I'm going to

Hell. I'm going to be Vincent's slave for all eternity, and this stunt guarantees the worst punishment. Had I just accepted things and acted like an obedient bastard, he'd have gone a bit easier on me. My soul wouldn't be moments away from discovering if taking a pounding from behind wouldn't require the training Dante teased me about. The bastard. Fuck him. He and Kase should've been here. Raven and the new devil Micah should've been here. Now I'm going to die alone and in misery, with an eternity of regrets.

Just when shadows try to steal my vision, the constriction on my throat loosens, and I hit my knees to the floor. I gasp in deep, painful breaths, but I'll take this new torment over what Vincent surely has in store.

"Elias, shit. Shit." Raven's gentle hand rubs between my shoulder blades, warming my skin. "Can you get up? We need to move."

I swallow the burning in my throat, trying to speak, but give up and nod my head instead. An ear-piercing roar quakes across the hallway, rumbling the floor with its vibration. Jerking my attention in the direction, I nearly shit myself at the raging boar-like beast charging after Vincent in his grotesquely bloody skeletal form—all bones and tissue without the skin.

"Hurry," Raven says, squeezing my hand. She wraps her arm around my waist and takes some of the weight off my aching body. "We need to get to the safe room."

"Safe room?" The words sound hoarse coming from my mouth. And fucking A. Why didn't anyone tell me there was a safe room in this gigantic house? I'd have spent my night in there rather than just screwing around everywhere else.

"It's at the end of the hall. Last door on the right." Raven nearly drags me the remaining dozen feet to the metal door that swings open by her presence alone. "I'm sorry no one told you. I just found out myself from Micah."

"The bastards," we both say in unison, and I can't stop the smile cracking across my face.

This isn't a happy moment, and as quickly as my smile comes do I force it away, but I feel so damn relieved watching the metal door swing closed, locking us in an...apartment-like suite. The studio setup looks ready to accommodate us for weeks with the non-perishable groceries waiting to be put away on the counter, the king-sized bed made and looking inviting as fuck, and a sectional couch with a TV in front ready to melt our minds.

"Here, let me help you to the couch," Raven says, half-carrying me forward as my body chooses now to give up on doing anything other than just hanging on to the last fragile strings of my life.

"Darlin', can I lie on the bed? I feel like I'm dying," I mutter, forcing my feet to work. It makes me feel pathetic as fuck with Raven needing to help me.

"You better not be," she responds, tightening her...bloodst ained features.

I stare at her in shock for a moment, drinking in the state of her clothes covered in blood. My eyes automatically search for injuries, but with the amount of blood? There is no fucking way she'd be hauling my ass around if it belonged to her. The amount looks like it came from a fatal injury. Spattering across her skin like she was aggressively stabbing someone.

I snap out of my thoughts and motion at the front of her shirt. "Where the fuck have you been and what the fuck were you and the raging asshole doing? Sacrificing virgins?"

She laughs in exasperation and pushes me a little too hard toward the bed. I lose my balance and land face-first on the comforter. It steals the giggles from her mouth. Sucking in a breath, she hurries to flip me over, my body relaxing under her touch. The second she bows forward, hovering her hands over me as she ensures she didn't cause more damage, I realize how thankful I am that the bastard angels denied my request for salvation at her expense. Her vibrant aqua eyes capture mine, and she swallows and wets her lips. I experience a moment of déjà vu, looking up at her like this with the light haloing the world around her soul.

Reaching up, I comb her hair behind her ear and say, "I'm okay. I promise. You didn't hurt me, darlin'. I'm still reeling from Vincent." I open and close my mouth, surprised by my ability to say his name. Maybe it's because we're alone and we're far more connected than I realized.

"I'm going to rip his insides out and strangle him with them when my devils catch him." Her eyes narrow at the thought. "He's going to regret ever getting within an inch of you."

My brows pinch together as the weight of her words sink in. I would've thought she'd gut the demon because hurting me put her eternity at risk. Hearing her say she'd go psycho hunter on his ass really digs into me in a good way. I'm used to being the one protecting people and not the other way around. It's fucking hot. It takes everything not to pull her onto me and kiss her. She even leans a bit closer like she wants me to. And damn. My cock hardens with the lust she awakens in me. I shouldn't want her like I do. It could be the end of me on more than a physical level with how dominating her soul keepers are. But the stupid, reckless part of me that makes me a good hunter thinks it's worth the risk.

But then my dumbass coughs, fucking ruining the moment.

Raven pulls me up and plops beside me, rubbing her hand along my back. It does nothing to chill my body out, and I swear to fucking God if my lungs collapse and I die with a damn boner, I will figure out how to give the universe Hell even if I'm a demon's little bitch.

"I don't know how to help you," Raven says, her voice lowering as she tries to hide her frustration. "I feel helpless."

I clutch her leg and remain hunched over, concentrating on slow, shallow breaths. It's getting harder and harder to inhale and exhale, my chest hurting with enough pain to make my eyes water. Fear rises the longer it takes to get myself together. What if I die right here and now? What kind of end would that be?

"Elias? Hey, Elias. Look at me." Raven shifts off the bed to kneel between my legs. "Elias."

My vision blurs with my slowing breathing. I blink me eyes dozens of times, trying to clear the haze, but nothing helps.

"Raven." I'm not even sure if I've said her name out loud, but bright light consumes me, and tingles prickle across my skin. The pain melts away, leaving behind a vision of Raven. But not as the woman I know. She is the woman I once knew. Grace.

Am I dead? No. If I were dead, I'd wake up surrounded in flames. This vision is a memory. A peek at what Heaven was for me in another life.

A smile lights Grace's beautiful face. "Elias, you gave me quite the fright. Are you well?"

I don't respond. I can't. Her beauty, love, and light entrance me just as it had the day I laid my eyes on her, crying alone in the rain at the gravesite of her lost Hope, her little sister, a young woman taken by the travesty of Scarlet Fever. Grace's prayers called to me in such a way I couldn't ignore. I stood over her, expanding my wings, protecting her from the rain in her moment of grief that wouldn't let me leave her.

"Elias, my angel?" Grace's eyes sheen over.

Still, I can't reply.

Light engulfs Grace, and I jerk my arms up, trying to catch her before the saviors steal her away. A surprised yelp sounds through the air. I blink in confusion, staring at Raven lying beneath me. My hands press into the tan carpet on each side of her head as I orient myself to what's happening. She clutches the front of my shirt in her fingers, keeping space between us.

"Elias, damn it. You scared the shit out of me. I thought you just died." Raven crinkles her nose, looking so breathtaking as she stares up at me.

The déjà vu hits me in full force as a dozen more memories click together. And this time, the knowledge comes with more than just facts. It comes with the all-consuming truth of who she is to me. How her soul matches mine, kissed by the essence of the heavenly power I once had.

"I'm sorry," I murmur, my mind now ultra-aware that I'm between her legs with our bodies touching. The intimacy turns me on, and my cock throbs, knowing how close it is to the sexiest woman in the universe. Of all time. "I'm not doing so good. My demonic soul keeper was right. I'm running out of time."

"We will get you out of this before that happens," she says, blinking until the sheen disappears from her eyes.

I force myself to roll off Raven and lie on the floor beside her. "I need to be prepared in case. I just…"

She shifts and rests on her elbow, staring at me in silence without prodding for me to finish my comment. Her messy hair veils her face, but I can still see her endless eyes capturing mine through her midnight tresses. I resist the urge to push the strands out of her face again, sensing she needs the protection from me as much as I need it from her. Because if I can see her clearly, peer right into her soul, I know I'll do something stupid. I'll kiss her and steal her away from her soul keepers. The persistent memories that spin through my mind make it hard to think of anything else.

There has to be another way to help her that doesn't involve the devils. If I can break my contract with Vincent on my own, it'll buy me a tiny bit of time to figure things out. My soulmate doesn't deserve this fate. She's at the mercy of Hell because of me.

If I could just get her away…

I sigh, shaking my head, knowing that if I draw out the silence any longer that I'll lose my nerve. This might be my only chance to be alone with her again because I don't even know if tomorrow will even come for me.

"Raven," I finally say, testing to see if she lets me cover her hand with mine. "If I die before you get things—"

"Don't." She scoots closer and touches my cheek. "My devils won't let that happen. They won't."

"You can't truly know that, darlin'. As much as I hate raining on your flame of hope, I have to. I have a dying request." I wet my lips with my tongue. "If I die before things get handled, will you ensure to return my body to my family? I want them to handle my burial. Your soul keepers might throw me in the trash or something, and I want my family to know what happened."

"I would never allow such a thing," Raven says, her eyes widening. "But I understand, and I will humor your request even though it won't be necessary."

I nod, remaining expressionless. "I wish I could see them, you know. They're probably assuming the worst." I feel guilty as fuck to bring this up, using Raven's concern for me like this, but I can't help it. These memories blooming in my mind get to me. I can't just sit back and watch as her soul keepers steal her away from me. She's my soulmate. That must count for something, even if our history isn't all unicorn farts and confetti rain showers.

"You're lucky you have family who cares for you. Mine hasn't answered my calls in months. They wouldn't even care if I died." She lowers her voice with her words and averts her eyes to gaze at my hand resting on hers.

I grimace at her admission. "I'm sure that's not true."

She shrugs. "It is. They hated my ex-fiancé and disowned me because of it. I should've listened to their warnings. I just—I don't know how to explain it."

Sorrow sinks into me, and I can't help wondering what our lives would've been like had the Higher Power not used time and death to keep us apart. Would I have found her sooner? Remembered on my own? Would it have been possible for us to have a normal life? I wish I knew.

"But whatever," she adds, bumping her shoulder against mine. "It doesn't matter. It also gives me a thought. What if I convinced Kase and Dante to allow you one more visit to see your family?"

I clench my jaw, both loving and hating how I predicted how her thought-process would work. She has an angelic soul with a devil streak, but in the end, she's always been mortal.

"A favor like that comes at a cost I can't afford and definitely would never ask you to pay," I respond, meeting her eyes again. Call me a selfish bastard, but I need this. I need her. The strange innate desire inside me won't allow anything else otherwise. This same need might have been the same reason I abandoned grace.

"There isn't a price for anything, Elias. Trust me. Let me talk to them. I'll get it worked out." Raven's expression lights up, a wicked grin widening her smile.

And damn it. She is sexy as sin.

I swivel my torso and meet her with my own grin that fades the second she sucks her bottom lip between her teeth. The urge to close the space completely overwhelms me, our moment together stirring something dark inside me. I crave to taste her lips. To see if my kiss can remind her of the knowledge burning a hole inside me.

I swallow and lean an inch closer, seeing if she'll be the one to come to me. "Darlin', you're going to get me in trouble all over again if you keep looking at me like that. I'm starting to remember our past, and it's getting to me in a good way."

She tilts her head slightly. "Yeah? Will you tell me what you know?"

"We were close. Inseparable. Alone together in that life just as we are now," I murmur, afraid to give more details. What if it pushes her away? But then again, what if she stays? "We saved each other in a way."

"It must be so strange." Raven eases closer, mingling her breath with mine. I'm glad I smoked my last cigarette hours ago. "I still can't imagine having a completely other life."

"I'm sorry I lost you then." I don't know why I say it, but the words never felt truer. "Grace."

"Grace," she repeats. "How fucking ridiculous, right? Grace stole your grace."

I chuckle, loving how she speaks like a woman after my heart. "I gave it to you. It was the final move for me as an angel. I gave it to you before I fell, which is why I returned as a mortal. At least I think. This is the first time the thought came into my head. Fuck, the things you do to me on a level I never knew possible."

"I wonder what else I could do to help break your past life free." She caresses her fingers over my cheek, making me shiver. Is that an innuendo, and I'm too chicken shit to flirt back? What if she's being genuine in her curiosity? I guess I'll find out. I'm already dying, so I might as well lose all my fucks toward the woman who has my soul but also is off-limits. Fuck forbidden love.

"Is that so?" I say, cupping my hand over hers, pressing her fingers harder to my cheek. I crave to feel the weight of her touch.

Her expression says it all as blush tints her cheeks. "Mmmh-mm. All the possibilities burn through me."

Fuck yeah. She wants me to make a move. I can feel it in the ache in my balls. How she licks her lips in anticipation. "I have a few in mind."

She tips her head and inches closer. "Show me."

My body buzzes as I lean in to kiss her, my whole being on the verge of exploding. I've never felt like this with anyone. This is different than a couple flings. Some dates. This is soul deep.

"Raven, fuck. Are you hurt?" Kase storms into the safe room

with Micah behind him. "Micah said the bastard got in."

"He used my soul," I say, speaking up. My palms sweat at the fire erupting in Kase's palm. I tense and grab Raven, instinctually trying to shield her from wrath himself. "If Micah and Raven hadn't come hom—" I snap my mouth closed. One look into Micah's glowing orange eyes screams I'm a damn fuckup for running my mouth.

Spinning, Kase punches Micah in the gut, sending him crashing into the wall. "What kind of bullshit are your trying to pull? Do you want Raven to fail? Do you really think Lucian will pick you as her punisher for eternity? I damn well know he won't."

Raven scrambles to her feet and braves getting between the two assholes. "Come on, Kase. It's not like that. We thought Elias would be safe here."

Kase blows hellfire in anger, sending it billowing across the room. "Angel-girl, Elias looks like he's about to drop dead. Why don't you help him to Dante's room, so he can help him the second he gets back?"

"And leave you two here to fight?" she places her hands on her hips.

Fear tightens my chest, and I cough, my whole body tensing at Raven getting in Kase's face. My hacking up a lung is enough to draw their focus from each other. Raven rushes toward me, a frown pouting her face.

"Micah, can you help me carry him?" Raven asks, glancing over her shoulder. "I don't think I can do it."

Striding past Kase, Micah stomps toward me. And damn. It's déjà vu all over again. A memory breaks free and I see Micah in all his angelic glory with his white wings and golden eyes. Features soft and easy-going and utterly familiar.

He manhandles me and lifts me off my feet. "I'm doing this for Raven, you treacherous, greedy, selfish bastard. Do you understand?"

"I guess?" My words come out as a question. I can't recall exactly what kind of history I have with Micah, but I know it's there, and he plans to hold it against me.

What the fuck ever.

"I'll be there in a minute," Raven calls, motioning for Micah to take me.

I don't get a chance to argue or do anything really.

I'm no match for a devil.

Micah carries me from the room like he's about to toss me out like the trash. Maybe I deserve it. I don't know.

"What's your problem?" I ask, using my arm to block my head from bashing into a doorframe.

"I don't trust you with this mission. You'll probably do what you've always done best. Put yourself first and let the rest of us clean up after you. But I swear to the depths of Hell. Leave Raven out of it. She doesn't deserve more disappointment in this life." Micah kicks open a door leading into what I assume is Dante's suite, and he drops me on the bed.

Storming off, he leaves me in a tornado of confusion.

I'm starting to think that this is how my life will be from now on—getting punished for a past life I don't fully remember.

I have to get out of here with Raven.

I'll do whatever it takes.

16

Family Reunion

RAVEN

"**Y**OU REALLY NEED to get a new car. This crap-mobile is a piece of shit. Raven is far too good to have to face this kind of torture." Kase smacks the steering wheel of Elias's car, scented with cigarette smoke.

Elias fiddles with the pack of smokes in his palms that he found in the pocket behind the seat. "Are you buying me one?"

I smirk without commenting, eyeing his nervous gesture. I would've once judged him for continuing to smoke even though he's dying, but it's his choice. He's going to make his decisions, and he's already living with the consequences. Plus, after smelling Hell, I don't think anything could ever smell so disgusting.

"No, but I'm fucking going to buy me something devil-approved and family friendly if I'm going to be chauffeuring you bastards around all the time." Kase drums his fingers on the steering wheel. He glances at me in his peripheral vision. "Come sit on my lap, angel-girl. I'm collecting your end of the deal now. It's going to be the only way I survive another moment."

I laugh and lock my fingers around his tail, stopping him from trying to tie it around me. "You haven't completed your end yet, so no. I said after you took us to and from Elias's family. Not on the ride there."

"You're one helluva negotiator, Raven," Kase muses, sliding his tail from my hand with a shiver.

"I've learned from the best," I say, snuggling into his side, teasing him by resting my hand on his thigh.

Dante follows my lead and sneaks his hand a few inches under the hem of my dress until I lock him out by squeezing my legs shut. "Don't make us regret this."

"It's fucking too late for that. We're here." Kase jerks the vehicle to a stop and kills the engine.

I flick my gaze from Dante's hand still trying to test my resolve and out the front window. A warehouse looms behind a barbed wire cinderblock wall at the end of the street. Searching the area, I look for signs of life but only spot a gray and white cat pouncing toward something on the sidewalk. I was expecting Elias's hunter family to reside in a home and not this old, industrial building. It's creepy and the kind of place I'd expect serial killers to drag their victims.

"Looks just as I expected." Dante swings the door open and climbs out, opening the backdoor for Elias. He offers him his hand, and the simple gesture warms me to my core. Dante can be a psycho, but he's also caring and helpful. "A shithole."

Kase laces his tail around my wrist, stopping me from exiting. "We have some rules, angel-girl. Do not leave our sides. Do not speak to anyone. Keep your eyes down. Tell no one anything."

"Okay, master. You say these things like I'm going to go running in there screaming that Hell is about to take control of the universe." I twist my hand and manage to lock my fingers around part of his tail. Stroking it, I wait for him to give me a reaction.

And damn it, does he.

Yanking me onto his lap, he kisses me, stealing my breath. His hands roam down my back, tugging the hem of my dress up until he can grab my ass cheeks. Micah groans and slams the door, his annoyance heavy in his voice. I don't know what he expected after our kiss, but I can already tell we might need to have a conversation about my relationships. *Relationships.* Shit. I never imagined such a thing as being involved with several men—devils—from my life, and it's been easier than I expected with Kase and Dante. While they're not technically together or regular lovers, especially with me in the picture, they are bonded. They've always had each other and have basically shared an existence. But with Micah? I worry. I can't survive Hell's rulers fighting over me and my soul. Without Micah having even a cordial friendship with Kase and Dante, things could get rough if we progress. I'll have to work on getting everyone to bond.

"Break it up, you two. You're not staying in the car to fuck while I escort Dead Man Walking into a compound of Hell haters." Dante expands his wings, blocking out the sun. "We had a plan, remember. We're not that kind and generous to grant final wishes without strings attached."

Kase breaks from my mouth but doesn't let me go. I'm horny enough and not really wanting to see inside the Serial Killer Warehouse now that Kase gets me worked up. Last night was rough as I stayed up with Dante and watched Elias sleep like angelic creeps...with pitchforks.

"You have Micah. Put him to work. He's on probation and needs to remember his place if he's going to stay and help Raven complete the mission," Kase mutters against my throat, his voice vibrating over my skin making me grind harder.

"Not happening." Leaning in, Dante locks his hands around my waist and tugs me out of the car. "We're all staying together."

"Out here. You can't go inside." Elias rests his palms on the hood of his car. His sickly pallor does nothing for my nerves, which immediately kills the desire Kase aroused in me.

"The fuck we aren't." Kase hops out of the car, not fazed by Dante dragging me away. "You didn't honestly think we came here just for you to tell these bastards goodbye."

Elias turns his gaze to me, pursing his lips. "Raven said she offered you a deal."

Tipping his head back, Dante laughs. "Not a deal. She bribed us, and the only reason we agreed, since she will let us fuck her any which way we please regardless, was because I want to know where the fuck you learned your hunting skills from. Not many mortals know how to create a demon trap."

I whack his shoulder. "You think I'm going to let you fuck me again now? That kind of comment is not the way into my pants."

Dante play-hisses and flicks his tongue at me. "Don't worry, pretty soul. I have other ways to ensure it."

Micah slams his hands on the roof of the car. "That's enough. We're wasting time better used on other things with this arguing." Glaring at Elias, he adds, "You better figure out a way to get us in. I know you have it in you."

Elias scrubs the back of his neck with his hand. "How about a compromise? Raven can go with me since I won't have to break the shields and—"

"No!" all three devils say in unison.

I hold my palms up at my devils and turn to Elias. "That's not going to happen. I'm still learning to protect myself, and you're in no shape to promise to keep me safe. The last thing we need is for one of the demon hunters to get killed because they invaded this imaginary devil claim bubble surrounding me."

"There is one other way to get them inside without too much trouble," Elias admits, shifting on his feet, probably feeling Kase's hellfire more intensely than I do as it crackles and dances a bit uncontrollably around our feet.

Kase releases another bout of hellfire, his devil form begging to break free, causing him to flick embers toward the ground. "We don't care about fucking trouble. Get us in or we're changing plans. I sense a horny fucking angel nearby."

I automatically peer around the street but don't catch sight of Andre. "Don't make me remind you of what you won't get if you break the deal. Come on, Kase. It's his dying wish."

Dante narrows his eyes. "You wouldn't."

I drop my arms to my sides and place my hands on my hips. "Oh, I will. I'll even tailor what I had planned to do for Elias."

Micah steps closer, looming over me. "He can't handle anything in his current condition."

Braving the devils, Elias tightens his jaw and offers me his hand. "You know what? I might just take it instead. Even if my body can't handle her like when I was healthy, it would be one helluva way to go."

I tip my head back and laugh, purposefully pulling Elias to me and spinning him away protectively. "Don't poke the beasts. They will not only spank me, but I'm pretty sure Dante would spank you too."

"And it wouldn't be with my hand." Dante expands his wings, towering behind me. "Though if you're Raven's soulmate, then you might enjoy it."

Fuck. Me. Now I can't get the visual from my mind. The only man I've ever seen Dante with is Kase, and he gives him dominance. But thinking about Dante using his control on Elias? I don't know how I feel about that. I'm willing to see though...but maybe not like this. I'd be a bit worried about Elias's fragility. And I'm suddenly feeling rather protective. It's strange.

"I'll pass." Elias snuffs out my curiosity. "With my luck, you'll kill me with my ass out, and that's not the way I want to go."

"I wouldn't let him spank you to death," I tease, laughter lightening my voice.

"Just to the brink. Raven has to be the one to take your pathetic life." Micah crosses his arms, his words wiping the smile from my face.

Whipping my attention to him, I glower. He really has something out for Elias if he's willing to risk my anger to say something we hadn't even told Elias about yet. Something I'm not sure I can follow through with, especially the more I get to know him. He's not as douchy as I thought he was.

Kase swings his fist and punches Micah in the gut hard enough to send him reeling. Striding between them, Dante creates a wall with his wings, stopping the impending fight. I step forward, but Elias laces his fingers through mine and tugs me back.

"Come on. We have to go," he mutters, tightening his grip on my fingers. "They'll never let us go without them, and I'm not sure I want to introduce the rulers of Hell to my family."

I flick my gaze to the three devils, still focusing on each other. "I told you, Elias. I can't go without them. It's not worth the risk."

"Please, you have to trust me. They won't hurt you." Tugging my hand, he hauls me with him, forcing me to walk or eat shit on the ground. "We'll be in and out in just a couple minutes. I don't want to stay long. I only want to say goodbye to my best friend."

I purse my lips and slowly nod my head. "Five minutes."

"You can stay by the door," Elias says, nodding his head.

I stop resisting and let him guide me along. Like Kase senses my sudden recklessness, he growls and lassos me with his tail, yanking me away from Elias. I screech in surprise, landing in Micah's arms. Fire lights his gaze and he shakes his head in annoyance.

So I kiss him.

"This had better not have been your plan," Kase snaps, keeping his attention on Elias.

"No, it was me trying to take advantage of an opportunity instead of convincing you to act as if you're my prisoner to get the hunters to allow us all in through the back and into the only non-warded room on the premises. It's where some hunters capture and interrogate demons." Elias combs his fingers through his tousled hair. "Which is what I meant about it being too much trouble."

"Me, your prisoner? No one will fucking believe that." Kase lifts an eyebrow and turns to me. "It's laughable."

It kind of is, but I don't say as much. "It wouldn't hurt to try. Please, Kase. Think of our deal. Just give Elias this dying wish. If you do, I'll add something to the bargain."

Red light warms Kase's gaze. "I'm listening."

I lick my lips. "You can leave your mark on me."

"I have something better in mind." A wicked smirk lights his handsome face. Uh-oh. "I want you to wear a ring from me too."

I glance at the one Micah gave me with the soul in it. I hadn't thought anyone noticed. "Deal." Turning to Elias, I reach out and touch his shoulder. "Enjoy this moment. I don't think anyone on Earth has ever had the chance to control a devil."

Elias lifts his eyebrow. "Except for Raven." Turning to me, he adds, "And I don't know how I'll repay you."

Micah grabs Elias by the shoulder and spins him away. "I'm sure we'll think of something."

"How in the world did you manage to get two demons to willingly come here, Elias?" a hoarse, masculine voice asks.

I stretch onto my tiptoes, trying to glimpse Elias with his hunter friend, but the window inside is far too dirty to see anything except the blurry forms within harsh lighting.

"I'm already a dead man, so I offered them a deal. Don't worry about it, Preston. Just get the holy circle ready. Make it quick," Elias responds. "They have a woman with them I want to steal from their sadistic asses."

The two figures separate, one heading in our direction. Micah releases a low growl, the rumble vibrating across my shoulder blades as he steps closer, touching his hands to my hips. His body heats me up, and I rub the sweat prickling along the hairline of my neck. I shiver as Kase twines his tail around my waist, ensuring I'm never out of his grasp even with space between us. Running my fingers over the smooth appendage, I absently stroke it for a moment before I realize it's probably not a great idea to get him worked up.

"Dante better have his act together," Micah mutters near my ear. "A holy circle can entrap us for a while if he doesn't, and I'm not absolutely certain we can trust Elias."

"We can. Trust me if you don't trust him," I say, grasping his hand to slide it more around me.

"I do, but you don't understand our history, Raven. He—he abandoned me without a single word. Never told me about you or his plans. He just vanished like the selfish disgrace he is." Micah huffs a breath through his nose, his familiar crisp ocean scent wafting over me.

I open my mouth to ask him more about it, but the cranking of a metal sliding door screeches through the air. I stiffen and reach for Kase, wanting both devils to hold onto me in case. If I wasn't so worried about something happening to Elias, I'd suggest we all go wait in the car, but the only way I feel even a little bit better is to stay close where I know Kase, Dante, or Micah can intervene. With the thought of Dante, I shift and try to peer over Micah's towering form for my favorite kinkster. He's hiding out of sight, and I realize I hate it. I want my eyes on him too.

"Hey, fuckers. In here. Don't touch anything if you want the book," Elias says, appearing in the wide doorway to a huge concrete storage room.

"We want to see it first," Kase says, falling into his demonic negotiator role. He makes playing along with Elias sound so easy and natural. If Elias had said something like that to me, my first reaction would have been to ask him what the fuck he's talking about. We never even mentioned anything beyond a fake deal.

"And we'd like a word with the hunter in charge around here," Micah adds, his gruff voice far from the angelic tone he used to speak to me in.

"That wasn't part of the deal," Elias snaps, glowering. If I didn't know any better, I'd think he wasn't acting any longer and that he and Micah arranged something without me knowing.

A loud whistle shrieks through the air, startling me, and I intake a sharp breath. Tugging me with him, Kase moves toward the doorway, inadvertently making Micah follow along like I'm the chain keeping the two of them together.

"Son, why don't ya let me finish up with this? I wish you'd have called, Elias. I'd have better prepared for our...guests. " The slightly accented, masculine voice booms from inside like the man thinks if he talks loud enough, it'll somehow intimidate my devils—though maybe if they weren't the rulers of Hell, it might work. I'm not sure. I don't deal with many demons.

"I got it, Pops. You don't know what we're dealing with, and I do. Just bring me the grimoire." Elias faces the man, his body slightly hunched forward like it's taking everything inside him to remain on his feet. "Trust me. These guys only want a specific page. They said they'd help me with my deal with my demonic soul keeper. Now go get it. You know it belongs to me. I was the one to get it."

The old hunter scowls. "Watch your tongue, son. You—"

"Enough!" Micah shouts, his body rippling against mine. "We don't have time for this."

Releasing me, Micah shoves past Kase and stomps into the storage room. I try to run after him, but Kase lifts me up from behind. My arms hang at my sides, his embrace pinning me to him. I don't fight and relax. I appreciate the hellish intervention because sometimes I react before I can process things.

And it's a good thing at least one of us thinks things through.

Fire explodes in front of us, igniting a circle around Micah before he can reach the old hunter and Elias. Widening his eyes, the old man takes a few steps back and scrambles to grab a gun from his belt. The fucker immediately starts firing the weapon, spraying bullets across Micah's chest. His devil form breaks free from his skin, and he roars and tries to ram through the fiery cage, but it only crackles under his attempts.

"Kase, he has two souls!" Micah shouts, colliding into the

fiery barrier again.

I frown and squint at the hunter as if I can see what Micah does. Kase whistles through his fingers and spins, tossing me right into Dante's outstretched arms as he lands a few feet away. Shouts echo from the building, and I whip my head around to watch several hunters rush into the room. Kase roars. Leaping around the demon trap, he smashes into the old hunter, snarling in his face.

"Stop! Don't hurt him!" Elias yells, braving Kase's wrath to lock his hands around his tail, trying to yank him back.

"Dante, let me go. We have to intervene," I say, wiggling in his arms. "Please. I don't want any of them to get hurt."

"Hang on, pretty soul. There are bullets flying everywhere." Dante folds his wings forward, shielding us as something pings off the metal frame.

"Then you go. I'll wait here. I swear. Just get Elias before he gets killed." I wiggle some more until he sets me on my feet.

Combing my hair away from my ear, he leans in, his warm breath tickling my skin as he uncontrollably hisses. "If I catch you running off with the horny angel while I protect your damn soulmate, that tight little asshole of yours is mine to do as I please later. Understand?"

I smirk. "Yes, sir. With so many of you dirty devils sharing a house with me, I guess it's time I let you train my body. I know you'll be extra naughty with me." I know I shouldn't prod at his desire, but I want him to know that no matter what, I'm his filthy soul even with others wanting a piece of me.

He hums and smacks my ass. "Fuck, you make me want to bend you over and take you now. Too bad I can't stuff you by myself like Kase can. The lucky bastard."

I shake my head and push him toward the frightened hunters as Kase herds them into a corner, not reacting to their weapons. It takes someone managing to pull out holy water to shake at him to get him to even back up a little.

Dante stretches his wings, expanding them almost from one side to the other. "Get your hunters to back down, and we won't kill them. We only want to talk to you, old man. You wouldn't want us to share your dark little secret, would you?"

Little secret? What is he talking about?

A gust of wind lifts up my hair from my neck and shoulders, sending the strands dancing in the angel-made breeze. If Dante hadn't told me Andre was nearby, and if I hadn't caught the fragrance of his coconut scent, I'd scream and run into the fray of things. His shadow looms behind me, but I pretend I don't notice his arrival.

Goosebumps prickle over my skin, and I tense in anticipation. Keeping my gaze trained at Dante and Elias managing to get everyone to stop fighting, I try to focus on anything and everything else even though my body begs me to turn around.

"I wonder how long the old hunter has been possessed,"

Andre muses from behind me, standing close enough to my back that all it would take is to shuffle my feet an inch to rest against his chest.

So I do. I back into his taut pecs and wait for him to steady me with his hands. When they touch my shoulders, I reach up and cover his fingers with my own. His scent engulfs me with the flap of his wings. I tip my head back until I stare at his handsome face upside down.

"What the fuck are you talking about? Possessed?" I scrunch my forehead in confusion. "By a demon?"

"Another soul. One who managed to cling to this realm instead of being ushered onward to their afterlife. It happens." Andre keeps his voice low, and he tips his chin a bit like he considers kissing me. But he doesn't.

I don't try either.

Not because I don't crave another taste of his lips or feeling his mouth on mine, but because an eerie silence creeps through the air a second before an ear-piercing shriek.

"Give us the holy relic, and we won't send you to Hell. Now!" Dante hollers, stealing my attention away from Andre.

"What is he talking about, Pops?" Elias asks, sounding far younger than he had before we arrived here. I know the old man isn't of blood relation, but he obviously means something to Elias.

"Son, do you trust me?" Pops says, keeping his blade drawn

and his gaze on the devils, watching as Dante manages to break the demon catcher from the outside with a gust of air from his wings. "You know I've always done right by you. Whatever these demonic bastards try to tell you, I want you to remember how I raised and taught you. It has always been me around you, and no one else."

Micah steps over the charred dust, the only reminder that the demon trap was ever there. "Because you don't allow the true owner of that body to come out and play. Now give us the holy relic, and we'll take it, along with Elias, and you can remain here with the hunters."

"We really don't give a fuck about the man," Kase adds.

I should feel bad about their words, but they're right. I don't care about whoever the hell managed to get possessed by a ghost. I only wanted to bring Elias here as a kind gesture to show him that I'm not some Hell-bound monster...shit. Maybe I am. How can I not care?

"Is that a deal? If I give you the holy relic and let Elias leave with you without trouble, you'll let me be, right?" Pops asks, confirming the bargain my devils try to make.

Kase smirks. "It's a deal." Uh-oh. His expression screams that the old man might've fucked up with his bargain.

Andre groans under his breath and pushes harder against me like he plans to rush past me to intervene. "Don't watch, little hellion. Please. It's going to get—"

"What in the actual fuck, Pops?" Elias shouts, throwing his hands out, staring into the trunk Pops had a hunter roll out. "Are those...wings? Angel-fucking-wings? This is how you've been managing to create weapons against Hell? Where did you get them?"

"None of that matters, son. You just have to know that without them, none of us ever stood a chance against Hell. We fight to help people, and who gives a fuck about the wings." Pops tries to close the space to Elias, but Elias steps out of his reach.

"Old hunter, tell him the truth," Micah says, speaking up. "Tell him whose wings those are. Have you had them in your possession long?"

Pops flares his nostrils. "It's not like he wanted them. I saw how he gave up his grace, and you damn well bet I wasn't going to let them go to waste. So what?"

I blink a few times in shock. Is he implying that the holy relic—the disgustingly shriveled, browning wings he has sitting in the trunk protected by strange symbols—belong to Elias? Holy shit. I don't believe it.

"Shoot me for all the good I've done with them. The Lord has let me hop from one vessel to another for a long time to ensure I could take care of you. It's how I knew where to find you to train you myself," Pops continues, trying to touch Elias's shoulder only to have Elias whack his hand away. "With enough good deeds, I can buy my ticket to the good place. You get it, don't you? I had to—"

"You destroyed him!" Micah explodes into his ferocious devil form, shaking the room with his hulking footsteps. "You destroyed everything!"

Swinging his giant hoof, Micah punches Pops in the stomach, lifting him off his feet in the process. The old man hugs Micah's thick arm to stop from flying across the room.

"Demon, we had a deal!" Pops gags and coughs the words out, hanging like a ragdoll.

Kase lifts and drops his shoulders. "Your exact words were, 'If I give you the holy relic and let Elias leave with you without trouble, you'll let me be,' and technically, letting you be doesn't include a body which doesn't belong to you. Your time on this plane is up."

"No!" Pops shouts, thrashing in Micah's hold.

The strangest noise—words, I think—escape from Micah. Andre tugs me back and tries to shield my eyes, but I reach behind me and cup his junk in my hand, throwing him off. He groans in lustful surprise, shifting his arm until it rests under my breast.

"Raven," he whispers, his hard body pulsing under my hand.

I ignore him the best I can, keeping my eyes trained on Micah, Dante, and Kase surrounding the old hunter as his skin shudders and moves and an ethereal light radiates from Pop's chest to spread over his skin as if his veins glow from within.

"What's happening?" Elias asks, his voice rising over the discordant collection of voices humming through the air.

Gunfire pops, piercing my ears and startling me. A couple of hunters try to intervene to save their leader, but it's too late. My vision blurs as Micah rips the light free of the old man's body, and it ignites in flames. Static buzzes over my skin.

"You murdered him!" someone shouts.

"Elias, this is your fault!" a woman yells. "You brought them here."

Pulling me back, Andre spins and shields me protectively. "Oh, no. I must intervene before the soul takes another." Andre abandons me outside and expands his wings.

Utter silence falls through the concrete warehouse. Every human stops fighting, and I know without having to ask that Andre reveals himself. Gathering brilliant light in between his palms, he shoots heavenly power at an inky shadowy spot hovering in the air in front of a man. The light engulfs the shadow, sizzling and crackling until a scream pierces my ears and flames burst across the floor.

"It can't be," a man whispers.

"Oh, blessed is this sight," says another. "We've been saved from these monstrous demons."

What the fuck?

I don't get a chance to tell these bitch-ass hunters that they never needed saving from my devils because Dante closes the distance to me and scoops me into his arms. Carrying the gross severed wings, Kase tightens his jaw. His fingers smoke and smolder, and I rush forward and try to take them from him.

He holds them over his head. "No, angel-girl. If you touch them, they'll mark you, and you might like what they do to you too much. I've had enough goddamn holiness for one day."

"Our savior," a few hunters say, drawing my attention back to Andre, stopping me from arguing.

Andre straightens his shoulders. "The Hell-bound cannot be saved. I'm sorry. I know that it sometimes takes a monster to kill one, and the Higher Power appreciates your work. Your sacrifices will not go unnoticed."

"What?" a hunter asks.

Kase tips his head back and roars a laugh. "Hilarious, right? The beings you bow and pray to don't even care—"

A loud groan cuts Kase off, and his eyes light with his red power. I shift and look at Micah, cradling Elias in his arms. My heart stalls at the sight of Elias convulsing, his eyes rolling back in his head.

"Oh, fuck. What's happening?" Panic rises through me. I search over Elias for signs of injury but don't see anything.

"Dante, take him. Go now. Get him as far as you can," Kase commands, using the wings to point.

I find myself stumbling toward Kase as Dante snatches Elias from Micah and launches into the air.

"What's wrong?" I ask, steadying myself. I tip my head back and stare at the sky, watching Dante's silhouette shrink with the distance growing between us.

"His essence recognizes his wings," Kase says. He shakes the gross wings. "We have to destroy them."

Summoning their devil forms again, Micah and Kase crack the ground open in front of me. Heat radiates from the open portal to Hell. I hug my arms over my chest, rocking nervously at the whispery voices humming from the fiery pit.

Together, Kase and Micah scorch the severed wings and toss them into Hell.

I heave a breath, a sharp pain in my chest winding me.

My soul aches.

So does my body.

It's like my essence is stolen away from me and succumbs to Hell with the destruction of Elias's wings.

Lifting me up, Micah cradles me in his arms. All I can do is stare at the sky, letting the whirlwind of emotions rage through me. Andre's light glows around me, and I tip my head back and stare at him as he watches me with the hunters pleading at his feet.

My devils take me away.

Fallen

RAVEN

I HOVER IN the doorway of Elias's room. Darkness shrouds his figure asleep in his bed, but I can't get myself to leave him alone. Kase, Dante, and Micah remain downstairs in the living room, discussing things that make my stomach twist.

I should leave Elias alone to rest. He's been weak and fatigued for two days now. I know it's best to let him be while we work on finding Vincent, but I can't seem to get myself to head to Micah's room to wait for him. Another part of me needs to close the space to Elias to prove to myself he's still breathing. So that's what I do.

I ease down on the edge of the bed and carefully rest my hand on his chest. It rises with a shallow breath, and I can't stop my eyes from watering. How is it possible for me to feel so sad for Elias despite the short amount of time we've known each other...in this life? At first, I worried about what his state meant for me, but now? I've already grown used to having him around. It's the strangest thing how familiar his presence alone feels. With him sleeping and the quiet of the world surrounding us, I can focus on just being here with him. How his heart beats beneath my palm and his body seemingly relaxes under my touch.

I don't know what comes over me, but the urge to sneak into his bed and just snuggle next to him while he sleeps consumes me. It's such a creep move, and I would punch him if he tried to climb into my bed while I slept. I can't help myself though. I want to support him the only way I know how, especially after discovering the man he treated like a father was a ghost possessing a mortal, imprisoning the innocent soul all to use Elias in this life.

Curling on my side, I scoot closer to Elias, curling against his side. My movements stir him awake, but he doesn't freak out and yell at me. He doesn't get into defensive fighting mode or anything like I expect. All he does is shift his arm away from his side and lets me rest on the crook of his arm while he hugs it around me.

"Everything okay?" he murmurs, his eyelids heavy with sleep. "We're not under attack by a demonic army or anything, right?"

I smirk and shake my head, drawing my finger across the front of his shirt. "My devils are currently devising plans and shit. Demonic affairs. I figured I'd check on you and…I don't know why I'm here."

Elias grazes his fingers up and down my arm. "I don't need a reason. It doesn't matter to me, Raven. I'm happy you did. It means that maybe I haven't fucked everything completely up. I never wanted any of that bullshit to happen, especially with you there. I just—I screwed up. I was selfish."

I frown, puckering my eyebrows. "You didn't know."

Turning over, he faces me, his eyes searching my face in the dimly lit room. "Every time I sit and think, fragmented memories of Grace return to me."

"What does this have to do with anything?" I rest my head on his pillow, sharing his minty breath, fresh from brushing his teeth. Cigarette smoke faintly lingers on his clothes, but it doesn't bother me, the familiarity of his smoky, citrusy scent soothes the worry digging deep into my soul.

Wrinkles crease his forehead with his frown. "It has everything to do with it. I asked you to take me to the hunters because I thought that maybe…I want—no, I need—to figure out how to keep us both safe. You carry a piece of me, and I feel it. It's strange and fucking terrifying. I just—I don't even know, Raven. Like I said, I fucked up. I'm selfish. I hate relying on demons, but even more so, it rips me open on a deeper level knowing that they get a part of my essence through you."

"Oh." I don't know what else to say. How to feel. "Elias..."

"Raven, I know I don't have the right to ask anything of you, but I have to know. If you could change things, would you? If there was a way out of Hell's clutches, would you take it?" Elias grazes his fingers along my jawline, combing the strands of midnight hair falling into my face. His question sounds so sincere, his face full of emotion I don't recognize.

I blink a few times, trying to break away from his gaze, but something about him grips me tightly, refusing to let me go. "I don't know."

His jaw tightens as he turns expressionless toward my response. I don't know what he was expecting for me to say. It clearly wasn't this.

"I never expected to...enjoy my life now as much as I do. Kase and Dante...Micah—"

"But Raven," he says, cutting me off, filling his thoughts with assumptions. Closing his eyes, he inhales a breath through his nose. "You're my soulmate."

"And neither of us has control over our souls. Hell does. The devils do. That's not something that will change for me. I've accepted it." My voice comes out a whisper. "At least this way

I don't have to suffer. I mean, as long as you don't go dying on me and I can finish this bullshit deal with Lucian."

"Raven, I..." He falls silent for a moment, sharing airspace with me.

I wish with everything in me that he'd open his eyes and look at me. Let me try to read him. Having recollection of a life I can't and am not sure I'll ever truly know or understand sounds the worst. I know I'm the reason he fell from grace and gave his essence to me—and the knowledge is already nearly impossible to accept—I just don't know how to handle all of this. A part of me knows that I shouldn't allow myself so close. If I get too close, how the fuck will I end his life when the time comes? Fuck. Another much louder, selfish part of me wants to say screw it all to Hell—quite literally—and to embrace this flawed, reckless desire suddenly coursing through every fiber of my being. I mean, who in their right mind can look at their soulmate and resist such a connection? I'm not a believer in love at first sight but I'm too old to deny something so obvious and true in front of me. At least, according to my soul...and my horny-ass vagina. Why can't she just be cool with the excellent, mind-blowing fucking she gets now? The greedy bitch. She's a sin enough herself that she could rule her own kingdom in Hell.

"Raven, how will I live my eternity with you in the arms of others? This is my eternal punishment, isn't it? God's given my soulmate to others." He's no longer talking to me. I don't think he's talking to the Higher Power either. "I deserve this. To think I almost lost you because of my own greed and self-ishness."

"You were an asshole psycho," I tease, smirking. Sliding my hand into his soft hair, I guide his face closer to mine.

"I'm sorry," he whispers, fluttering his lashes to gaze into my eyes. "I'm sorry for everything. For how we met. For nearly getting you and me killed. For thinking I could save you from the men you clearly don't need saving from."

"You don't need to apologize. You had your reasons the same as I had mine. I'm just happy you're not a dickhead anymore." I wet my lips, turning my attention to his mouth.

"What about a psycho?" His voice lightens with his comment.

I release a breathless laugh. "You know I apparently have a thing for them."

"Then I guess I'll have to sacrifice virgins in your honor." The corners of his eyes crinkle with his smile. "I'll do anything for another reminder of how sweet and soft your lips are. What they feel like against mine."

"I prefer vengeance on twisted sickos, to be honest," I say, "but maybe tomorrow. Right now, I think you deserve to get something you want as much as I do."

Leaning in, I brush my lips to his, kissing him slowly, sensually, exploring and tasting his mouth. He slides his hand around my waist and pulls my body flush to his until our legs tangle and our pelvises meet, sending passion through my core. Our kiss sparks a dozen sensations across my body as if my soul remembers his closeness despite the absence of our past life in my mind. Before everything terrible that happened in this life, I would've slowed down, feeling his body awaken with desire. I would've eased away and smiled, saving the pent up desire for another time. My reserve would've forced me to make him wait for any sort of progression in a physical relationship.

But now?

I'm too damn old.

I don't need to live by these self-imposed standards all set on the notion of maybe waiting is what I'm supposed to do. Some would call me easy, slutty, or a frustrating woman who can only think with what's between my legs as if there is something wrong with enjoying all the fucking. Maybe that's why I'm going to Hell. What the fuck ever. At least I'm having fun. I'm fully prepared to have all the sinful dick for eternity. That's currently my idea of paradise.

And I'm ready to discover exactly what Elias and our bonded souls have in store.

Hooking my fingers to his shirt, I wait for him to ease up, so I can drag it over his head. I undress myself next, taking control of the moment. I'm not used to having this sort of power, taking whatever I want. Elias moans and caresses his fingers over my boob, playing with my nipple. I kiss him harder with the sensation and roll onto him, straddling his waist between my thighs. Rocking my hips, I grind on him, watching the lust sharpen his handsome features. Arching forward, I run my fingers over the edges of his chest tattoo. It's my first time seeing the skull with wings, and I can't help thinking how fitting it is. A barbell glints in the light, pierced through his nipple, and I graze my finger over it, wondering how sensitive it feels for him. His breathing quickens under my intensity, and I bite my lip and smile, bowing the rest of the way to his chest to lick my way down.

"Raven, I want you. I want you so fucking bad, but what if someone comes in? There isn't a lock on the door." Elias massages his fingers into my hair, gathering the wild strands in his hand. He holds it out of the way, his voice deep and breathy. "They'll do something crazy if we don't stop."

"They're busy. Even if they come looking, the worst that will happen is they might ask to join or watch." I shimmy my way lower, kissing his taut stomach.

Fuck, his body is hot. I don't know what I was expecting—because the previous men in my life never looked like this—but it wasn't this. He might carry himself like a dead man walking, but he's built with the body of a devil despite being slightly thinner.

"That's fucking weird," he murmurs, groaning under his breath.

I slow down as my mouth grazes the waist of his jeans. "Want me to stop?"

"And risk you turning to one of them to finish? Hell no. You're my soulmate. If you say we're good, I believe you." Elias leans up, curling his torso. He pulls me to his face and crashes his mouth to mine, sucking my bottom lip hard enough to bruise before pulling away. "But turn your ass around. You're going to fucking sit on my face. If they barge in, there is no way in Hell they're going to catch you on your knees."

I clench my body at the thought. Elias's unexpected dominant side turns me on, and I don't argue, giving him what he wants. He undresses me in a mad rush like our clothes are our enemies. One second I'm trying to unbutton his jeans, and in the next, he tugs me backwards to his face and tastes exactly what he does to me. And damn. I thought my devils acted starved for me—Elias licks and sucks my clit like he's famished and I'm the only one who can satisfy his cravings.

I moan as he pinches my hips, rocking my body forward and back, going wild with his tongue. His passion sets me off. I grab at his jeans and nearly rip the button off. Unzipping his pants, I slide my hand into his boxers and lace my fingers around his hard-on. He hums between my legs, sending a burst of vibrations over my skin. I clench him between my thighs and gasp, reaching my peak, my whole body exploding with my orgasm.

But he doesn't stop or give me a break. I can barely concentrate to lick my lips and suck his cock into my mouth. It's the only thing to slow him down before he leaves my clit tender and aching from all his eager attention. Bobbing my head, I deep throat him, inhaling as I take his length all the way into my mouth, feeling him in my throat. I cup my hand around his balls, stroking them with my thumb.

"God, you are perfect, Raven. It feels so fucking good," he murmurs, rubbing his palms on my ass cheeks, kissing my thigh with his lustful moan. His hand shifts and he slips his finger inside me, slowly finger-banging me, familiarizing himself even more with my body.

I pick up my pace, rolling my tongue as I suck him in and out, creating more pressure with my mouth. His muscles flex, the soft skin of his hairless balls tightening. Adding another finger to his pleasuring me, he strokes my G-spot, obviously aware of how to get me off every possible way. I tense, scratching my nails into his hips, now more determined to make him cum before I squirt on him. I know I will. I feel the sensation building in my nerves. I never knew it was possible until recently, and fuck. Here it comes.

I yank my head up, afraid I might hurt him or something as another orgasm rips through me, stealing my breath and voice.

I can't scream my ecstasy because it's so intense that even my soul feels it. Warm liquid splashes across my face, startling me, and I automatically lick my lips and taste the slight saltiness of Elias's cum dripping from my forehead.

He sucks in a breath. "Fuck, Raven. Shit. I tried to aim away."

I swipe my hand over my face and blink. He couldn't move if he wanted to because I'm pinning him down. The sheer craziness of it sends bubbling laughter rolling through my body and I release my thigh's death grip on his head and flop off. He spins me around and uses his sheet to clean my face the best he can, an amused smile lighting his face as I continue to laugh.

"You are something else, darlin'," Elias says, his voice rumbling with the lust still clinging to him. I love the way darling drawls with his words, his pet name for me sneaking out. He doesn't say it often because of his reservations with my devils, but I love when he does.

I giggle again, my face warm with slight embarrassment and my lingering desire. "So are you. You look ready to cuddle instead of suggesting I clean up."

"Because I am. I'm not wasting this time, worrying about shit I don't care about. I wanted to kiss you since you saved my ass from Vincent. I didn't care about the blood all over you then, and I sure as fuck don't care about this shit." He pulls me to him and kisses me, proving how serious he truly is.

"You're crazy," I say, crinkling my nose.

He eases away, his light gray eyes searching mine. "And self-ishly wanting you all to myself for as long as I can manage it. For as long as life is willing to let me before death wins."

I blink a few times at his words, a wave of emotions crashing through me. I never expected to feel so conflicted over something in my life. It pains me to think about how fragile our existences are and how easy they can be stolen.

"Hey, no. No, Raven. I'm sorry. I didn't mean—" Elias kisses me again, cutting off his own words. "I just meant I will enjoy every damn minute I have with you."

I inhale a shuddering breath, trying to control my voice. "This whole situation outside of what's around us now sucks. I didn't sign up for this. You were supposed to be an angel that I was going to corrupt and bring over to the fun side. You weren't supposed to be human. You weren't supposed to be sick and dying."

"And indebted to a demon," he whispers, engulfing me in a hug. "I really fucked up this life, haven't I? Fucked up the last one too."

"I just—I don't know how I'm going to do this." I groan and rest my head in the crook of his arm. Reaching over, I trace my finger over the pentagram—his demon mark—on his bicep. "It might kill me."

Elias shifts and peers at me, his brows furrowing together.

"I don't know your soul keepers well—at least not now—but I'm damn certain they won't let anything or anyone kill you, Raven."

I close my eyes. "They can't protect me from this mission. I know you know what must happen. Why haven't you asked about it? How can you look at me like you do, knowing that I have to be the death of you if I'm going to save myself?"

Elias sighs and sits up, pulling me with him. "Raven, you know I'm dying already. How it happens? I would honestly prefer to have my life end by your hands. At least I know you won't make me suffer like the rest of the damn universe. I can't hold it against you. You're my soulmate, and if this is the sacrifice I have to make to ensure you don't burn because of me, I will do it. It's the least I can do."

If only his words made me feel better. I don't think anything can. So I need to stop thinking about it. I need to shove the morbid thoughts away like I do with all the other fucked up things in my life. Dwelling on the things out of my control doesn't accomplish anything. It changes nothing.

But being here and giving a dying man reprieve from the weight of his impending death? I need the distraction as much as Elias.

I nod slowly and lean in, kissing him again. "Okay. If this is something you've accepted, then I'll accept it too. But don't think I'll let your soul abandon me in this life. When we get it back from the bastard demon, I'm keeping it for myself."

A smile plays on his lips. "Is that so?"

"Yeah. It's mine. Stealing it from you is the only way I can be certain it stays safe." I roll on top of him and squeeze him between my thighs. "I think it's why you gave me your essence to begin with."

He grabs my hips and pushes me lower. "You don't have to steal it. It's yours. I'm yours. Do with me as you please."

I laugh and blush, feeling his body awaken all over again. "Are you sure?"

"Mmmhmm."

A loud roar echoes through the room, shaking the windows. I'd recognize the guttural beastly noise of Lucian anywhere. My heartbeats pick up pace, pounding hard enough to make me clutch my chest. I hadn't expected Lucian to show himself, especially after he ignored Kase and Dante's summons before, and it freaks me out that he's suddenly here.

"What the fuck was that?" Elias asks, grabbing my clothes from the bed and handing them to me. He rolls off the bed and pulls his pants up, buttoning his jeans in place. He wobbles for a moment, steadying himself on the edge of the bed as he peers at the closed curtain of the window. "Do you think we need to go to the safe room?"

"No, it's Lucian. He can't escape the summoning circle." I follow Elias to the window, shrugging on his shirt. Pulling up the blinds a couple of inches, Elias stands close and we hunker down and peek outside. "I think the devils might have called him, and he finally decided to get off his ass to come here."

"Shit," Elias whispers, clutching my arm as he follows my line of sight to Lucian in his human form instead of the scary beast he usually comes to the Mortal Realm in. "That's Lucifer?"

"Lucian," I correct, my voice low. The last thing I need is for someone to hear me. I don't know exactly what Lucian is truly capable of. "He will gut you for calling him by the name he despises."

"I wonder what they're meeting about." Elias flicks the lock on the window and eases it open. The putrid smell of Hell trickles in through the crack, but we both pretend like we can't smell the rancidness of Lucian's arrival.

"Me too. Let's go find out." I lace my fingers through Elias's hand and try to tug him with me. "We can sneak around front. If they think I'll show up, they'll expect me to strut through the backdoor."

He plants his feet to the floor, resisting me. "I knew you were crazy, but going out there? That's fucking nuts, Raven. You don't know what's going on. They could be plotting something you aren't supposed to know and hurt you for finding out."

"Now, look who's crazy. They would never. At least, not

Kase, Dante, and Micah." I drop his hand and cross my arms, so he can't latch onto me. "If you're scared, you can stay here. I'll go alone. I don't trust Lucian not to do something despicable. I've seen him beat the shit out of my devils and I won't let him get away with it ever again."

"What the fuck?" he mutters, his eyes widening with my words. "You can't say shit like that and expect me to let you go alone out there."

"Sure I can. I'm capable of taking care of myself. Lucian doesn't scare me any longer. He just pisses me off." Without waiting for him to respond, I stride toward the door.

Elias rushes after me, his footsteps clomping loud enough to make me slow down. "Raven, wait. I know you can. I just...I don't want you to have to. I can help."

I press my lips together and close my eyes for a moment. I don't want anyone to know we're heading their way, but Elias seems determined to back me up. Spinning, I face Elias. "It's better if you don't, but I get it. Just stay behind me and keep quiet. I only want to eavesdrop if I can manage."

He frowns, scrunching his nose and rubbing his scruffy facial hair. "They're going to punish you if they find out."

I shrug and motion for him to follow me. "So what? You know I like that shit."

Groaning, he laces his fingers through mine, pulling me in close. "I'll remember that for when the fucker leaves.

This tough-babe attitude infuriates and turns me on. I never thought I'd be jealous as fuck of the devils. They're the last beings who need your protection."

"I think you've forgotten. I want to protect you the most." I smile teasingly and nudge him to start moving his ass, striding to the stairs and heading down.

We exit through the front door and stick to the shadows as we stroll to the backyard of the expansive property. Muffled voices sound through the air, and I duck behind one of the huge trees. Kase, Dante, and Micah stand outside of the fiery summoning circle with Lucian throwing his hands up in the middle, looking as if he pitches a tantrum once again for not getting his way.

"I should gut the lot of you for being bested by a fucking bottom feeder. If you want my help, one of you must take my place." Gathering hellfire in his palms, Lucian chucks it at the devils, but it only explodes against the shield. "Otherwise, no."

Kase scratches his hand on the back of his neck. "Raven will not—"

"Her opinion doesn't matter!" Lucian hollers, his skin rippling with his fury. The tips of his horns peek through the skin of his forehead. "She's made you lose sight of our mission. You've given her far too much power. I want her dead. We don't need her help any longer."

"Now look who has lost fucking sight. You have a contract

with her. If you break it, you know what will happen." Dante hisses and flashes his long fangs. "Raven must claim the throne of Purgatory. It can only be someone of light and dark. She's who we've chosen."

"I don't care," Lucian snaps, fisting his hands. "Go get the bitch now. You will give her to me to care for through the remainder of the mission."

Elias tenses beside me. "We have to go, Raven. Now."

Lucian sends another blast of hellfire at the summoning circle, causing the ground to shake. I stumble and crash into Elias. Dropping to his knees, Elias coughs and tries to scramble out of sight, but it's too late. The four devils stare at us.

Lucian morphs into his beastly form. Towering several feet above us, he snarls and points. "Bring them to me now!"

Elias yanks a dagger from a sheath attached to his belt and throws it at Lucian, hitting him with perfect accuracy in the chest. "Go back to Hell, Lucifer! Go, or I'll send you myself!"

Fire sets the world aglow.

Demonic Bonding

RAVEN

MICAH BLOWS ANOTHER breath of fire, creating a second flaming wall between Elias and Lucian. Whipping his tail, Kase lassos it around Elias's torso and drags him off his feet. Elias hits the grass and coughs, slumping on the ground. I rush forward, my heart thrashing in wild beats as panic over Elias's health consumes me. He'd never admit it, but he's not resilient. He's weak, in pain, and absolutely no match against the rulers of Hell.

"Be careful with him!" I shout, huffing a breath, dodging past Dante.

I drop to my knees besides Elias and pull him onto my lap,

combing his mess of hair from his forehead. He winces, his features twisted in pain. Seeing him hurt and in agony ignites annoyance through my very being. This is Lucian's fucking fault.

"Get away from the traitor and come to me, Raven." Lucian's command echoes through the air, sending heat over me despite him being trapped in the summoning circle several feet away. "I need a word with you."

I scowl and whip my head up, glowering at him. "Fuck off, Lucian. I'm not going anywhere near you. I know you want to go back on our contract. If you're not here to help us with a mission I thought you were hell-bent on completing, then leave us alone. We're trying to get shit in order."

Kase and Dante stiffen at my tone and immediately form a muscular barrier between me and Lucian, adding even another layer of protection even though Micah's fire barricade and the summoning circle still block Lucian's way.

"Angel-girl, now isn't the time to poke the beast," Kase mutters, keeping his voice low. "Your ass is in so much trouble for coming out here."

"Dressed in Elias's shirt and—that better not be what I think it is in your hair, pretty soul." Dante's eyes flash green and he strolls closer, leaning down to get in my space. He growls under his breath, the rumble reverberating through my being. "That fucker better have just had bad aim and didn't ask you—"

"Enough with your envy. It helps no one and fucking proves Lucian's point about Raven's role in your life if something like Elias ejaculating on her face sets you off," Micah says, punching Dante in his ribs. Fuck. If death didn't mean Hell servitude, I'd beg the universe to kill me now. Turning to me, Micah offers his hand. The sudden sensation of his presence prodding at my mind opens me up to him, and our thoughts intertwine. "Come on. Your attitude and disdain of Lucian doesn't help anyone either. He embodies envy as much as Dante. Give in a little to his power and he might not be such a monster toward you." His voice remains even in my head like he wants to be sure no one knows we're communicating telepathically.

I flare my nostrils and lock my gaze to Micah's. "You're joking, right?" I think to him.

His steely eyes flicker with firelight, and he silently responds, "Trust me, Raven. I've been around him in Hell for a while. He craves control, and it enrages him that he gets none. At least pretend. Please. Do it for all of us."

"Kase and Dante would never ask this of me," I mutter under my breath, unable to concentrate to think to him.

"Because they don't know what it's like to have been alone." Raising his hand toward the devils, he gets Kase and Dante to remain calm while he guides me closer to Lucian. "Now just follow my instructions and say what I tell you to."

My soul and mind already scream inside me, wanting nothing more than to shout my protest. But I suck up my innate desire to disobey and finally nod.

Micah presses his palm to the small of my back and guides me to the summoning circle, stopping just outside of it. "Raven," he says aloud, his stern voice lashing me like my name on his lips is my punishment alone. "You will obey Lucian as your soul keeper. If you do not speak to him and give him the moment he asked for, I will push you to him. Do you understand?"

He sounds so serious that I can't help but wonder if his reasoning in my mind was all just a figment of my imagination.

I swallow my nerves, trying not to pray, and say, "Yes, Micah. I'm sorry."

"Don't say it to me." Pinching my chin, he eases my head to turn to Lucian, half transformed into his devil form. "Lucian is who you must ask for forgiveness from."

Taking a deep breath, I steel the roiling emotions waging a war inside me and give Lucian my undivided attention. Goosebumps prickle over my skin under his scrutiny, and he cracks his neck, completing his transformation into all his demonic glory like he wants to make everything about this situation even more unpleasant than it truly is.

I force my mouth to work. "Lucian, I owe you an apology. My attitude and purposeful disobedience is uncalled for. I'm really sorry. I just—"

"You need to bow before me and prove to me that you're not saying all of this to appease me. If you are truly remorseful and want to fall in line, you must accept my punishment. Only then, will I reconsider ending our arrangement." Lucian straightens his shoulders, flicking his attention behind me. Without having to look, I know Kase and Dante—possibly even Elias—are ready to put up a fight on my behalf.

I blink a few times and shudder at the thought of whatever kind of punishment Lucian could have in mind. I've seen him beat and whip both Kase and Dante. If even they broke under his sadistic actions, what does that mean for me?

I wish I could get myself to look Lucian in the eye and accept my fate.

I wish I were strong and had enough faith to survive that I could bow like he demands.

But in this moment? I'm utterly and cowardly human.

My bottom lip trembles at the thought of the pain, and my heart crashes against my ribcage. And then, I start bawling my eyes out like a child who knows they've done something wrong but doesn't quite understand the consequences. I just know it's going to be horrible. I feel it on a soul-deep level.

Damn it.

Fuck. My. Life.

I need to be brave.

"I knew you were unworthy of the power my brethren want to bestow on you," Lucian mutters, sending the flames of the summoning circle reaching toward the sky. "Pathetic."

Anger rises inside me at his words. He purposefully makes me feel unworthy and incapable, and it reminds me of Joel and all of the times he belittled me and twisted things to make me feel like I was worthless.

But I'm not worthless. I'm stronger than I ever realized. I can face Lucian and handle whatever he tries to do to break my will.

I won't let him.

My will might be the only thing I have left that solely and irrevocably belongs to me.

Clenching my fingers into fists, I tighten my jaw and face Lucian, peering up at him since there is no way I could ever look at him straight on. "You can fuck off, Lucian. If it takes you punishing me—a supposedly worthless mortal—to feel powerful, then you're the damn pathetic one. So go ahead. Torture me. Beat me. Whip me. Show me what a big, scary monster you are, because in the end, that's all you'll ever be."

Lucian roars in anger, yanking out his whip made from the flames of Hell and lashes it at the barrier, sending fire crackling and popping through the night. "Micah, push her in now. She will bow!"

Kase and Dante growl in warning, and heat swells around

me. Before Micah's forced into proving his disloyalty to Lucian, I force my feet to work and step through the barrier, the heated air sending sweat prickling over my skin.

I heave a few breaths and turn my back on Lucian, meeting everyone's gazes. Micah remains expressionless, though his thoughts seep into my mind, begging me to brace myself for the fight. He plans to launch himself at Lucian, as does Kase and Dante. It's written all over their faces. And then there's Elias, clutching his chest, his face grimacing in horror.

"You will accept a lash for every day you have failed me," Lucian snaps, shoving his clawed hand into my back hard enough to force me to my knees. With a swipe of his nails, he rips open the back of my shirt, exposing my skin to him.

"You're a monster," I repeat, scratching my fingers into the concrete. "A coward. A dickhead who thinks he can push me around when I'm the one who will make Hell's Kingdom rise."

"If any of you try and intervene, you will face punishment far worse," Lucian says, ignoring me. "I will take her head."

I still at his threat.

My devils hesitate, their fury as palpable as the heat of the fire around me. It's in this moment that I realize they take Lucian's words utterly and completely seriously. They don't trust him not to act and do the one thing that will end my life and eternity.

"God, help me," I whisper under my breath. "Please."

The Higher Power doesn't answer my prayers.

But Andre does.

Bright ethereal light blasts through the sky above us, and Lucian jerks his attention toward the glow of Andre's wings. I knew he was around. He's been following me everywhere. Except the last thing I expected was for him to reveal himself.

"Raven, run!" Elias shouts, rushing toward the summoning circle.

Lucian roars and tries to whip me, slashing the ground inches away from my feet. Andre swoops closer with a ball of heavenly light glowing in his hands, his distraction enough to keep Lucian's attention split between us. I scramble away on my hands and knees. Locking his fingers under my arms, Elias drags me the rest of the way from the flames.

Kase, Dante, and Micah shock the hell out of me, transforming into their devil forms to counter-attack Andre even though he saved me from unbearable agony at Lucian's wrath. Dante launches into the air, chasing after Andre. Kase and Micah split up, abandoning me and Elias with Lucian trapped within the hellfire.

One look at the devil asshole sets me off.

I straighten my shoulders and glower into his fiery eyes. "If you ever put your supposed brethren in this position again—having to choose between two fucking horrid options—you will regret it, Lucian. You think you're as powerful as the Almighty, but you're weak. You're a bastard and I know that you rely on me to give you the power you crave."

"I don't. You are not irreplaceable, Raven," Lucian snaps.

"It doesn't fucking matter. I'm not going to stand for this damn bullshit and all your threats. Micah thinks you act this way because you're jealous of Kase and Dante and the bond we've grown, but I don't think it's that at all. I don't know what you think you're doing, but I swear to God that if you ever pull this again, I will give your brother Cassius what he wants. I'll let him take my life as a sacrifice to ensure you never, and I mean, never-fucking-ever get the power you need. I will make sure he knows every damn detail of your plan, so you stay trapped in your miserable eternity."

"You're lying," Lucian says, lowering his voice.

Cupping my mouth with my hands, I shout, "Cassius!"

Lucian snarls and stomps the ground hard enough to knock Elias and me off our feet. Without another word, Lucian ignites into flames, disappearing from the Mortal Realm along with the summoning circle. I kind of wish he'd have stuck around to beg me not to ruin his plan, but fuck it. The universe clearly doesn't want to give me that kind of satisfaction.

Arms encircle me, and Elias hugs me from behind, spinning me back toward the house. "You're fucking insane. I don't know whether to scream at you or cuddle the hell out of you. What you did—fuck. I was about to throw myself to Lucian."

I shiver, trying to push the thought from my mind. "Don't you ever do anything that stupid, understand? He would have killed you."

"No, he would've killed *you*," Elias says, spinning me in his arms. "He's far too proud to admit that he's wrong. I know it."

"Andre must've too." I tilt my head back and look at the night sky. "I never expected him to grant me a miracle."

"You can thank that sweet pussy of yours, angel-girl." Kase strolls from the side of the house, dusting off his arms. "He will do anything for you. The fucker is falling."

My chest tightens at his words. "You think so?" How the thought makes me feel? I have no idea.

"You'll be boning him by next week. He won't be able to resist you much longer." Kase closes the space and slides right between me and Elias, acting like a wall to keep the two of us apart. "And neither can I." He fingers a couple strands of my hair. "But the fucking mortal jizz has to go."

I can't stop laughing in exasperation. "Don't even start. If you bring it up ever again—"

"No more threats. I've had enough of them tonight." Kase scoops me into his arms and motions to Elias. "Let me take care of you instead. The jizz-master can join."

"We'll make it a party." Dante lands in front of us, folding his wings. "A celebration of our badass soul."

"Don't you think we should all sit down and talk?" Micah

comes from the other side of the house. "I don't know how much longer I can manage until we do. All of this unnecessary drama could've been prevented."

Kase and Dante glare, and Kase says, "Fucking fine. We'll talk. But let's get one thing straight. If you ever put Raven in danger like that again, I will hang you up by your tail and gut you."

"Kase," I say, trying to get him to focus.

"I mean it. This goes for all of you." Kase points toward the sky. "Do you hear me?" he shouts as if he speaks to the universe. "Don't fuck with our soul. She's ours."

Dante slides his arm over Kase's shoulder. "And it will always stay that way."

If only the universe didn't feel as if it will send me to Hell.

Or that Lucian will eventually win.

"Do you all agree to our house rules?" Dante says, leaning on his elbows with a contract in front of him.

I stare at Kase and Micah as they each nod their heads and sign their names where Dante points. It's the strangest thing to see, but as soon as I sat down to eat with Elias, the three devils joined us and insisted that the only way this was all going to work was to ensure a new agreement involving me was put into place.

"What about you, jizz-master?" Dante asks, using Kase's new nickname for Elias as if they've been calling him that for all of eternity. "Do you agree to the terms? One dedicated day to Raven, protecting her above all else even if she doesn't want it, and accepting all punishment on her behalf from now on?"

Elias drops his fork and opens and closes his mouth in surprise. "This bullshit is for me too?"

"Yeah, dickhole. You're on the verge of getting murdered by that sexy soul, and upon your descent and resurrection, we need shit in place—especially with your greedy ass. I can already tell you'll be worse than Micah, shouting that she's all yours because you're soulmates." Kase tosses the pen to Elias. "Sign it, or I'll guarantee you don't die with a bang. I thought she could fuck you while choking your ass to death."

Dante chuckles. "Damn. That's one helluva way to go."

It's my turn to drop my fork. "Seriously?"

"What about sitting on his face until he suffocates?" Kase smirks as his tail finds its way to my lap. "I can join you and fuck you with my tail. It's been a while."

Linking my fingers to his weird-ass appendage that I've grown to like, I stroke the smooth skin until he tugs it away from me. "And it still will be. We are not going to sit here and plan Elias's death. He might have a particular way he wants to go." This is fucking morbid. It goes against every last mortal fiber of my being to think about killing him, even if it serves a purpose—shit, even if he agrees. The fear of not knowing for certain what happens to him after makes me want to prolong his life as long as I can. There are three other angels who must fall anyway. Elias can live as long as his body allows.

"Which isn't much longer," Micah's voice murmurs in my mind.

Elias bumps me with his shoulder, drawing my attention back to him. "Come on, darlin'. Don't let it get to you. His ideas are exactly how I'd love to go."

I sigh and laugh, shaking my head. "You're a bunch of pervs. What else is in your damn contract anyway?"

I snatch the thin stack of papers away from Elias the second he scribbles his name. Kase lunges at me, trying to grab me. He locks his hand around my wrist, but I yank away and tumble backward out of the chair. Instead of falling on top of me, he stabilizes himself with his tail. The papers scatter across the floor and I rush to gather as many as I can. Dante and Micah stand from their seats, wicked smiles lighting their faces. They stalk me like the cocky-bastards they are, knowing that I can't get far.

"Dante, get some restraints. Our naughty soul needs to be tied up for trying to get involved in something that doesn't involve her," Kase says, sliding off the table.

"Doesn't involve me? I live here too. The house rules are my concern," I say, turning my back to flit my gaze over one of the middle pages. "Especially rule number twelve. I mean, what the actual fuck? You can't decide on shit like joining in to fuck me when it's my first time with Micah or Elias or anyone else for that matter."

Dante's eyes flash green. "You're not reading it correctly. It's only stating that they can't expect to have your sole attention when and if you choose to bang them."

I groan. "And what about this? My ass is exclusive to you and Kase?"

"You knew that," Kase says, wagging his eyebrows.

I throw the contract into the air. "This is ridiculous and will not hold up in the court of Raven, you assholes. I'm going to write the damn contract and you will sign it without complaint."

Silence responds to my demands as the four of them stare at me with a mixture of emotions. Elias stares at the wall, his lips smashed together like it's taking everything in him not to laugh at me trying to put the devils in their places. Rubbing his palms together, Dante looks like he's warming his hands to give me a spanking hard enough for the universe to hear. I can feel the heat of Kase's annoyance, so I don't meet his red-glowing gaze. Micah rests his arms on the table and winks at me.

"I'll accept whatever you have in mind, heathen. Write it up, and I'll sign it. You already know where I stand in regards to our eternity." He twirls his finger at my hand, drawing everyone's attention to the ring he gave me. Like he still controls the soul he placed inside, it lights up with an ethereal glow, sparkling like a beautiful rainbow prism.

"Don't think we didn't notice your attempt to steal all her attention from us," Dante says, glancing at Kase.

Kase subtly nods at him and they each summon glass boxes in their palms. Inwardly groaning, I slump into my chair, already sensing that Micah's gesture might have started some sort of competition between the devils.

"Which is why we have our own gifts to give you, Raven," Dante says, setting his box in front of me. "Open it."

"How original," Micah mutters under his breath. "A soul stored in jewelry. I wonder who came up with that first?"

Ah, hell.

"At least we didn't make Raven acquire it herself," Kase says, popping the lid open on his box, revealing what is definitely not a ring, bracelet, necklace, or even damn earrings.

"Uh, Kase?" I ask, tapping my glittering nail on the table. "How am I supposed to wear that? I'm not pierced anywhere besides my ears."

Kase's smile widens. "We had a deal that you would wear a ring from me, remember? You never stated what kind, so I took creative liberty. One of my contracts is coming to help get you ready. You're not pierced yet, but come tomorrow…your pussy is going to look even more—"

I whack him, cutting off his words. "Seriously?"

"Dead serious."

I groan and close my eyes. "This was all unnecessary. You don't need to give me anything, and you don't have to worry about each other. I like being around all your psycho asses. We're going to be ruling Hell together. I'm pretty damn sure I can handle all of you, okay? I'm not going to choose or be forced to deny the attention each one of you craves from me."

"So if we all asked to fuck you right now, you'd—"

"Be fucking stuffed," I say, laughing. "But don't you dare ask. That's one of my rules. Only I can." Picking up the pen, I turn one of the papers over and scrawl the words 'House Rules' across the top. "As for how everything else is going to work…" I add the number one beneath it and write the only thing I can think of in the moment. I hold it up for the four of them to see. "I'm making all the rules. The first one being that you need to get your shit together and go on a demon hunt since Lucian is acting like an ass."

"I don't like it when you tell me what to do, pretty soul," Dante teases, flicking his tongue. "Your naughty ass hasn't even opened my gift." He lifts the lid and shows me the cylindrical metal rod on a chain with a ruby on the top. "So we can have extra fun anywhere." He presses the ruby, sending the necklace vibrating.

I flush. "You're too much, Dante. And...thoughtful. So you better hurry and bring me a demon."

He narrows his eyes. "Then we expect you to have an angel tied up and begging to bone you when we return."

"I'll help her ensure it," Kase says, hugging me from behind. "Isn't that right, angel-girl?"

Warmth continues to blossom across my chest and through the rest of me. "You guys are crazy. You know I like chocolate, trash TV, and cuddling as gifts too."

"Wet dreams as well," Kase teases.

"Orgasms," Dante adds.

I groan and wave my hands. "That's enough. Let's just get shit done, so we can really celebrate or new arrangements. I expect you to protect Elias as if he were me."

Micah gets to his feet. "You have my word."

"And if he fails, I got you, pretty soul," Dante says, draping his arm over Micah's shoulders. "Who fucking knew I'd ever be okay with this bastard on our team."

Our team.

Fuck. The saviors have no idea what's coming.

Addicted

ANDRE

"WHY ARE YOU here, Andre? I thought you were going to stay away from her?" Zade strolls up beside me and stares at the side of my face.

I keep my eyes trained on the devils' mansion, far more gaudy and grand than anything I've ever seen them acquire over the years. "She prayed for help, and I couldn't deny her of my divine intervention. Lucifer, he—" I scrub my hands over my face, the image of Raven on the ground, her back exposed, and completely defenseless against Lucifer's wrath hurts me at my very core. Her soul keepers stood there and denied her mercy, proving how devastatingly helpless she is. Anger swells inside me the longer the image of Raven brands in my mind. "I couldn't let him hurt her."

Zade opens his wings, his feathers caressing against mine. "I understand. It's impossible to stand by and ignore such a brilliant soul. I would have done the same."

Finally breaking my gaze from the flickering light in the living area, I turn and meet Zade's turquoise eyes. Raven's mark mars his cheek, the glow of the brand looking as fresh as it had on the day she gave it to him. Like he senses me studying it, Zade massages his fingers to it and offers me a reassuring smile.

"She is unlike anyone I've ever met, Zade," I murmur, nervous to say the words out loud, but I can't lie to him. He's been by my side for as long as I can remember.

"Because she is. She carries the essence of grace inside her," he reminds me as if I don't know.

I shake my head. "It's not only that. I've been in her dreams. I've felt her soul. I wish I could show you what I see. She—"

"Was to be left alone." Cassius's deep voice cuts me off, his arrival going unnoticed by both Zade and me. He did it on purpose, sneaking up on us and not announcing his coming appearance. "What have I told you, Andre? We have greater priorities to focus on. As long as we stay away, the devils will not get what they want. It won't be much longer until things fall apart and they discover they were never a match against the Higher Power's grace."

"Lucifer was going to whip her with hellfire," I say, ignoring his comment. "She needed me. She prayed to me."

"To you?" Cassius asks incredulously.

I tighten my jaw. "Yes." The word comes easily, instinctively, despite me knowing that Raven prayed to God. But even so, it didn't feel like she was praying to the Higher Power. Her soul called to me. It felt as if her very essence wrapped around me, tugging me to her like a force I had no control over. "She prayed for help after standing up to Lucifer."

"No mortal would stand up to Lucifer," Cassius says like I'm capable of speaking anything but the truth to him. And who knows. Maybe I am. I haven't tried much or ever needed to.

"Raven did. She threatened him with our grace," I add, feeling a wave of something strange pulsing through me.

Seeing her confront the most feared devil did something to me on a level I never knew possible. Remembering the moment triggers the same sensation and need inside me, awakening my body with a desire to be near her.

"I'm not sure I follow." Cassius follows my line of sight and steps forward to the edge of the sidewalk. He stretches his glorious white wings out, blocking my view of Raven's glowing soul, calling to me.

"You know she doesn't truly want to help Hell and has chosen to do so out of self-preservation, but I think being around the devils has reminded her that there is a world outside of her soul. She threatened him with telling you everything." I bounce on my feet, growing more anxious by the second.

"Perhaps I was wrong about my concern of you being here. It sounds as if your presence might be influencing Raven." Cassius folds his wings, his comment bringing me far greater relief than I had expected such a thing would.

"I think you're right, Cass," Zade says, offering me a smile in encouragement.

"As long as you remain uninvolved," Cassius adds, turning to peer at me. He motions toward the mansion as Dante, Micah, and Elias emerge. His features harden at the sight of them, and he instinctively gathers heavenly power in his palm. "I will not lose you like I've lost them."

"I promise you won't," I say, reaching out to squeeze his shoulder. "I'll even prove it to you by following the devils. It's not often they leave Raven. Something must be going on."

"I think you're right, Andre," Zade says, speaking up.

Cassius clenches his hands into fists. "Zade, go with Andre. I need to leave the plane for guidance. If what you say about Raven standing up to Lucifer is true, then I need to find out more. I have an idea that could change things. Can you manage while I'm gone?"

"Yes," Zade says for the both of us.

I open my mouth, wanting to know what thoughts cross his mind, but Cassius launches into the air and disappears in a flash of light. Zade turns to me and squeezes my shoulder. A dozen thoughts flicker through his gray eyes. He shifts his jaw back and forth, silently waiting for me to give him directions. I know I should do as Cassius commanded. It's in our best interest to keep watch on the majority of the devils when we can. If only Raven came rushing out the door to join them. I can't get myself to leave her without finding out if she's really okay after her confrontation with Lucifer.

"Andre, if we don't leave now, we might lose sight of them," Zade says, expanding his wings.

I wet my lips and nod. "I'm sorry. I have a lot on my mind."

"Raven?" he prods, his brows lowering on his forehead. "Trust in Cassius to work things out for her. She might be hell-bound, but we all know that miracles can and do happen—ones even out of our control. Keep your faith, Andre."

"Would you mind if I caught up with you?" I break his gaze and turn back to the mansion. The lights turn off in the living area, turning the property completely dark apart from the glowing moon overhead. "I'd like to peek in one more time to assure myself she's okay and then I also need to return to the hunters I abandoned. Some could be of use to us—at least, the ones not already hell-bound."

Zade ruffles his feathers and rubs his palm over Raven's brand on his cheek. "We can call upon someone else for that. I'll go with you to look in on Raven, and I'm sure we'll still have time to catch up. The devils are on foot."

Until they reach the shopping center they abandoned their vehicle in. How I know? I watched them myself. I don't know why they do strange things like that, but I'm sure they have their reasons.

"I need to do this alone, Zade. She's been scared enough, and after what happened with Micah...please. I'm still earning her trust." I silently pray for Zade to agree. If he knew how desperately I wanted a moment alone with Raven and why, he'd try to intervene. He's not as worried as Cassius, but his reluctance shines clearly in his gaze.

"Andre..." He scrubs his face again. "Are you sure everything is okay? You can tell me anything on your mind."

Except this. I can't tell him this.

"I know, I can, and I will if something were wrong. I just—please let me go. I need to know the miracle the Higher Power granted me to give to her hasn't gone to waste. I know truly and deeply that it was my purpose tonight, and I must do this alone." Opening my arms, I engulf my dearest companion in a hug. "I will catch up, Zade. Be safe."

"The same goes to you. Call upon me for anything. I will listen." Zade gives me one last look and launches into the air, spreading his ethereal white wings, glittering with tips of gold, wide overhead.

I wait until he disappears from view, watching the dark

mansion as if it'll come alive with the flames of Hell, but it remains quiet. Gathering my nerve, I remain on foot and cross the street to the vast property. I hop over the wrought-iron fence, using my wings to give me height, and sneak around, narrowing my vision to gaze past the exterior in search of Raven's soul, the only thing I can see in my heavenly view. The bright light of her soul shifts and moves on the upper floor, drifting across the room. I blink my eyes, clearing the light and replacing it with the mansion's sturdy walls once more in search of the nearest window I can peer in.

The soft click of a door closing draws my attention away from the window directly above me, and I still at the sight of Raven wagging her finger at Kase. She flicks her fingers at him, motioning for him to go back inside. My heart picks up pace as he leaves her alone on the balcony, and a huge part of me knows that he does so on purpose. I haven't been exactly stealthy in watching over Raven, and despite my good senses not to mistake Kase's dark thought-out plans as small mercies to visit with Raven, I can't help myself. I will take advantage of it. I know as long as I remain clear-headed and aware of what the devils want from me and expect from Raven, I will never fall to their darkness.

There is nothing wrong with getting to know the most tragically beautiful soul like this. If there was, then it would feel as such. If anything, staying away will be the only cause of my downfall. She needs me. She needs my grace and my company to remind her that there is more to her life than completing the devils' deeds. There's me.

"Andre? If you're going to be a creep, at least come up here and be a creep I can see," Raven says, clutching the railing to peer over the side.

I smirk at her silly comment and bend my knees, flying the short distance to where she stares at the backyard below. My boots thump on the balcony, and I fold my wings, concealing them from sight. A wave of something strange washes over me at the sight of this breathtaking mortal in a silk robe over a nightie, the sheer fabric tight and revealing, showing off the curves of her body. I never noticed how perfect she was before this moment, and I can't stop my feet from shuffling me closer.

My heartbeat pounds, and I raise my hand, feeling the thuds in my chest. "I'm sorry for the intrusion but I couldn't get myself to leave until I knew for certain you were okay. What Lucifer almost did—" I snap my mouth closed and shake my head. I shouldn't remind her of the dreadful moment I'm sure will remain present as an invisible scar on her very soul. No one can face Lucifer's anger and not feel the aftermath, even if he never touched her.

Raven surprises me by sliding her fingers through mine and squeezing my hand. "I'm okay because of you. I don't know how I'll ever repay you for risking your life and wings to save my ass."

I pull her closer to me, wanting her to feel the thumping of my heart like I do. She catches herself against me, pressing her free hand to my chest, steadying herself. Her bottom lip quivers as whatever thoughts or comment she had planned to say disappears with one look into my eyes. Like her body and soul call to mine, I give in to my deep-seated need to close the space, and I kiss her softly, her lips against mine being the only thing to stop me from scooping her up and flying away. I can sense Kase lurking nearby, but he remains out of sight.

Easing away, Raven smiles, her whole face lighting up brighter than the silver moonlight. "What was that about? It should be me who kisses you," she says, sliding her hand up to my shoulder.

The thought of her lips on mine again awakens my body. "I'm unsure exactly. I can't seem to keep away from you. And after tonight? After you prayed? I'm not sure I will ever leave again. Who else will protect you?"

Her smile falters, and she flicks her gaze toward the balcony door. A rumbling growl trickles through the air, and usually, I would heed to Kase's warning, but a shift inside me weighs me down, keeping me in place.

"Careful, Andre. Lucian put us in a terrible position tonight. My devils wanted to help me, but it was impossible. It was either watch me be punished or watch me die." Her voice cracks with her words, the darkness of her thoughts stealing away her beautiful smile completely.

"I do not need a warning, little hellion. I need you to know that I'd never stand by and watch you suffer as they had. I do not fear the dark deeds of Lucifer. I fear that you can somehow accept that it is all your life could ever be." I unfurl my wings, my muscles rippling with the foreign emotions crashing over me. I dislike how they make me feel, so I do the only thing I know can shoo them away. I bow down and cup Raven's cheek. "I'm sorry for speaking my mind. Being near you does strange things to me. Will you kiss me? The closeness of your body seems to be the only thing that forces this disconcerting emotion away."

Raven doesn't hesitate and stretches on her tiptoes, brushing her lips to mine again. Parting her lips, she glides her tongue into my mouth, sending a new wave of feelings exploding through me. I devour her offering as if her affection is the only thing important in this moment and the only thing that'll keep me fighting for her for the rest of existence.

With her body so close and the sweetness of her soft tongue exploring mine, the chaotic world around us settles. My heart stops racing, and I can finally think clearly and without the dark rage threatening to consume me.

I release a deep breath and bow my head, resting it against hers. "I'm sorry. I should go. Your soul keeper will grow tired of this game he plays, and I don't want you getting hurt if you get trapped in the middle."

Grimacing, Raven pops out her bottom lip as if my words pain her as much as they pain me to say. "Kase would never put me in..." Her voice trails off with her words. She won't lie to me about something we both know might not be true, even if it might not be intentional. "Fuck me."

My eyes widen at her words, and I lean back and meet her gaze. "Raven, I don't think that is the best idea right now."

Her frown melts away and she gasps a laugh, covering her mouth to stifle the sound. "Andre, you sweet angel. I wasn't asking you to have sex."

I blink in confusion, warmth burning up my cheeks as if the gates of Hell open nearby. "I'm sorry. Your comment...I don't understand it. I thought..." The heat intensifies, and I step back and touch my cheeks, making sure I'm not on fire.

She releases another breathy laugh, the sensation of her whispery voice sending goosebumps prickling over my body. "Don't be embarrassed. It was cute. So...innocent and honest. And now I want to know if you won't fuck me now, when were you planning to?"

"I—I—" I ruffle and expand my wings, growing flustered as she continues to beam her radiant smile. "You're teasing me."

She laughs. "You've made it so easy. I couldn't resist."

"Like I can't resist being near you, especially seeing how

much happiness joking with me brings to you." I push away my embarrassment and return her smile, losing myself in her gravitational pull that reels me in to keep me close to her.

"I love it more than I thought I would. I look forward to corrupting you, Andre. It's already so much fun." She flicks my shoulder.

I grab her hand, pulling her flush against me. "You truly are my little hellion, aren't you?"

"You haven't seen anything yet." Once more, she stretches up and kisses me like it's now impossible for her to resist. Maybe it's the both of us unable to keep from each other.

I can't help myself, and I slide my hands around her, lifting her off the balcony and into my arms. She hugs her legs around me, kissing me deeper as she slowly rolls her body against my pelvis, creating explosive tingles over the hardness of my erection.

She feels so good in my arms, everything about this moment stilling the fear that had clung to me after my confrontation with Lucifer.

"Andre, no. No. You can't be doing this. You told me you were only going to check in on her." Zade's voice sounds from behind me. "Please, stop. We have to go."

Raven tenses in my arms and pulls away. "Oh, shit. Ka—"

I cover her mouth with my hand, silencing her call. "It's okay, Raven. Zade would never hurt you. He's my most trusted friend."

Raven locks her fingers around my wrist. "You probably say the same thing about Cassius."

I turn to Zade. "Please, just go."

"I'm not leaving without you," he argues, folding his arms across his chest.

Shimmying out of my hold, Raven drops to her feet. I prepare to cover her mouth again if she screams, the last thing I want is her calls to summon the rest of the devils back from wherever they might be.

"Please, Andre. Come with me. We can talk this through. I can help you," Zade says, offering me his hand.

"I don't need help." I nudge Raven to my side, pulling her to me protectively.

"You do. You can't see it because of the light of her soul, but she's not good for you." Zade straightens his shoulders. "You saw for yourself what she did to Micah."

Raven huffs and steps forward, poking Zade in his chest. "I did nothing to Micah, you asshole."

Zade's turquoise eyes narrow. "He fell because of you. I won't let Andre face the same fate. I won't."

I can't move fast enough. I can't even tell him to stop.

Hooking his arm around Raven's waist, Zade restrains her against his chest.

He takes flight.

Glass explodes from the door behind me, and the weight of Kase's heavy hellish form crashes into my back. I stumble forward and fall over the railing. He launches into the air, lunging at Zade and Raven.

I collide into the ground, the wind knocking from my lungs.

Staring up at the dark sky, I try to clear the haze from my vision. I watch in shock as a dozen of my feathers scatter on the wind.

20

Gates of Heaven

KASE

IF THAT FUCKING angel leaves even a scratch on Raven's skin—a tear in her robe even—I will pluck every damn feather from his wings, shove them down his throat until they explode out his ass, and then I'll start the process all the fuck over again. It was one thing allowing Raven to spend a few torturous minutes with Andre, who looks ready to cum at just the thought of getting his cock wet inside my angel-girl. It's a whole other thing that Zade had the audacity to intervene and be the Divine Cock-block.

I didn't think the bastard had it in him, especially after how Raven slapped him and left Lucian's mark on his skin, an eternal reminder that he's a shitty angel.

"Zade, let her go! The devil will hurt you with his wrath. Please! I can't stand the thought. Just let her go," Andre shouts as I fly over his head and sink my claws into the sturdy trunk of a tall tree before catapulting toward Zade again.

Raven screams and thrashes, trying to break free from Zade. If he launches any higher, the fall will kill her.

Roaring, I holler my anger into the night, hoping that all of Heaven can hear my fury. "Return her now or I will torture Andre until you do. I will push him toward the ledge of faith until he loses it and abandons you just as Micah had."

Zade whips around, freefalling with Raven a few feet. She screams and hugs him with her entire body, freaking out about the sudden drop. Blowing a breath of fire, I encircle the grass around Andre in red flames.

Jumping from the high branch of the tree, I prove to Zade that he shouldn't ignore my threat. I don't fucking care if Raven might have a growing thing for Andre. I don't care if this might piss her off. The only thing that might stop Zade from carrying my angel-girl off is doing something he won't be able to live with himself over if he knows he can prevent it by obeying me.

"Three seconds, Zade!" I shout, landing in the hellfire circle trapping Andre. He doesn't move or fight, keeping his gaze locked on Zade and Raven.

"Please, Zade. Don't test his wrath. You know there is another way," Andre says, straightening his shoulders.

"Time's up," I say, growling from deep in my chest. I whip my tail across Andre's chest, slashing open his shirt.

"Kase, stop. Don't do this," Raven says, her pleading voice echoing from above. "It's not Andre's fault."

"Release her!" I shout, ignoring her pleas. She can't help the feelings crashing through her, but I'll accept her rage over my actions to ensure she stays safe with us. "Now!"

Colliding into Andre, I knock him onto his back, impaling my claws into his wings and shoving them inches into the ground. Andre hollers as my touch burns over his feathers. A gust of cool wind blows over me. I ignore Raven's cries and bend down, staring at Andre in my devil form. The red power crackling over my skin reflects in his glassy eyes. He doesn't beg me to stop, taking every ounce of my wrath.

"Bring her back now!" I shout again, the guttural tone of my voice making Andre flinch. "This is your last chance, Zade. Raven is mine. If you take her, you will be the one who faces my fury next."

Because I can't lose her. I can't even imagine an eternity where she doesn't claim the throne in Purgatory to bring balance to Heaven and Hell and offer humanity a change. With her bringing Hell to its intended glory and purpose, we will have the power we need to be the Higher Power's equals. I will not let one blasted, righteous, idiotic angel get in our way. I will do whatever it takes, even if I have to rip Andre apart and make a point that I don't fucking care who takes my wrath. I will destroy the world for Raven. I didn't realize the truth of my thoughts until this very moment.

"She is mine!" I sink my teeth into Andre's shoulder, biting him hard enough to burn my lips and tongue because of the holiness of his being.

Thrashing in agony, Andre finally tries to fight back, unable to suffer through another round of the torture I have planned. Raven screams, her voice catching on the wind. A thud sounds from beside me, and Raven's familiar fingers grab onto my tail and yank. I whip around and snarl, snapping my jowls, but not at her. Zade stands behind her with glowing heavenly power swirling between his palms. Raven charges me and slaps her palms to the sides of my head, trying to break my focus. She looks me straight in the eyes, her body stiff, her muscles flexing as she braces for my reaction.

"I will do anything to ensure no one takes you from me," I say, heaving a few breaths as I transform back into my human façade.

"I brought her back, so let Andre go," Zade says, scowling at me.

"Let him go? He was not my prisoner. He could've fought me and chose not to." I growl, releasing a breath of smoke about Raven's head. "If anything, it's you who should let him go."

She sinks into my arms, snuggling close. I thought she might hold my actions against me, but her body and soul prove me wrong. If anything, she liked it. She enjoyed seeing exactly what I'll do on her behalf and what lengths I'll reach to keep her with me and safe, even at the expense of the damn angel she clearly lusts after.

"Andre," Zade says, ignoring my quip. "Come on. Let's get out of here. We can call Cassius."

Andre groans, rolling onto his side to push up onto his knees. Spots of glowing hellfire pepper over his wings where I stabbed him with my claws, but he doesn't try to touch them. He just gets to his feet and dusts his pants off.

Turning to Raven, Andre gives her his attention instead of showing an ounce of gratitude to Zade for bringing Raven back. Andre risks my wrath all over again to stand only a foot away from us. I growl in warning, ready to shove him away if he considers touching her, but he keeps his righteous hands to himself.

"Are you okay, Raven?" Andre asks, tightening his jaw. "Zade didn't hurt you, did he?"

"Andre!" Zade snaps, his voice lacing with shock and anger. "Of course I didn't hurt—"

Flaring his nostrils, Andre swivels and faces Zade. "Leave us.

I will catch up. I'm doing what I told you I was going to do, and you need to accept that. What you did, Zade...you could've hurt her."

Zade frowns, unfurling his wings. "But Andre—"

"Leave! I will call you when I'm through." Andre expands his burned wings, blocking Zade from us.

I narrow my eyes, wondering what his plan is now that he sends his brethren away. Zade launches into the air, the flapping of his wings sending more of Andre's feather's scattering across the lawn. Raven grimaces and catches one, quickly dropping it as it burns her with the lingering grace.

"Let me," I murmur, catching her by the wrist. I tug her hand to my mouth and kiss her palm. If the feathers were still swirling with the full power of his grace, she might've faced another angelic brand. Andre's lucky it didn't. I might not tear his wings apart for such a thing, but Dante would. I know he still thinks about how Micah branded her before his jump.

"Raven, I'm sorry," Andre whispers. "I didn't mean for any of this to happen."

I glower and tug a demon blade from my jacket. "It doesn't change that it did. I want you fucking out of here, Andre. I was being nice by not intervening while Raven had her fun, but that's over. You're done fucking with my girl since you proved how worthless you truly are."

"Kase, hold on a sec. Andre didn't know Zade would follow

him," Raven says, getting between us.

I growl at her. I can't help it. "He should've expected it like I had. Now get your sexy ass inside. No more angel games tonight."

"Is that an order?" she asks me, placing her hands on her hips. And damn. The naughty little soul. She's testing me. "Because if it is, you're going to have to make me. You know I have a job to do. Andre isn't a threat to me."

Her blue-green eyes sparkle as her pouty lips curl into a smile. Andre stands quietly a couple of feet away. The fucker is a goner. If he still had any damn angel sense left inside him, he'd have gone already. He'd have bailed with Zade. But he hasn't. And since he's here, I might as well give Raven a little taste of what she wants. What Andre might need to dive head first from grace and straight between her legs to taste what real paradise is like in that tight, sexy pussy and ass of hers just waiting to get fucked as much as she craves.

"Is that what you really think, angel-girl?" I ask, rubbing my hands together. "If that's the case, I want you to prove it."

Andre shifts on his feet, expanding and folding his wings a few times. One look at his crotch shows how much Raven already gets to him. It's almost pathetic how obvious his desire is. This will be easier than with Micah. Andre won't be able to resist. Hell, now I want to see if Raven can break his ass by morning. I'll help her.

"That won't be necessary," Andre says, clearing his throat. He steps back under the weight of both our stares. "I should go."

"You don't have to. You can't fly." Raven strides away from me and closes the distance to him. "Maybe I can help. I can drive you—"

"I'll walk." Andre shuffles back, his sudden nerves obvious.

"Let him go, Raven. You're going to scare him off. I think he realizes how much power you have on him. I mean, look at his raging boner," I say, pointing.

"Kase," Raven chides, swinging her hand to hit me, but she misses. "I'm not the one going to scare him."

Andre scrambles back, a strange expression crossing his face. I laugh and snake my tail around Raven, tugging her into me. I grab the front of her nightie and lock her in place, using my tail to sneak around to her ass. Andre's gaze burns over us, and I kiss Raven in front of him, sliding the back of her robe up to expose her ass. She gasps as I slip the tip of my tail between her legs, wetting it with her excitement.

Andre intakes a lusty breath and tries to rush away. A shock of Hell power crackles through the night, sending sparks through the air. Raven grabs my tail, stopping me from trying to slide it into her ass how I like right in front of Andre but only because the fucker releases a husky groan as he realizes his mistake.

Our property not only has defenses against demons and the Hell-bound mortals who work for them now. We also set up some angel traps and Andre walked right into one.

"Looks like you're not leaving after all, you righteous bastard," I say, leering at him with my wicked smile.

Raven furrows her brows. "Kase, what is this?"

I drape my arms over her shoulders and guide her along until we stand in front of Andre. "Consider it a present. This asshole was just going to abandon you after all that teasing but now he can't."

She sighs. "What did I tell you about gifts?"

I flick my gaze to Andre, watching his expression morph from nervous and into acceptance. Of what exactly? He'll be damn grateful to find out how much I want to push his grace and to discover if Raven's angel-kissed pussy can truly make angel's fall.

"Fine. Consider this his punishment then. The bastard nearly got you taken from me and must pay." I narrow my eyes at Andre. "The consequences are up to you, angel-girl. You will either let me punish him or accept him as your reward for being a good girl and learning to control him by his cock."

"Seriously, Kase?" she asks. "What do you expect for me to do? Bone him? I'm not going to do that out here or like this."

"What about suck his cock like I know you want to?" I ask, smirking.

"Kase," she says again, though her glare breaks from mine and her gaze wanders down Andre's body. She's considering it.

"It'll make us all happy, angel-girl. You'll get what you crave for me in return." I tease her with my tail, and she clenches her body.

She exhales a sexy breath and shivers. "You don't want me alone and all to yourself?"

Hell yeah, I do, but I also love how the thought of lacing her soft lips around an angelic cock has her soaking her panties. "I want what you desire. Why don't you ask the bastard if he wants you to make him cum?" I say, encouraging her to embrace the sexy, wild side I know vies to break free. I step forward and grin at Andre. "I mean, what kind of fucking question is this, huh, Andre? You've been thinking about Raven's pouty mouth sucking on your cock, haven't you? You won't deny her. Not with what you put her through tonight."

Raven slides between us, bumping her ass into my pelvis, pushing me back. "Don't let him get into your head. I don't want to push you." She's full of shit and we both know it. She's already crossed the line with him, kissing him and touching him in a way he can't get enough of. But that line must not only be crossed. It must be annihilated.

"Tell her what you really want, Andre. She doesn't think you desire her. She thinks she'll corrupt you, and it scares her. We both know that isn't true. So tell her. Show her how angels don't lie." I nudge her closer to him in anticipation. "Show her how hard she makes you. She loves to see."

Raven remains quiet, her curiosity far too controlling for her to continue to act as if Andre is some innocent being when we all know he's horny as fuck and needing to experience the kind of pleasure only my angel-girl can bring him.

"I bet he aches just waiting for you. He won't ask you. He wants to follow your lead," I add. "Come on, angel-girl. Give him the relief he needs. Start with another kiss. If he kisses you back, then you'll know. Right, Andre?"

Andre groans and slides his hands around Raven's back, pulling her body to his. I knew all it would take was a little push, giving him an opportunity to give in to his lust without outright asking for Raven to get him off. I grin and stroll closer, breaking the angel trap to admire how sexy Raven looks slipping her tongue into Andre's mouth, her nipples hard and pressing against the soft, sheer fabric of her lingerie.

"Fucking finally," I murmur, shifting Raven's hair off her shoulder. "Just imagine how soft and hot her mouth will be on your dick. Tell her you want her, Andre. Tell her and I'll let her have you how she craves."

"Do you want to taste me, Raven?" Andre asks quietly instead of saying exactly what's on his mind.

Raven bends her neck slightly, exposing her throat. I give in to her offering and kiss her skin. "I need to hear you say that you want this. It isn't about me. You already know my answer."

My perfect woman. I love how she says what's on my mind, not oblivious to the fact that he hasn't admitted what he wants yet.

Andre moans and adjusts his junk, his nuts probably throbbing in desperation. "I want you to do this. More than I realized, and so much so that I'm happy to give you what you want."

"Do what?" I ask, leaning closer, meeting Andre's gaze. The fire in my eyes reflects back to me, and he flares his nostrils. "Tell my sexy soul exactly what it is you want. She does not leave things to interpretation. Tell her you want her to suck your cock."

He exhales and shudders, his body trembling at the thought. "I want her to."

"That's not what she wants to hear, isn't that right, angel-girl?" I ask, sliding my tail around her leg, loving how instead of clenching and keeping me out, she shifts her stance and invites me in. "You want his mouth to sound as filthy as his thoughts are."

"Mmmhmm," she murmurs, trailing her hands down his chest, lowering her body to her knees, leaving her body open as I stroke her through her panties. "Tell me you want to fuck my face. You want to see how good my mouth feels."

Andre moans, his hands moving to Raven's hair as he gathers the dark strands in his fingers. "I want you to taste me. I want to feel what it's like to fuck your mouth and feel you on the level I already feel your soul."

She moans at his filthy desires and unzips his pants, pulling his dick out. "Tell me more."

Damn. I love how much she enjoys dirty talk. I suddenly can't wait to see if that fucking enormous angelic cock can even fit without dislocating her jaw.

"Do to me what you'd do to Kase. I want to know what it's like to be a devil. What it's like to have you always," Andre says, moaning and watching as Raven glides her tongue over the length of his shaft before sucking the tip of his cock into her mouth.

Satisfaction courses through me at his words. Usually I'd prefer to have someone watch Raven suck me off, but I get a fucking boner just seeing Raven on her knees and showing this bastard how incredible her mouth is. He won't even know what to do with her, which means that I can have my way, doing as I please and as she wants. Fuck, this is going to be fun.

I hum under my breath. "You want me to fuck you with my tail, angel-girl? Show this bastard how good your moans of pleasure feel vibrating on his cock?"

She responds by shifting on her knees, widening her hips. Snatching the back of her silky robe, I undress her for Andre, showing how sexy she is in her lingerie. I hook my fingers to the front of her nightie and pull it up until she raises her arms, letting me tug it off her. I want Andre to know what Heaven prevents him from having, and how Raven is worth his eternity. He groans, rocking his hips to her mouth like he needs to feel her throat with his tip. I smirk at him as he stares in anticipation, watching my tail slide over her thigh until I slip it into the waistband of her G-string.

Pleasure zings through me at the wet heat of Raven's pussy welcoming my tail with her slick desire. It takes everything in me not to drag her away from Andre and lift her up, so I can fuck her tight ass from behind as I stroke her G-spot with my tail. She clenches me with her body, moaning as I ensure my tail rubs her clit hard and fast as I sink inside her over and over.

"You're such a dirty girl, aren't you?" I ask, tipping my head, watching how sexy she looks taking in Andre's cock like the goddess she is. I rub my fingers just below her temples, massaging her in a way that will keep her going. "Do you think he'll taste like Heaven? I bet he's dripping for you, my insatiable tease. Do you want him to cum?"

She hums her agreement, and Andre tightens his fingers through her hair with one hand and grabs my fucking shoulder for support. He'll explode at any second. My fascination over seeing a savior come keeps my attention on Raven's sexy lips stretching over his wide girth that it doesn't bother me that he hangs on to me and tips his head back, his eyes rolling with the building of his release.

"Oh, God. God. Raven. Beautiful Raven," Andre murmurs, calling upon the fucking High Power like he is thanking it for Raven's glorious mouth. "I think I'm ascending. You're my paradise on Earth."

Raven bobs her head, her lips and chin glistening with her spit, making her look ravishing and sexy as sin in the pale moonlight.

"Brace yourself, angel-girl," I say, picking up the speed and pressure of my tail.

Andre tries to pull away, his eyes widening, but I dig my fingers into his shoulder at the same time Raven clutches onto his hips. He moans her name so fucking loud that his voice echoes through the night. She freezes, accepting his angelic load in her mouth and swallows as much as she can until she jerks away and plants her palms to the grass. She screams out in pleasure with her orgasm, squeezing her thighs shut so tightly that I can't even pull free until she finishes.

"Raven," Andre says, falling to his knees beside her, a strange look crossing his face. "Have I hurt you?"

I tip my head back and roar a laugh. I almost forgot that the bastard angel doesn't know what it's like to see a woman cum. Scooping Raven into my arms, I lift her up, not giving Andre a chance to do anything. I'm not allowing him to ask her anything more. Fuck, I'm taking her away to torment him. He's gotten enough.

"Raven's fucking great because of me. There was no way I was going to let her get you off without rewarding her myself. Now, get the fuck out of here. She's mine. I'll take damn good care of her while you're off begging for forgiveness." I turn my back on Andre, leaving him standing in confusion.

Raven strokes my cheek, her eyes rolling for a second as she blinks and finally focuses. "Fuck, Kase. I think I saw Heaven."

I flick my gaze to Andre, staring at us with his cock still out and already looking like he's ready for more.

"Tell me all about it. I'll let you know, angel-girl," I say, carrying her back inside. "And then I'll fuck the thoughts right out of you. I'll give you a glimpse of my favorite parts of Hell."

21

Devil's Bargain

RAVEN

I HAVEN'T BEEN able to sleep all night, my body continuing to buzz no matter what I try to do. I only pretended to fall asleep because my clit needs a break from all of Kase's attention. I hate to imagine how insatiable Andre will be when he falls. I might have to ask Dante for help with his toys. I'm sure there is a flesh-light out there to accommodate the biggest dick I've ever seen. My jaw is still tired from me stretching it.

I roll over and into Kase. His arms slide around me, and he pulls me on top of him, already excited, hard as stone and ready to go at it again. I groan, my body aching with the pressure of his shaft rubbing between my legs.

Bending down, I kiss him. "If you plan on fucking me every way you please again, I'm going to need extra lube. I think you've forgotten I'm a mere mortal."

He flips me onto my back and grins. "Let me get Dante while you stretch."

I laugh and grab his wrist, dragging him back to me. "No. Why don't you draw me a bath while I get Dante and something hot to drink?"

"But you sound so sexy all hoarse from screaming in pleasure," he teases.

I wag my finger at him and scoot toward the edge of the bed. Fuck me. My body wants nothing more than to slide to the floor where I'll remain for the rest of eternity. I don't know if Andre got to Kase or what, but we have never fucked so long—and uninterrupted as we had last night. And me? Fuck. Maybe it wasn't all him. I don't know what's up with angel cum but it was like the world was perfect and right. Heavenly. Actually, I'm pretty sure I glimpsed it. Or at least felt it. My mind is foggy the harder I try to remember.

"Looks like you need me to carry your tight ass around," Kase says, crawling from his spot to me.

I force myself to my feet, not wanting him to know how weak and achy every muscle in my body is. It's a good pain, and I get wet just thinking about everything we did to make me hurt this way.

I shiver and grab Kase's unruly hair, yanking his head back to look up at me. He play-growls and teases me with his tail, nearly making my legs give out on me. "Not happening. I'm good. Great. But draw my bath. You do it the best, and I want you and Dante to massage my entire body. I bet he will even suck your dick if I ask him while you do so. I'd love to watch."

Kase spins me around and slaps my ass. "You naughty girl. You better fucking hurry up. If you're not back by the time the tub fills, you're going to need the lube you bring for something a bit thicker than my tail."

I widen my eyes and shake my head with a laugh. "But it's my favorite."

He hugs me from behind, aligning his tip between my ass cheeks, gently poking me. "Just be grateful I don't have Andre's cock, angel-girl. You'd really be in trouble."

I gasp a laugh and stumble away. "That thing is huge, right?"

He chuckles. "Monstrous. I can't wait to see your face when you finally break the bastard and take him like the queen of cock you are."

"What a filthy honor." I laugh again and manage to dodge away from him and stumble my way to the door.

"Just wait. I can imagine it now. We will fill up every hole on your body. Your hands. Fuck, with enough stretching, we might really fill up that addictive twat of yours. Wouldn't you love that? Feeling how fucking hot you make us. Letting us have our way." Kase glides his tongue over his bottom lip. "A real bonding experience."

"You're a psycho if you think I'm going to just let you stuff me with cock. You all have holes too." I fake-glare and open the door. "And plus, I don't think Andre's going to want to participate in a devil orgy. Elias either, for that matter."

He strokes his hard-on like he can't help himself as the fantasy drifts through his mind. "You forgot Micah."

"No, I haven't. I'll have fucked him how he desires by then. Maybe tonight. I haven't decided." I stick out my tongue and close the door, cutting off his growl at my teasing.

The more I think about Kase's kinky-ass fantasy, the more I realize how he's gone from possessive to acceptance, knowing that I'm attracted and feel a connection with others outside of him and Dante. I don't know if it's because my soul knows what my future holds, but I realize now more than ever how much I want this twisted existence for eternity. I love having these protective, possessive, psychotic devils around, and I love how they're all mine and I'm theirs.

Strolling past Dante's room, I peek inside and see him on his side naked, watching porn, and...fuck. I'll come back. I know if I enter his room now, I'll end up restrained to his bed or in his swing and wearing the butt plug he's obsessed with that says 'spank me' on the base. I think I need coffee before I set forth on another ass-adventure, especially with Kase waiting.

If Dante hears me, he doesn't look, and I manage to ease the door closed. Stopping at Micah's room, I notice it empty—as well as Elias's—so I make my way downstairs. I find Elias in the kitchen, hovering over a cup of coffee. He glances up and smiles, grabbing the coffee pot to pour another cup without asking me.

"Have you seen Micah?" I ask, slumping forward to rest my elbows on the counter. "He wasn't in his room."

Elias tightens his jaw. "Uh...he went to Hell for a bit. When we came in last night—"

"You heard me and Kase, didn't you?" I ask, my cheeks flaming with heat.

"I think the entire galaxy did." He rubs his hand over his scruffy face, trying to stop himself from smiling. "How was Heaven anyway? Did Kase manage to get it out of you?"

Holy shit.

My face is never going to recover.

"Usually, people get Hell exorcised out of them," he adds.

I tip my head back and release a loud ass laugh. Swinging my hand, I smack him in the arm, turning his smirk into a full-blown grin. "Shut the fuck up."

"Not until you tell me. Come on, darlin'. I'm desperate to know." He turns me toward him and lifts me up, setting me onto the counter. "Don't deny a dying man his one wish."

"You're just as crazy as the rest of them, Elias," I say, resting my hands on his shoulders.

"I'm pretty sure you're into that kind of thing." Elias surprises me by sliding his hand into my hair and tightening his fingers enough to hold me in place. Bowing forward, he kisses me like he's been doing it forever, and I hook my legs around his waist and pull him closer until we're flush together.

I hum and suck his lip between my teeth, nipping him. "I enjoy other things too. You don't have to summon Hell or Heaven. Sometimes, I enjoy just being here on Earth. It's my piece of normalcy, you know. Which isn't a bad thing."

He offers me a whisper of a smile and loosens his fingers from my hair to run his hands down my back, bowing into me in a sweet embrace I never want to leave. "I'm glad to hear that. I was a bit afraid that I couldn't compete with—" He waves his hand around, motioning to our surroundings. "All of this."

"It's not a competition, Elias," I remind him, snuggling my face against his throat. "I need all of you, remember? I want you too."

"You already have me, Raven," he murmurs, stroking his hand up my spine. "My very being is yours, my gorgeous soulmate."

"I do, don't I?" Warmth rises from my middle, and I brush my lips to his again, savoring the sensual caress of his affection. I imagine what it would be like for him to carry me upstairs to shower me with his gentle attention, the perfect cure for the incredible aches caused by the dark wildness of my devilish passion.

"Mmmhmm."

A phone rings and buzzes, stealing our focus away from each other. Groaning, Elias scoops up a cell from the counter and glances at the screen. He shows me the name and number like I might know who the Hell it is, but I shrug.

"I can call him back," Elias says, setting the phone back on the countertop. "Preston probably wants to check in to see if I'm still kickin'."

It dawns on me who Preston is, and I snatch the phone and hold it out to him. "You can answer it. He's your best friend."

Releasing a sigh, he taps the screen and puts it on speaker. I'm surprised by his actions, because my ex would've never done this and would have walked into another room. Joel would've yelled and told me to mind my own business. I'm almost nervous to listen to this guy, the hunter Elias loved like family enough to trade his eternity for.

"Hey, man. What's up?" Elias asks like there isn't tension after what happened with the leader of the hunters.

"Is it okay that I'm calling?" Preston asks, his gruff voice rumbling through the speaker. "You alone?"

"Yes to both. I won't lie to you, Pres. I'm surprised. I wasn't sure you'd reach out to me after all the bullshit." Elias eyes me, running his fingers up and down my arm. Once again, he shocks me by lying to Preston about my presence.

"You're my brother. I know what kind of shit you got yourself into. I want to help you if I can...which is why I'm calling. We caught Valeka. He showed up at Jose's bar, looking for souls. Gil, Tek, and Viper snagged him." Silence hangs in the air.

Turning his gaze to mine, Elias captures my eyes, a mixture of disbelief and hope crossing his face. After another couple of heartbeats, he finally says, "No shit? You have him?"

"Your angel buddies gave us a few new toys to play with. Demon restraints blessed by Heaven's fiercest angel. We were supposed to call Cassius if we caught a monster, but I thought you'd want first dibs." Hearing Preston say Cassius's name feels as if a stone sinks in my stomach. Of course the angels had gotten involved. I bet Andre told them everything when we had left him to deal with the aftermath of the ghost possession.

But fuck. If Preston hadn't called us first...I hate to think what would've happened. If Cassius sent Vincent to Hell, I'm nearly certain there would be no saving Elias from demonic enslavement. Or me.

"I fucking love you, man. I'll come get him now. You have no idea what we've been dealing with trying to get the bastard. I think he has negotiated something with Lucifer himself to avoid our entrapment." Elias frowns with his words.

"What?" I whisper. No one told me this, but it makes sense

how one damn demon could keep a step ahead of our reach.

Elias presses his finger to my lips, forcing me to wait to speak. "You've just saved my soul, brother. You have no idea. I'll be there—"

"Nah, man. I'll bring him by. The guys don't want the Hell that follows your unlucky ass around," Preston says, cutting him off.

I glower at the phone. What an asshole.

"Okay. I'll text you the address. Thanks again." Elias's handsome face beams with his smile.

Preston clears his throat. "Anytime. You did save my life. Now I have to at least help save your soul."

The line drops as Preston disconnects. I watch in silence as Elias texts Preston our location and sets his phone on the counter next to me. I don't have a chance to react before he scoops me into his arms, kissing me with enough passion to awaken my body. And damn. I might be sore from Kase, but feeling his excitement and relief is worth walking funny for the rest of my life.

"This doesn't look like you getting a gallon of lube from Dante," Kase says, leaning against the entryway to the kitchen butt-ass naked. His cock jewelry glints in the morning light coming in through the curtain-less window, totally stealing my attention.

Elias nearly drops me to my feet, and I clutch onto him,

steadying myself. "Sorry. Don't get mad. It was my fault."

"Mad at her? Never. I already do blame you for the delay in our morning fuck-session. Maybe I should make you watch." Kase cocks his eyebrow and strolls the rest of the way to us, hugging me as he tugs me away. "But the clothes have to go. She likes her men a bit pervy."

Oh jeez. I hate that he might be right.

"As fucking intriguing as that sounds, hard pass. I heard you all night and it was freaky as hell. I don't want to know what kind of kinky shit you begged Raven to do that got you purring like a damn cat. I'm good." Elias flicks his gaze to mine. "Though I wouldn't mind finding out what had her—"

"Elias, don't encourage him. Have you already forgotten we have a visitor coming over?" I can't stop the smile from crossing my face. "We got news that the hunters caught Vincent Valeka. They're bringing him here."

Kase's face twists in anger, his skin rippling as his devil façade tries to break free. "How? There is no fucking way they could've. And bringing him here? Damn it. What were you thinking?"

I frown and ease between them as Kase flexes his biceps. He's about to unleash his wrath solely on Elias. "Uh, we were thinking this was kind of the miracle we needed. You haven't been able to trap the bastard."

Kase throws his hands out, flinging red power in opposite

directions. Still, he doesn't look at me. "You don't get a miracle, Elias. Did you honestly think that some damn hunters could do something we couldn't? Yeah-fucking-right."

This time, I reach up and grab his face between my hands, forcing him to stop glowering at Elias. "Kase, chill. It wasn't them alone. Cassius helped them. He—"

"Now I know for fuck's sake that this is bullshit." Kase whistles through his fingers, calling for Dante without yelling. "When did they say they were coming? I bet you a good ass fucking that this is a trap. Your damn demon probably offered them something they couldn't refuse."

I swivel and slap my hand over Elias's mouth. "Don't even humor him. He means what he says when it comes to betting, and I can tell you wouldn't be down for that."

"Be down for what?" Dante asks, strolling into the kitchen. And damn. He's naked too.

"Is this going to be a thing?" Elias waves his hand at Dante's junk, swinging with his movements. Even only partially hard, the damn rod of flesh manages to hypnotize me. "The whole rock out with your cock out bullshit."

"Our pretty soul loves it," Dante comments.

Kase slams his hands on the counter, startling me. "Enough! Where is Micah?"

"Hell," Dante and Elias answer in unison. "He'll be back on his night," Dante adds, shifting his gaze to mine.

I frown, puckering my bottom lip. He never mentioned he would return to his kingdom. I thought he would remain on this plane until all of his old brethren fell. And the more I think about it, the more hurt I feel simmering inside me. He left without even saying goodbye. Why?

"The fucking bastard. I knew we couldn't count on him. He still thinks he has a right to a sole claim on Raven." Kase combs his fingers through his hair. "What the fuck ever. I'll handle it alone. I want you to take Elias and Raven upstairs to her bedroom and stay there."

My bedroom? Oh. He means the safe room.

Elias's phone rings from its place on the counter, drawing all of our attention to it like it'll suddenly explode and start spewing holy water. Kase growls from deep in his throat and snatches it, slapping the phone to Elias's palm.

"Answer it," Kase says, his wrath forcing his blunt horns to break through his forehead. He turns to me. "Start heading upstairs. Dante will make sure Elias gets there."

I open my mouth to argue, but one look into Kase's smoldering gaze ties my tongue in invisible knots. Swallowing my nerves, I head upstairs and stop in Dante's room, grabbing some clothes. I toss them over the banister, knowing Dante will see them coming up. There is just something about thinking of my devils confronting hunters naked that gets to me. No one but us should ever get a look at their amazing bodies.

They're mine.

Whoa. Where did that jealousy come from? I need to get my shit together.

I stride toward the safe room, wishing Dante would hurry up. I wish I knew exactly what Kase is getting worked up about with the hunters. Even if they were lying, we shouldn't have anything to worry about. We're Hell's rulers, after all.

Swinging the door open, I startle and screech. A tall figure looms in the darkened room, the sunlight of day not penetrating through the heavy black-out curtains. Micah spins to face me, holding his hands up. I gasp, shuddering and shaking out my nerves.

"You scared me," I snap, strutting into the room. "I thought you went to Hell."

He tightens his jaw. "I couldn't stay away from you, but I couldn't stand listening to Kase have his way. So I came in here. It's the only spot I could get some peace without leaving the realm. This room has most of your possessions that you had before Lucian's deal, and...I don't know how to explain it. It reminds me of my purpose."

"Micah," I say, stepping closer. I don't know exactly what to say, but I know I need to say something. Splitting my time and energy between each of my devils is harder than I expected—at least with Micah. He doesn't share the same bond that Kase and Dante do. I know he feels it the same as I do. "You know I care for you, right? Even when I'm with Kase or Dante—with Elias or even one of the angels as I complete this mission—I don't forget about you. You are mine, and a part of me is yours."

A soft smile smooths out his hard features at my words. "I just—I'm impatient to be with you on a mortal level."

I slide into his arms and hug him. "Well, if you get your ass downstairs and help Kase handle the hunters Elias invited over, I think I'd be happy to reward you."

The front door bangs, and Kase's ferocious roar cuts through the mansion, vibrating the walls and windows. I tense, wondering what the fuck is going on. Grabbing a curved dagger from his jacket, Micah hands me the strange knife and gets in front of me. A loud explosion shakes through the room, and the door clatters on the wall. Rushing forward, Micah tries to close it, but gunfire makes him hesitate.

Shit.

"Raven!" Dante yells from somewhere I can't see. "Raven, get to Kase's room. I'll meet you on the balcony. We have to go."

"What's happening?" Micah shouts, stiffening and exposing a part of his monstrous true form.

Dante hisses. "The fucking hunters crashed a damn truck through the front. They have a death wish. Just get Raven out back. I'll meet you there with Elias."

Thank unholy Hell. I'm glad he has him.

Instead of running through the house and to Kase's room with the nearest balcony, Micah slams the door and heads to the window. With a swing of his now hooved hand, he shatters it, sending glass raining everywhere. He doesn't flinch as he sweeps it away with his arm.

"I'm going to jump first, so I can catch you," Micah says, kicking away the glass from the floor the best he can. "Will you be able to do that for me?"

I nod my head. "I'll do anything. You know I'm ready to go to Hell to rule with you. If that doesn't scare me, jumping from the second story won't."

Except figures move down below as hunters swarm the backyard. A huge winged shadow cuts across the back lawn, but it's no angel.

"Fuck. Why are they surrounding us?" I ask, pressing my lips together.

Micah leans out of the window, unfazed by the spray of bullets thunking into the exterior. "Good question." A crash sounds outside the bedroom door. "Looks like we get to find out. Just stay behind me."

"Micah, we should just wait it out." I grip the back of his shirt.

Pounding bangs on the door. "Raven! Raven, I know you're in there!"

Micah growls deep in his throat. "Doesn't sound like they'll be giving up. I think I know why they're here."

I groan. "For me, right?"

He transforms completely, getting onto all fours like the wild beast he is. His tusks scratch over the floor, leaving behind burning trails. I clutch the curved blade in my hand, preparing for an army of hunters to come shooting up the place. I expect to have to murder all of them by Micah's side.

"Raven! This is your last chance. Come out here alone and by your own freewill. If you don't, we'll make you." I recognize the voice. It's Preston.

Micah roars and smashes the door wide open with his big head. He freezes in his tracks and backs up, whipping his attention to me.

I don't have time to react, scream, or even brace myself as Micah charges toward me. With all of his strength, he smashes the wall around the window and catapults us into the air. The concrete cracks under his weight, and fire explodes in a circle around us.

"Fuck! What are you doing?" I shout, trying to orient myself to what's happening.

"I'm taking you to the one place I know you'll be safe," he says, his voice rumbling.

The putrid smell of rotting eggs permeates the air.

"Micah, please. Don't do this," I beg, clutching onto his

tusks.

"We can't stay here," he argues, stomping the ground again, sending more hellfire soaring toward the sky from the summoning circle. "Now, don't let go. I promise this is only temporary."

At least for now.

I squeeze my eyes shut and brace for the wave of evil to engulf me. For the tormented souls to scream my name.

Because shit.

I'm going to Hell.

22

The Hellhole

RAVEN

BRIGHT LIGHT SETS the world aglow, blinding me. Roaring, Micah's hold on me loosens, and I stumble, falling through the hellfire and out of his summoning circle. I land on my palms, scraping my hands on the rough concrete. Fear seizes my heart. The loud pops of gunfire kick my body into action, and I drop to my stomach and scramble around, searching for Micah.

Cassius towers in front of me, cutting me off from Micah. He raises his flaming sword but not at me. His wings shield my view of his confrontation with Micah as he snuffs out the summoning circle with his heavenly grace.

And then he swings his sword, sinking the blade into Micah's shoulder. It sparks against his devil form, Micah's tough skin protecting him from the sharp edge. If only it could protect him from the angel's grace. Smoke smolders from Micah's body, and he hollers, ramming his hoof into Cassius's gut.

I cover my head protectively as Cassius stumbles backward and trips over me. It's the chance I need to get my ass in gear, and I crawl toward Micah, my body refusing to brave the chance of getting shot in the cross fire as the hunters shoot at anything that even moves.

I don't make it far.

A cool hand locks around my ankle, dragging me out of Micah's reach. I scream and thrash my body, trying to break free of Cassius's hold. If he manages to take me, my life will be over. He won't hesitate this time to kill me in the name of the greater good. I know it.

"Zade, catch!" Cassius shouts, throwing me into the air and farther away from where Micah snarls. "The hunters deceived us."

What?

The world blurs as I freefall toward Zade. My stomach twists and makes it impossible to scream for help.

Two muscular arms catch me, cradling me like a hysterical child. I whack Zade on the side of his face, trying to get him to release me before he launches into the air. All he does is grip me tighter and fold his wings around us, protecting me with his body as another hunter attacks and opens fire.

"What the actual fuck!" I shriek, tensing as Zade shudders. "Are they shooting at you? You're an angel!"

"They've been recruited by Hell," Zade responds, his breath tickling my cheek. "Whatever they were offered must've been far more tempting than the chance of redemption. I'll never understand it. Why risk your eternity for—"

Zade jumps and huffs, expanding his wings long enough for me to see a familiar hunter jab a dagger into Zade's brilliant wing. Anger rushes through me at the sight of Preston. Is this real? Is this truly happening? I can't fucking believe the bastard has the nerve to fight Zade, damning himself to Hell after Elias gave up everything to save him.

I break, my panic over being hurt in the crossfire melting away. Searching around the vast property, I catch sight of Micah fighting with Cassius. Kase tears at a hunter's arm, ripping it off with his teeth, sending blood cascading across the grass. He snarls and whips his tail, throwing another hunter at the side of the mansion. A shadow crosses overhead, and I spot Dante jumping from the roof, where he abandons Elias to zoom toward me.

Zade notices too, surprising me by dropping me on my ass and unsheathing his flaming sword. With his free hand, he blasts Preston back with heavenly light, disarming him. Another wave of angelic power destroys the gun, ensuring Preston can't shoot me. I'm nearly fucking certain Zade only does it to stop Preston from killing me while he faces Dante, the obviously bigger threat.

"Run, Raven! Get as far as possible. I'll catch up," Dante shouts, extending his fangs and projecting venom across Zade's wing. "Go!"

His command pushes my impulse to collide into Preston away, and I scramble to my feet. Dante's wing grazes my ass as he pushes me in the direction he wants me to run, and I bolt away and toward the long stretch of lawn leading who knows where on the property.

"Fuck. Fuck. Fuck." I chant the words over and over again, resisting the urge to peek over my shoulder.

But even with my focus on the world in front of me, I still miss the strange shadow crossing the grass until I'm only feet away. The warm air freezes around me, causing my breath to fog. I gasp and jerk my attention toward the sky, but nothing is there. My skin crawls, my soul shouting that something is wrong. I jump over the growing shadow, treating it as if a monster will stretch its clawed fingers out to snatch me from this world if I don't.

I lose my footing and stumble, skidding across the grass. Goosebumps prickle over my skin, and I push up and get to my feet, spinning around.

That's when I see the shadow spread and grow with nothing in the area able to cause such a sight.

"Raven, raise your arms!" Dante shouts, his expansive wings drawing my attention from the slithering shadow.

I do as he says and raise my arms, strolling backward to keep space between my feet and the shadow. "Hurry! Something's wrong!"

Kase's roar echoes through the air and he shakes the ground as he lands thirty feet away. Micah builds a wall of hellfire, cutting the hunter's off. My devils all head in my direction at once.

And then Zade and Cassius land behind me.

"Raven, don't let it touch you," Cassius says, his voice erupting over my devils' shouts, demanding I run toward them.

"Come to us, Raven. Please. You'd have to cross through it to reach your devils, and all it would have to do is touch you to take a host," Zade adds.

I step back again, watching as the shadow continues to grow, creating a thick barrier too wide to cross. "I can't," I whisper. "You'll kill me."

"Raven!" Dante shouts, stretching his arms out to me.

"No!" Cassius launches from his spot, but Dante spits venom at him, burning his chest and face.

Locking his hands to my hair, Dante flaps his wings, propelling backward from the ground. My feet drag across the grass, an icy sensation engulfing my toes. I tremble as it slides up my calves, swallowing me inch by inch as Dante gathers me in his arms.

I open and close my mouth, struggling to form thoughts. "Dante...something's wrong."

Dante lifts me up in front of him, his eyes widening. "Fuck!"

He descends so fast that I can't do anything—not speak, scream, move, maybe even breathe. My heart pounds in my ears, the world exploding in utter and complete chaos as my very being screams.

Dante's quick movements aren't what incapacitate me.

It's something else. Something dark and deadly.

"Hello, sweet thing," a deep voice says, swirling through my mind. My eyes blink out of my control and I stare in frozen horror as I carve something with a discarded dagger into my arm. "If you try to shove me out, I'll stick a knife right through this fragile beating heart racing out of control for me."

Holy fuck.

The edges of my vision shadow. I'm being possessed. I can't believe it.

The strange shadow fills up my very being, restraining me with dozens of invisible knots and chains I can't fight. I can't do anything.

And then an unrecognizable language hums through the air and fire explodes at my feet.

"Do something!" Micah shouts.

"I can't. The fucker carved an anchoring mark on her arm," Kase snaps.

"Someone's summoning the bastard." Dante shakes my body, peering into my eyes. "Raven? Fight. I know you can hear me. You need to resist."

But I can't.

Flames swallow me whole.

I gasp as my world turns from a fiery abyss to shadows, only to be spit out in the middle of...Heaven? No, this can't be. If I die, Lucian would drag me to Hell. There will be no saving me from a tortured eternity for failing. This place, this breathtaking, colorful world belongs to Andre. It's his Heaven. I know it because I've seen it, a crazy-ass reaction to swallowing his angelic cum—or maybe just getting nearly drowned in his sweet, sugary ecstasy, tasting like my favorite coconut cream pie I used to order from Blue's Diner on Cherub Drive in Angel Canyon when I thought I had finally had my shit together before losing my job.

Damn. What I wouldn't give to have one last meal there before whatever fucking being stealing my willpower sends me flying straight down to bend over Lucian's knee and beg him to let me call him master and do what he wants. I'm not against groveling. Hell, at least Lucian is hot when he's not all asshole Satan.

"It pains me to hear you plan such an eternity, little hellion. I thought you had way more fight than that." A bright light engulfs the sunset-colored clouds stretching out before me and Andre materializes into view. "What do I have to do to remind you that just because a soul managed to bargain with a demon to drag him back from Hell to do his bidding doesn't mean it's over for you? Have faith in your devils. I know they'll come."

Rushing forward, I jump into Andre's arms, praying with everything in me that this moment is as real as when Micah took me to his home away from Heaven. Tingles explode through me at Andre's touch, warming my very being as his light dances with mine.

I groan and rest my head on his shoulder. "Fuck. You're not here. This is a dream."

"You're not sleeping, but you're in a state of unconsciousness. And I am here for you. Just not physically. The hunters have warded the place against angels and demons." Andre strokes his cool hand along the length of my back. "This is all that I can do until either your devils or Cassius figure it out. Either way, no matter who gets to you first, you'll be okay. I will protect you."

"Wait, Cassius is trying to find me?" I search his gold-rimmed, brown eyes for answers he's not rushing to give. "Is that why he sent the hunters? He wanted to use them to get to me? Is that why you weren't there?"

Andre's grimace hardens his face, stealing the light shining in his eyes. "It is my fault, Raven. I—I have found it impossible to stay away from you, and Cassius grew concerned. I made a mistake by sharing with him how you confronted Lucian. He thinks you might be persuaded to help the Higher Power and sacrifice your soul to do so."

"What the actual fuck, Andre!" I exclaim, my whole soul releasing my fear only to fill up with anger. "I was only threatening Lucian to try to save my ass from getting whipped into oblivion. I'm not sacrificing my damn soul for the ones who already declared me a lost cause and unredeemable."

Andre bows into me, hugging me closer instead of releasing me and growing defensive like I expect. But he's not the type of man I'm used to—the mortals like my ex who would never hold himself accountable, always twisting the blame onto me.

"Please forgive me. I've wronged you, and I'm sorry. I let my feelings for you consume me and put you in this danger." Andre breathes into the crook of my neck, cuddling me close.

I can't help giving into his affection and brush my lips to his temple. "Andre, I forgive you. I don't blame you either. I haven't exactly been subtle at my attempts to corrupt you.

Your lust for me—"

"Lust? No. It's far more powerful than that. I don't only yearn to feel you on the same intimate level as your soul keepers do. I crave to be with you in every which way for all of eternity. I can't deny it any longer. You're the most magnificent mortal and soul I've ever laid eyes on. I think I'm in love with you. Cassius and Zade agree with me. You've changed me, and there is nothing anyone can do to keep me away from you. Even trying to force me to leave the Mortal Realm." Andre tilts his head, aligning his mouth with mine, his words awakening my essence on a soul-deep level. "Cassius thought I crossed between planes, but you've anchored me here, little hellion. You've captured me with your whole being, and I swear to the Higher Power that I'll never let you go. We belong together."

A wave of Andre's emotions crashes over me, igniting my body like fireworks crackle in every molecule of my being. His pouty mouth invites me closer, I mold my lips to his, kissing him with every fiber of my being until it feels as if our essences merge into one.

I comb my fingers through his hair, sliding my tongue into his mouth kissing him deeper, more desperately and with the same sizzling passion from his strangely exciting, yet fucking possessive as hell, declaration.

"I'm nearly certain it's me who won't let you go, Andre," I murmur against his mouth, running my fingers down to his neck and over his taut shoulders. "I am your hellion after all."

"And so perfect. Wickedly divine. The woman I will gladly get on my knees and pray to before I worship every inch of your body and make it mine. You're all I need to survive this existence, Raven. You bring me light and life and everything I never knew I wanted until this moment. You. You and your intoxicating body and soul." Andre shifts me in his arms, sliding his hand lower until he reaches my bare ass cheeks, peeking out from my nightie and robe, the same one I was wearing last night as I kneeled at his feet.

"Release her body. I have your vessel as we agreed upon." The deep, sultry voice booms through the world, fissuring the pure goodness Andre brings to my state of unconsciousness. "I need her in control to summon Lucian."

I yank away from Andre and search around for something, anything, to prolong this moment in the safety of my mind. "Fuck, Andre. I think the ghost fucker is releasing me. I'm going to wake up."

"I'm coming for you. Just try to hold onto my presence the best you can until I break through the protection shields, okay? I'm not far," Andre says, flickering in and out of existence.

I don't get a chance to respond as my body explodes in pain, jolting me into consciousness. A scream rips from my mouth, my body, mind, and soul crashing back together as if the fucking ghost who possessed me had to tear me open to escape. My stomach twists in agony, and I dry heave. I hurt everywhere, from my fingers to my toes, and even my fucking hair cries in misery.

"What a delicious morsel you are, Whore of Hell's Kingdom. Let me get a better look at you." A thin, willowy man towers over me within a strange blood painted circle. His deep-set eyes bulge from their sockets, the dark color indistinguishable between brown and black.

"Fuck off," I snap, planting my palms to the sticky floor, trying to push to my feet.

Bony fingers pinch my chin, tipping my head back. I recognize Vincent Valeka and his creepy demeanor. He stretches his gangly arm out and uses his free hand to rub the pads of his fingers over my mouth before he shoves them in, sliding his thumb over my tongue. I gag at the salty taste and snap down, biting him as hard as I can. He doesn't jerk away like I expect and instead locks his fingers to my teeth.

Pressure builds in my jaw as he stretches my mouth wider, pinching my front teeth hard enough to freak me the fuck out. A wicked smile stretches across his face, splitting the corners of his lips, sending blood trickling down his chin.

"I'm not very fond of your teeth. If you keep trying to bite me, I'll remove every single one of them to ensure you can't use them when I shove my cock down your throat and see what the fuss is about. I don't know why your keepers haven't done so yet, considering how pleasing your bloody gums will feel." The demon flicks his blood-red tongue over his bottom lip.

My heart stalls, and I close my eyes and try to keep my shit together when all I want to do is scream my head off at the torture this monstrous fucker plans to inflict.

"Maybe it'll get Lucian to finally pay me a visit," the demon adds. "Do you know I've been trying to reach him for months?"

"Raven, stay calm. I won't let him hurt you." Andre's soft voice trickles through my mind. "But I need you to let go. Let go and invite me in. We're already connected on a soul-deep level that I can put you into a trance and take control."

"Do whatever you have to," I say, cringing at the sound of my voice echoing through the room.

The demon adds more pressure to my teeth, and I scream, trying to yank back.

"Let's find out what it takes to summon the dark lord himself." Vincent's skin bubbles and moves as if bugs crawl through his veins. "Maybe having you ready for him will allow me to reap the benefits."

"No! No!" I scream, kicking his shins and scratching my nails into his wrist. "Andre, help! Please! Please!"

Fire erupts across the demon's fingers, and he sheds his human façade, revealing the horrifying skeleton-like creature beneath, covered in muscle and blood. He whacks his bony fingers against the front of his vest, trying to rip the burned tissue away.

My ears pop, the weight of the world no longer suffocating me, Light radiates from my core and pours through the rest of me. Electricity dances through my hair. Andre's intoxicating presence captures my wild soul and cages it within undeniable love and devotion. Obsession. Different emotions that steady my soul, bringing me comfort instead of fear.

My vision shakes as my body moves without my permission and Andre takes complete control. Vincent screeches, his ear-piercing calls stinging my ears. My palms glow, bursting with light, and heavenly power blasts toward the demon, making him duck.

"You will destroy your contract to Elias or I'll make you regret ever clawing your way out of the bowels of Hell." The words come from me, but I know I didn't say them. It was Andre.

The blood on the floor ignites on fire, setting the summoning circle glowing with hellfire. Lucian's deep, guttural growl rings through the air. It didn't take torturing me to get the asshole devil off his ass. All it took was an angel getting ahold of me.

Fury crashes through me, ripping control away from Andre and returning it to me.

Lucian doesn't turn to look at me fast enough.

Launching from the floor, I land on his back and clutch his big horns with my hands. "Lucian, this has to fucking stop. I'm starting to think you don't want the seven sinners to take their thrones."

He locks his hands around my arms and flips me over, slamming me on my back. "Of-fucking-course I don't want the assholes to rise. I don't want balance. I want the saviors gone and Heaven to crumble. All the other devils will fail. Their kingdoms are mine."

23

The King Sinner

RAVEN

"**R**AVEN." ANDRE'S SOFT voice trickles through my mind.

It's like how Micah speaks telepathically to me, but yet, it's somehow different. I feel the shadow of his presence lingering inside me. I don't know if it's because the pain of Lucian's weight crushes my chest, pinning me beneath him as he speaks to Vincent or if it's because we're truly bonded. I guess it doesn't matter. The small blip of light brings me relief.

"Raven, will you allow me control? Give me permission to possess your body. I can fight with you," Andre pleads.

I blink, trying to clear the haze from my vision. Lucian presses his hooved foot into my ribcage hard enough to hurt but not with enough pressure to kill me. I don't think he can. I'm sure in this moment if it were possible, I'd already be dead.

"What is it you want for her body? You've summoned me here, so I assume you expect the reward for bringing me her soul, yet you delivered her with her tie to the Mortal Realm," Lucian asks, peering down at me. Fire lights his eyes. "So what is it you want for her body?"

"Nothing. I'm keeping her alive for my enjoyment. Your brethren haven't been able to pinpoint me, and I thought it would be entertaining to leave behind clues for them until no piece of her remains." Vincent paces back and forth outside the circle. "I gave up Elias's soul for this. I'm going to reap the benefits as long as possible. Now release her."

A throaty growl escapes Lucian's mouth, his devil form shifting into a man until his bare foot holds me down. He stands naked over me, his cock swinging with his movements, reminding me of the first day we met where he sunk his darkness into my soul and touched me on an intimate level I try not to think about—not because it was bad, but because I still can't forget it. He shouldn't have this sort of power over my headspace. It's like being at the mercy of Joel all over again. Micah claimed that Lucian might be a douche because of the circumstances, but hearing him declare wanting to abandon the plan he, Kase, and Dante formed together proves otherwise.

"What is it you want in exchange for her body?" Lucian repeats, ignoring the demon's comment. "You won't be able to enjoy your throne for long if you think I'm going to allow you to keep her. You have far too much confidence in yourself. My brethren are already on their way."

"As I said. Nothing. I'll take my chances." Unsheathing a long spear from his hidden hellish façade, Vincent jabs me in the calf and drags me from beneath Lucian.

Agony burns through my leg, and I scream in pain. I jerk upright, locking my hands around the pole, but I can't yank it free. Snarling, Lucian sets the room aglow with the flames of Hell. All Vincent does is smile, watching as the barrier of the summoning circle traps the devil and all of his power.

Standing over me, Vincent twists the spear harder, listening as I scream and wail. I blackout and find myself in a world of pure white. Cool relief soothes my soul the longer I remain lost in this world of light. A shadow emerges out of nowhere in front of me. I reach out, sensing Andre, and caress my being to his.

"Please, Raven. I can't stand it. Give me control. I want—no, I need—to protect you from this hellish evil," Andre says, materializing more clearly in my vision with his words.

"I don't know how to let you." I'm also afraid. Not of Andre but of the pain. Will I still feel things with him possessing me?

What will happen if Lucian and Vincent figure it out?

"Just say yes. Give me your consent to possess you and use you as a vessel. I vow to protect you, no matter the cost. Please, Raven." Andre's glorious light radiates across my skin, igniting me aglow with a pure goodness that eases the fear traveling across my soul.

"Okay. Yes." The words come out before I even think about them. What he means by cost? I have no idea. I don't even care. All I know is that if I don't get the strength that Andre can bring me, my living life will turn to Hell. I know it. I feel it in the agony stirring through my body as I break through and regain consciousness.

But the pain doesn't last long.

Utter and complete peace soaks deep into my bones as a pure, familiar presence fills me up and bathes me in faith, love, and protectiveness. Where pain once burned, now only remains the soothing sensation that banishes my misery. Light glows from my skin and fades with my control.

I watch in fascination as my fingers curl and uncurl without my command and then proceed to grab my boobs and strum my thumbs across my nipples.

"This is so strange and exhilarating," Andre thinks, his thoughts echoing around me as if they're my own.

A growl vibrates through the air. "What the—"

Summoning heavenly light, Andre gathers a radiant orb between my palms, smoldering my skin over Lucian's mark. I can't feel the pain, but I know Andre does, because he's quick to chuck it at Vincent, sending the demon crashing across the room. Throwing another blast of heavenly light, Andre sends it flying at Lucian, but misses him by inches. Streaks of electricity crackle in the air as the heavenly power ricochets back to us, knocking my body off its feet.

The world spins, and my soul tries to evacuate my body. Lucian bares his teeth with hellfire shining brightly in his eyes. Locking his claws to the front of my nightie, he hoists my body higher into the air. Smoke wafts from his devilish features.

"Release her!" My own voice echoes through the room as Andre commands Lucian as he uses my body to protect me. "Raven will never be yours."

Two horns cut through Lucian's skin with his hellish transformation. Not a single inch of him holds onto his mortal façade, and he glowers, capturing my soul with his burning gaze. "Get out of Raven, or I will cut you out myself."

Igniting heavenly light in my palm, Andre uses my vessel as if it is his true body, and slaps Lucian across his face. A smoldering handprint glows red, and Andre kicks, trying to break free of Lucian's hold over my body. But he can't. I don't know if he's afraid of hurting me or if he can't manage to embrace his power. Whatever it is, Andre's fight falters, and Lucian smacks my face so hard that Andre's presence shoots right out of me.

I scream in dizzying agony, my chest tight and refusing to suck in enough air. It's like my body betrays me, trying to kill me instead of giving me any sort of strength to challenge this infuriating devil.

Swinging me toward the wall, Lucian tosses me through the fiery barrier and toward the wall. The world darkens once more, the sweet nothingness a relief that doesn't last long. I flutter my eyes and open my mouth to scream again, but a hot hand silences me as Vincent pins me to the floor and climbs on top of me.

"Keep screaming, and I'll rip out your vocal cords. The only thing you can say is my name as I find out what the devils enjoy so much about you," Vincent says, leaning into me.

I couldn't scream if I wanted to. The weight of him on my chest suffocates me.

"Kill her and I will give you control of the Mortal Realm," Lucian says, his voice bellowing through the air. "Kill her and send her soul to me, and you'll be a king."

Vincent nods his head and grins, his demeanor suddenly changing with Lucian's deal. "Done."

Fiery pain explodes in my heart as he impales me with his spear over and over again.

I lose consciousness, the world melting away once more.

Instead of Andre's light, cacophonous yells of agony and

regret explode in my ears, and I gasp and stare at the fiery pool of souls in front of me. Claws dig into my shoulder, whipping me around, and I face Lucian in all his hellish glory.

Oh-fucking-no.

I died.

My body couldn't handle the trauma. The possession. It couldn't handle the thought of getting raped and tortured by a demon who would've kept me alive to keep me from Lucian's hands just to show him that he's not the all-powerful being he thinks he is.

"Despicable." Lucian leers, capturing me in his fiery gaze. "I knew Kase and Dante were lying, trying to tell me that you were a worthy soul. I knew otherwise. You are nothing but a desperate, shameful whore who will spend eternity on her knees unless you would prefer to burn."

Fuck my life. Sucking off Satan or burning? My knees will never recover.

"You're full of shit, Lucian. If you thought that then you'd have never wasted your time with me." I clench my teeth, summoning my anger at the situation. I still can't believe it. No, I won't believe it. "I was doing fine before this mess. You'll be the reason your damn mission fails."

Lucian sets me on my feet only to tower over me. "I won't fail. Now that I have your soul in my possession, I can use you to get my brethren in line. I don't need all seven sinners. All I needed was for them to lose their sight on the universe and fall to mortal desire. They will bow to me. They will do anything for a moment with you. You'll see."

Anger bursts through me, and I swing my leg up and kick his monstrous devil dick as hard as I can. Apparently he enjoys the pain, because all he does is laugh and grab my wrist, forcing me to touch the appendage that looks like a mortal man's cock but is bigger, thicker, and the same shade of velvety dark skin as the rest of him. Thick dick veins glow with molten color, joining the rest on his beastly body as they gather and radiate power in his chest, sending his evil heart aglow.

His cock flexes in my fingers, hardening even more, and I gawk at how my nail polish sparkles in the fiery light around us.

"Feels good, doesn't it?" Lucian asks me, his deep voice turning husky. "You want it. You'll beg for me over everyone else. I own you, Raven. You might fight it now, but I will break you in a way you'll enjoy. You'll beg me to feed your soul with my darkness."

My mind jumps from thought to thought, my insides a jumbled mess. How the fuck do I respond to his words? Micah once told me that he's such an asshole because he wanted me in the same way as Kase and Dante. Maybe he was right. Maybe that's the only way I'll manage to save my soul from suffering. I guess I'll find out.

Without responding, I gather my resolve and shove my fear away. Lucian was once an angel. He might now be a devil, but I'm sure there must be a way to get to him. I might not have to make him fall from grace, but maybe, and this is a longshot, maybe I can make him fall for me. Crave me. I know there is something about the lightness of my soul that attracts darkness. The fucked up part of me will do anything to save myself. If it means sucking Lucian's cock and calling him master until the rest of my devils destroy him...fuck. Here I go.

I tighten my fingers, unable to close my hand completely, and stroke the length of Lucian's cock from the base and to the tip. His fingers loosen on my wrist, and he remains silent as I rub my palm over the head, exploring the smooth skin.

"I knew you wouldn't fight. You're as weak as I suspected," he mutters, shifting from his devil form and into the achingly beautiful angelic façade he carried before he abandoned his grace. "Unfit for ruling Purgatory."

Still, I don't respond.

"Tell me what it is you're good for, Raven," he continues. He trails his fingers up my arm and pushes my hair over my shoulder. "Right now, I think it's nothing...unless you want to prove to me otherwise."

My soul buzzes with his words. I never expected to be standing in Hell in front of Lucian with him trying to get under my skin. He thinks I'm going to break. He thinks he can push me until I lash out, so he can punish me. But he doesn't realize that I might be just as fucked up as him. I'm not afraid of his cock. I'm not against doing things I have to, even if it means demeaning myself. I'd have to care enough about that kind of thing for it to get to me. I've already come to terms with the lust and mortal desires both angels and devils crave. It's how I can get on my knees for angels like Andre. How I would get on my knees with my ex just to get him to shut up. I have complete control over my body and have learned long ago that I will not give up my power. So fuck human standards. Fuck the shame that comes with embracing my sexuality. Lucian's an asshole. He's a monster. But so am I.

Clearing my throat, I tip my head back and gaze into Lucian's wicked eyes. "I am good for nothing." I shake my jaw, making my lip tremble. "I don't know what you want from me to prove otherwise."

Fire sparks in his eyes. "Undress for me."

That's not what I was expecting. I thought he'd demand I get on my knees.

I blink a few times and inhale a small breath. "What do you plan to do?" I can't help it. I would prefer to prepare for whatever he plans to do to my soul.

Fury twists his features, and he grabs me by the throat and lifts me up. My body reacts by hooking my legs around him. It's strange feeling his fingers around my neck. Pain sizzles over my skin, but I can breathe. I'm dead. The way I see things as if I'm physically here is all in my head.

Sparks fly as our essences connect more securely, my ankles locking me in place around his waist. Something comes over me, and I fight against his restraint on my throat. Lucian's eyes capture mine and he shifts his hand to hold my ass, allowing me to overpower him and kiss him. I kiss him with my entire being, merging my light with his dark, doing the only thing I can think of to fight against his control without him fighting back. I don't kiss him out of desire. I kiss him in desperation, stealing his focus over his control to give into his innate need to fall to mortal desires. I kiss him to hold onto my control. This kiss will cement my place above him and not as a soul he can destroy. He won't want to.

I can feel it. I can taste it in the sweet, spiciness of his lips.

"Fuck me," I murmur against his mouth. "Let me feel what kind of power the most notorious devil has."

Lucian releases a deep growl-like moan, the noise vibrating from his chest. He wants me. I can feel it on a soul-deep level. I just need to give him a push.

"Fuck me anyway you want, Lucian. Fuck me until I can't walk. And then after, let me serve you. Let me show you that you can use me to get what you want." I kiss him again, sliding my tongue into his mouth.

"I want the saviors annihilated. I want Hell and Earth to

be solely mine. I want my brethren to bow down to me," he mutters against my lips, his desires escaping him as if my kiss and body pull them out of him. He can't resist me. I'm the one with power over him, and I will use it.

"I want that too." I reach between us and open my soul to him, my clothes suddenly vanishing as if they were never there. "Now fuck me and let me help you. I will bring the saviors to their knees for you. I never wanted Purgatory. A part of Hell. I just never wanted to suffer."

I expect him to fuck Hell right into me, but he doesn't. He meets my gaze, his dark eyes searching mine. "And what of my brethren?"

"What about them? I know why they've kept me away from you," I murmur, my body aching at even the thought. A lie has never felt so painful.

"Why?" he prods. "Tell me, and I'll give you what you desire. You will feel my power in your soul."

I lick my lips. "They've kept me from you because they're weak. They're afraid. They—"

Bright light ignites the world aglow around us, and Lucian roars, dropping me from his arms. I hit the ground, my soul screaming. Spinning, Lucian rips a flaming sword from his back and flings it inches away from me.

I scramble away and stare in shock at the sight of Andre unfurling his brilliant wings before Lucian.

"You can't take that soul before her time," Andre says, gathering heavenly light. "I'm taking her back to where she belongs."

Summoning hellfire, Lucian transforms into his devil form. He unleashes his fury on Andre, engulfing him in the fires of Hell.

My soul erupts in agony.

My very essence weeps.

A cool hand touches my cheek, pulling me from Hell and the fire engulfing everything. I snap my eyes open and find myself in Andre's arms in the now empty room, lying in my own sticky blood.

What the fuck?

"It's okay, Raven. You're okay. I healed your body and brought your soul back. Lucian can't have you," Andre says, stroking his fingers over my cheeks. "I'm sorry I couldn't get in as fast I should've."

I open and close my mouth, my body exhausted, my mind whirling.

He leans down and kisses me. "Just relax. You've been through a lot. Your soul keepers are coming."

I nod, savoring the sensation of his arms around me.

If only I could be sure this is all over, but I can't. I might've made things worse with my attempt at controlling Lucian.

God, what have I done?

Andre winces, and I search his face, confusion battling inside of me. I know I didn't say the thought out loud, but I know he felt it. But why did he react the way he did?

And then I see it. The spark of fire in his eyes.

"Andre," I whisper, touching his cheek.

"I'll never leave you, Raven. I swore I'd always protect you," he replies, offering me a sad smile.

My heart fissures and breaks. Fuck. Andre has abandoned grace.

He has fallen.

24

Long May He Reign

DANTE

I SOAR OVER the warehouse the hunters call home, cir-cling to get a better view. There is only one way for me to get in, and even then, I'm sure they've shielded the place. Fury turns my vision red, and I adjust my prisoner in my arms, bringing the man up from his dangling place clinging to my leg.

"Please, don't drop me," he cries, his tear-stains satisfying to study, glistening on his cheeks.

"You mean, like this?" I toss the man away from me and savor his high-pitched scream as I let him freefall a dozen feet. I dive and catch him by the wrist, dislocating his shoulder in the process.

He hollers and sobs, praying to the Higher Power he turned his back on. "Please, I'll do anything," he says, blubbering with snot dripping from his nose.

"Fuck yeah, you will. You're taking me to Raven. You better pray to me that she's unharmed because I will inflict on you all the injuries she sustained because of you fuckers." I hiss and flash my fangs, startling the man.

The fucker pisses himself right in my arms, setting me off even more. Don't these damn hunters know to go to the bathroom before they enter suicide missions against Hell? Flipping him around, I face him outward and flip him upside down, hoping his piss drips onto his face like it did my boots.

He screams again, waving his arms. "Please! God, please!"

I descend, swinging him by his ankles, testing how strong his heart and body are against the fear I ignite in his wretched being. Dropping him to the grass, I land a few feet away and unsheathe my blade, taking a moment to peer around the empty property.

"Where did the fucking ghost take her?" I ask, stomping forward, revealing my devil façade.

The hunter cringes and freezes as I tower over him. "He was being summoned here. Preston arranged a new vessel for him if he'd help kidnap her. He agreed to do this in exchange for Elias's soul."

I holler in anger and shoot venom over his head, watching as it smolders the dry grass. I don't need to know anymore to know the reason. The demon wanted Raven's body for something, and by the lingering presence of Hell buzzing through the ground around me, I know it involves Lucian. The fucking bastard devil.

"Now please, just let me go," the man pleads.

I will not show mercy to the man who helped get my pretty soul taken from me. I can think of hundreds of ways the demon could hurt Raven without killing her, and I know he would try to do every single one of them.

"No. The only place you'll be going is to my kingdom in Hell. I will finish this later. Your soul is mine." I aim my blade at him, aligning it with his stomach. I want his death to hurt.

"No!" he shouts.

The bang of a door closing shut steals my attention, and I stop short of gutting the man. He squeezes his eyes shut, crying and snotting, praying to the Higher Power. It takes everything in me to leave him, but I can always come back and finish him. Right now, I need to get to Raven. It's been long enough already. If I could murder time for keeping me from her, I would. I'd show it exactly what it's like to mess with the devil of envy.

I jog around the massive building and to the back, catching sight of Vincent leaving out a door and heading in another direction. His human façade barely hangs on to his skeletal body, his skin smoking and smoldering with…grace. I can sense the lingering presence of Heaven—of Andre. He wasn't with his brethren when I left the hunters, going after Raven.

Taking flight to stop Vincent from hearing me, I soar toward him, my need for justice and revenge controlling me. Right now, grabbing this bastard is all I can think about. He's the reason we might lose Raven. He's the reason Hell might not get the chance to rise because of his deal with Elias. I can't let him get away. I will cut him up inch-by-inch until he gives me Elias's soul.

I flap my wings, pushing me forward. Vincent turns his head, peering behind him. I'm too fast and slash my blade at his back, cutting his jacket open to see his baked skin. Crashing into him, I knock him off his feet and we skid together over the sidewalk. He growls and thrashes, but he's no match for me.

"Where is she?" I ask, my gruff voice echoing through the air. "What have you done with Raven?"

A leering smile crosses his face. "I killed her and sent her soul to Hell to be ravaged by Lucian."

My eyes widen at his words, and I slam my blade down on his arm, severing it from his body. He howls as black blood sizzles across the pavement. Spitting my venom at the appendage, I disintegrate it into a pile of black slime.

Vincent wails and tries to scratch me with his claws. I spit venom in his face, melting the rest of his human flesh until I see his demon façade and...fuck. He wears Lucian's mark, the pentagram etched with his molten power on Vincent's skull. Slamming my dagger on his neck, I sever the bastard's head and kick it several dozen feet. Rage consumes me, gripping me to my core. Betrayal runs hotter than the pits of Hell. Lucian made a deal with Vincent. And a powerful one.

I stab the demon over and over again, my muscles flexing and craving to destroy this fucker. Flames lick over Vincent's body, fissuring the ground beneath him. The concrete splits open and the flames of Hell snatch his body away from me. The ground shakes under my boots, the scent of Hell engulfing me.

Shit.

I expand my wings and fly into the air, putting two dozen feet between me and the ground as it explodes wider and Vincent crawls back out, whole again, glowing with molten power. His eyes glow red and a smile crawls across his face. I clench my fingers into fists and prepare to send him to Hell again.

"You can't destroy me! Lucian gave me control of the Earth Realm in exchange for sending Raven to Hell," he hollers, gathering hellfire in his palms.

"The fuck I can't!" I shout, dead-set on tearing him apart over and over again until he decides to remain in the bowels of Hell instead of facing me. And even then, I'll hunt him down.

I'll show him Kase isn't the only one capable of wrath.

Like the coward he is, Vincent throws power at me and spins, bolting away instead of fighting. I let him go. I need to find Raven's body. I need to see the truth for myself before I open the gates of Hell and tear the fucking place down to get her back. I will not let Lucian get away with this bullshit. I won't.

Tugging out my cellphone, I call Kase as I rush toward the door. If Vincent came through it, I can enter it. The hunters must've destroyed the protective shields to keep Hell out.

"You get our girl?" Kase asks, his voice growling through the line. "You better have fucking got her."

My insides twist, and I hesitate.

Agony rolls through me. I can't tell him. I can't do it over the phone.

I run deeper into the building and fling open another door, catching the lingering scent of Hell.

"Dante, you fuckhead. Answer me. Now!" Kase roars.

I exhale a breath, my whole body buzzing.

And then I see her.

Raven rests in Andre's arms, blood covering her, but she's not dead.

"I got her. Get your ass here quick," I finally respond to Kase. I disconnect the line without waiting for his response. Holding my arms out, I reach for Raven. "Give her here."

Andre glowers and hugs Raven tighter, unfurling his featherless wings, seared by hellfire but as tough as ever, reminiscent of bat wings. His Hell façade peeks through, and he flares his nostrils, showing off his hellish features.

Raven flutters her eyes open, and Andre banishes his devil façade, not letting her see him. "Dante..." Her voice caresses my ears.

I ignore Andre's warning glance and kneel beside them, touching her face. "Let's get you home, pretty soul. I meet Andre's gaze next. "You too, you awesome fucking bastard. I think we need to talk."

Raven wiggles from Andre's arms and onto my lap. Her big blue eyes sheen with tears. "You have no fucking idea."

"Just look at that cock. It's huge. Like a stacked set of soda cans." I flick my fingers to Andre's thigh. "I feel bad for you. Half of that thing will never get wet inside Raven. I thought I had it bad."

Andre rubs the back of his neck. "Please stop. I can't think about that."

I cock my head, staring at his swinging dick in the mirror as he studies his naked body. Raven wanted to be in here, hugging and loving up on Andre, but I knew he needed time to get himself in control. I know how fucking horny she makes me, and damn. I can't imagine what it'll be like for Mr. Lust the second he finally sheds the rest of his heavenly thoughts.

"Why not? I love thinking about that sexy woman. All the time. I love her. How she licks her lips when she's turned on. How her hands tighten stronger than you expect when she rubs one out for you. How fucking hot her snatch is and how she creams so much that she'll glaze your damn face with her just as sugary sweetness. Elias's essence infused her with fucking Heaven, and we get to have every part of it without all the other bullshit." I adjust my junk while watching Andre grow even more. And damn. He's lucky I have the perfect toy for him.

"Shut up!" he yells, fire licking across his skin. A deep growl escapes his mouth, and he unfurls his webbed wings, his features shifting. "My erection hurts. My testicles throb. I can't stand this. It's torture."

I chuckle, striding across my room to my special He-Shelf, dedicated solely to my cock. Grabbing my mega stroker, I toss the ring-like contraption toward Andre. He catches it, furrowing his brows. I scoop up a bottle of my favorite lube next and shake it at him.

"This will do the trick, at least temporarily. Hurry up, though. Everyone's waiting for you to get your shit together." I slam the bottle of lube on the dresser. "Who knows? Maybe

Raven will want to love up on all of us."

Andre doesn't even hesitate or wait for me to leave as he slathers on far too much lube, moaning before figuring out the toy.

I clap my hands once and laugh. "Damn. Look at you prep. I might allow you to try to convince Raven to spread those smooth, biteable ass cheeks of hers for you to see that monster slip inside her backdoor. But I'm getting her first."

Andre waves his hand. "You're going to get me first if you don't leave."

I howl in amusement and thrust the door open. "And make both Raven and Kase jealous? No fucking way. You're on your own unless they invite you to join."

Andre releases the loudest fucking moan—and I mean, Raven getting fucked by Kase's horns and tail loud—and I shake my head and leave the door to my room wide open. This fucking house is going to turn into a constant orgy fest, and I'm here for it. I have enough toys to keep any extra cocks busy if Raven's body is maxed out at cock-pacity.

"That son of a bastard!" Kase shouts, his voice shaking the chandelier over the entryway. "If he thinks we're going to stand by and do nothing as he attempts to rise as the Higher Power, I'll shove the bastard Vincent so far up Lucian's ass that he'll choke on him. This is what we abandoned Heaven for. I will not fucking allow him to change things now."

"I won't let that happen, Kase," Raven says, her soft voice stirring my insides around in a good way. "You should've seen him with me. He's not immune to my angel-kissed soul."

"He was manipulating you." Micah steps into view, leaning his back on the doorway.

"It didn't feel like it," she argues. "I just need more time. You all need to stop treating me like a fragile soul. I can face Lucian again. You can coach me how to make a devil fall like you have been with the angels."

"No," Micah and Kase say in unison.

"Seriously? Now's the time to do something. I mean, Cassius and Zade are going to be on guard for a while, and Elias's contract with Vincent was voided. Let me do this." Raven stands and waltzes to Micah and places her hands on her hips. "Please. What can I do to convince you? Want me to bend over?"

Oh, that naughty fucking pretty soul. Spinning around, Raven hikes up her dress and bends over, stretching to touch her toes. Her smooth, lickable pussy lips show through the sheer fabric of her thong. Micah stiffens, his body flexing, and if Kase didn't whip him across his burly chest with his tail, I'm fucking certain he'd have whipped his cock out and thrust it in. No foreplay or nothing. The fucking virgin bastard still has a lot to learn, and Raven's going to learn real fast that Micah's carnal innate nature is to consume to the point that everyone else gets nothing. He needs to learn restraint.

I yank him back and take his place, swinging my palm at her ass. If I didn't grab her panties, she'd have fallen face-first on the tile. I hum, appreciating the silhouette of my handprint blossoming across that bubble butt of hers that I lean down and lick it to blow a cool breath over her skin.

"I'm so fucking jealous by how easy you're making it for Micah. He hasn't earned a dip into that sex pool between your legs yet. At least sit on his face first. Learn what it's like to have the gluttonous bastard eat you out. I bet he'll go for a week." I grin at Micah and flick out my tongue between my index and middle finger. "Once you get one taste of the true angel lips, you won't ever want to stop."

Raven wags her finger at me. "Dante, enough. We have more important things—"

"You bent over first," I tease.

Kase growls and he chucks an empty decorative vase at the wall, shattering it into sharp pieces. "I'm going to bend you both over and give you each a damn turn if you don't chill out. I can't stand here another moment and let Lucian believe he is the cocky, powerful dickhole he thinks he is. I need you to gear up. We're going home."

I raise my eyebrows. "You don't think he was just fucking with Raven's head to get his way?"

Red energy crackles over Kase's skin. "I don't give a damn.

Maybe the fuckhead was right and we're too far removed from Hell. We should've never been fucking bested by a demon, hunters, or the shitty saviors either."

Ah fuck. Kase has already made up his mind. After all this time, I know him just as good as I know myself. He won't stop going on about this until he can unleash his wrath where it belongs. But returning to the crappiest place I own? Damn it.

"Don't be so hard on yourself, Kase," Raven says, sauntering away from me. She holds open her arms and ends up embracing Kase's moody ass instead of the other way around. "We're all still figuring everything out. Most of this bullshit was unexpected. I mean, I got possessed by a ghost. I never in a million years expected that bullshit."

"You forgot possessed by an angel too." Andre's voice sounds from behind me, and I swivel and peer over my shoulder at what will surely be Raven's most exhausting devil. I should be jealous, insecure even, but something is different this time around with Andre than it was with Micah.

Raven graces Andre with a smile, but she doesn't leave Kase, continuing to smother him with her affection until he lifts her up and buries his face between her perky tits. "That was fucking nuts. Can you still do that? Maybe we can use it to our advantage against Lucian."

Kase eases his head out of her cleavage. "Fuck no. You're not coming. There is only one way I'm allowing any of these bastards inside you, and it's not through your soul."

She tips her head back and laughs. "You're crazy."

Kase leans in and kisses her. "I just want to protect you. You've dealt with Lucian enough."

I stroll to the two of them, wanting to feel Raven between our bodies like it was before she managed to bring these other bastards to their knees. Raven reaches behind her, running her fingers over my jaw, her touch awakening my body. "He's right. Plus, Micah's going to need help babysitting the jizz-master. Maybe together they'll succeed to get it in your mouth."

She groans. "I don't want you guys to leave. Just stay. We can plan something for tomorrow."

Andre clears his throat, drawing everyone's attention. "I can't wait until tomorrow. I need to claim my throne."

Raven purses her lips. "It can't wait even a day?"

"If I wait, I don't know if I could fight for it. But for you? I'll do anything. Lucian must pay." Andre reveals his wings to Raven for a few seconds before concealing them. "I won't sit around and let him do more damage. Kase is right. Lucian needs to be reminded of who he is, even if it's me having to do it. I didn't fall for nothing."

Raven bobs her head. "You didn't," she repeats.

Kase shudders and transforms, not wasting another minute. "Let's hurry the fuck up." Turning to Raven, he brushes her hair from her shoulder and kisses the spot. "And be a good little angel-girl, will you? I don't want you to fuck Elias to death by accident."

She gasps a breathy laugh. "Kase!"

I grab Raven and toss her toward Micah. "You don't have to worry about that. Micah's got her."

"And I don't plan to let her go," he says, hugging her in his arms. "You got that, heathen?"

She smiles. "I'm not letting go of any of you." She waves her hand at Kase, Andre, and finally me. "I mean it."

"You couldn't even if you wanted to. I'll have you in my favorite restraints soon enough." I flick my tongue at her, watching her squirm.

"Okay, okay. Enough. Hurry up already." She waves her hand at me. "Go the fuck to Hell."

25

Eternal Bond

MICAH

SAY SOMETHING EROTIC. Something unexpected. Raven needs something to get her attention away from the gates of Hell I hold open with my mind.

The thoughts tumble through my head over and over again.

I need to do something. The silence sinks into my skin, unnerving me. I feel like I'm failing her by not keeping her attention and instead letting it wander to the dozen scenarios I know flit through her mind. I can hear bits and pieces of her thoughts, and I need to change them. She should trust that Kase, Dante, and Andre can take care of themselves and let me learn how to take care of her like they do.

"Why don't you come over here and straddle my face. I'd enjoy performing cunnilingus on you," I say, licking my lips, my body awakening at the thought. "I want to discover if your labia tastes as Dante describes."

Damn. Raven's expression morphs from concern to shock.

I messed up.

I just wish for my mouth get on board to speak the vulgar terms she favors.

Jerking his head back, Elias howls a laugh hard enough to make him cough. He wheezes and clutches his chest, his face reddening from the effort. Annoyance rushes through me, and I curl my fingers into fists, preparing to punch the loveseat he sprawls out on to send him flying backward.

Raven raises her palm at me, moving from his side to mine. "That's really tempting. A bit clinical sounding, but tempting."

"Shit, Micah. Your attempt to talk dirty will be the literal death of me." Elias gets up and surprises me by plopping down on my other side. He bumps his knuckles into my shoulder, still grinning in amusement. "This is gonna be weird as fuck, but I have a strong need of self-preservation. Let me teach you."

Raven whips her head, sweeping her black tresses around. "Don't you dare. It's my job to corrupt Micah."

"We can't have a pity corruption on you. Make him earn it."

Elias chuckles again and leans in close. "Repeat after me."

I turn and glance into his eyes, testing my ability to get into his head to listen to his thoughts. He's open enough toward me that I don't have to pry my way in. It could also be because he's Raven's soulmate, and their connection and our past life—one I don't want to think about—aids the new bond we share with Raven tying us back together where time and life had torn us apart.

"You can just think the words," I say into his mind, smirking at his reaction. "Don't worry. I don't listen to your thoughts. Just now."

Elias closes his eyes like he thinks he needs to concentrate. "This is fucking weird. God, what do I think? What would make Raven cream? If she likes it from him, then she might like it from me."

It's my turn to laugh.

Raven groans and climbs onto my lap, straddling me with one of her knees between Elias's leg and mine. "This is too weird. Knock it off and kiss me instead."

"Go on. Kiss her and get her worked up a bit. Make her forget that I'm coaching you," Elias thinks to me.

I lift my eyebrow and do what he says, giving in to Raven's request. She hugs her arms around my neck, deepening our kiss until I give her what she craves and slip my tongue across hers. Easing away, she bites her lip with a smile, turning her attention to Elias.

"Do you want to kiss him too?" I ask, studying the desire crossing her face.

"Damn, look at you. You don't need my help after all," he thinks, stretching closer to pinch Raven's chin between his fingers.

She hums in agreement and brushes her pouty mouth to his. I thought I'd be more jealous, but I'm far from it. It only makes me crave more of Raven. I've always learned from watching and listening to mortals, and seeing how beautiful and sensual Raven is wrapped in Elias's arms does something strange to me.

"Tell her you're going to kiss her throat, and then ask her how it feels," Elias thinks, kissing Raven passionately with her on my lap.

"I want to taste more of you," I say out loud, shifting Raven's hair from her neck.

She grips the front of my shirt in her fingers and bends her neck, exposing her supple skin to me. I pull her closer by her hips, wanting her to feel what she does to my body. The pressure of her weight makes my testicles clench in anticipation, the ache sinking into my core.

"Not testicles," Elias thinks. "Too proper. And tell her what she does to you. Describe what you want to do. Make it dirty. Tell her you want to lick her pussy and won't stop until she squirts all over you."

I groan at his words, the thought of experiencing Raven in such a way consuming me. "Raven," I say, licking her throat before kissing the exposed spot on her shoulder. "Look what you do to me." Grabbing her wrist, I guide her hand lower until she continues on her own and strokes my bulging hard-on. "You make me so hard."

"Let him find out what he does to you," Elias murmurs, sucking Raven's bottom lip. "You'd like that, wouldn't you, darlin'?"

Raven bobs her head and straightens her body, stretching up on her knees. "Only if it's okay with both of you."

"Fuck yeah, I'm good," Elias says, eyeing me.

"Only if you tell me you want this." I trace my finger along her bare thigh, her dress hiking up.

She shifts, spreading her body wider. I tilt my head for a view of her sexy underwear. I wonder who she chose them for. For Kase or Dante, or maybe Andre.

"I wear them for all of you," she responds, hearing my thoughts. I realize now that I'm open to her.

"I want them off you," I murmur out loud, sliding my fingers into the string of lace over her hip, tracing my way down, enjoying the smooth, softness of her skin. She's completely smooth and utterly wet, the warmth of her body dampening my fingers.

"She's so fucking sexy, isn't she, Micah?" Elias asks, grabbing the hem of her dress.

Raven raises her arms and lets him tug it off of her, showing off her sheer bra that matches her G-string, her nipples like perfect peachy-pink pebbles I want to strum with my thumb. She grazes her fingers over her breasts like she hears my desire. Elias tugs the strap of her bra down and kisses her shoulder.

I lean in and lick between her cleavage. "Her tits are impeccable. Delicious. Think I should work my way down?"

"Hell yeah." Elias slides his arm around her waist, tugging her off me and resting her against him. "You want her pussy, don't you? You're going to eat her out until her legs quake, aren't you?"

"And then you'll have your turn," I muse, shifting to kneel between Raven's knees. I reach out and caress her cheek, loving how her sheer lingerie teases me. "Would you like that?"

She shivers and nods, goosebumps prickling over her skin. "I'd love it."

"Damn straight, you will, darlin'," Elias says, turning her head to caress his lips to hers. "You'll cream yourself for the rest of eternity at even the tease of our tongues when we're through with you. Tell her why, Micah. What are you a glutton for?"

"For you, Raven." I bury my face into her cleavage again, nipping her skin. "I can't get enough of you. No matter how much you give me, I'll always want more. Your kisses, your touch."

Unhooking her bra, Elias lets it fall forward, the simple act exciting me to the core. "What about her tits?"

I drink her in slowly, memorizing her body as she smiles at me in anticipation, a flicker of hellfire in her blue eyes, making it look as if the sun sets in her gaze. "That's where I'm going to start. Your tits are ours."

Elias flicks his fingers over her hard nipples, encouraging me to follow through. "Listen to her to learn what she likes," he thinks to me. "Start soft and work up your pressure."

I hum my agreement, remembering a time I forgot I missed when we were once brethren on the same path before he chose another. And now? We're together again, bonding over the same soul that changed both of our eternities forever. It's strange how he encourages and helps me through acts I'm unfamiliar with, but I know he does it for Raven. I'm well aware that she's fragile compared to my devilish brawns and strength, and I don't even know her boundaries or what she'd go for with me.

Raven rubs her fingers over my cropped hair, guiding me to her body. I glide my tongue over her nipple and suck it into my mouth, slowly and gently at first, working my way up until she moans and tightens her fingers to my shoulders.

"Now work down," Elias thinks, sliding his hand over one of Raven's breasts to roll her nipple between his fingers.

"Want more?" I murmur, licking a line down her stomach. Shifting, Elias holds one of her knees, spreading her body wider to accommodate for my broad shoulders.

"So badly. You're just teasing me," Raven says, squirming and panting on Elias's lap. I imagine she feels so good grinding on his shaft. The thought shoots desire right to my groin.

"What else are you a glutton for, Micah?" Elias asks out loud, drawing his hand down Raven's stomach.

"Her pussy. I can't stop thinking about it. What it tastes like. How it feels. What I can do to make her scream my name." I follow his gesture with my eyes, my throbbing erection pressing against my pants.

"Are you dripping in anticipation, darlin'?" Elias asks.

"Mmmhmm," she moans. "See for yourself."

I can't stop from touching myself, the act of seeing Raven lift her hips up, allowing Elias to slip his hand into her panties...

"Damn," I whisper, needing to see more. To experience more.

I bow forward and kiss her thigh, working my way up until I bite the waistband of her underwear and drag them down until I singe the fabric and rip them free. Raven gasps in pleasure, shifting her legs as Elias strokes his finger between her legs until he spreads the folds of her body open.

"Have you ever seen a clit, Micah? This is the magical button to get her to cum with your mouth," Elias thinks to me. "You'll learn what she likes really fucking quick if you listen to her."

I don't respond and dive right in, desperate to taste her and have her how I want. Raven releases the sexiest moan and digs her fingers into my shoulders, the bite of her nails feeling so good on my skin. I've never felt anything so soft against my tongue, so smooth and sugary. I know my desire for her and her soul enhances everything addicting about her, and I'll never get enough. I'm addicted. Obsessed. Something more.

"Micah," she whispers, her words breathy with her moan. "That feels so good."

I smile and peek up at her, stroking my tongue up and down, keeping it flat and wide to get every inch of her. Elias watches me with intensity from over her shoulder, massaging his fingers into her breasts and playing with her nipples. She pants and squirms, her legs trembling, her sexy moans filling the air.

And then she tenses and cages my head between her legs. "Micah, fuck. Oh, fuck. Fuck. Micah!"

Her pleasure courses through me with her scream of ecstasy, and I watch her soul intensify, brightening under my touch. Elias grins and wags his brows, thinking about how impressed he is by how fast I got her off even with my lack of experience.

I wait for her to loosen her body. "Hold her still. I need to taste her again."

Raven blocks me with her hand, her chest rising and falling. "I can't be the only one getting off. You next."

"And it's my turn to make her cream," Elias says, making her shiver.

I narrow my eyes, releasing a low growl. "No. I need more. I need to hear her say my name like that again."

Elias chuckles. "Can't argue with a damn devil."

"But—fuck. Fine, just one more time," Raven says, sucking her bottom lip between her teeth. "And with you naked. Both of you."

Elias shrugs his shoulders. "Oh-fucking-kay. Whatever you both want."

I lock my fingers to my pants, popping the button and zipping them down. My erection throbs in anticipation. I can already imagine Raven's fingers stroking the length of my shaft. It's now that I realize it doesn't have to be me or her. We can both get what we want. Snatching her from Elias, I flip her around to face him and drag her onto my face. She shrieks with surprise and moans as I unleash my wild nature, my devil façade breaking free. My tusks slide against her naked thighs, and she automatically grips onto them to brace herself. She doesn't freak out like I expect, embracing my darkness with her light, unfazed by the shift in my body.

Elias sucks in a breath. "Whoa, what the—"

"Don't you fucking say anything or you can leave. They can't control it, and I don't care. He's my gluttonous devil. Mine." Raven cuts Elias off, not letting him finish his comment about my sudden shift.

"No, not that. No shame here. But look," Elias says, stealing my attention from Raven's body before I can get started again. "Someone's outside."

"Fucking pervert angels," Raven snaps.

I growl at her words, the vibration of my voice against her making her clench and intake a sharp breath of pleasure. As much as I want to continue, my rage and annoyance overtake me, and I lift her off me and set her on the couch. Fire courses through my veins at the bright light seeping in through the closed curtain. The bastards are closer than they should be, and they're probably squirming in misery crossing our Hell boundaries like they are.

The floor quakes as I stomp across the living room and to the foyer, only glancing at Raven and Elias once as he helps her dress. I clench my fingers into fists, preparing to fight and knock Cassius and Zade back to the high heavens. I will never forgive them for taking my wings and denying me the one thing that would've stopped me from abandoning my grace—and now, I'll be damned if they try to get within a dozen feet of Raven and her soul.

Unsheathing my Hell dagger, I yank the door open and charge forward. Cassius flies back out of my reach and launches into the air. Zade touches down in front of him protectively, his narrowed eyes focusing on Raven behind me. I can sense her in the doorway peeking out.

Zade surprises me and drops his flaming sword. "Micah, we're not here to cause problems. We just want to talk."

"Talk? You want to talk? After everything you did to me?" Fire escapes my mouth, and I torch the grass in front of him.

"Yes, please. We realize we've been going about all of this wrong." Zade motions behind him at Cassius slowly shuffling closer.

"He's right, Micah. And I'm sorry. I'm so incredibly sorry. I should've paid better attention to the signs. I shouldn't have forsaken you like I had. But I was scared." Cassius raises his hands, showing he is unarmed. "I couldn't see what you see."

I clench my jaw. "And now?"

"I've made a grave mistake. I let things go too far, and now I've lost not only you but Andre." Cassius scrubs his hand through his beard, reminding me of Lucian from long ago. Though where Lucian's eyes look like obsidian, Cassius's glow purple like amethysts, reminding me of a winter sunset behind a stormy sky. "We're devastated."

Rage bursts through me, and I charge forward, smashing into Cassius. He doesn't put up a fight or anything as I swing my hooved hand and clock him in the jaw. "You're devastated, you selfish bastard?" I ask, raising my voice. "What about me? About Raven? You stole my wings!"

Cassius glows with his grace, his mere existence burning me.

"And I regret it. You just—"

"Enough! I don't want to hear it. Regret changes nothing. Apologies do nothing. I've claimed my throne in Hell, and it won't be long until I tear those wings from your back and toss you in the pits myself."

"Please, Micah. Listen to me. If you continue down this path, Heaven will be lost. I spent time reflecting on the situation and was given a moment to share a vision of Lucifer. What I saw...we can't let it happen. It goes far beyond the prophesized nine kingdoms. Lucifer will not allow the seven sinners to rise, nor will he let the light of the brightest soul in existence to create Purgatory." Cassius turns his gaze from me to Raven. She slides up beside me and nestles herself in the safety of my side. "You have to believe me. I will give you what you've been praying for."

I frown, unsure if he is speaking to me or Raven. "You have nothing we want."

Cassius crosses his arms over his broad chest, narrowing his eyes at me. "Not even Raven's redemption? I can grant her the miracle...if she's willing to help."

Raven stiffens next to me. "You mean you can save my soul? I don't understand. Lucian owns it until I complete my mission."

"Things have changed," Cassius says.

"You're lying," she argues.

I tighten my fingers around hers. "He can't lie. If he says there is a way to redeem you, then there is a way."

"How?" Raven steps forward but not out of my reach. "How the fuck can you redeem me?"

"You must get the original devils to fall by your hands, including Lucifer. Only then will Heaven bring you the peace you deserve." Cassius tightens his jaw, flicking his gaze from mine to Raven's. "I will assist you in any way I can."

"And what of me? Andre?" I swivel and motion to Elias, hovering inside the house, clutching onto the doorframe. "Of Elias?"

"You will still be Hell's keepers, but under Heaven's guidance. It'll be the true balance of the universe Hell's brethren somehow think doesn't exist." Cassius extends his hand to Zade, drawing him closer. "We wouldn't have to fight."

"It sounds like you'd be in control," Elias mutters, his voice raspy. "The same beings who think we are lost and forsaken."

Cassius clasps his hands together. "It doesn't have to be this way." Turning his attention to Raven, he adds. "Please, Raven. You'll have your soul and peace."

"No. You can fuck off, you righteous bastard," Raven snaps, surprising me.

Cassius brings his hand to his chest. "What?"

"You said you could redeem me if I destroyed the original devils, so no. I will not hurt Kase and Dante. I won't do it.

They're mine." Raven waves her hand. "So fuck off."

"Raven—"

She grabs my dagger and rushes forward. "I said, leave!"

"This is the only way, Raven. It might be our only chance," Cassius pleads.

"Go!" Raven yells, swinging her arm.

Cassius and Zade erupt in a burst of light, vanishing from in front of her. Spinning on her feet, she searches the sky above, but they've concealed themselves from us. They disappear like the cowards they are.

Raven groans and pulls at her black tresses. "The fuckers. How could they ask that of me?"

I press my lips together, my words lost to me.

"It's fucking crazy, right?" she asks, speaking her thoughts out loud. "I could never do it. Not for him."

I rub my chin, trying to still my racing heart. "But what about for you?"

She groans. "I don't know, Micah. I fucking don't know."

26

For Hell's Sake

RAVEN

THE FUCKING ANGELS just love ruining everything. Not only did they kill my spirit boner, they decimated any chance of corrupting Micah and bonding with Elias. Tonight was incredible with them, and I felt like everything would work out with our eternities since Micah and Elias seemed to be getting along.

Damn Cassius.

Damn him to Hell with Lucian.

The two of them deserve each other and can spend the rest of eternity arguing over who's right and wrong while I help my guys bring real balance to the universe. Because Elias was right.

There is no way there will be balance if the saviors were guiding the devils' rule over Hell. And for me to kill Kase and Dante in the process? That would be like ending a piece of myself. They hold a piece of my soul as well as my heart, and I will not destroy the two men who have been fighting against the entire universe for me while managing to fulfill my needs and also welcome in the other devils as part as our family.

I don't know how else to describe it. We're together and will rule together. I can't just give in to the righteous bastard who tried to tell me there was no hope in saving me. Who threatened to make it his sole purpose to end me. Who went through great lengths to try to set things his way, thinking he knows it all, and what he knows is all.

"Raven," Micah says, his low voice wrapping around me a second before his arms do.

I twist around and fall into him, desperately wanting him to pick me up and hold me. To drown me in affection and anything else he can do to pull my mind out of my spinning thoughts.

"Why don't you come to my room and get some rest. Elias is already in there, and I think he could use your attention. He doesn't look great." Micah eases away and peers into my eyes. "I'm not sure what to do without my grace."

My heart stalls, my soul screaming in fear that maybe I pushed him too far earlier. Maybe Cassius and Zade stressed him out. Whatever it is, I can't help worrying that something will happen to him before Kase, Dante, and Andre return. I need them here. I need to be surrounded by the strength of all the devils to ensure everything goes as planned.

Micah groans and hugs me tighter. "Relax. He's not dying tonight. Soon but not before Kase and Dante return. I would sense it. See it even. His soul clings onto his body." Micah scoops me up and carries me from the balcony of Dante's room. "He just needs you. Your presence helps."

I rest my head on his muscular shoulder, savoring the sensation of his protective arms around me, and within them, the promise of a powerful eternity with him by my side. "How much longer do you think the others will be?" I ask, wishing Micah would just bring Elias to me, so I can continue to watch the summoning circle.

"I don't know. They're not as connected to Hell as Lucian is. It could be hours or even days, but don't worry. The longer it takes, the more powerful they'll grow. And who knows, perhaps they've chosen to check in on their kingdoms." Micah clicks open his bedroom door. "It's an enormous place, you know."

"I really don't, though," I muse, straightening up to catch sight of Elias, lying on his side on the edge of Micah's bed. "Not yet, at least."

Micah crosses his room and climbs onto the bed with me in

his arms, sandwiching me between him and Elias. I turn on my side and caress my fingers to Elias's cheek, stirring him awake long enough to smile at me. Sadness clings to my soul, seeing him like this. Some moments he seems fine, well even, and then in others such as now, he looks fragile and weak, summoning sorrow from my soul.

Pushing away my morbid thoughts, I lean in and caress my lips to his as Micah spoons me from behind, twining his fingers through one of my hands while I cup Elias's hand in my other. The soft sounds of crickets chirp in through the open window, allowing in fresh air from outside. I tilt my head, letting my hair fall away from my neck, and wait for the sensation of Micah's lips on my throat.

How can a moment feel so good yet so...miserable? I shouldn't worry about Kase and Dante. I shouldn't worry about Andre taking his throne in his kingdom forged from lust. I damn well shouldn't allow Cassius and Zade to take up any more of my headspace either. But fuck.

"Raven, can I ask you something?" Micah's voice trickles into my mind as he opens his thoughts to me. "It's about Cassius's offer."

I close my eyes for a second, trying to summon my nerve to let him open this door. "Yeah, sure, but there isn't much to talk about."

Sliding his arm under me, he gets me to roll over and face

him. I rest my head on his pillow and lose myself in his gorgeous brown eyes, lit with soft firelight. We share the same breath, his scent still crisp and fresh, though hints of smoke, like a bonfire on the beach, waft over me. In this moment, Micah looks nearly angelic again—his features soft, his expression embodying concern with his furrowed brows and oh-so-pouty full lips.

"I just want to know what your soul is worth to you," Micah says, surprising me. "If you didn't have a contract with Lucian, what would you exchange it for? Family? Elias's life? Something I have yet to learn about you?"

I pucker my lips in thought. His question throws my guard off that I have no idea how to respond. What would I trade my soul for? Had he asked me weeks ago, I'd have said nothing. I didn't want the contract with Lucian in the first place. But now? I don't know.

"If I had a soul, I'd trade it for you. I'd give up everything to ensure you could find peace in your eternity. It's why I fell, Raven. You were my purpose and still are. I feel my darkness siphoning your light, and as much as I enjoy it, the part of me still clinging onto my life in Heaven's grace knows that I'm bad for you now. I don't want to see you in Hell, even if it means I lose you." Micah's words crack as his eyes sheen over.

I thought seeing an angel cry was heartbreaking. But this? It's torture. I hate it. "Micah, please never try to do that, and especially not for me. I know you think I deserve more than Hell, but it sure as shit isn't Heaven. Not with fucking Cassius. Not without all of you."

His frown deepens. "But—"

I cut off his complaint with a kiss, waiting until his muscles loosen and he pulls my body closer, pressing his hardening cock to my pelvis. "I have made my decision. Purgatory is mine. I'm tired of the fighting between Heaven and Hell and all the assholes in between, which says a lot considering I've only known about this crap for weeks. If I traded my soul for anything, it would be for Purgatory. It would be for the chance for souls not to feel stuck like I feel I am under Lucian. I'd trade my damn soul to get Lucian to knock his shit off and let us finish the plan he, Kase, and Dante came up with before Hell got to his head."

Micah's eyes flicker with a dozen thoughts. "Heaven really screwed up, losing you. That is the most unselfish thing I've ever heard. Cassius was wrong. He thought you were selfish for not sacrificing yourself for Heaven, but in reality, what you want is far more powerful and greater, no matter what anyone thinks."

"Which is why Lucian doesn't want it. He doesn't want me to have Purgatory. He doesn't want Purgatory at all." I crinkle my nose at the thought.

"I didn't jump from Heaven to see you lose your soul to him.

I will fight with everything in me to see it come to fruition, if this is truly what you want, my beautiful heathen," Micah says, closing the space to caress his lips to mine again. "My queen."

"Say that again," I tease, smiling.

"You're my queen. My purpose. My everything. I'll even bow." Micah hooks his arms around me and rolls with me off the bed, setting me on my feet.

I have no idea how Elias sleeps through my laughter, but I cover my mouth, trying to muffle the noise as Micah gets on his knees in front of me. He bows forward and kisses my feet. My laughing turns into psychotic cackling that only worsens when he crawls forward, grabs my leg and puts it on his shoulder, looking ready to devour me like he survives off eating me out.

The scent of sulfur trickles to my nose, and I grip Micah's head, stopping him from continuing. He flares his nostrils and glares toward his window for a moment before pulling himself together.

"It's them," I say, excitement coursing through me. "Save that tongue. I'm going to want it later."

Micah chuckles and shakes his head, smiling at my happiness instead of getting annoyed. I beat him to the door and dash ahead of him, teasing him by swaying and spinning and ensuring he gets a show as I rush downstairs and toward the backdoor.

I hesitate and spin toward him. "Let me handle telling Kase

and Dante about Cassius, okay? I don't want them to inadvertently take out their anger on you, especially with everything you've been through. I'm afraid you'll say something that will end with one of them stabbing you or some shit. I don't want them worrying, okay?"

Micah cocks an eyebrow. "If they're that insecure—"

"Micah, stop," I say, clasping the doorknob. "I don't want them to think you'll do something insane. Not that you will, but you all just started getting along."

"For your sake." His jaw twitches with his words.

It's like something shifts inside Micah, his devil side threatening to steal away the softness he's been showing me tonight. Firelight dances in the corner of my vision, and I realize why. Hell's gate is open, and as much as I want to pretend it doesn't mess with him, I know it does.

"Well, keep it up." I twirl my finger at him. "And maybe stay here until the gate closes. You're hot enough."

That gets him to smile, and he remains firmly in his spot a couple feet away with his muscular arms crossing his chest. I fling the door open and stride outside, only to slow down at the sight of the summoning circle lit with no one inside. My stomach twists, my nerves tightening. If Kase, Dante, and Andre were returning, they would've put that shit out and be waiting for me.

I stop in my tracks, glaring at the flames of Hell as they

explode and reach toward the sky. I open and close my mouth, trying to summon my voice to call for Micah, but Lucian's hulking form appears before me, his horns glowing like molten lava swirls within them. He stomps his hooves, shaking the ground hard enough to send me to my knees. I scramble away, trying to get up.

The world quakes again, and the earth splits open, shooting a crack right toward me. Hell peeks through, the fire burning away from the gateway and to me.

"This is not how you should greet your master, Raven. Bow forward and worship the ground before me until I'm content," Lucian says, his grumbly voice humming through the air.

I tip my head up and glower. "What the fuck?"

A smile curves his lips, and Lucian shudders, ridding his devil façade to take on his human form. "Crawl forward to me. Do it now before I make you."

My heart ricochets around my ribcage and my mind whirls with a million racing thoughts. What is going on? Where are Kase, Dante, and Andre? If they're not here, does that mean ...no. I refuse to believe it.

"No," I say, pushing up to my feet. "You actually can't make me. You can't leave that damn circle."

Lucian's eyes flash with firelight, sending my heart sinking into my stomach. Oh, fuck. Ah, Hell. Damn it. Something has changed, and the dread coursing through me explodes into full-blown panic.

Snarling, Lucian gathers hellfire in his hands and winds it into a whip like the one he threatened me with before. The same whip he's lashed across both Kase and Dante's backs. "It is your last chance to bow to me willingly, Raven, or were you deceiving me when you asked to be by my side as I destroyed Heaven and took Earth in my control?"

"I—I wasn't," I lie, choosing to be smart over brave in this moment, watching as the fire around him lowers to a circle of calm flames. "I'm just—where are Kase and Dante? Andre?"

"I said to bow!" Lucian flicks his wrist, lashing the whip at me.

To my utter horror, it breaks through the barrier and stings across my shins, knocking my legs out from under me. I shriek in pain and drop to my knees as tears burn my eyes. I toss my hair out of my face, tipping my head back, my body stiffening at the sight of the summoning circle extinguishing completely.

And then Lucian strolls toward me, leaving the closed gate and Hell.

I cover my mouth, trying not to lose my shit. "Oh, God."

"Don't speak of the Higher Power!" Lucian roars, his devil façade rippling over his skin as his horns jut from his forehead as the rest of him remains in his mortal form. Fire licks over his smooth, bald head and dances down his thick beard. Locking his fingers into my hair, Lucian drags me upright and bows into my face. "Do you understand? You are no longer in control, and it's time you realize your place."

I swallow and inhale a few deep breaths, staring at the empty ash ring where the gates of Hell would be, praying that I'm hallucinating or something. "I don't understand," I repeat, wishing the fucker would answer my questions.

Lucian releases an exasperated laugh as if my comment is the stupidest thing he's ever heard. Tightening his fingers through my hair, he yanks me closer until I look directly at his cock, the hunk of flesh growing immediately under my attention. I stretch back, afraid he might poke me in the eye to fuck my brain, not caring what hole he puts it in me because he can surely ravage my body with just a flick of his finger.

"What is it that your mortal brain can't comprehend? You are mine to do with as I please until you complete your mission—if I allow you. Perhaps you can earn the chance. Show me that you'll be an obedient soul now that there won't be any interference from those who wouldn't fall where they should've." Lucian guides my head back, forcing me to look up at him. "What will it be, Raven? Earn my forgiveness by worshipping me as your master and show me what it is about you that had my brethren swollen with lust and with clouded judgment or be a petulant, weak mortal who never rises to your feet again and will die on your knees. I don't care either way. Your body and soul are mine. You will give me what I want."

I blink a few times, trying to process his words. Fury explodes through me, and I yank away, wincing through the pain of getting some of my hair ripped free. I crawl until I manage to get to my feet and dash away, running toward the house.

"Micah!" I screech, trying to see his towering frame. Where the fuck is he? "Micah!"

I try to pull the door open, but the knob doesn't turn. I'm locked out. A burst of pain lashes across my calves, the fire of Lucian's whip lassoing around my legs. He drags me away from the house and across the grass. My dress rolls up, exposing my ass, and I cry out, wishing with everything in me that this is a nightmare. That I'll wake up at any second to realize I had fallen asleep waiting for my devils to return.

The heavy foot kicking my side jolts agony through me, proving that this isn't in my head. This is real. Lucian has managed to escape Hell.

"Stop acting like you don't want me, Raven," he says, his guttural voice vibrating over my skin. He stands above me, naked and terrifying, just as he was the first moment we met. "I've felt your soul. You resist only because you cling to your humanity. Let it go and give in. This doesn't have to be torture unless you make it that way."

I shield my body from him, curling in on myself. "Please, Lucian. Where are the others? If you tell me, then I'll stop resisting you. I just need to know."

"Gone," he responds. "They are finally where they belong. Now be an obedient soul and come here. It's time for me to truly claim you how I desire. How you crave in the dark facets of your soul." Grabbing his cock, the bastard strokes himself like he gets off on my shock and disbelief. On my anguish.

I guess he would, seeing as he is the notorious Lucifer after all.

I lick my lips, peering around the quiet yard. Regret courses through me. What if this is it? What if this is my eternity now and I just lost my chance at redemption because I refused to think of any other possibility.

"Come on, Raven. Don't be shy for your master," Lucian says, his voice turning from sharp to teasing. He enjoys this way too much.

I shake my head. "Fuck off, Lucian. You'll never have me."

His eyes narrow. "Want to bet?"

Launching from the ground, I crash into him, the strength of my connection to Hell giving me the chance to catch him off guard. "I'd rather go to Hell than be with you here."

He growls and grabs the front of my dress. "You're lying."

I lock my fingers around one of his horns and jerk it closer to my stomach. "I'm not. At least now that you're here, going there means I can get away from you. I know you won't fucking follow. You think you know me, but I know you too, Lucian. I'm not worth you returning to Hell for."

"Raven, stop," Lucian says, grabbing my wrist.

I close my eyes.

I brace for death.

27

Hell's New Ruler

RAVEN

"I SAID, STOP!" Lucian roars, shoving me down the length of his torso until I straddle his waist.

I scream and punch his hard stomach, his abs hard like knocking my fists into bone-like walls, but it doesn't stop me. I'm pissed that he stopped me from doing the only thing I could think of—no matter how awful and heart-wrenching it is to even consider—to get away from him. I mean, who the fuck runs to Hell to escape from fucking Satan? What was I going to do? Fight all of the forsaken souls until I found Micah's kingdom, the only one I might recognize, and hope he might have already left this world, knowing Lucian escaped.

I think I'm going out of my mind. Lucian's already gotten to me.

"You son of a bastard!" I yell, smacking him over and over again, scratching and punching at his naked body, now fully aroused and loving what I do to him.

A wicked smile beams across Lucian's face, his anger melting into a masochistically beautiful smirk. The fucker doesn't even stop me, a bark of laughter filling the air and pissing me off more.

"At least shift your damn panties and let me fuck you if you want to tear me to pieces," Lucian says, grabbing my hips. "Just give in, Raven. It'll be easier on you to accept me as your soul keeper. You only resist because that's what you've been molded to think. I can fix that. You have five seconds to make your decision. Will you live the rest of your life in anger and madness or will you choose pleasure with your pain?"

"You're a psycho!" I shout, swinging my hand, slapping him across his face.

"Come on, Raven. Fuck me. Fuck me until you see what kind of Hell I have in store," Lucian says, his smile frozen on his face, the fire of Hell still lighting his eyes. "Choose to obey me. Choose to obey me as your master, so I don't have to break you and piece you together how I please. Fuck me! See the glory of Hell through my eyes."

What is wrong with me? How can I even consider it? I'm

suddenly trapped in his gaze, my body awakening with his twisted commands. It's like he already knows the dark side of me that gets off with this kind of thing with Kase and Dante. He went from trying to push me with fear to trying to manipulate me by pushing the right buttons on my body. And what the actual fuck?

Lucian digs his fingers into my hips, biting my skin with his nails. "Give in, my little soul slut. Fuck me. Fuck me how you desire! I'm the only devil left. Fuck me!"

My eyes blur, my mind and body at war. The only thing I can focus on are his words commanding me and how his hard cock presses into my panties like he'll tear through them at any second. Fire erupts around us, licking and destroying the grass. I struggle to think about anything else apart from the eternity he forces on me. My resistance already weakens as if my soul just wants for me to give in and be this monster's filthy little whore to protect myself. Fall in love with the being hell-bent on destroying me. Eternity won't be so bad if I lie to myself so much that I start to believe that maybe Lucian's right. Maybe I have it in me to be his obedient soul slave as long as I convince myself that I like it.

"All you have to do is say yes, and this torture will be over. Fuck me! Feel the power of Hell," he repeats, grabbing me by the back of the neck, pulling me closer. His eyes burn brightly, reflecting my startled gaze back to me. "Tell me you want me, and you'll be mine. You are mine. Let me give you a taste of my Hell."

My lip quivers, and I stare at his mouth. It could be so easy. My life is already destroyed regardless. Lucian's here. He somehow managed to escape Hell and come to the Mortal Realm. What that means? I have no idea.

I open and close my mouth, trying to let go of everything that binds me to hope. Hope for an eternity with the devils I chose to be mine. Hope to create a place where humanity isn't just disregarded and thrown to Hell if they don't meet Heaven's standards. Hope for something more than the life thrown at me.

But I can't give away my hope and fall to Lucian's commands.

I can't and I won't.

What he's asking of me erases the one thing I have left. Freewill. It's the one thing that he can't take from me as long as I'm living and breathing and strong enough to resist him.

"Raven—"

"Lucian, you fucking bastard." Dante's gruff voice cuts through the air and over the crackling fire. "You're already fucking trying to twist our agreement?"

Something slithers around my waist, hoisting me off of Lucian. "Don't let the power of his Satanic cock compel you, angel-girl. That's my job."

My whole body relaxes the second I land in Kase's arms, and he pulls me in close, waiting for me to hug him with my whole body. I kiss his throat a dozen times, squeezing my burning eyes shut, so tears don't spill. Another warm body sandwiches me to Kase, and Dante tilts my head back to kiss him.

"I thought something happened to you," I squeak out, my voice shaking. "Where the hell were you? Why is Lucian here?" I stretch up and peer around. "Andre?"

"Take a deep breath, angel-girl. Give us a moment to bathe ourselves in your light and love up on you. I knew how important you were to us, but fuck. I was going crazy being away, even if it wasn't that long. Shift your legs a bit. I'm going to fuck you with my tail until we get to my room." Kase glides his tail along the seam of my ass.

I clench my body. "Don't you dare. That can wait. My questions can't. Tell me everything like how the fuck Lucian is here?" I clench my jaw, sensing the asshole standing a few feet away, his annoyance as palpable as my anger and fear. "Why would he tell me he destroyed you?"

"Because he's evil incarnate and was trying to get to all of us. He thinks you have an undeniable and irresistible bond to him that will sway you to give your eternity to him. He slammed the gates of Hell on us. It took us a minute to remember how to unlock it from inside. Sorry, pretty soul. Want me to hold Lucian down? I'll grab a strap on and you can peg him and show him what your power is truly like." Dante smiles, yet his eyes flash green, and I know it bothers him on a deeper level he doesn't want to display in front of Lucian.

I rub my lips together, the idea not turning me on but piquing my curiosity only because Lucian should fucking know the power I possess. "No, thanks. I'm never fucking or getting fucked by that devil."

"I will prove your disobedient ass otherwise, Raven," Lucian says from behind me. "You won't be able to control yourself, especially given the fact that you are mine. I've only agreed to allow my brethren to occupy your time as you've already arranged, but I am taking a day and night with you for the rest of your existence."

What the actual fuck? I shake my head. "No fucking way."

Kase growls at Lucian. "Shut the fuck up. Don't test my wrath. I'm holding you to the agreement, and you need to stay the hell out of it and keep your damn mouth closed until we have a moment to explain everything to Raven."

"Then hurry the fuck up. I don't agree with all this coddling bullshit. Learn how to get that soul in place. You know she will obey you with enough punishment. She's weak. Needy. The Mortal Realm and the people in her life made her mind malleable. She lives to be on her knees." Lucian steps closer and peers at me from behind Kase. "Isn't that right? It's the only way you think you'll ever be wanted."

Dante hisses and flashes his fangs, launching at Lucian. Turning me away, Kase strides toward the door, ignoring the fighting unfolding behind us. I cling onto Kase's shoulders and peer at Dante as he grabs onto Lucian and launches into the air, taking him up two-dozen feet to drop him.

Lucian roars and transforms, impaling the grass with his claws. "You cowardly bastard. Get your ass down here and fight me like a devil. I'll take those wings from you if you can't."

"We have better things to do. I don't need to prove myself to you. Now fuck off and go terrorize your mortal servants until we're ready for you," Dante says, landing beside me and Kase at the back door. He shrugs out of his pants and tosses them at Lucian. "Cover that cock up until you know the realm better."

"You have one hour," Lucian snaps, dusting off his naked body. He slides on Dante's pants, the leg hems a bit long. "When I get back, I'd like a word with Micah and Elias. Alone."

"What the fuck ever," Kase says. "Just leave."

Lucian crosses the distance and tilts his head, grinning at me. "After I say goodbye to my soul."

I remain utterly still in Kase's arms, trying not to shiver as Lucian combs my hair behind my ear and leans in, kissing my cheek.

"I'll see you in a bit. Wear something red for me. It's my favorite color," he murmurs, breathing in my ear. "Be my perfect, obedient slave and maybe I won't destroy your life. My brethren can't keep you to themselves forever. You are mine."

I jerk away and slap his hand, stopping him from touching me. "I'm not. Just because you have my contract doesn't mean anything."

He smirks again. "I guess we'll see."

We'll see? We'll fucking see?

Lucian shoves past us, not giving me the chance to respond. Kase bonks his head against the doorframe until he's out of view. Covering my mouth, he stops me from losing my shit. My mind whirls a mile a minute. I can't believe this is happening.

And then it dawns on me.

Where's Andre?

My heart races alongside my mind, and I wiggle and slam my hands into Kase's chest, using my sudden strength from my Hell-bound soul to escape his arms. Neither he nor Dante try to catch me, letting me hit my ass on the back patio. I scrape my hands on the concrete, ignoring the pain, the ache in my legs from Lucian's fire whip more dominant but not as consuming as the agony coursing through my mind, body, and soul at the realization that Andre hasn't returned from Hell with Kase and Dante.

"Andre!" I shout, rushing to the summoning circle. "Andre! Damn it! Show yourself."

Upon my command, Hell's gate bursts open, sending flames

shooting toward the sky. My breath catches at the sight of Andre unfurling his black wings, his veins lit with molten liquid that gathers at the center of his chest like it had with Lucian.

"Oh, God. Fuck. No, please tell me. Please tell me you haven't traded places with Lucian, tethering yourself to Hell, so he can walk free." I drop to my knees, my insides twisting, knowing that my nightmare is true.

"Little Hellion, I did what had to be done to protect you. It's not forever. The others will have their turns as long as you agree to Lucian's adjustment in your contract. I volunteered to be first up, because I thought Kase and Dante would better serve your needs at this time...and I'm not ready to leave. It's...difficult. The craving—it's better this way." Andre rests his palm against the fiery barrier, unable to pass through.

I raise my hand to touch my palm to his, but hot fingers link around my wrist, stopping me. "Careful, angel-girl. He has a lot of Hell coursing through him and no one to help balance it. Don't let that angelic smile trick you."

I frown. "What? I don't understand. Andre wouldn't—"

A snarl from beside me startles me, and I fall into Kase. Andre's intense anger burns hot around me with the rising flames. "You fucker! She can make up her own damn mind. Give her here. I get her for one day a week like the rest of you. As the watcher of Hell, I'm taking my turn now. Raven, come to me. I need you. Don't let him take you."

My heart stalls at his words, my soul trembling as much as my body. "What? I have to go to Hell? You guys are swapping turns?"

Kase lifts me up and drops me on his shoulder. "We'll discuss it inside. You need a clear head to look over everything, and Andre won't help with that."

"You bastard! Bring her back! I'll die without her!" Andre shouts, setting the world behind us aglow in flames. He's already consumed with Hell, far more than Micah was, and it opens a hole inside me, knowing he won't be here to fill it.

I hang like a ragdoll, not bothering with fighting. I should be used to these kinds of decisions being made without me, but it doesn't hurt any less. I'd have never agreed to freeing Lucian. I know my devils had their reasons, but are they more important than mine not to want him around? I have no idea.

"Make room. Our soul needs some serious attention," Kase says, drawing my attention to the living room.

Elias leans on the armrest, his heavy lidded eyes struggling to remain open. Dante sits beside Micah, and I can't help frowning at him.

"I'm sorry, Raven. It wasn't my place to intervene with Lucian. It would've been worse had I fought him." Micah's words trickle into my mind, his apology doing nothing for the wild heartache coursing through me. He purposefully left me at Lucian's mercy. How could he?

I ignore him and wait for Kase to put me on my feet. Without looking at any of the devils, I stroll to Elias and get him to shift enough to slide beside him, using him as a shield. My emotions run all over the place. I'm still in shock. I don't even know how to deal or if I can.

"Here's the deal, Raven," Kase starts, kneeling on the floor in front of me, not allowing me to avoid him. "We've made arrangements with Lucian to stop an impending war within Hell. I know he's a dickwad douche, but this was the best way to stop him from trying to destroy everything we've worked hard to accomplish."

I keep my gaze pointed at the floor. "You couldn't leave me out of it? How can you expect me to live like this? He's going to try to break me, and—I'm fucking scared. He's going to get fed up if I don't give in to his unwanted advances."

"We felt you were strong enough to keep him in line, and it's clear in the arrangements that none of us can force you into anything you don't want," Dante says, his voice coming out quietly. "I can assure you that if he tries to do what he did to you tonight again, I'll fucking seduce him only to bite his cock off."

I pout my bottom lip. "I don't want his dick near your mouth."

"Then Micah will do it," Kase says, smirking. "You'd do anything for Raven, right?"

Micah cocks an eyebrow. "I have my own methods of punishment and will handle Lucian how I see fit."

Groaning, I hang my head, wishing this was all just a hallucination brought on from Dante's bite. A cool arm rests over my shoulders, and Elias leans into me. I hug his side, wishing he'd wrap me completely in his arms, but something holds him back.

"We'll find a way to get through this. As soon as I crap out and claim my throne, I'll throw Lucian into the pits of Hell for you, okay? This is these assholes' contract, not mine," Elias murmurs, kissing my cheek.

"Don't go trying to be the hero, jizz-master. You don't know what you're up against," Dante says, flicking out his tongue. "Leave it to us."

Except I can't.

It's my life and eternity. It's my time.

I won't just stand by and allow Lucian to steal everything from me.

He might be a force of Hell, but I'm a force of humanity. I have my stubborn will and determination. My faith.

It's all I need.

Hell will rise as it should, putting Lucian back in his place, even if it takes me until my final breath. Purgatory will be mine.

28

Soul Crushed

RAVEN

WARM ARMS SLIDE around me, and I turn onto my side, meeting Andre's gaze. Stars light up the night sky like thousands of diamonds. I can't stop the smile crossing my face. I've missed seeing Andre outside of flames. But now? He's here, visiting me in my sleep.

"Miss me, little hellion?" Andre asks, stroking his fingers along my cheek. "Because I've missed you. I've missed all the hours you've denied me of filling myself up on the pleasure our bodies together can bring. I suppose this dream will do for now."

I bite my lip, tingles blossoming from the spot on my cheek

his fingers caress and to the rest of me. "It will have to. Kase told me what can happen. You survive on my desire and lust not unlike the incubi demon you freed last week."

"Someone must do my bidding," he teases, a smile lighting his velvety brown eyes. "Until you're ready."

"I want to. I'm just…I don't know. So much could happen." I graze my lips to his, relishing the sensation of his exhilarating darkness tangling with my soul.

"Let me show you it'll be worth it." Andre rolls on top of me, planting his hands on each side of my head. Bending down, he crashes his mouth to mine, kissing me with enough passion to set my body off.

The sensation steals my breath, and I gasp in the fragrant air that turns me on without Andre even touching me yet. And what the hell? What is this magic? Is it the dream or Andre? Whatever it is, a strange desire courses through me, and all I can think about is fucking his brains out. My clit aches, my body in desperate need of relief. Andre hums and arches up, extending his nails a bit to shred my clothes right off of me. His features shift, his jaw turning sharper and more angular as hard plates sprout across his cheeks in a deep onyx color like armor.

"You want me, little hellion, don't you?" he murmurs, his muscular body bulking up as he pushes away and slinks around me. Then I notice his extra-appendages jutting from his sides. Whoa. It's strangely seductive and a bit frightening. Not because I'm afraid, but because if he's anything like Kase and his tail...damn.

I stare in surprise, his devil façade massive and rock-hard, his ribbed tail arching up and over his head like a scorpion. Bulging veins snake over his body gathering between his thighs to set his cock aglow in a way that entrances me. It's unlike anything I could imagine, the glowing flesh hardening to point at me.

My body zings at the sight, and Andre uses his two hands to stroke the length, but instead of growing, it returns back to what I know of him in his mortal form.

"Turn over. I want your ass in the air," Andre says, his crude demand weakening my knees. "It'll be easier this way."

"To do what?" I ask, squirming, my whole body out of whack with all-consuming desire.

"Do it and find out." Andre strokes the length of his cock again.

Doing as he says, I roll over and bow, sticking my ass into the air. He mounts me, his cock sliding between my legs without going in, and he tightens his hands around me, pinning me in place. Just his touch sends pleasure cascading over me, and I pant and imagine what it will be like to let him fuck me doggy-style and if it'll hurt. Because damn. I'm about to take a pounding.

"Are you ready?" he murmurs, aligning his body to mine. "I'll go slow."

I hum my agreement, digging my fingers into the strange spongey ground of my dream world.

My muscles spasm with my sudden orgasm, the intensity knocking Andre away from me.

I jolt upright, my body humming, the blanket under me wet with the lingering ecstasy aroused in me by Andre. What the fuck? Damn. He gave me a wet dream that affected my reality, and I clench my thighs together, a moan escaping my lips.

I blink my eyes, trying to orient myself to Lucian's room, the fog of lust consuming me. I expect to see him staring like a perv from his bed, but it's now empty. I'm alone and on the floor where I fell asleep since I refused to climb into bed with the cocky bastard.

"Raven," a soft voice whispers. "Raven, wake up."

I rub the heels of my hands into my eyes, clearing away the sleep. I spot Zade flying outside the open balcony door, flapping his wings to stay in place.

"Are you crazy?" I ask, abandoning the mess of blankets on the floor. I hug my arms around myself and cross the room. "If Lucian catches you—"

"He won't. He's busy outside. Please, let me have just a moment to speak with you. Andre was visiting, wasn't he? I could sense him." Zade's heavenly glow dims with his words.

Grabbing onto the railing, he balances on the ledge instead of joining me on the balcony. "How is he?"

His question throws me off. It wasn't exactly what I expected from him. I thought he'd come with a message from Cassius, wondering if I was ready to accept his deal for my soul. But even after everything, I'm not.

"He's bound to Hell. That's how he is," I snap, annoyance rushing through me. Andre has been visiting me almost every night for the last six days since I refused to go to Hell and remained outside the circle for our time together. He wasn't happy, but I'm done bowing to crazy-ass demands. I'll go to Hell when I'm ready, and not a moment sooner.

"Will you give him a message from me?" Zade asks, ignoring my comment like I didn't say anything at all. "I want him to know—"

"Just keep him away. I will string your intestines across the city if anyone finds him before he dies." Lucian's voice rings through the air, stealing my attention from Zade. "Do you understand? He must die unbound. I need time."

Lucian's words ignite fear inside me. What is going on? Time for what? Shit. I need to find out. Without thinking, I launch at Zade and cling onto him, using his need to catch himself to save my ass from possibly breaking my leg in the fall from the second story.

"You fucker! Help! Micah!" Elias hollers. "Mi—"

A loud slap reverberates through my bones, followed by silence.

Fuck.

"Hurry, Vincent. Get him out of here. Now," Lucian says.

I dash toward the side of the house, fear and anger exploding through me. Zade snatches the back of my nightshirt and pulls me into his chest, using his free hand to cover my mouth.

"Shhh, don't let him hear you," he whispers. "If he does, I can assure you, Elias will be dead by morning."

Tears burn my eyes. "Let me go."

"And do what? You can't follow a demon, Raven...but I can." Zade releases me, still keeping his hand across my mouth. "I just need you to do me a favor. Please."

I slowly nod. "What is it?"

"I'll find out where the demon is taking Elias, so you can tell your soul keepers, but then, I need you to allow me to use your soul. I need to speak with Andre," Zade says. "I need you to agree to let me use you to get into Hell."

I blink a few times. "Deal."

To be continued...

Other RH Books

OMEGAVERSE SERIES

Saint Vista Pack Regimes

Bonds of Steele Omegaverse

PARANORMAL

The Seven Sinners of Hell's Kingdon

The Pack Mates of Lunar Crest

The Wolfpacks of Shadow Moon Island

The Fated Mate of the Dragon Clans

The Divine Vampire Heirs

The Royale Vampire Heirs

The Academy of Vampire Heirs

La Vega Vampire Showstoppers

Rise from the Flames

About Ginna Moran

GINNA MORAN IS the *USA Today* Bestselling author of over seventy novels including the popular Knotty Lessons and The Seven Sinners of Hell's Kingdom novels.

She always carried a fascination for all things paranormal and wrote her first unpublished manuscript at age eighteen. Her love of the supernatural grew stronger through her adult life, and she now spends her days with different creatures of the night. Whether it's vampires, werewolves, dragons, fae, angels, demons, or mermaids, Ginna loves creating and living in worlds from her dreams.

Aside from Ginna's professional life, she enjoys binge-watching TV, crafting and design, playing with her daughter, and cuddling with her dog. Some of her favorite things include chocolate, mermaids, anything that glitters, learning new things, cheesy jokes, and organizing her bookshelf.

9 781951 314453